Sadie

Sadie

Jane Elliott

W F HOWES LTD

This large print edition published in 2008 by
W F Howes Ltd
Unit 4, Rearsby Business Park, Gaddesby Lane,
Rearsby, Leicester LE7 4YH

1 3 5 7 9 10 8 6 4 2

First published in the United Kingdom in 2007
by Harper

A CIP catalogue record for this book is available
from the British Library

ISBN 978 1 40741 721 9

Typeset by Palimpsest Book Production Limited,
Grangemouth, Stirlingshire
Printed and bound in Great Britain
by MPG Books Ltd, Bodmin, Cornwall

'Happy families are all alike;
every unhappy family is unhappy in its own way.'

Leo Tolstoy, *Anna Karenina*

PROLOGUE

A Manchester Prison, 1985

Something was going to happen today.

The screws could tell. The inmates could tell. Nobody knew when or where; they just knew. Whispered rumours in the corridors of the prison had not gone unnoticed by the authorities, but it's hard to put out a fire when you don't know where the flames are. All they could do was watch and wait.

The air of the canteen was thick with the smell of grease and eggs. It would have turned the stomachs of most people, but the prisoners queuing for their breakfast hardly seemed to notice it. They smelled it every Sunday, after all, when their cereal and yoghurt was replaced by fatty bacon, eggs and fried bread. Normally there were boisterous shouts as the inmates queued, but not this morning.

Something was going to happen today.

Vic Brandon was eight years into a life sentence, so he was more used to the bland stodge of prison food than most of the small-timers around him. It still wound him up, though, queuing for his meals with everyone else. He'd been in six prisons since the day he went down for shooting some copper who got in the way of him and a waiting VW – an occupational hazard of being an armed robber – and in each of those prisons he had stamped out his authority within forty-eight hours of arriving. It was amazing how all you had to do was take a blade to some hapless lag if you wanted to have everyone else eating out of your tattooed hands.

'Bacon?'

Vic looked up unsmilingly at the inmate who was serving. New face, he thought. Didn't know who he was. It wouldn't last. He said nothing, but held his tin tray in front of him.

'Just give him some,' another server whispered to the bacon man, before turning back to Brandon. 'All right, Vic?' he asked with a slightly nervous smile.

Vic nodded curtly as food was placed on his tray, and then went to take his seat at the place that was always reserved for him.

Respect. Hierarchy. That was what it was all about in these places. The screws might insist that he queue up with all the others, but he had his own ways of keeping things the way he liked them. No matter that half his eight years had been spent in isolation wings; no matter that his violent behaviour meant that his chances of parole were minutely small. Cop-killers always served the full stretch anyway. Look at Harry Roberts. Besides, he liked it in prison. On the outside he was a nobody; in here he was a somebody. His missus turned up once a month, done up to the nines and turning heads the way he liked her, and his eyes on the outside told him that she was keeping on the straight and narrow. If she was a trophy in the real world, she was double that in here.

Every now and then, though, he needed to make his presence felt. Today, he had decided, was going to be one of those days.

Something was going to happen today.

Of course, he was spoiled for choice in this place, as it was one of the few lock-ups he'd been in that housed a Vulnerable Prisoners' wing. The VP wing was like jam to an insect as far as Vic was concerned. Bent coppers, convicted paedophiles – it was where they stuck all the scumbags whose very presence offended both inmates and screws alike. They were kept apart from the rest of the prison population – different sleeping quarters, different recreation times – for their own safety. The only space they shared was the canteen on a Sunday morning, when the promise of bacon and eggs lured them out of their protective bubble. There had never been any doubt in Vic's mind that his next target would be one of the dogs from the VP wing: that way he could reassert his authority and do everyone a favour at the same time.

He had even chosen his man.

His name was Allen Campbell, another new boy,

and if ever one of these sick fuckers wanted the smile wiped from his face, he was it. The word on the corridors of Brandon's wing was that he was just starting a five-stretch for spiking the drink of a fourteen-year-old with Rohypnol and then doing God knows what with her. Five years, out in two and a half. It wasn't right. Made Vic's flesh creep just to think about it, and he saw it as his duty to make sure those two and a half years were as bad as they could be.

The prison authorities were doing their best to keep him safe, but nobody was untouchable. Not if you wanted to get at them badly enough.

Brandon chewed his breakfast slowly as two other inmates came and sat with him. They made a mismatched trio. Brandon was short and sinewy, his balding hair closely shaved. On his left sat Matt, an ageing bare-knuckle fighter doing a six-stretch for GBH, much of his muscle bulk now turned to fat, but still useful in a fight. To his right was a thin, bookish, bespectacled man with a deeply lined face. This was Sean, a counterfeiter at the start of a sentence for flooding the streets with a wave of funny money. A weaselly sort of man who would do whatever it took to ingratiate himself with the right people – not the type Brandon would usually associate himself with, let alone let sit by at mealtimes. But Sean had no history of violence, which made him essential for today's work. Neither Brandon nor Matt would be allowed to walk out of the workshop without being searched down; Sean was a different matter, and had been instructed to smuggle something out during one of his woodwork sessions.

'Well?' Brandon asked eventually.

'Philips screwdriver, Vic,' Sean informed him in a reedy cockney voice. 'Small one, like you asked for.'

'Where is it?'

'In my pocket, Vic.'

'Hand it over.'

There was a fumbling below the table as Sean passed the tool over to Brandon. Vic grasped the handle and ran his finger along the business end of the screwdriver. It was a good weight, and small enough for him to conceal up his sleeve. Not as sharp as he'd have liked. But sharp enough.

'Off you go, then,' he told Sean.

Sean looked nervously at him. 'I thought I might stay, Vic,' he chattered. 'Give you a hand.'

Vic just gave him one of his looks.

Sean read the signs well. He stood up from the table, took his half-eaten breakfast over to the slop bucket and then left the canteen.

As he left, the men from the VP wing shuffled in, flanked by three bored-looking screws and ignoring the unfriendly stares from all the other inmates. A youngish man, in his mid-twenties perhaps, Allen Campbell was halfway down the line. His dark hair was close-cropped, his skin closely shaved. A handsome man in his way, but Brandon watched him with loathing. As Campbell accepted his breakfast, a misty calm descended on the lifer. He clutched the screwdriver in his right hand and watched with satisfaction as his prey took a seat at the end of a long table.

He turned to Matt and nodded subtly. 'Let's do it.'

The two men scraped their plates into the slop, and then casually walked over to where Campbell was sitting and concentrating on his meal.

'Nothing like a fry-up, eh?' Brandon asked quietly.

Allen's fork stopped halfway to his mouth, and he turned to look up at the two men towering above him. He looked each of them in the eye, sneered faintly and then turned back to his bacon and eggs.

Brandon bent down and whispered in his ear, 'Not ignoring us, I hope.'

'Fuck off,' Allen murmured in a heavy Mancunian accent, not even bothering to look up this time.

Brandon felt the mist descending a little further. '*No one* talks to me like that, you sick little bastard,' he spoke even more quietly.' 'Specially not sex cases like you.'

Allen still refused to look at him. 'And what are you in for, bad boy? Speeding?'

'It ain't the same,' Brandon hissed through gritted teeth. He felt a nudge in his ribs and looked up. Matt was pointing to two screws in the corner of the room: they had spotted what was going on, could clearly sense trouble and were closing quickly in.

'Do it, Vic,' Matt urged in a low growl.

Brandon needed no more encouragement. 'Hold the screws back,' he told Matt.

Allen Campbell became instantly aware that the situation was about to explode, and he started to push himself up from the table to try to get away. But he was too late. With a deftness that seemed to belie his squat frame, Brandon grabbed Campbell with his left hand around the neck and pulled him up from his seat. The buzz of voices in the canteen suddenly fell silent, and one of the screws shouted as he ran, 'Put him down, Brandon!'

But Vic wasn't going to do that. Gripping the screwdriver firmly, he used his right hand to punch the tip into the belly of the squirming Campbell. As it punctured the skin, Brandon felt his victim's T-shirt become saturated with blood, and his hand became warm and sticky. Campbell exhaled sharply, like a bellows. Vic twisted the weapon fiercely, first one way and then the other. Campbell shouted out in pain and fell to his knees. The screwdriver slid out of his body as he did so, and the blood started to seep out even more copiously, forming a shallow puddle around his midriff.

Brandon looked around. The screws were nearly on him, but he might as well be hanged for a sheep as a lamb, he thought. Matt would be able to hold them off for a little bit. He bent over the weeping Campbell, picked up his meal tray and crashed it down on his head. The metal tray had a small, jagged nick on the edge that tore coarsely into Allen's skin just above the eye.

Suddenly Vic felt the screws' coshes raining down on him. With a roar, he pushed his arms out to the side, but the screws soon grabbed him, one to each arm. 'All right, all right,' he shouted, but as he struggled with them, he could not help aiming a kick firmly in Campbell's side. Blood stuck to his shoe as Allen groaned loudly, but the screws seemed more intent on dragging Brandon away than helping the bleeding inmate on the floor. They started shouting to their colleagues, 'Lock down! Lock the place down!' The hubbub had returned, and there was a palpable feeling of mutiny in the air as a siren started up.

And above it all, there was one voice shouting. It was Vic Brandon.

'Fucking nonce,' he yelled. 'You got what was coming to you. You're lucky you ain't dead. *You fucking nonce!*'

PART I

CHAPTER 1

Wandsworth, south London, five years later

The woman who held the door open was still in her dressing gown and already on the third Rothmans of the morning. Her skin always looked a bit greyer before she'd done her lipstick, but her daughter was used to that. It didn't worry her too much nowadays. It used to, after the funeral and everything, but her mum seemed better now. Happier.

'Don't be late back, love.' Smoke billowed from her nostrils as she spoke.

'But I wanted to go round Carly's.'

'Not tonight, love. I've got a surprise for you.'

She had such a mysterious twinkle in her eye when she said it that the girl immediately relented, looking up at her with a mixture of suspicion and pleasure.

'All right, Mum,' she said quietly.

Sadie Burrows kissed her mother, and then slung her beaten-up leather school satchel over her shoulder. It didn't contain much, but Sadie would never be persuaded not to use it. Her dad had proudly presented it to her two years ago, and even though she knew it was off the back of a lorry, it was her most prized possession. Even more so now he wasn't around any more.

She slammed the door shut and ran down the path of the tiny front garden of the run-down house that Dad had blagged so hard for them to get; then she hurried down the road that led through the centre of the estate. It was just past eight o'clock, but already the sun was warm and bright as Sadie half ran, half skipped to the small playground where she met her friends before school every morning. As usual, she was the first one there, so she slung her satchel on the ground and sat on a graffiti-covered swing to wait.

Sadie liked it at this park, but it made her sad too. Her dad used to bring her here almost every day. No one ever dared push her as hard in the swing as he did, and sometimes, if Sadie was persuasive enough, there was ice cream on the way back. But it was also here, in the same park where they used to have such fun, that Sadie heard the news. That had been a couple of years ago, on a much colder day than today when she and her friends were wrapped up in mittens and hats. They had seen the ambulance scream past them, but of course they hadn't paid it much attention – ambulances were always for other people, after all. Perhaps there had been a fight; maybe one of the junkies on the estate had overdosed. Minutes later, though, old Mr Johnson from next door had come hurrying out to find her.

'Sadie, sweetheart,' he'd said, out of breath and in a voice made rough by the stinky brown cigarettes he smoked, 'you've got to come with me.'

She was only eleven years old at the time, but she could tell something was wrong. 'What is it?' she asked, her eyes wide and her lips trembling.

'It's your daddy, sweetheart. He's not well. The ambulance is taking him to hospital now.'

The rest of the day had been a horrible blur. Mr Johnson had taken her in a minicab to the hospital, where her dad was lying in intensive care, an oxygen mask on his face and tubes coming out of his hands. The nurses had been nice to her, bringing her glasses of orange juice and even some chocolate biscuits, but she knew that people were only that nice when something was really wrong. She kept asking what was the matter with her dad, but nobody wanted to tell her. It was only afterwards that she learned that it was a heart attack. At about six o'clock in the evening, the machine to which her unconscious father was wired started to beep alarmingly. Doctors were called and Sadie and her mother were ushered away from his bedside.

Ten minutes later he was dead.

They didn't want Sadie to see the body, but she had insisted. She was thankful that they had removed the mask and the tubes – it made him seem more human. More like her dad. In fact, he didn't even look as if he was dead. Just asleep. Sadie stood on a chair so that she could see him more clearly, but she didn't cry. She just stared at him, drinking in the sight of the face that she knew she would never see again.

Not until she got home, under her duvet, did the tears come. Then she cried until she could cry no more.

That was two years ago, but it felt like yesterday.

Carly was the first of her friends to arrive at the playground this morning, her hair pulled back tightly as it always was and her face made up so that she appeared older than her thirteen years. She was closely followed by Anna, whose black skin and closely plaited hair always seemed somehow exotic to Sadie, even though black faces were as common as white ones on the estate. None of them greeted each other; they just fell into conversation, which was casual at first but soon became excited and loud as they made their way to school. None of them had any money, but they all had an appetite for sweets. And they had a plan.

'Who's going to do it?' Anna asked as they walked to the edge of the estate.

'It's your turn,' Carly told her.

'No, it's not.' Anna's voice became louder in her own defence.

'I did it last time,' Carly insisted.

'Yeah, but—'

'It's all right,' Sadie interrupted them quietly. 'Leave it to me.'

In the old days, Sadie had been able to get anything anyone at school wanted. Or to be more accurate, whatever Sadie brought to school everyone wanted. Her dad would indulgently let her take what she asked for from his ever-changing stocks, and she would supply them, mirroring his wheeler-dealer attitude with stardust that fizzed on your tongue and erasers that came in every shape, colour and smell under the sun. Sometimes she would sell them, sometimes she would give them away – making herself the most popular girl in the school. For a while.

Now, though, she had to find other ways of coming by her stash of goodies.

They were outside the newsagent's by now. It was part of a parade of shops in the main road that led to the estate, between a dry-cleaner's and an off-licence. Carly and Anna loitered to one side while Sadie marched brazenly in. It wasn't a big shop, but there were two small aisles selling groceries and a huge counter of sweets, behind which sat the shopkeeper, who eyed Sadie with suspicion. He had dark skin, white hair and a deeply lined face.

'Got any milk?' Sadie asked with a smile.

The shopkeeper pointed in the direction of a tall, glass-fronted fridge in the aisle furthest from him. 'In the fridge,' he told her.

Sadie nodded and wandered over to where he had indicated. She opened the fridge, and although she saw three cartons of milk on the lower shelf, she made the pretence of scanning up and down as though unable to find them. Then she shut the door and walked back up to the shopkeeper. 'Couldn't find it.'

'It's in the fridge,' the shopkeeper repeated with a frown.

Sadie shrugged, and continued to smile at him.

The shopkeeper muttered something beneath his breath; then he stood up from his stool, walked out from behind the counter and made his way over to the fridge. Sadie watched him carefully. As he opened the door and bent down to take out the milk, she quietly snatched two big handfuls from the sweet counter, shoved them into her satchel, grabbed another couple of handfuls and slipped outside again. She had left the shop before the man had straightened up to close the fridge door.

The three girls ran silently round the corner of the parade, stifling their giggles. Then Carly and Anna huddled excitedly around Sadie.

'What did you get? What did you get?'

'Did you get any ciggies?'

'Course not,' Sadie scoffed, but not unpleasantly. 'Ciggies are behind the counter. Anyway, you don't smoke, Carly.'

'Course I do.'

'Since when?'

'Since last week. Tom gave me one of his, didn't he?'

Sadie and Anna looked at each other with raised eyebrows, and then exploded with laughter.

'What?' Carly asked defensively. '*What?*'

'We knew you were after Tom,' Anna screeched.

'I'm not *after* him. He just gave me a ciggie, that's all.'

'Bet that's not all he gave you,' Anna laughed.

'Shut up.'

'Look,' Sadie interrupted them, more to defuse the argument than anything else. She opened her palms to display her haul – chocolate bars, gum, sweets. Carly and Anna moved to grab what they could, but suddenly they heard a man's voice behind them.

'Oi, you lot!'

As one, they turned their heads to see who was calling them. The newsagent was running towards them. 'Give me that stuff back. I'll call the police on you.'

The three girls were like pigeons dispersing at the sound of gunshot. Quick as a light switching on, they ran in three different directions, Anna and Carly disappearing in opposite ways down the street, Sadie speeding down the alleyway that led past the bins and back into the estate.

As she ran, she nervously congratulated herself on not risking their little shoplifting escapade on the estate. Everyone knew her there, even the shopkeepers – it was difficult to get away with anything. She looked back over her shoulder to see the shopkeeper running after her, and felt a little surge of adrenaline in her stomach as she upped her pace. The alleyway turned a corner and then led out on to an area at the foot of a grey concrete tower block where people parked their cars. There were about fifteen vehicles, all fairly old and run-down. Without stopping to think, Sadie hurled herself into the middle of the car park and hid down by the side of a rusty old blue Fiesta. She tried not to breathe too heavily as she crouched, holding her sweets, and she strained her ears to hear the patter of the shopkeeper's feet as he emerged from the alleyway – only to find that she had disappeared. She heard him swearing to himself in his pronounced Asian accent. 'Bloody kids. Always the bloody same.'

Suddenly, to her horror, she saw someone approaching. He raised an eyebrow at her just as she heard the shopkeeper calling to him, ''Scuse me, my friend. You seen a young girl running through here? About thirteen, maybe a bit older, long brown hair.'

The man paused, and seemed to be wondering if he should reply or not.

'She just stole something from my shop, you see,' the man continued, a bit desperately.

Sadie threw an imploring look up at the man.

'Sorry, pal,' he replied in a northern accent. 'Didn't see anyone. She can't have come this way.'

The shopkeeper breathed out in annoyance. 'Bloody kids,' he muttered again.

The man watched him go. 'It's all right,' he said finally. 'He's gone.'

Slowly Sadie stood up, flashing the man her

most winning smile. 'Thanks,' she said. As she spoke, the alarm on her digital watch beeped twice. Nine o'clock.

'Shouldn't you be going to school?' the man asked her.

Sadie's grin grew a bit broader. 'Yeah,' she replied, clutching her sweets and starting to slip away. 'Yeah, I suppose I should. Um . . . Anyway, thanks again.'

The others, she knew, would be back at their usual meeting place by the swings. Flushed with the success of her adventure, she ran off to meet them.

Stacy Venables had wanted to be a teacher ever since she was a little girl. Her mum had been one, and her dad too, so she supposed it was only natural. Of course, teaching now wasn't as it was then. Her mum had never had to deal with pupils using four-letter words to her face, and whenever Stacy told her about the things she had to put up with, she would shake her head, tut and start talking about standards. But standards in the cosy corner of Wiltshire where the Venables family lived were very different to standards in inner-city London. Stacy remembered the time her parents had given her what for when she had asked if her eighteen-year-old boyfriend could stay the night. If they only knew what kids nowadays were up to: drugs, sex – they needed so much more than education, she always thought.

They needed a bit of care – a bit of what they weren't getting in the home. That was why she tried to make herself seem accessible to the children. Unlike her female colleagues, who wore severe suits in rough, cheap material, Stacy wore jeans. In summer she wore a white T-shirt and a black leather jacket – much to the disapproval of the disciplinarian headmaster, Mr Martin; for winter she had a succession of thick, woolly thigh-length cardigans that seemed to match her full head of long, curly hair and made her appear, she thought, a bit more homely.

Of course, she was still a teacher, and subject to the disdain and abuse most of the kids at school gave anyone in authority; but every now and then she felt as if she had made a difference, and that made her efforts worthwhile.

Miss Venables stood patiently at the gates to the school. It was ten past nine now, and the two police officers who stood outside the school every morning and afternoon to keep away undesirables had just left. It saddened her that they had to be there, but she knew it was the right thing. Prevention was better than cure, even if some of the older kids were savvy enough to arrange meets with their dealers just round the corner, where there were no uniforms. Last year a boy had been excluded for having a wrap containing three rocks of crack cocaine. Bright enough kid, decent family – you never could tell who was going to go down that line. The police had been called, a fuss had been made and the children had been told that this sort of behaviour was not to be tolerated. Stacy had argued that he should be given help, not exclusion, but hers was a lone voice, soon drowned by the head. She had received a letter from the lad's parents just a couple of months later, saying that he had gone missing and that the police weren't hopeful of finding him unless he wanted to come back, but thanking her for everything she had done for him.

It saddened her, too, that they had to lock the main gates to the school, not so much to keep the children in as to keep other people out. You could never be too careful these days.

She looked at her watch. Another minute for the stragglers and then she'd lock up.

Just then, around the corner, came three familiar figures.

Miss Venables had a soft spot for Sadie Burrows. It wasn't just that she looked appealing, with her glossy long hair, olive skin and those beautiful almond-shaped eyes. Some kids just had something, a spark, call it what you will – when you'd been in the job for a while you found you could recognize it easily, and you knew how rare it was.

It didn't make her a goody-goody. Far from it – more of a charming tearaway, and plenty of the teachers in the school had marked her out because of that. She was neither brilliant academincally, nor poor – just average, although here that almost made her stand out. Sadie could be cheeky and mischievous, just like any other kid. But she was definitely the daughter of her father, a man well known all over this part of London as being able to sell umbrellas in July and sunscreen in December. Just don't ask where it came from. Tommy Burrows had a twinkle in his eye that he had passed on to his daughter, which meant that whenever she was caught crossing the boundary, it was impossible to stay angry with her for long.

'Come on, you three!' she shouted at the girls as they approached. 'You're late. I was just about to lock up.'

'Sorry, Miss Venables,' Carly and Anna intoned in unison.

'Why are you late? What have you been doing?'

'Nothing, miss,' the two of them told her rather guiltily.

'Sadie?' Miss Venables turned to the ringleader with a raised eyebrow.

Sadie looked straight at the teacher. 'Carly had to get the little ones ready for school, miss. Me and Anna said we'd wait for her.'

Miss Venables looked at each of the girls in turn. 'Are you sure?'

'Oh, Miss Venables. Would I lie to you?' Sadie looked innocently at her.

'Probably, Miss Burrows.' She couldn't help smiling at Sadie's banter, perfectly aware that she was being twisted round the finger of this little thirteen-year-old, but somehow not minding. And who was to say that they weren't telling the truth?

She knew that Carly's mum was off the rails: a child protection officer had informed the school that she was under observation by social services. Single mum, too fond of the bottle – it was a story they heard all the time, and too often the eldest daughter ended up with the responsibility of looking after her younger siblings.

'All right, girls. In you go, quickly. Straight to your classes.'

Carly and Anna hurried inside, but on a sudden whim Miss Venables called out, 'Sadie!'

Sadie turned. 'Yes, miss?'

'Is everything all right?'

Sadie looked confused.

'At home, I mean.'

'Oh.' She smiled at the teacher in appreciation. 'Yes, miss. I think so. Thanks.'

'Good. Well . . . Off you go.'

Sadie nodded and ran across the playground into the school building, while Miss Venables thoughtfully locked the main gate and wandered back inside, slowly so as to enjoy the warmth of the morning sun on her face.

After lunch she noticed Sadie again. It was Friday, so Miss Venables was on playground duty, doing her best to keep some sort of order among the couple of hundred screaming kids working off their lunch in the early-afternoon heat. Frankly, she dreaded playground duty: it was hard enough keeping a class of forty kids quiet, let alone a schoolyard full of them. And especially on a Friday, when everyone was looking forward to the weekend.

In the far corner, something was going on. A boy – she couldn't quite make out who it was – was being circled by three other kids. Even at a distance, she could tell it wasn't a friendly game. He was being pushed about from one to the other and being jeered at. It was going to escalate into something nasty. Miss Venables started to stride across the playground, blowing her whistle. But, as usual, the kids paid her no attention.

Now she could see the boy who was being bullied. Poor little Jamie Brown. He didn't stand much chance in this place. He was so badly cared for at home that his skin was always dirty and his clothes stank of urine and filth. She suspected physical abuse, and knew that he was being closely monitored; but he would never admit to anything – he was too scared – and the mother always seemed to have a story to explain away any suspicions people had. But Jamie's peers didn't know about all that, or if they did they didn't care. All they saw was a smelly little boy who cowered at every harsh word, and for whom barely a day passed without tears and fights and traumas. Even Miss Venables had to admit that standing too close to him was a bit of challenge, so the moment he had arrived at school she had known what a rough ride he was likely to get from the kids. And she knew that even if she stopped this little fracas, another one wouldn't be far behind. That didn't mean she shouldn't try, though.

Suddenly she stopped.

She narrowed her eyes as she saw Sadie step confidently into the ring.

Ordinarily she would never have stood back to let other kids enter a brawl, but something encouraged her to keep her own counsel for a few moments.

Sadie was older than the boy who was being bullied, but the kids who had formed the ring were her own age and outnumbered her three to one. With casual confidence, she stood beside Jamie Brown.

The bullies sneered. 'What are you then? His girlfriend?'

Sadie's face didn't flicker. 'What do you know about girlfriends?' she asked quietly.

A blush came to the bully's cheek. His eyes moved from left to right as he looked to see what reaction Sadie's comment was getting from his companions; then he made forward as if to attack Jamie Brown. Miss Venables saw the little boy flinch and, in her most authoritarian voice, started to call out the bully's name. But as she did so, she saw the bully's friends grab him by the arms and pull him away. They started scuffling among themselves for a moment, but then they caught sight of Miss Venables bearing down on them. Each of them threw her a scornful look, and then turned and hurried away. A final insult – 'At least I don't piss my pants!' – reached her ears, but she let it pass, choosing instead to hurry up to Jamie and Sadie.

'Are you all right, Jamie, love?' she asked, kneeling down so that she could be more at the little boy's level. But Jamie simply looked angry and confused; he turned and ran to the other end of the playground, where he sat with his back to the wall, alone and avoided, as he always was.

Miss Venables turned to Sadie. 'You should leave that sort of thing to the teachers, Sadie,' she chided.

Sadie looked calmly at her. 'Sorry, miss,' she said, but there was no apology in her voice. She looked over at Jamie. 'But I don't see why they have to be so horrible.'

'I know, Sadie,' Miss Venables agreed. 'But sometimes it's the easy targets that attract the weakest people. Jamie will be all right. I'll keep an eye on him. Now run along.'

She watched as Sadie made her way back to Carly and Anna, who were laughing good-naturedly. They didn't seem to have noticed what had just happened, and Sadie rejoined them quietly, only occasionally glancing across the playground to where Jamie Brown was still sitting by himself.

CHAPTER 2

The afternoon passed slowly. Sadie sat at the back of the class with Carly and Anna, her chin resting in the palm of her hand; she stared into space as the teacher at the front droned on and on, his monotonous lesson frequently punctuated by barks of reprimand and tellings-off. It was a typical Friday afternoon.

Carly slipped a note under the table. Her childish handwriting asked Sadie in misspelled English if she still wanted to come round to her house after school. Sadie thought about writing a reply, but instead she just whispered back.

'Can't,' she told her friend. 'Mum says I've got to go back home.'

Carly shot her a surprised look, and Sadie understood why. Her mum never told her when she should be back.

Even when Sadie was younger, she had been allowed to wander round the estate by herself. People came to expect it of her. She was forever knocking on doors, fixing her neighbours with her most appealing smile and flogging whatever goods or goodies her dad had a run on that particular week. She understood how difficult grown-ups found it to refuse such a chirpy young girl and she'd got a taste for it. She would always come home, of course, but she never had to be told.

After the funeral, though, things started to become a bit different. Mum would still never tell her when to be home, and at first that was just because it was the way things had always been. But the loss of her man hit Jackie Burrows hard. Sadie would never forget the first time she got back after school to find her drunk. The bottle of cheap vodka on the smoked-glass coffee table wasn't quite empty, but it wasn't far off. An ashtray was full of stubs, and the television was on. Sadie's mum was comatose on the sofa and, try though she might, the little girl couldn't rouse her. She shook her, tears streaming down her face and crying at her to wake up; but when she did open her eyes, they just rolled unconsciously to the top of her head before closing again. Sadie had been on the point of calling an ambulance when her mother rolled off the sofa and started vomiting on the carpet.

It had taken her two days to get back on her feet again. Sadie stayed away from school to nurse her, bringing her glasses of water and painkillers. Jackie had begged her daughter not to be angry with her, but Sadie was not angry. In her child-like way she understood. At times mother and daughter held each other and cried and cried, but they never spoke of their sadness. How would they have known what to say?

Since then Jackie had never been that bad. But for several months not a day went by when Sadie didn't come home to find the ever-open bottle of vodka depleted and the ashtray brimming over. And more than once, when the booze had run out and Jackie was in no state to leave the house, she handed Sadie one of the precious ten-pound notes that arrived in her purse courtesy of the benefits office, and begged, 'Get us a bottle of voddy, love.'

The first time it happened, Sadie was reluctant. 'I can't, Mum. I'm not old enough.'

But Mum looked imploringly at her, a horrible, pitiful desperation in her eyes, and Sadie agreed because she didn't know what else to do. She took the money down to the off-licence with the grey metal grilles on the front where on a number of occasions she had gone with her dad to sell cheap cases of spirits. The first time she tried to buy vodka the owner had been nervous; but she told him it was for her mum, and she soon ceased to have any problem.

Jackie's habit grew from bad to worse, and soon she was able to drink the same quantities she had that first time without the devastating effect.

And then, a few months ago, it simply stopped. Sadie returned home one day to discover that for the first time in ages her mum had dealt with the washing – a job Sadie had taken over in some unspoken agreement, knowing that if she didn't she'd just have to wear dirty clothes. Jackie had folded the clothes and placed them on the kitchen table, and as Sadie walked in, her satchel slung over her shoulder, Mum was standing proudly by her handiwork, dressed and sober. She almost managed to look proud of what she had achieved. No matter that the dirty dishes were piled in the sink; no matter that the house stank of cigarettes. Sadie could tell it was a turning point.

That night Jackie even went out. Sadie lay alone in the darkness of her bedroom, wondering where she was and waiting for her to come back, but towards midnight sleep overtook her; she awoke the next morning to find her mum still asleep. She left for school quietly, without waking her up.

At first Jackie's evening outings were few and far between. But as the weeks passed, Sadie found herself alone in the house of an evening increasingly frequently. Now and then she would ask her mum where she had been, but Jackie would reply evasively. She was lonely in the house by herself at night, and the creaks and cracks that always sounded ten times louder when the lights were off were frightening. But she never said anything to Mum: she was just glad she had stopped drinking. And when they did spend time together, there would be kisses and cuddles and affection; sometimes they even managed to talk about Dad without crying.

Life was getting better. They were going to be OK. Just the two of them.

The bell rang for the end of school, and there

was a sudden cacophony of chair-scraping. Sadie closed the book that she had not glanced at since the start of the lesson and tossed it into her satchel. Most of her share of the chocolate bars she had pinched that morning were still in there, she noticed, as she heard Carly speak.

'So, why does your mum want you home?'

'Dunno,' Sadie shrugged, affecting less interest than she felt.

They wandered out into the corridor and walked towards the exit.

By the time they got there, most of the other kids had left. As they walked through the school gates, Sadie saw little Jamie Brown, the boy she had helped in the playground. He seemed to be in a world of his own, scuffing his shoes as he shuffled along and humming dreamily to himself in that tuneless way that always attracted so much derision from the other kids.

'You all right, Jamie?' she asked as they passed.

Jamie looked up as though noticing the girls for the first time – which he probably was. The pungent odour of stale urine hit Sadie's nose, and she did her best to stop her distaste from showing in her face; but next to her she heard Carly's voice, half-choking, half-sniggering. She glanced at her in momentary annoyance and then turned her attention back to Jamie. As soon as he had heard Carly, he had hung his head straight back down and started to walk away, his cheek twitching nervously. Sadie strode after him. As she did so, and on a whim, she thrust her hand into her satchel and brought out a bar of chocolate. She shoved it into Jamie's hand. 'Here you go,' she told him. 'You can have this.'

Jamie stopped once more and stared in astonishment at the foil wrapper in his hand. He looked to Sadie as though he had never seen a bar of chocolate in his life.

'Go on,' Sadie said to him, half laughing. 'It's not poison.'

A look of indecision crossed the little boy's face, but eventually he shook his head and handed it back to Sadie. 'No thanks,' he said in a small voice. 'I can't.'

Sadie and Carly shared a surprised glance.

'What do you mean, you can't?' Carly asked. 'She just gave it to you, didn't she?'

'I'm not allowed,' Jamie said firmly, handing the chocolate bar back.

'Who says?' Sadie asked him gently.

'My mum.'

Sadie looked at him in confusion. 'But it's only a bit of chocolate.'

'Yeah, but I'm still not allowed.'

'But she won't know.'

Jamie looked away, embarrassment shadowing his face. 'Yeah, she will. She always knows. She gets . . . angry.' As he said the word 'angry', his voice went hoarse.

Sadie and Carly stood awkwardly, unable to think what to say.

'Anyway,' Jamie mumbled, his voice a little aggressive now, 'it's nothing to do with you.' And he strode off, walking with more purpose than before and resolutely not looking back.

'Weirdo,' Carly observed, but without much conviction. Sadie said nothing.

It was a ten-minute walk back to the estate, and the two girls remained quiet all the way home. Sadie couldn't speak for Carly, but she had been shocked by the look on Jamie's face when he spoke of his mother. It was a look of sadness, certainly, but also of confusion and fear. She couldn't imagine what it must be like to feel those emotions when you were going home.

That thought brought her mother's farewell words this morning back to her: 'I've got a surprise for you,' An involuntary smile flickered across Sadie's face – like all children, she liked surprises. She liked the anticipation. And most of all, she liked the idea that her mum had thought about doing something for her. It was like the old times, when her dad would arrange little treats for her if he'd made a bit of money.

As they arrived on the outskirts of the estate, Sadie and Carly said goodbye and went their separate ways. In the bright afternoon sunshine, the faceless grey tower blocks almost managed to look cheery, and Sadie continued to daydream as she wandered home, her mind full of what-ifs. What if she were to get back to find the flat as it used to be: full of boxes and the life that her dad breathed into the place? What if they were going out, to the cinema, or McDonald's? Maybe her mum had rented a video from the shop, and bought them Coca-Cola and crisps.

She wandered up the pathway, put her key in the door and walked inside.

Jackie stood in the kitchen. It was a large room, big enough for a dining table, which they never used. As Sadie stood in the door, her always-present satchel hanging around her neck, she blinked in astonishment. When she had left this morning, the sink had been brimming with dirty plates and pans, and Sadie fully expected to find it so when she returned. Jackie might have kicked the booze, but she was still a long way from being the perfect mum, and it was just a matter of course now for her to have to wash up whatever she needed when she made her sandwich for tea. But this afternoon, the kitchen was pristine. Even the large ashtray had been emptied, although Jackie still had a long, slim cigarette burning between her fingers.

'Are they new trousers, Mum?' Sadie asked, a bit disconsolately, as she had been telling her that she needed new school shoes for ages now.

'Oxfam.' Jackie smiled a little nervously, stubbed out the half-smoked ciggie and walked forward to embrace her daughter. She planted a kiss on Sadie's cheek, and the girl turned to look at her mum in suspicious amusement. Mum never kissed her when she got home from school – it just wasn't something she did.

'What's going on, Mum?' she asked, removing the satchel from round her neck and plonking it in the middle of the floor.

Jackie took her daughter by the hand. 'Come with me, love,' she said, unable to hide the quiver in her voice. 'I want you to meet someone.'

She led Sadie through the kitchen and into the sitting room. As she did so, Sadie felt a lurch in her stomach. Her childish instinct told her what was coming.

The man standing in their sitting room had very closely cropped hair. His face was slightly round and clean-shaven, and his sideburns were sharp and angular. There was a scar, about an inch long, above his right eye, and his lips were pale and pursed. He wore brown trousers, pleated below the waist in such a way that they gave the impression of hiding a bit of tummy, and a pale blue shirt that complimented his piercing eyes. It was his eyes that struck Sadie most of all. They were surrounded by black bags and stared straight at her with a flatness that seemed to contradict the thin smile that spread across his face.

And within seconds of seeing him, she realized that she had met him before. That very morning. He was the man who had sent the shopkeeper packing. The man who had stopped her copping it.

She stared at him awkwardly, her dark eyes narrowing a little and the inside of her mouth suddenly becoming dry. Then she heard her mum speaking.

'Sadie,' she said in an emphatically friendly voice, like a hostess introducing two people at a party, 'I want you to meet Allen.'

She waited for Sadie to say something, but Sadie didn't.

'Say hello, Sadie, love. And remember your manners. Allen's going to be your new dad.'

CHAPTER 3

'What do you mean?'

Sadie looked round at her mother incredulously. What was she saying? They were in this together, weren't they? They were mourning her dad *together*.

Jackie seemed surprised by Sadie's reaction. 'Don't be like that, love.'

Silence.

Allen spoke for the first time. His voice was deep, quiet and not unfriendly; Sadie could not place his faintly Mancunian accent, but to her it sounded almost musical. 'Why don't we have a nice brew, eh, Jackie?' he suggested to Sadie's mum.

Jackie responded a bit too quickly. 'Cuppa, Sadie?' she asked, even though she knew perfectly well that Sadie had never drunk tea in her life. When Sadie didn't reply and just remained staring at Allen, she turned. 'I'll put the kettle on,' she said, almost to herself, as she walked back into the kitchen. But instead of making for the kettle she first picked up a packet of cigarettes on the side, took one out and lit it with a deep drag.

Sadie's emotions were running riot, and a feeling of physical sickness arose in her gut. She spun round and walked back into the kitchen, wanting to ask her mum a million questions but somehow unable to find the words for even one. Allen followed her and stood in the doorway. The silence was filled by the clattering of her mum getting the tea things together.

When Sadie could bear it no longer she finally spoke. 'I wasn't doing anything,' she whispered.

'What's that, Sadie?' Allen replied, his voice loud enough to be heard by Jackie.

Sadie shot him a spiteful look as her mum turned round to listen. 'We just met before, that's all,' she mumbled.

Allen raised an eyebrow and smiled. 'No, pet,' he said. 'I don't think so.'

'Yes, we have,' she insisted.

'Sadie,' her mum reprimanded. 'Don't answer back to Allen.' She turned to her new man. 'I'm sorry,' she told him.

'It's all right. She's just getting confused, aren't you, pet?'

'I'm not getting confused, I . . .' Her voice trailed away as she realized that Jackie was now suddenly too busy making the tea to listen.

Allen approached her, and Sadie became aware of his strong-smelling aftershave. He put his hand into his pocket pulled out a cuddly toy, pink and floppy-eared, and pressed it into Sadie's unwilling hand. She looked at it briefly. It was not new – she could tell that instantly – and it was the sort of thing that might have been of interest to a child half her age.

'Squeeze it,' Allen said.

She did so, and the cuddly toy started to laugh. The laugh lasted for about thirty seconds, during which time the three of them were silent. When it stopped, Sadie looked from the toy back to Allen. He was obviously expecting a 'thank you', but she didn't have the voice to give it to him, and his eyes tightened in momentary annoyance. He looked over her shoulder, across the kitchen and into the hallway. 'Don't you think you should pick up your school satchel, Sadie?' he asked.

Sadie stared at him in astonishment, and then glanced at her mum for some sort of support.

'Do what Allen asks, love,' was all she said.

Sadie blinked. She handed the cuddly toy back to Allen, and then turned and walked to her satchel as calmly as her turmoil would allow. She picked it up and hung it on the creaky stair banister where she always kept it; then she ran up the stairs, her feet thumping the floorboards, and slammed her bedroom door behind her. She threw herself on to her bed, hugged her pillow and burst into tears.

After some time – Sadie was not sure how long – she heard the stairs creak as they always did when someone walked up them. There was a knock on the door and, without waiting to be asked, Jackie walked in. She was holding the cuddly toy. 'Come on, love,' she said, sitting on the bed beside Sadie and gently stroking her hair.

Sadie continued to whimper into her pillow.

'I thought you'd be pleased,' Jackie continued. 'To have a man in the house, I mean.'

'What about Dad?' Sadie asked accusingly through her tears.

'Oh, love. No one's forgetting about your dad. It's just . . .' Her voice trailed away, and she continued to stroke Sadie's hair as she waited for the crying to subside. Eventually Sadie sat up and put her head against her mum's shoulder. Jackie handed her the cuddly toy. 'You should say thank you to Allen for this,' she told her daughter.

Sadie looked at it in distaste. She could hardly explain to herself why she found it such an unpleasant thing, let alone to her mum. 'I'm too old for things like that,' she said finally. 'It's babyish.'

'I know love, but Allen . . . He doesn't have any children, and he just wanted to do something nice for you.'

As she spoke, Sadie felt a hot wave of guilt passing over her, and she knew she had behaved badly. She stared hard at the frayed carpet on the floor in a gesture of apology, but she prayed her mum wouldn't make her go down and say sorry. 'Is that where you've been going? In the evenings, I mean. To see him?'

Jackie nodded, and brushed a strand of Sadie's long hair off her face. 'Allen's going to look after us, love,' she said in a half-whisper. 'He's going to make sure we're not lonely, you and me.'

Sadie continued to stare at the floor. 'Is he going to live here?' she asked.

'Yes. If that's all right with you. Is it?'

For a moment Sadie thought about telling the truth – that she didn't want anyone else in their house, that she didn't want anyone else in their life. But then she looked up at her mum and saw the anxiety in her eyes. 'All right,' she muttered.

Jackie squeezed her hand. 'Shall we go down?' she asked.

Sadie nodded mutely.

Allen was sitting on the sofa downstairs, his hands behind his head and his legs stretched out in front of him. When he saw the two of them in the door he sat up straight. Sadie felt her mum give her an encouraging little push, and stepped forward. 'Thank you for my present,' she said, without fully catching his eye.

Allen stood up, walked over to her and slid the palm of his hand momentarily down the back of her head. When it reached her neck, she felt him stroke her gently on the shoulder and then squeeze slightly. He stepped over to Jackie. 'You ready?' he asked her.

Jackie shot a guilty look at her daughter. 'Um, me and Allen are nipping out tonight. You'll be all right, won't you, love?'

The corkscrew in Sadie's heart twisted a little further. 'Yeah,' she said sullenly. 'I'll be all right.'

She pushed past them and hurried back up to her bedroom.

By six o'clock she was alone in the house. It was a light, sunny evening, and from her room looking out over the front of the house she could hear the sounds of other children playing in the street. There was nothing to stop her from going out and joining them, or phoning Carly or Anna, but somehow she didn't have the enthusiasm. Her mind was saturated with the confusion of her mother's bombshell; it was like a piece of blotting paper that had soaked up so much ink that you couldn't see its original colour. She could concentrate on nothing else. At times she found herself crying; then she would find herself unable to cry, even though she felt as though she ought to. She made herself a sandwich, but two mouthfuls in she realized she wasn't hungry, so she left it half-eaten on a plate by the sink. She ran herself a deep bubble bath – that always made her feel better – but it did no good. She put on her night-dress, which was a bit too small for her, and climbed under her duvet in an attempt to shut out the persistent evening light. Clutching her teddy bear, she bit her lip as the words her mother had spoken echoed in the chamber of her mind.

'Allen's going to look after us.'

But they didn't need looking after.

'He's going to make sure we're not lonely.'

But they weren't lonely, as long as there was the two of them.

'Allen's going to be your new dad.'

But she didn't want a new dad. She just wanted her old one.

The following morning was a Saturday, and Sadie woke early. The ugly feeling that had been with her until she had finally fallen asleep the previous night had not gone away, and she didn't feel as if she would ever want to get out of bed. But she was thirsty, so, still wearing her nightdress, she crept downstairs, doing her best not to wake anyone.

Allen was already up, leaning with his back to the sink, a mug of tea in his hand. As Sadie walked into the kitchen, she saw his eyes look her up and down and she felt a sudden prickle of discomfort. He looked at her in an enquiring way, and Sadie found herself almost apologizing for her presence.

'I just wanted a glass of water,' she told him.

He acted as though he had not heard her and, instead of moving to allow her access to the sink, he looked meaningfully at the kitchen table.

Sadie followed his gaze. There, on the table, was her beloved satchel. It was lying on its side, the sturdy leather straps unbuckled and the contents spilling out. On top of her few school books, neatly arranged in a precise line from smallest to largest, were the sweets from yesterday.

'Who said you could look in my satchel?' Sadie whispered, horrified that anyone would do such a thing and moving swiftly to pack her things up. But again Allen seemed to ignore her.

When he finally did speak, it was slowly and smoothly. 'That's a lot of sweets for a little girl whose mam only gives her two pound a week,' he observed. He sniffed, his nose wrinkling as he did so, and then took a sip of his tea. The blue eyes continued to look at her over the rim of the mug.

Sadie looked at him with what defiance she could muster, but she couldn't help glancing guiltily back at the table. 'Yeah, well, I've been saving up,' she retorted.

Allen smiled humourlessly. 'I don't think so,' he said. 'Don't worry, I won't tell your mam.' And then, almost as an afterthought, 'I don't think she'd be very happy, do you?'

He turned and poured the dregs of his tea into the sink. Sadie started to pack her things back into the bag, but stopped when Allen spoke again.

'You didn't clear your dinner things away last night.'

'I'll do it this morning.'

Allen breathed out heavily through his nose, a contemptuous sound. 'It's no good doing it this morning,' he said in a suddenly irritated voice. 'You made the mess last night. No one likes messy children.'

A thousand different retorts popped into Sadie's head. 'I don't care what you like or don't like.' 'This is my house, not yours.' 'What makes you think you can talk to me like that?' But suddenly she was tongue-tied. She gazed at his back for a few moments before continuing to pack up her satchel. When she had finished, she looked back at him to see that he had turned and was moving towards her; but he stopped in his tracks as soon as she noticed him.

'You should go and get dressed,' he told her, his voice quiet again now. 'Nice girls don't walk around the house wearing next to nothing.' He smiled, and the expression seemed out of place to Sadie. 'Go and get dressed. Then come back down and we can have breakfast together.'

Sadie gathered her satchel in her arms and, feeling suddenly uncomfortable with the shortness of her nightdress, ran back up the stairs. She threw her stuff carelessly into her room, and then she shut herself in the bathroom and slid the lock closed. Half of her wanted to run into her mum's room and slip into the bed next to her, but she knew she wouldn't be able to face seeing the ruffled sheets on the side where Allen had been sleeping, or lying on the linen where his skin had been. She could hear him moving about in the kitchen, but she vowed that she would not leave the bathroom until she heard her mum getting up.

She didn't have to wait long before Jackie walked down the stairs. Sadie knew what she would be doing – going to find her cigarettes. She listened to the creaking of the floorboards before unlocking the bathroom door and slipping back into her room. She removed her nightie and dressed in a tracksuit – quickly, though she wasn't sure why.

Then she took a deep breath and went back downstairs.

As soon as she walked into the kitchen she could tell that something was wrong. Allen sat at the head of the table, stony-faced, and Jackie seemed unwilling to look her daughter in the eye. A third place was set, with a side plate containing a slice of toast and jam. As Sadie walked in, Allen stood up, picked up the piece of toast, took it to the other side of the kitchen and dropped it in the bin.

'Sadie, love,' her mum said, breaking the tense silence. 'Allen told you he was making you your breakfast, and you let it get cold.'

Sadie was silent, too stunned to speak.

'What do you say?' her mum insisted.

The little girl's eyes flickered between the two of them. 'I didn't know,' she murmured. 'I'll get my own toast.'

Jackie glanced at Allen, who almost imperceptibly shook his head. 'No, Sadie, love. It's too late now.' Jackie's voice was subdued. 'Try and be quicker next time, all right?'

Sadie opened her mouth to object, but as she did so she caught Allen's eye. There was something about the stern look he gave her that made her feel suddenly frightened of this man in their kitchen. Too angry and upset to say anything, she turned and left the flat, slamming the front door behind her.

As she made her way to the estate playground, she felt hot tears of indignation welling up in her eyes. Someone called her name in a friendly way, but she didn't want to speak to anyone and picked up her pace; by the time she reached the playground she was running, and the tracks of her tears were horizontal along the side of her face. It was still quite early, so the playground was deserted as she took her usual seat at the swings.

Sadie just couldn't understand why her mum was taking his side against her. She hadn't been out of order, had she? She hadn't done anything wrong. Then she thought guiltily about the chocolates. It was true that she shouldn't have stolen them, but they hadn't done anyone much harm, had they? Not that she thought her mum would see it that way. Sadie really didn't want Allen to tell Jackie his suspicions, and she hated the fact that this man suddenly had a hold over her.

As the morning wore on, the playground began to fill up – mums mostly, with their kids, but also a few older teenagers, loitering and sharing cigarettes there because there was nowhere else to go. Sadie was used to these people – she recognized most of them and certainly never felt threatened by them – but she didn't want company this morning; and as the nearby tower block started casting a shadow over the playground, she left with a vague shiver and wandered round the concrete jungle of the estate. By lunchtime, though, she knew she would have to go back: she was getting hungry, and had no money to buy food. And even though she knew she could knock on the door of a neighbour, somehow she didn't feel like sharing what was bottling up inside her. She headed home.

Allen was still in the kitchen when Sadie walked in. She looked around to see if her mum was there but, as though reading her mind, Allen said, 'She's gone to the shops.'

Sadie kept her lips tightly closed.

Allen walked towards her, and suddenly his frowning face lightened up and he smiled down at Sadie. 'I've been out and got you something,' he told her. He smiled a little more broadly as he reached into his pocket and pulled out a small chocolate bar. He bent down and gave it to the reluctant Sadie. 'If you want sweets,' he told her in a conspiratorial whisper, 'you only have to ask.'

Sadie winced slightly under his piercing stare, but Allen ignored it. He held her chin gently between his thumb and first finger and lifted her face slightly. Sadie couldn't help but notice that his hand was shaking slightly. Once more she smelled his after-shave, and she suppressed a wave of nausea.

'Just keep it a secret from your mum, eh? She doesn't have to know everything, does she?'

Suddenly a key could be heard in the door. Allen quickly stood up, turned his back on Sadie and walked swiftly into the sitting room. By the time Jackie was in the house, Sadie was alone in the kitchen.

Last night Sadie had been shocked and upset that Mum and Allen had gone out; tonight she wished they would. But they stayed in, and on Sunday they didn't leave the house at all. Sadie spent most of the time in her bedroom, only coming down for food which her mum – uncharacteristically – prepared for them. They would sit round the table in silence, eating ready meals and drinking water. Occasionally Jackie would try to goad them into conversation, but never with success. It was the longest weekend of Sadie's life, and she couldn't wait to get to school on Monday morning.

She met up with Carly and Anna as she always did, but they could tell instantly that Sadie was subdued and not her usual self.

'What's up with you?' Anna asked when Sadie appeared not to hear something she had said.

Sadie blinked. 'Nothing.'

'Don't look like nothing. You look like you're sucking a lemon.'

'I'm fine, OK?' she snapped.

Anna and Carly looked at each other, their eyes mock-wide. 'All right, all right!'

They walked in silence for a bit.

'What d'you reckon?' Carly asked finally. 'We going to help ourselves to some chocolate this morning? There's that mini-mart on the side of the main road – we haven't tried that yet, and I reckon we could get our hands on the ciggie counter if someone distracted the girl there.'

Anna sucked her teeth. 'What d'you reckon, Sadie? I'm up for it if everyone else is.'

They waited for Sadie to answer, but she seemed

to be in a world of her own. Suddenly she realized what they had been saying and snapped out of it. 'No,' she said. 'Not this morning. I don't feel like it.'

'Why not?' Anna asked, her voice rising several notches.

'Yeah, come on, Sadie. I'm starving. I haven't had any breakfast.'

Sadie snapped, 'I don't want to, OK?'

Sadie never usually raised her voice, and the sound of it was enough to silence Anna and Carly into submission. But Sadie felt suddenly guilty that she had lashed out at her two friends, so she put her hand into her satchel and rifled around. After a few moments she pulled out a chocolate bar. With an unpleasant pang she realized it was the one Allen had given her – she didn't remember having put it in her schoolbag – and as though dropping a hot coal she handed it to Carly, before rummaging around and finding another one for Anna. Like hungry kittens being given a plate of food, they fell silent and ate their treats as they continued their journey to school, although Sadie could sense them glancing warily at her from time to time.

In class Sadie was more unwilling than usual to concentrate, and when the bell rang for morning break she found herself in the unfamiliar position of being by herself in the playground – clearly Carly and Anna were giving her a wide berth after this morning's little outburst. On this occasion, she didn't really mind. She kicked her heels around for a few minutes before she became aware of someone following her. Looking round, she saw little Jamie Brown. He was pretending not to notice Sadie, but she could tell that he knew she was there. 'All right, Jamie?' she called.

Jamie looked up and nodded at her; then he walked a little more quickly in her direction. As he approached, the unmistakable odour he carried with him assaulted Sadie's senses.

It was hot. Most of the other children in the playground – Sadie included – were wearing T-shirts, but not Jamie. He had on his usual tatty corduroy trousers and thick, stained sweatshirt that was several sizes too small, and he looked stifled. As he fell in beside Sadie, he said nothing, and the two of them carried on walking in silence. As they walked, however, Sadie threw the occasional glance down at the younger boy.

'Aren't you hot in that top?' she asked him finally.

Jamie shook his head, and clumsily pulled the sleeves of his sweatshirt down further towards his wrists. As he did so, Sadie noticed something: just below where the cuff of his sweatshirt finished was what looked like a purple stain. For a moment she couldn't work out what it was; then it struck her that it was a bruise. She stopped, and turned to take hold of his hand, but the sudden movement made her companion flinch and draw away.

'Let us see your hand,' she urged gently.

Jamie shook his head, and his cheeks flushed with embarrassment; but when Sadie made a second attempt to look at his wrist, he relented. She peeled back the dirty sleeve of his sweatshirt and he winced as she did so. She was horrified by what it concealed. The bruising continued all the way up his arm, and it was mottled and ugly. In places it was a deep almost-black; elsewhere it was yellow and faded. Sadie had no idea if it continued beneath the rest of his sweatshirt, and she couldn't bear to ask. But she had to say something.

'Who did it?' she asked.

Jamie said nothing: his lips were pursed and he was shaking his head stiffly.

Sadie looked around her. She could see little groups of people looking in her direction and talking, so she put her hand round Jamie's shoulders and moved him to a further corner of the playground.

'Was it your mum?' she asked the boy.

Jamie looked away. He hadn't said yes, but it was acknowledgement enough for Sadie.

'Why don't you tell someone?'

Jamie shook his head.

'I can tell someone for you, if you like. There's that social worker who comes in sometimes. Or what about Miss Venables? She's nice –'

'No!' Jamie spoke forcefully. 'I wish I never showed you now.'

He stomped off, but Sadie followed him. 'It's all right,' she said. 'I won't tell no one.'

Jamie stopped and looked at her with an anger that seemed almost comical on his tiny frame. But he couldn't keep it up for long, and soon his gaze dropped back down to the ground again. 'She'd only say it weren't her,' he muttered. 'Any case,' – his eyes flickered up to Sadie then back down again – 'I don't want her to get into trouble. And they'd only get me kicked out, wouldn't they?'

Sadie felt a sudden pang of pity. The little boy's plight made her own problems seem inconsequential; and without knowing quite how, she understood his desire to keep things to himself. Ever so gently, more out of a wish not to frighten him than not to hurt him, she rolled his sleeve back down so that the bruise was covered once more.

'And anyway,' Jamie continued with a weak smile, 'I have told someone, ain't I?'

Sadie looked at him in confusion. 'Who?'

'You,' the little boy said, and he wandered away into the heart of the playground, ignoring the unkind comments from the children he passed.

CHAPTER 4

'Why?' Sadie watched her mum wiping down the kitchen surfaces, and wondered why she wouldn't catch her eye.

'Because we need the money, Sadie,' Jackie replied irritably. 'Stop asking so many stupid questions.'

It was three weeks since Allen had moved in, and apart from that first night he appeared barely to have left the house. The sitting room had become his domain, where he would sit on the settee, his legs stretched out in front of him, the TV remote never far away. And since his arrival, the room had become immaculate – not just the room, in fact, but the whole house. Sadie found it weird: for as long as she could remember she had lived in a chaotic house, and her mother was not one for tidying up and cleaning. But one look from Allen seemed to be enough for her to clear up a dirty coffee cup or wipe crumbs from the now perpetually empty kitchen table. Sadie herself had always kept her room tidy, but since Allen's reprimand about the dirty plate on his first morning, she had been extra fastidious. There was no way she was going to give him an excuse to tell her off again.

'But you're always saying there's no point you getting a job. What about your benefits?'

Sadie heard her mum start to swear under her breath. 'For fuck's—' But then she checked herself, and turned to her daughter. 'It's more complicated than that, Sadie. Grown-up stuff, OK? I've got a job in a pub up the road, and that's that.'

At the word 'pub', Sadie's stomach gave a little lurch. Whatever else she thought of Allen, she had to be thankful that he seemed to have got her mum off the booze. The ciggies too, although she knew from the smell on her mum's clothes and skin that she still had the occasional crafty fag outside, despite Allen's ban on smoking in the house. The idea of Mum working in a pub filled Sadie with a sudden fear that she would slide back into her old ways.

'But he doesn't do anything,' Sadie complained, 'apart from watch the telly.' She kept her voice low so that Allen wouldn't hear her in the next room. 'Why can't he be the one to go out to work? Why does it have to be you?'

Still Jackie refused to look directly at her daughter, and she avoided her questions. 'You'll just have to get used to it, Sadie. Lots of mums go out to work.'

'But—'

'No buts, Sadie.' Allen spoke quietly from the

doorway to the sitting room. Sadie and Jackie both turned their heads to look at him at the same time, and waited for him to speak again. 'Have you thought that your mam might actually *want* to go out to work, Sadie? You shouldn't be so selfish.'

Sadie jutted her chin out forcefully, but she didn't reply.

'Tell her, Jackie,' Allen instructed.

Jackie hesitated, but kept her eyes on him. 'It'll be nice for me,' she said in a slightly monotone voice, 'to get out of the house and all.'

'Just as long as you keep off the sauce,' Allen said rather contemptuously. 'Putting you in a boozer is like putting a cat in a mousehole.' As he went back into the sitting room, Jackie's face flushed with embarrassment and she turned back to her cleaning.

'So when do you start, Mum?' Sadie asked in a small voice.

'This afternoon. Late shift. Three till twelve. You can get your own dinner, can't you?'

Sadie nodded, but her mum didn't see her, so she slung her satchel sullenly over her head and left.

School was uneventful and passed quickly. It always did when she didn't want to get home. As she sat daydreaming in her lessons, she thought about what had happened that morning. It made no sense. She loved her mum, but she knew her well enough to doubt that she really wanted to go out to work. And yet she had heard her say so herself. Maybe her mum wanted to go to work so that she could get away from Sadie. She wouldn't have thought that before Allen had arrived, but in the last few weeks she had been different. Distant. Not the mum she knew or wanted to remember.

What was more, Sadie didn't relish the idea of being in the house alone with Allen. She couldn't work him out – sometimes he was nice to her, sometimes mean, and she almost didn't know which Allen she liked the least. He was always walking up quietly behind her, appearing out of nowhere, getting in the way. Even when she hid herself away in the bedroom, he was always coming in to check on her, knocking gently – three measured raps that she had grown to dread – and entering without waiting for a reply.

The weather had turned. It was still warm, but the dry summer had become wet and the day was punctuated with thunderous showers. The rain started as soon as the school bell went for home time and was torrential on the way home, so Sadie, Anna and Carly barely spoke and concentrated on running back to the estate and its rain-stained concrete as quickly as possible.

Soaked to the skin, Sadie sprinted up the pathway to the front door. Her key was already in her hand – it had been in readiness ever since she entered the boundaries of the estate – and almost on autopilot she tried to open the front door with it. The key slid easily into the lock, but when she tried to turn it, it wouldn't budge. She tried again, wiggling the key gently at first and then with more force, but it was no good. She rang the bell instead.

The door opened almost immediately. Allen stood in the doorway and observed Sadie as though she was a stranger or a cold caller. After an awkward few moments, during which he did not step aside to let her in, Sadie was forced to speak.

'Can I come in?'

Suddenly Allen looked as though his attention had been snapped into focus. His lips flickered into a smile, and he stepped aside slightly, though not quite enough for Sadie to be able to enter without her sopping clothes brushing against him.

'My key wouldn't work,' she mumbled as she entered.

'No,' said Allen. 'It wouldn't.'

'Why not? It's always worked.'

'I've changed the lock,' Allen said as he walked back into the kitchen. Sadie stayed in the hallway, watching him.

'What for?' she asked, but Allen didn't reply, instead walking into the sitting room. Sadie followed him, water dripping off her coat on to the kitchen floor. 'What did you change the lock for?' she asked again. She knew she sounded insolent, but she couldn't help it.

By now Allen was sitting on the settee again, his legs stretched out in his usual position. 'You're too young to have your own door key. I've discussed it with your mam and she agrees with me.'

Sadie could hardly believe what she was hearing and found herself unable to speak. She'd had her own key for years – Mum and Dad had trusted her, and she'd never done anything to betray that trust. Tears started to brim in her eyes.

'No use crying about it. It's about time we knew where you are and when you're coming back. I know for a fact that you get up to no good when you're out on your own. I haven't told your mother what I suspect yet, but if it carries on, I will – don't you worry about that.'

Sadie was shivering now, half from the wet clothes, half from the way he was speaking to her. Unable to trust herself to open her mouth, she spun round and ran, not for the first time since Allen had arrived, up to her bedroom. Outside the rain continued to hammer on her window and the sky was a deep, felt-tip grey. She slammed the door shut and started to peel off her sopping school uniform. She felt her long wet hair cold against her face.

As the clothes fell to the floor, she froze. She could hear Allen moving around downstairs, his footsteps sounding heavy and impatient. And then she heard a sound she recognized – a click. It was the front door being locked.

A sudden panic arose in her. She held her breath and remained deathly still as she listened with all her concentration. At first there was silence; then there was an unmistakable sound.

It was the sound of footsteps coming up the stairs.

Feeling an irrational burst of terror, Sadie jumped on to her bed. Goosebumps arose on her skin as she crouched in the corner, hugging her knees, wanting to remove her wet underwear and yet somehow not wanting to. As she did so, she counted the footsteps up the stairs.

One.

Two.

Three.

Four.

Five.

And then they stopped – about halfway up, Sadie calculated. For a few moments there was silence and then, more quietly this time, the footsteps disappeared back down the stairs.

Sadie did not move until she was sure that Allen had finished walking around. Instead, she remained on her bed, her skin clammy and her limbs shaking, the sickness of fear suddenly replaced with the hot flush of relief.

After a few minutes, she dared to creep on to the landing. Standing at the top of the stairs, she strained her ears and could make out the low hubbub of the television. By now she knew his habits. She knew that once he was installed in front of the box, he would not move from it willingly, so she crept back to her room, removed the rest of her clothes and put on the blue dressing gown that hung on the back of her door. Then she crept back on to the bed.

How she wished her mum were there. How she wished she could wordlessly snuggle up to her, feel her arms around her shoulders and put her head in her lap. She wished now she hadn't been so mean before she left for school. When she saw her, she would be really nice. She would make things better between them. Jackie might have been different these past few weeks, but she was still her mum, and Sadie wanted her. It all seemed wrong, being stuck in the house with this man she hardly knew and liked even less – a cruel inversion of the way things were supposed to be.

The rain continued to pound on the window. For a precious minute or two, Sadie allowed herself to be transfixed by the droplets falling like tears down the windowpane.

Unbidden, the image of little Jamie Brown popped into her head. She suppressed a shudder as she remembered the bruising up his arm and wondered, not for the first time, what sort of hell he had to endure when he was at home. All of a sudden she felt slightly ashamed of herself. The little boy who had taken to following her around the playground at breaktime surely had to endure more than she did: Allen might be mean, but at least he never hit her.

Maybe he was right. Maybe she *was* selfish. Maybe this whole situation was her fault.

How long Sadie sat there, huddled in her dressing gown, she couldn't say; but she was snapped out of her daydream by the sound of

Allen's voice: he was calling from the bottom of the stairs, 'Your tea's ready, Sadie.'

Sadie blinked. He never made her tea; it was normally up to Jackie or Sadie herself to prepare meals for all of them. She felt like calling down to say she wasn't hungry, but something told her that would not be a wise thing to do, so she quickly pulled on her pink tracksuit and went downstairs. A plate of spaghetti hoops on toast was waiting for her on the kitchen table, with a glass of water.

Silently she sat down and started to eat. The food was only lukewarm, and she barely had an appetite, but she knew that if she didn't eat it would only cause aggro, so she soldiered on, aware of Allen's gaze on her all the time.

'You don't say much, do you, Sadie?' he asked after a while.

Sadie chewed her food and didn't reply.

'You like spaghetti?' Allen tried again.

''S'all right,' Sadie said, her mouth still half full.

'Me too. Mind if I have a bit of yours?'

Sadie did mind, but she knew she couldn't say so, so she shrugged and watched as Allen stood up and fetched himself a fork from a drawer. He walked back to the table, put his left hand on Sadie's left shoulder, and then leaned over the other one and lifted a forkful of food into his mouth. Sadie felt her muscles seizing up and she stared intently at the plate in front of her. Allen's hand remained lightly on her shoulder. When he had finished his mouthful, he helped himself to a second, gave her a little squeeze and went to wash up his fork.

Sadie started eating more quickly. As she heard Allen put his fork by the sink, somehow she could tell that he was looking at her from behind. The moment she had wolfed down her last mouthful, she scraped back her chair and picked up her dirty plate. Allen was leaning against the sink, a strange smile on his face.

'Excuse me,' Sadie muttered. 'I have to wash up.'

With a nod, Allen cleared out of the way and wandered back into the sitting room.

Sadie washed up quickly, and hurried upstairs. She felt a chill. It was not particularly cold in the house, but she had got soaked earlier on, so maybe that was why. She felt like having a bath, hot and soapy, to warm her up and wash away the uncomfortable feeling Allen had just left her with. Then she would go to bed – early. Changing back into her dressing gown, she took the towel that was hanging on the end of her bed and went into the bathroom.

Immediately she noticed that the sliding lock that had been there ever since she could remember was not there. All that remained were four screw holes and a patch of unpainted wood where the lock used to be. Sadie stared at the door, puzzled: why would anyone take the lock off the door? Admittedly it had always been a little stiff, but it had never been a problem – although she knew Allen never locked the door behind him when he used the bathroom. Looking around her, her eyes fell on the dirty-washing basket that was always kept by the sink. She dragged it across the floor and propped it against the door – at least that would make it clear that someone was in there. She turned the taps on and the sound of running water filled the room.

When the bubble bath that she had poured into the hot water had transformed itself into huge snowy peaks, Sadie let her dressing gown fall to the floor and climbed in. The hot water stung her skin, but she liked it – it felt as if it was cleansing her all the more thoroughly. Slowly she allowed herself to sink beneath the suds and stretch out, closing her eyes to block out the harsh glare of the plastic strip lighting on the ceiling. She slipped gently further down into the water, allowing her head to become half submerged and her long, dark hair to splay out. She loved the feeling of being under water, and the way all the sounds became muted and muffled; she felt as if she was in her own little world, away from it all. She started drumming her fingernails against the bottom of the bath, and focused on that regular, rhythmic, under-water sound.

But then she heard something else. A voice. It could only be one person's.

Spluttering, she pushed herself up from under the water and wiped the suds from around her eyes. Her pulse was suddenly racing, her breathing heavy, but she was relieved to see nobody in the bathroom. Perhaps she had imagined it. She sat still in the bath.

Suddenly, the dirty-washing basket in front of the door nudged forward a couple of inches as the door was pushed ajar. It nudged forward again. She could see Allen's fingers curled round the edge of the door. 'Let us in,' he said, his voice echoing slightly against the yellowing tiles of the bathroom. 'Let us in to use the toilet. I'm desperate.'

Sadie found that her breath was shaking, and all of a sudden something snapped in her as she started to scream. 'Get out!' she yelled. 'Get out! Get away from me!' Her screams degenerated into a whimper. 'Get out!' she repeated, her wet hands covering her wet face.

When she looked up again, Allen's fingertips were no longer round the door; but she had not heard him walk away, so she could not tell whether or not he was waiting for her on the other side. For an unrealistic moment she considered staying where she was, safe under the water, until her mum came back. But of course that would not be for hours: she had to get out.

Still catching her breath through sobs that escaped involuntarily through her throat, she stood up in the bath and, her hands covering herself to afford her some sort of modesty, stepped over the side. She grabbed her dressing gown and tried to pull it quickly over her wet skin, but her fingers were fumbling and the more she tried to hurry, the slower she seemed to go. Eventually she had herself covered, and she wrapped her towel around her shoulders to give her extra protection. She wanted to be in her bedroom. Now. So she pulled the dirty-washing basket away from the door and, with a deep, shaky breath, stepped out on to the landing.

Allen was there.

He was standing at the other end of the landing, at the top of the stairs. His head was bowed slightly, but his eyes were looking straight at Sadie and his breathing was heavy. His lips seemed stuck in a position that was almost a sneer, but not quite. For an instant he looked away from her, but then he blinked again and his eyes were on her once more. She found herself unable to move.

When he spoke, his voice was even quieter than usual. 'I thought you said come in.'

Sadie shook her head faintly.

'I thought you were done in there,' Allen repeated. 'I thought you said come in.'

'I didn't say anything,' Sadie whispered hoarsely. She returned his gaze as coolly as she dared.

All of a sudden, Allen lashed out. He banged the flat of his hand hard against the woodchip wall, and Sadie jumped. In an instant his face had transformed. His eyes were flashing and his lip curled into an ugly mockery of the expression Sadie was used to. And then he was shouting – not particularly loudly, but forcefully, and with unbridled contempt. 'I was calling you for ages. You should have shouted back.'

His hands appeared to be shaking, and Sadie took a frightened step backwards into the doorway of the bathroom.

'Anyhow,' he hissed, more quietly now, 'what makes you think I want to see you in the first place? You're too fucking cocky, Sadie. You're lucky I don't see to it that you go into a home.'

Sadie felt her lower lip wobbling. She watched, wide-eyed, as Allen struggled to control his sudden burst of fury. With a hateful look, he turned and stomped down the stairs. As though his disappearance had released her from a lock and chain, Sadie rushed into her bedroom.

Dusk was falling, as was the rain, though less heavily now, and her room seemed saturated with gloom. Sadie did not want to turn on the light, feeling that the half-darkness somehow protected her. She quickly dried herself, pulled on her nightdress and buried herself under her bedclothes, clutching a soft teddy bear her dad had bought her many years ago. She breathed in its smell. Normally it was so comforting, but tonight for some reason it just made the tears come, and it didn't take long for the bear's matted hair to become quite wet. And even when she could cry no more, she remained under the covers, curled up and clinging desperately to the soft toy which could not offer her the comfort that she craved.

It was fully dark outside by the time she dared to poke her head out from under the duvet. Late, though sleep seemed only a distant possibility.

Slowly, tentatively, she put her head on the pillow and closed her eyes.

Time passed.

After a while, a warm blanket of drowsiness fell over Sadie; but it was ruffled before she could truly fall asleep by the sound of footsteps coming up the stairs once more. They were not heavy footsteps this time, but her eyes sprang suddenly open when she realized they were approaching her door. And then came the sound she dreaded.

Knock.

Knock.

Knock.

She said nothing – she knew there was no point. She heard the sound of the door brushing against the carpet as it swung open, and she closed her eyes, lying desperately still and pretending to be asleep. Despite not being able to see anything, she could sense Allen walking across the room to her bed. He sat on the side of it, and the sickening smell of his aftershave filled her nose.

Then, with a start, she felt him brushing his hand across her hair.

'I know you're not asleep, Sadie,' he whispered.

Sadie wanted to jump out of bed and scream, but some unseen force pinned her to the mattress and she kept her eyes resolutely closed. The stroking of her hair stopped, and suddenly she felt Allen's warm breath near her face. It smelled of the tinned spaghetti from earlier.

'Goodnight, pet,' he breathed, before planting a

kiss on her closed mouth, leaving a vile feeling of the wetness of his lips.

Then he stood up and walked out, leaving Sadie alone in the darkness of her room.

She awoke with a start.

It was pitch black in her room, and she had no idea what time it was. In the darkness, however, she heard the front door closing and assumed that it must be her mum coming back from work. That would make it a bit past midnight; she could only have been asleep for an hour or two. The rain had stopped now, and she could quite clearly hear her mum shout 'I'm back' before moving through to the sitting room and out of earshot. Sadie wanted more than anything to go down and see her – to hug her – but she couldn't bear to be in the same room as Allen.

So she just lay there, protected by her duvet and the darkness of the night.

All of a sudden she heard voices from downstairs. Raised voices. Allen was shouting at her mum. Sadie couldn't hear what he was saying, but she could detect the fury in his voice. Her mum said something – or shouted it, rather – but it was short-lived. There was an immediate and ominous silence; Sadie found herself holding her breath. The silence was broken by the sound of footsteps up the stairs – running, this time, and Sadie recognized the rhythm of her mother's steps. She sat up in bed, hoping that Jackie would come into her room to say goodnight; but she was disappointed: all she heard was Jackie's own bedroom door slamming shut.

Something told her that she shouldn't go in to see her. She lay back down in bed and, despite the turmoil in her mind, soon fell asleep.

If Allen came up to bed that night, Sadie was not awake to hear it.

CHAPTER 5

The next day dawned bright and clear, but Jamie Brown had been awake long before the sun rose.

It was his birthday the following day, and last night he had gone to sleep cosseted by pleasant fantasies of a birthday present, and even a chocolate cake with candles. He had never had either, of course, but that didn't stop him from hoping each time his birthday came around. Maybe Mum would have had a change of heart this year; maybe there would be a bit of spare money; just maybe he would have a happy day.

But the maybes had dissolved from his mind a little before dawn when he awoke with the familiar feeling of horror. The thin mattress which lay on the floor of the tiny box room he called his own was wet, and so was the stained sheet that covered him. He didn't dare move for fear of waking his mother up; all he could do was hope that it dried before morning. But morning had come, and the bedding was still damp. The little boy shivered, not just because he was cold.

Perhaps he could hide what had happened.

Perhaps if he got up now and pulled the frayed blanket over his sheet, she wouldn't notice. He quietly slipped out of bed, removed his damp pyjamas and put them under the pillow; then he put on the underwear he had been wearing for the past week. He crept out of his bedroom and into the bathroom. It was filthy, as it always was. The taps to the bath were broken, and he wasn't allowed to use the shower unless Mum said so; instead, he took his flannel, which had fallen down beside the toilet and become encrusted hard, and soaked it under cold running water. He squeezed it and rubbed it over his skin, taking care not to press too hard where the bruises were. When he had finished his ineffectual wash, he moistened his toothbrush under the running water. The bristles were worn and flattened, and the handle stained with lime scale; there was, of course, no toothpaste, but he brushed nevertheless, pressing so hard that his gums started to hurt. He placed the toothbrush back on the side of the sink, and then turned round and left the room.

His heart jumped.

Standing in the doorway of his room was his mum. She had a cigarette in one hand and his damp pyjamas in the other.

Jamie cowered, shrinking against the wall under the withering heat of her gaze.

'What the fuck is this?' she asked, her voice deathly quiet.

Jamie was too terrified to speak.

'Don't fucking ignore me, Jamie. What the fuck is this?'

'I'm s-s-sorry, Mum,' Jamie stammered. 'I think I wet myself.'

His mum hurled the wet pyjamas at his head. 'I can fucking see that!' she screamed.

Jamie struggled to remove the clothes from around his eyes. As he did so he saw his mum bearing down on him. Instantly he crumpled to the floor, rolling up in a little ball like the hedgehog he had seen in a book at school. 'Please don't hit me, Mum,' he whimpered, but it was too late. As he spoke he felt her bare foot against his abdomen. The thought flashed through his head that at least she wasn't wearing shoes; but he still felt a shriek of pain as she kicked him on the bruises from his last beating. He found himself gasping as his mother shouted at him again.

'It's no fuckin' wonder everyone hates you. *I* fucking hate you, and I'm your mum, more fool me.' She stomped back into her bedroom, but the shouting continued. 'Now fuck off to school. I'm sick of the fucking sight of you . . .'

The blue sky made yesterday's rain seem like a weird dream; indeed, to Sadie, everything about the previous evening had a nightmare quality about it, almost as though none of it had happened. As she walked sleepily to the bathroom, however, she was reminded of it all: the bath water was still there, as she had been in too much of a hurry to get to her bedroom to pull the plug out. It seemed that nobody had been into the bathroom since; or if they had, they wanted to make a point. She removed the plug, and as the water drained out of the bath she cleaned her teeth and washed her face. Then she returned to her bedroom to get dressed.

It was quiet in the house, for which Sadie was extremely thankful. If she crept downstairs, maybe she could get her cereal and leave the house without anyone waking up. She tiptoed down, avoiding those parts of the staircase that she knew were creaky, and made her way into the kitchen, where she poured herself a bowl of cornflakes. There was only a drop of milk left, so she doused the cereal with what there was before turning to sit at the kitchen table.

She stopped in her tracks.

Allen was sitting at the head of the table, with his chair turned ninety degrees so that he could face her. He had been so quiet, so immobile, that she hadn't seen him until now. His face was blank, but he looked tired, and he was wearing the same clothes that he had been wearing the previous night.

'Good morning,' he said.

Sadie walked brusquely to the other end of the table, where she sat down and started to eat with big mouthfuls; but the faster she tried to eat, the more the cereal stuck in her throat.

'Aren't you talking to me, Sadie?' Allen asked.

Sadie swallowed her mouthful. 'Where's Mum?' she asked.

‘Don’t worry about your mam,’ Allen told her. ‘She’s still in bed. Tired. She needs her sleep, now she’s working and all.’

‘I want to say goodbye before I leave for school.’

‘I told you, she’s tired.’ He stood up, and walked over to where Sadie was sitting. The girl put her hands on her lap and looked down at the now empty cereal bowl. He was standing too close now, invading her personal space. He lifted his hand and made as if to put it on her shoulder, but Sadie shrank from him and instead he picked up the bowl. ‘Off you go, then,’ Allen said. ‘I’ll wash this up for you.’

Sadie watched as he took the bowl to the sink and stood there, running the water, resolutely not looking back. As quickly as she could, she got her things together and left.

‘Miss Venables, you are not this school’s child protection officer. I can assure you that we are fully aware of the concerns about Jamie Brown, and they’re being dealt with through the proper channels.’

‘But Mr Martin,’ Stacy said, her frustration with the headmaster taking the edge off her politeness, ‘social services aren’t doing a thing.’

‘They’re *monitoring the situation*,’ the headmaster said emphatically, as though speaking to a child. ‘They can’t just storm in and remove the child from his mother – there’s no evidence of maltreatment, there’s been no disclosure from the child.’

‘But you only have to look at him . . .’

'Enough!' Mr Martin said forcefully, and she was stunned into silence by the sudden raising of his voice. The headmaster collapsed heavily into his chair and pinched his forehead momentarily before speaking again. 'We're keeping a close eye on Jamie Brown,' he said more quietly. 'It's really not your concern.' He looked her up and down. 'I see you've chosen to ignore our last conversation about what constitutes a suitable dress code for teachers in this school.'

Stacy smoothed her white T-shirt. 'Will that be all, Mr Martin?' she asked coldly.

'Yes, Miss Venables,' the headmaster said wearily. 'That will be all.'

Stacy's footsteps echoed off the hard floor of the corridor as she stomped, seething, to her next lesson. Her cheeks were flushed with the embarrassment of her dressing down and also her frustration. She knew instinctively that all was not right with that kid. Why could nobody else see what was so obvious to her?

It was a long lesson. The children were distracted – it was always the way when the weather was sunny – and Miss Venables spent more time calming them down than teaching them English. There were the usual troublemakers: Anna and Carly felt the sharp end of her tongue, as well as a few of the boys. Curiously, though, Sadie Burrows was not sitting with the girls but had installed herself at the front of the class and was working quietly. It wasn't like her to be by herself.

As the bell rang, the familiar sound of chair-scraping filled the room. 'Don't forget you have homework to do tonight,' she called above the noise, but few people paid her any attention, and in any case her mind was on something else.

'Sadie,' she called to the girl sitting at the front. 'Could you stay behind, please?'

Sadie looked up suspiciously at her teacher. 'I'll be late for my next lesson,' she said without much enthusiasm.

Miss Venables approached her desk. 'It won't take long,' she told her. 'Just a couple of minutes.' She looked around at the few children who were dragging their heels, clearly hanging around to see what she wanted with Sadie. 'Was there anything?' she asked them with a raised eyebrow. As one they shook their heads, muttered and left the room.

When it was just the two of them, Miss Venables' face softened. 'Is everything all right, Sadie?'

'Yes, miss.'

'You seem quiet, that's all.'

'I'm fine, miss.'

Miss Venables furrowed her brow slightly and nodded. 'I was going to ask you if you could do me a favour, Sadie.'

She watched Sadie's face twitch slightly and knew that she felt uncomfortable being asked this by a teacher. But give children a bit of responsibility, she always said, and it's amazing how often they rise to the challenge. Besides, she really did need her help.

'You know Jamie Brown?'

Sadie nodded cautiously.

'Does he talk to you?'

'Sometimes, miss.'

'That's what I thought. I've seen the two of you in the playground. Has he ever told you anything about what happens at home?'

Sadie looked straight into Miss Venables' eyes, and the teacher found it impossible to read what she was thinking. She did notice, however, that the girl took a little bit too long to answer. 'No, miss. We don't talk about things like that.'

The teacher's eyes narrowed slightly. 'No, of course not.' She turned and walked back to her desk at the front of the class. 'So what do you talk about?' she asked lightly.

Sadie shrugged. 'Just stuff, miss,' she said.

Miss Venables nodded. 'The thing is, Sadie, I'm a bit worried about him.' She smiled at the girl. 'I'm sure I don't need to tell you why that is. He seems very down today. You're a sensible girl. I'm sure you'd tell me if you thought there was anything I should know, wouldn't you?'

'Yes, miss.' Miss Venables noted that Sadie avoided her eyes as she spoke. She thought of quizzing her a bit further, but at the last moment decided against it.

'Well, you always know where to find me if you need to. Go on, then. You'd better get to your next lesson.'

Sadie nodded her head, slung her satchel over her neck and left the classroom.

Anna and Carly were waiting for her a little way up the corridor. 'What she want?' Anna asked immediately as Sadie approached. 'What you done wrong? You in trouble?'

'It's nothing.'

'Oh, c'mon, Sadie,' Carly needled her. 'What she say?'

'It's nothing, OK?' Sadie snapped. Her two friends looked at each other in surprise, and then back at her. 'Just leave me alone,' Sadie muttered, and she stormed off without them.

As a result of her outburst, Sadie found herself alone again in the playground at lunchtime. Carly and Anna were pretending to have a good time, but she could tell by the sidelong glances that were coming her way whenever she was near them that they felt as uncomfortable as she did. Somehow, though, she couldn't drum up the enthusiasm to go and make her peace with them. They would only ask her yet again what was the matter, and she didn't want to talk about that. She hadn't told them about Allen moving in, or any of the other stuff: for some reason she was embarrassed about it, and she wanted to keep it to herself.

Sadie had been surprised by Miss Venables' questions – teachers weren't supposed to talk like that. Maybe there was something really wrong with Jamie. Maybe she should find out: even if she didn't tell anyone, perhaps she could do something to help. And it would take her mind off other things. Looking around, she saw the little boy walking along one of the walls of the playground, his finger tracing the shape of the mortar between the bricks. He looked just the same as usual. She crossed the playground to talk to him.

'Hi,' she said, as she fell in beside him.

'Leave us alone.'

Sadie blinked at him. 'What d'you mean?'

'Just leave us alone,' Jamie replied. There were tears in his eyes, and to hide them he took a couple of quick steps forward. Sadie stood still, watching him go and feeling a hot creeping embarrassment rising up her neck. In her little fantasy she had thought she could make everything all right for Jamie Brown, but she couldn't.

How could she, when she couldn't even make things all right for herself?

Carly and Anna continued to avoid her, even after school. She wanted to make up with them, but she was embarrassed by her outburst and didn't know how to; besides, now that she no longer had her own key, something told her that if she was late back home she'd get a grilling from Allen. The thought of seeing him was repugnant to her, but not as bad as the memory of his fury the previous night. So as soon as school finished, she walked home by herself.

It felt strange having to ring the bell, as though this was not even her home any more. In the event she had to ring it twice before Allen deigned to answer. When he did so, Sadie looked aghast at him.

He was wearing no shirt, and the pungent odour of his aftershave was worse than ever. Sadie's distaste must have been obvious from her face, because a shadow instantly fell over Allen's expression.

'What?' he asked.

Sadie looked away. 'Nothing.' She pushed past him and ran straight upstairs to her bedroom.

Closing the door behind her, Sadie sat down on her bed and pulled a book out of her satchel. Homework for Miss Venables was to read a chapter. While Sadie would never normally have rushed to do schoolwork at home, it was a more attractive option than being downstairs with Allen, and if he came up to nag her, at least she had an excuse for staying in her room. She opened the book and started to read. For the next twenty minutes, though, she must have read the opening paragraph a hundred times, and still she had no idea what it said. Her mind was too distracted, and her ears were waiting to hear the sound of footsteps on the stairs that she knew could not be far away.

Eventually they came, followed by the predictable three knocks and the opening of the door. His shirt was still off.

'What you doing?' Allen managed to look almost revolted at the book in Sadie's hands.

'Homework,' she replied curtly, furrowing her eyebrows and pretending to continue to read.

'Never mind that now,' he told her. 'Come downstairs and talk to me. Nobody likes sulky kids.'

'I can't.' Sadie tried to sound apologetic, but in fact she just sounded panicky. 'It's homework. I –'

All of a sudden Allen was striding towards her. Sadie flinched as he grabbed the book from her hands and scrunched a handful of pages in his fist. 'What's the fucking matter with you?' he fumed. 'Think you're brainier than everyone else, do you?' He stared furiously at her before throwing the damaged book on the floor. 'You see what you've made me do?' he asked, his voice quieter now but no less dangerous. 'You'd better stop being so fucking arrogant – otherwise I'll tell your teachers it was you did that. Are you coming downstairs or what?'

Sadie bit her lip and nodded her head.

'Well, go on, then,' Allen urged. She pushed herself off the bed and then walked downstairs, never looking back but feeling him close behind her nonetheless. When she got to the kitchen, she simply stood there, not knowing what to do. Allen made his way into the sitting room, and he heard his voice drift out, calmer now: 'Make yourself useful, then, and make us a brew.' He switched the television on.

Sadie found herself filling the kettle full to the brim so that it would take longer to boil and she could stay out of the sitting room for a few extra precious seconds. But there was only so much time she could take making a cup of tea until she provoked his anger again, and before she knew it she was carrying a mugful into the sitting room and handing it to him.

'Ta, Shakespeare,' he said with a forced smile, apparently trying to be pleasant, before placing the mug on the arm of the settee. He then tapped the seat next to him. 'Sit down next to me,' he ordered, his eyes fixed on the television screen.

Sadie did as she was told.

They sat there in silence for a long while, Allen sipping his tea and watching the television, Sadie increasingly feeling the urge to shrink from him. But although she was repelled by the very presence of the man sitting next to her, she found that she couldn't help looking occasionally at his bare skin. It was white and slightly podgy, with a wispy dusting of brown hair. What had caught her attention was a patch on one side of his belly that was even paler than the rest of his skin, where no hair grew. Sadie found herself wondering what it was, but pulled her eyes away when she realized Allen was watching her.

'You looking at my scar?' he said in a voice that was little more than a whisper.

Sadie shook her head.

'Yes you were. I saw you. It's all right, pet. You're allowed to look.'

'I wasn't looking.'

'I suppose you're wondering where I got it.'

Sadie remained tight-lipped.

'It's a knife wound,' Allen said. 'I got it in Manchester. There were a couple of scallies attacking an old lady for her handbag, so I stepped in. They went for me instead. Three weeks in hospital it cost me.' He took another slurp of his tea, and then placed the mug back down on the armrest. 'It still hurts sometimes, but rather me than an old granny, eh?'

Suddenly Sadie felt his hand on her wrist. She tried to pull away, but he just gripped harder. 'You're hurting me!' she squealed, but that only made him squeeze tighter. He pulled her arm towards him and placed her clenched fist against the scar; then he moved it up and down, forcing her to caress it against her will. The scar tissue felt smooth compared to the rest of his downy skin, but the sensation made Sadie shudder with revulsion and she continued to struggle, despite the increasing fierceness of his grip. 'Let me go,' she said, feeling tears starting to stream down her cheek. 'Please let me go.'

But he didn't let her go. Instead, he was whispering in her ear, his lips brushing against her lobes. 'You don't want a scar like that on your pretty little body, do you, pet?'

'No,' she whimpered.

'No,' Allen confirmed. 'So you'd better do as you're told. Understand?'

Blinded now by her tears, Sadie nodded. Her wrist was burning, and if she had wanted to speak, she knew the words would choke in her throat.

As quickly as he had grabbed her, he let go. 'Go on, then,' he spat. 'Fuck off back to your bedroom. Go and pretend to read your book.'

Sadie fled.

For the second time in as many days, she found herself trembling in her room, her ears straining to hear the sounds Allen was making downstairs. She deduced that he had turned the television off – or muted it, as he sometimes did, leaving the picture silently playing – because she could hear him walking around. His movements seemed more chaotic than usual, as though he was stomping around angrily. Sadie tiptoed to her door, opened it a little and put her ear to the gap: she jumped as she heard the smashing of a glass and then ran back to her bed, where she automatically grabbed her teddy bear and squeezed it with all her might.

Yesterday, she had been given some warning of Allen's arrival in her room: his footsteps had stopped halfway up the stairs before he finally decided to intrude on her. Today there was no such hesitation. Out of the blue, Sadie heard a rush of clattering footsteps as Allen ran flat-footedly up the stairs and burst in. His shirt was back on now, but it was not his state of undress or otherwise that made Sadie freeze, statue still.

It was the look on his face.

There was a wildness in his eyes, an anger and a loathing that Sadie had never even dreamed of in her worst nightmares. One eye seemed to be open slightly wider than the other; his lips were fixed in a snarl that suggested the deepest contempt; and his whole head seemed to twitch intermittently. He took deep, shuddering breaths, as though he was trying to bring himself under control; but everything about his demeanour suggested that he was not being successful.

Sadie's skin prickled with fear as he stood there and looked at her.

Finally he spoke. His voice was not loud, as the fury in his face would have predicted: he spoke in a forced whisper that was all the more sinister for its quietness. 'You're a fucking tease,' he breathed.

Sadie shook her head, not trusting herself to reply, nor quite knowing how to.

'Don't look at me like that, you little bitch.' His voice was dangerously soft now. 'I've met your type before. You think you can do anything. You think you can prance around wearing next to fuck all. You think you can sit on the settee and touch me and then fuck off back to your bedroom.' He took a step nearer. 'You're a worthless little slag.' He licked his lips, almost nervously. 'I suppose you've got a string of boyfriends at that school of yours.'

'No,' Sadie said in a small voice.

That seemed to mollify Allen a little, but he still spoke viciously quietly. 'You should count your fucking blessings I don't tell your mam what your game is and have you taken into care.'

Sadie allowed a sob to escape from her throat, and all of a sudden Allen smiled – a vicious, humourless smile that was even worse than the snarl.

'Touched a nerve, have we?' He walked right up to the bed and bent over so that his face was only inches from Sadie's and his breath was hot on her skin. 'It'll happen, you know,' he whispered. 'Put one step wrong, and it'll happen. You know I can make it happen, don't you?'

Sadie nodded, her eyes brimming.

Allen smiled again. 'Good,' he said. His voice was calmer now, and as he stood up and stepped backwards towards the door, the beast in him seemed to have been tamed somewhat. When he spoke again, he had lost the whisper and managed to sound almost matter-of-fact. 'I wouldn't bother telling anyone about our little chat, Sadie. You'll just show everyone what a lying little slag you are. And I'd hate to have to tell anyone all the things I know about you.'

He gave her an oily grin, and left.

Sadie sat perfectly still on her bed. She felt tears dribbling down her face, but could not summon the will to wipe them away; instead she simply stared into the middle distance. Allen's words had cut through her like barbed wire in her veins, exposing her very worst fears. 'I'll have you taken into care.' 'I'll tell all the things I know about you.' She didn't doubt that he would.

How long she sat there she couldn't tell, but after a while a massive, body-shaking sob arose in her chest and she crumbled, prostrate on her bedclothes and weeping into her hands until they were quite as wet as they had been when she was caught in the rain yesterday. She felt as wretched as she had when her dad had died: Allen's poisonous words made her miss him more than ever.

She didn't risk going into the bathroom that night, and she certainly didn't want to go down and make herself any dinner. Even before it was dark, she was underneath her duvet, sometimes crying, sometimes shivering, sometimes just lying there in shocked exhaustion, listening for footsteps up the stairs. But they did not come.

The evening passed with excruciating slowness. Sleep would be impossible until her mum got back, of that she was sure. When she finally heard the door opening it was with a surge of relief and yet she felt a slight lurch in her stomach when she realized in an instant that it didn't really change things. All she wanted to do, though, was to see her mum, to have her put her arms around her and kiss her goodnight. A hug – it wasn't much to ask. She slipped out of bed and, remembering Allen's words about walking around in next to nothing, pulled on a jumper and her dressing gown before creeping downstairs.

It was not until she was in the kitchen that she was able to distinguish the murmur of the grown-ups' voices from the babble of the television. She held her breath and stood with her back against the wall next to the door – unseen and unheard – so that she could determine if it was a good moment to walk in. Her mum was speaking, and Sadie immediately recognized a slur in her voice that told her she had been drinking. The little girl strained her ears to hear what she was saying.

Jackie was rambling. 'It was only a couple of voddies. Ray from up the road – you know Ray, him with the white beard and the Rottie on a lead – was in, bought us a drink. They're good like that down there, always someone to stand you a drink. I know most of them, course, from before.' Jackie sounded carefree, as though she had been enjoying herself. 'Don't worry,' – her voice was suddenly heavy with mock exaggeration – 'they won't dock my pay or nothing.'

'I don't give a fuck about the money,' Allen replied quietly. 'I told you I didn't want you drinking any more. You stink of it.'

'Oh, c'mon, it was only a couple of voddies,' Jackie repeated. There was the rustle of movement on the sofa. 'I'm sorry about last night, love. I didn't mean to make you so cross. Why don't you let us make it up to you?' Her voice had suddenly turned almost kittenish, wheedling, as if she was trying to talk him into something. Sadie was not so naïve that she didn't understand what was going on, and the sound of her mum making advances of that type to Allen made her feel nauseous. She didn't want to hear any more, yet somehow she couldn't drag herself away.

'Your breath stinks of tabs,' was the only reply Allen gave her.

'Never mind that, eh?' her mum breathed. 'You ain't hardly touched me since you moved in. You don't have to be shy, you know. I won't bite.' Her voice was husky now, but there was something about the way her words drunkenly ran into each other that made her sound faintly pitiful.

'Get away from me,' Allen snapped. 'I'm not fucking interested. Can't you get that into your thick, ugly head?'

Before Jackie could cajole him any further, Sadie heard the unmistakable sound of someone getting up from the sofa and approaching the door. She panicked, spinning around to look towards the stairs and work out if she could get there before she was caught eavesdropping, but it was too late. Before she could move, Allen was there, standing above her.

'You little . . .' he whispered as his eyes narrowed. Then he smiled unpleasantly and raised his voice. 'Hey, Jackie, look at this.' Her mum appeared at the door. 'Not quite the fucking angel you think she is, eh? Listening in on us – listening in on you making a fucking fool of yourself.' He shot Sadie a warning glance, as if to say 'I told you so', and then disappeared upstairs.

Sadie didn't watch him go. She turned to her mum with outstretched arms and teary eyes, hoping to receive the hug that she had been aching for all night. But before she knew it, her mum was bending down, taking her by the shoulders and shaking her like a rag doll. 'What do you think you're doing, Sadie?' she shrieked, all restraint dissolved by the alcohol in her system. 'Why the hell are you listening in on us?'

Sadie tried to speak, but all that came out was a breathless whimper.

'You're just a kid, Sadie.' Her mum was raving mad now. 'You shouldn't be listening in to grown-ups' stuff that you don't understand.'

Jackie had stopped shaking her daughter now, but she was still bending down. Sadie looked directly into her mum's face. Jackie was embarrassed; of that her daughter was sure. Ashamed of what Sadie had heard her say. Then, through her tears, Sadie looked closer and for the first time was shocked to see a bruise to the side of her left eye. She wanted to ask her where it had come from, but now Jackie was shouting at her again, breathing the smell of booze over her as she did so. 'You can be so selfish sometimes, Sadie. A naughty little girl. Get to your room now, and I don't want to catch you doing this again.'

At first Sadie didn't move, but then her mum started screaming even louder, and she found herself running quickly up the stairs, slamming the door to her bedroom and retreating once more under the duvet.

Two minutes later, she heard Jackie stumbling drunkenly upstairs, and then the house fell silent.

Silent, apart from the sound of a small girl crying all the tears that were in her, feeling more desperate, more filled with self-doubt and more alone than she had ever done before.

CHAPTER 6

Sadie left the house at six o'clock the next morning, before anyone else was up. As soon as the door clicked behind her, she ran down the pathway and along the street in case the noise awoke her mum or Allen and she was summoned back into the house. There was hardly anybody about on the estate, and once she stopped running she realized that there was a chill in the air – the sun had not been long up, and although the sky was blue, it would be a while before she felt warmth on her skin. She headed straight for the playground without even thinking, and sat on the swings, waiting for Anna and Carly to show up.

But Anna and Carly didn't come.

She had known it was going to be embarrassing to see her friends this morning after the awkwardness yesterday, but she ached to see them, to laugh and joke with them and try to forget about all the stuff that was going on at home. She had even prepared herself to apologize. But as it became increasingly obvious that they had arranged to meet elsewhere, Sadie started to feel the hot prickle of shame and solitude; she left it until the very last minute before making her way into school.

By the time she arrived at the classroom, the teacher had already started the lesson and all the pupils were sitting down. Only half hearing the teacher's reprimand, she glanced to the back of the room, where Carly and Anna were together, but they studiously ignored her. Feeling her cheeks redden, Sadie took a seat at the only space available – by herself.

The teacher droned on and Sadie neither heard nor cared what he said. When the bell rang, she packed her things up slowly, giving her friends the chance to come up to her and chat; instead, they walked straight past her and out into the corridor. Sadie felt the familiar sensation of tears filling her eyes, but she knew better than to cry in front of her classmates, so she fought it back and walked alone to Miss Venables' English lesson, where again she found herself sitting alone at the front.

'All right, ladies and gentlemen,' Miss Venables called briskly above the hubbub when everyone was sitting down. 'Reading books open at page twenty, please.'

Without thinking, Sadie pulled her book out of her satchel and placed it on the desk in front of her. The spine fell open on account of the crumpled pages, which for some reason looked a lot worse now than they had done the night before. Miss Venables noticed the state of Sadie's book immediately.

'Er, Sadie Burrows,' she said, her voice not quite so loud now but certainly audible to the rest of the class. 'What have you been doing to your book?'

Sadie looked guiltily down at the damage Allen had done. 'Nothing, miss,' she mumbled.

Miss Venables picked the book up from her table and held it up between her thumb and forefinger. 'This doesn't look like nothing to me, Sadie.' It was a reprimand, but it was kindly spoken in the way that only Miss Venables could manage.

There were a few giggles from the class behind her, and Sadie felt her skin redden again. 'What d'you do to it, Sadie?' a voice called out. 'Use it to wipe your—'

'That's enough!' Miss Venables said sharply, and the class quietened down again. She laid the book back down on Sadie's table and said, under her breath, 'Don't let it happen again, Sadie.'

The rest of the lesson passed without incident. When it finished, Sadie left quickly, so as to avoid having any further conversation with Miss Venables about the book, and went straight out to the playground for breaktime. Anna and Carly had made it impossible for her to approach them, she decided, by the way they had been ignoring her. It was up to them to make up with her. But from the way they had positioned themselves at the far side of the playground, it didn't look as if that was part of their plan. So Sadie found a place away from everyone else, laid her satchel on the ground and sat down, clutching her knees with her arms. At first she started watching what was going on in the playground, but after only a few moments everything became an unseen blur as her mind concentrated on all the things that were preoccupying her.

She didn't want to go home. She couldn't bear to. The thought of being in the same house as Allen – let alone the same room – was horrible to her. It made her muscles clench and her stomach churn; it made her thoughts become confused and jumbled. Now Mum was never there, and even when she was she took his side all the time. If she told her the things he had said to her, she'd never believe her anyway. The image of the bruise on the side of Mum's face flashed into her mind. It was perfectly obvious to Sadie where it came from, and she knew that she couldn't leave Mum to that sort of treatment. She was too weak; she'd never survive it.

But what could she do? She was only thirteen.

Her thoughts were interrupted by the sound of a small voice. Shaking herself from her reverie, she looked round to see Jamie Brown, standing alone and awkward, a couple of metres away. The smell of his dirty clothes hit her, but she was used to that by now. He looked nervous – more nervous than normal – and Sadie suddenly remembered the way he had walked away from her yesterday. With everything else that was going on, Jamie's troubles had barely entered her head. She forced her lips into a thin smile.

'All right, Jamie?'

Jamie nodded, his wide, bloodshot eyes fixed firmly on Sadie. 'Um, sorry,' he said.

'Forget about it,' Sadie told him.

He shifted his weight from one foot to the other. 'It's me birthday,' he blurted out, blushing as he spoke.

Sadie felt a pang of renewed sympathy for the little boy. Jackie had taken her to McDonald's on her last birthday; she had no doubt that Jamie would not have been treated in any way by his mum. She smiled at him. 'Sit down, birthday boy,' she said, indicating the ground next to her.

They appeared to come from nowhere. Before Jamie could sit down, he was suddenly rushed at from one side by a tall, lanky ginger-haired boy who pushed him roughly so that he fell to the ground. Jamie shouted in sudden pain as his hand scraped against the rough tarmac, but his cry was soon drowned by the jeering shrieks of his sudden assailants.

'Gross!' one of them shouted out. 'You fucking touched him!'

Two other voices howled with laughter as the ginger-haired boy grinned at them. Sadie looked up at the gang. There were three of them, a little older than she was and quite a bit older than Jamie, and they started taunting him with chants, which he must have been used to by now.

'Fucking tramp,' one of them laughed.

'Don't get too close to him,' another warned, 'or you'll start to stink as well.'

The insults continued, like a barrage of gunfire; Jamie remained immobile on the ground, clutching his grazed hand and refusing to look at the bigger boys. Sadie saw tears of indignation and frustration streaming down his face and she silently urged him to stand up for himself. He never would, though – she could see that. And she understood.

Very calmly, she stood up. Her mouth had gone suddenly dry, and she found herself feeling Jamie's shame. There was something about the bullying she had just witnessed that reminded her of her own secret bully. She couldn't watch any more of it: either she could walk away or she could interfere. There was really no choice: if he wasn't going to do anything about the situation, she would.

Almost as if in a trance, she placed herself between Jamie and his assailants. For a stunned moment they fell quiet; then, with an amused and sarcastic sidelong glance, the ginger-haired boy took a couple of steps forward.

'What's your fucking problem?' he asked.

Sadie didn't reply.

Suddenly the boy's face became more serious. He clearly understood Sadie's silence for the rebuke that it was, and now he risked losing face in front of his friends. He took a step closer. 'I said,' he repeated, 'what's your fucking problem?'

'I haven't got a problem,' she replied calmly.

'Apart from the fact that your boyfriend stinks of piss.' He smiled at his friends, who guffawed encouragingly.

Sadie waited for the laughing to die down before she spoke again. 'I think you should leave him alone.'

'Well, *I* think you should mind your own business.'

'I've just made it my business.'

The argument was attracting attention now, and a ring of children congregated around the two of them. Sadie felt a chill of ice down her spine as she realized that there was only one way this could go. The boy was taller than she was, and probably stronger. The only way she could come out on top was if she struck first. She felt her fists clenching of their own accord and prepared to go at him.

But she never got a chance.

To a cheer from the audience, the boy hurled himself at her. Sadie hit the ground and felt the wind being knocked out of her by the fall; the boy fell heavily on top of her, and she gasped with pain as he grabbed a clump of her long hair and twisted it hard. She writhed violently and managed to poke two fingers into one of his eyes. He let go of her hair, but recovered quickly enough to raise his clenched fist and start to bring it down with all the brutality he could muster.

'Sadie!' She recognized the panicked voice from the crowd as Anna's. 'Look out!' As deftly as she could manage, Sadie rolled away, and with a grim satisfaction she heard the boy's fist clunk on to the rough tarmac. He shouted in agony as she jumped to her feet. From the corner of her eye she saw Anna and Carly struggling to enter the fray but being pulled back by others; she couldn't pay them much attention, however, because the ginger-haired boy was getting to his feet. His fist was bleeding, but he had a look of blind determination in his eyes. Sadie kicked him hard in the shins and he winced – but he didn't stop getting up. His face sneering and dirty, he started staggering towards her. Sadie realized the crowd had gone quiet now – this was getting more serious than anyone had intended.

She had to stand her ground.

'Break it up!' A severe voice barked from beyond the crowd, which split open and started to dissolve. Sadie and the ginger-haired boy looked in the direction of the voice and saw Mr Martin, the school's headmaster – brown-suited, bespectacled and his face a picture of fury – storming towards them.

Both assailants froze.

The headmaster took the situation in at a single glance, although his gaze seemed to linger on the boy's bleeding fist. 'My office, now,' he ordered in a voice that could not be refused. He turned and marched back towards the school building. Sadie and her opponent had no choice but to follow, still seething and emanating an aura of hatred towards one another, while listening to the gossiping babble that had started up behind them.

It seemed an age that the two of them were

standing in the echoing corridor outside the headmaster's study, not daring to take a seat on the plastic chairs that were lined up there; in reality it was only a couple of minutes before they were called in.

When they were standing in front of his desk, the headmaster stared at them before announcing without emotion, 'Two days' suspension each. And if I see it happening again, it'll be expulsion.'

'But sir—' Sadie started to say.

She was instantly interrupted. 'Shut up, Burrows. I'm not interested. You're worse than him – look at his hand. Hardly ladylike behaviour, is it?'

Crushed, Sadie shook her head. 'No, sir.'

'No, sir,' the headmaster repeated. 'Now, your parents have been called and the situation explained. Burrows, your mother has to go to work, so she's asked your stepfather to come in . . .'

'He's not my stepfather,' Sadie said through gritted teeth.

'Well, your mother has arranged for a' – he consulted a piece of paper – 'a Mr Campbell to pick you up. You know Mr Campbell?'

Sadie nodded.

'Good.' He turned his attention to the boy. 'You, go to Miss Venables,' he said, his voice slightly less severe. 'She'll patch you up and your mother will be here to pick you up in half an hour. Burrows, wait outside my office to be picked up. I'd like to have a word with Mr Campbell when he arrives.'

It felt cold in the echoing corridor, though whether or not that was to do with the temperature or Sadie's state of mind she could not tell. She took a seat on one of the uncomfortable plastic chairs, sitting on her hands to warm them up and stop herself from picking at her already frayed nails, and staring at the floor to avoid the curious looks from the pupils who passed by. Occasionally someone shouted something out at her, but she ignored them. In fact, she barely even heard them. Her mind was trained on just one thing: Allen was on his way here. She felt a sickness in her chest at the very thought.

He arrived sooner than expected. Sadie pretended that she hadn't noticed him as he appeared at the end of the corridor with the school receptionist, being led silently to the headmaster's office, but as he drew closer it became increasingly difficult to keep up the pretence. Allen walked a pace or two behind the receptionist, a kindly woman who always had a smile for Sadie and who gave her an encouraging look now. His eyes were fixed on Sadie, but he neither smiled nor frowned as he approached her; nor did he utter a single word of greeting.

The receptionist knocked on the headmaster's door, and then opened it and stuck her head round the corridor. 'Mr Campbell is here,' she informed her boss.

The headmaster's response was inaudible, but the receptionist closed the door and turned to Sadie and Allen. 'Mr Martin will be with you in just a minute.' She nodded at Allen, smiled at Sadie and was on her way.

The silence between the two of them crackled as they waited for the headmaster to beckon them inside. Sadie could hear Allen's heavy breathing, and could tell by the way his lips occasionally twitched that he wanted to say something but was holding it back. She was almost relieved when the door opened and Mr Martin, unsmiling and dour-faced, appeared. He looked down at Sadie with a shocked expression, and she immediately started wondering what she had done wrong.

'Why are you sitting down, Sadie?'

She looked at him blankly, not knowing what to say.

'You know the school rules. If an adult is standing, you stand unless you are told otherwise.'

Sadie's eyes flashed down to the floor again. 'Yes, sir. Sorry, sir.' She stood up.

The headmaster nodded his head in satisfaction; then he looked at Allen with a brief, business-like smile. 'Do come in, Mr Campbell.' He held the door open for Allen, and indicated with another nod of his head that Sadie was to follow. Once inside the office, he offered Allen a seat while Sadie remained standing, and then took his place on the other side of his desk. 'Mr Campbell,' he said, addressing Allen. 'I'm afraid Sadie was found fighting in the playground during break. Now, children can be boisterous, I know; but this was rather more than that. The young man involved was quite seriously hurt, and I'm sure you can appreciate that this is not the sort of behaviour I wish to encourage in my school.'

'Of course not, Mr Martin,' Allen replied smoothly.

'I've issued a two-day suspension. Today is Wednesday, so Sadie will be welcome back in school on Monday morning.' He turned to Sadie, who was standing with her head hung. 'I hope, young lady, that this punishment will make you realize what will and will not be tolerated in my school.'

Sadie looked up at the headmaster. Don't leave me with him, she longed to say. Don't make me go home with this man. But Mr Martin looked so severe that what will she had simply crumbled. 'Yes, sir,' was all she managed.

The headmaster turned his attention back to Allen. 'It's very important, Mr Campbell, that Sadie understands that a suspension is not a two-day holiday. I'm a strong believer that firm discipline in the school needs to be followed up in the home. I trust I can rely on you and Mrs Burrows to back the school up in this matter.'

Allen glanced sidelong at Sadie. 'Her mam and me will take it very seriously,' he assured the headmaster.

'Good.' Mr Martin stood up and proffered his hand to Allen across the desk. Following the headmaster's lead, Allen stood up and shook his hand; then he turned to Sadie. 'C'mon, you,' he said, his eyes flashing. 'Home.'

As Sadie stood up, he put his hand on her shoulder and squeezed it. She wanted to shrink from him, but she knew how much trouble she would be in if she appeared disobedient in front of the headmaster and so didn't.

Sadie and Allen walked home in silence. Not a word was spoken between them; indeed Allen kept several paces ahead of her and walked so briskly that she almost had to run to keep up. His arms were stretched straight by his side, and she noticed that his fingernails occasionally dug into the palms of his hands. It would have been easy to run away. At no stage did Allen stop to look back at her, and she knew these streets as she knew her own home. More than anything she wanted to get away; but she was scared. Scared to leave and scared to stay. She trotted along behind him, breathless not only from exhaustion but also from the sickening anticipation of what awaited her back home.

When they arrived the garden gate was swinging open. Allen strode through it, unlocked the front door, held it open and, for the first time since they had left the school, spoke. 'Inside,' he growled.

Sadie did as she was told, stepping through the front door. As soon as she was in, she tried to hurry up the stairs, but Allen was too quick for her. He pulled her satchel and she fell backwards heavily into him. Grabbing her by the hair, he shut the door with his free hand and clicked the latch, locking the door. Sadie whimpered as he clenched his fist a little tighter, turning her head round so that she was looking at him, but she did not struggle, as it would only have hurt more.

If she had thought that there was a wildness about Allen's face the previous night, it was nothing compared to the madness in his eyes now. He looked tormented, like an animal trying to control itself but unable to do so. His fist was clenched even tighter and Sadie gasped; but suddenly he yanked his hand down and let go. She fell to the floor and curled up tightly, like a foetus. Trembling with shock, she dared not look up at the man towering over her; instead, she kept her eyes tightly shut and covered her head with her hands, fully expecting to feel the full force of a blow from his foot or his fists.

But there was nothing.

It was perhaps a minute before she dared to peek up at him. He was still standing just where he had been, the madness in his eyes barely assuaged. 'Get up,' he instructed, his voice a forceful whisper.

Sadie stayed where she was.

'Don't make me force you,' Allen warned.

Slowly, Sadie pushed herself to her feet.

'What happened?' Allen asked.

For a moment Sadie didn't know what he was talking about – the events of the morning seemed a million miles from where she was now. But then she realized that he was referring to the fight. 'Someone was being bullied,' she stuttered through her tears. 'I stepped in to help him . . .'

'Him?' Allen pounced on the word.

'Yes,' Sadie replied hesitantly, unsure what she had said wrong.

Allen nodded gently. 'Get upstairs,' he said, his voice still low.

Sadie felt a surge of relief that she was to be allowed to go to her bedroom, and she started climbing the stairs without complaint; as she did so, however, she realized with a shudder that Allen was close behind her. And when they reached the landing and she headed for her bedroom door, she felt his hand on her shoulder again.

'Not your bedroom, Sadie,' he whispered. 'Mine.'

Sadie turned to look at him. His brow was furrowed and his eyes half closed. She didn't dare disobey him.

She had barely set foot in this room since Allen had moved in. Before, it was always untidy; today the bed was made and the duvet neatly smoothed. The curtains were shut and no light was on. As Sadie's eyes got used to the semi-darkness, she realized that there was what looked like a freshly laundered towel draped immaculately across the bed.

Then Allen spoke. 'You've been asking for this, girl,' he breathed. 'You're not so stupid that you don't realize that, are you?'

Sadie bit her lip and shook her head. A terrifying numbness had descended upon her, the dreadful feeling that she knew something awful was going to happen but she had no power to stop it.

He reached out and held her chin lightly in his fingers. Sadie was too scared even to pull her face away and he smiled, as though satisfied that he was enjoying her touch.

'Take your clothes off,' he ordered, his voice barely audible now.

Sadie's skin went hot, then cold; still biting her lip, she shook her head again. In a flash, Allen's hand moved from her face to her neck. He squeezed the flesh tightly, and in a moment she was chocking, unable to breathe. He pushed her and she fell on to the bed.

'Take your clothes off,' he repeated.

Her hands trembling, Sadie did as she was told.

When she was down to her childish underwear, she sat on the edge of the bed and cried. Her fingers touched her neck where Allen had grabbed her: it was still sore. Through her tears, she was vaguely aware that he was getting undressed too. She turned her head away, unable to let herself look at his pasty, naked body.

His fingers touched her skin again, stroking the side of her cheek and ignoring the wetness. 'You might as well try to enjoy it,' she heard his voice saying, 'because it's going to happen. You know it's going to happen, don't you, Sadie?'

The little girl nodded.

And then Allen pushed her on to her back.

The towel felt rough against her skin. Sadie

closed her eyes tightly as she felt his heavy body press against hers. With trembling hands he tore at her underwear; it dug sharply into her skin before he ripped it away with a second fumbling tug. She tried to keep her legs closed, but his knee poked viciously into her inner thigh and she was forced to open them; and her desperate struggling was useless against the weight of his body.

It hurt as he entered her, and she screamed; but Allen was clearly expecting that, because he had covered her mouth with one hand to muffle the sound as, in a few short minutes, Allen Campbell brutally and agonizingly robbed Sadie Burrows of her childhood.

He didn't object when she stood up to leave; having rolled off her on to his back, he just lay there, staring at the ceiling.

Sadie picked up the towel, ashamed of the stains she had left on it, and went straight into the bathroom. She didn't want to look in the mirror, but as she passed she couldn't help noticing that there were the beginnings of two bruises on either side of her neck. She climbed into the bath, ran the tap and, ignoring the scalding temperature of the water, took a limescale-encrusted nail brush from the side. She scoured it roughly into a bar of soap and then rubbed the hard bristles all over her body. It didn't matter to her that the brush made her skin sore; indeed it bled in places. All she wanted to do was scrub away all traces of his touch. When she had finished, she rubbed herself down with her ordinary towel; then she grabbed the soiled one and walked back into her bedroom. She tucked the towel under her bed, where her mum wouldn't find it, and found some fresh clothes from her drawer and pulled them on.

Then Allen was there. He was dressed again, and his cheeks were red.

'It's your fault, pet. You know that, don't you?'

Sadie looked away.

He approached her and took her face in his hand once more. 'No one will believe you,' he whispered. 'Not your mam, not your teachers. Breathe a word of it to anyone and you'll show yourself up for the lying little slut that you really are.'

He waited for a moment while his words sunk in. Then he turned and walked out of the room, closing the door quietly behind him.

CHAPTER 7

The packet of cigarettes in Jackie's pocket pressed against her skin. Perhaps she should nip out and have one now, to calm herself down before she confronted him. Then again, perhaps not. If he smelled it on her, it would only make him angry. He'd been in a strange mood ever since she got back last night. She took a deep breath and stepped into the doorway of the sitting room.

'I'm not going to work today,' she said, her arms by her side and her nails digging into her palms. She sounded uncertain, as though afraid to say what she was saying.

Allen appeared not to hear her. He used the remote control to change channels.

'She's not very well. She hasn't come down all morning. I think I need to stay here.'

'You're a fucking idiot,' Allen told her, not taking his eyes away from the screen.

Jackie blushed. 'No, but . . .'

'You're a fucking idiot,' he repeated. Only now did he turn to look at her. 'And you're a soft touch. That girl is a liar and a thug. I can see it, her headmaster can see it – you're the only one who can't. Of course she doesn't want you to go out. She's in a lot of fucking trouble.' He turned his attention back to the television.

Jackie lowered her eyes to the floor. 'I just thought . . .'

'You're going to work, Jackie, and that's that.'

'But . . .'

'Don't make me angry, Jackie.' His voice grew dangerously quiet, but he continued to stare at the television.

Jackie hesitated. 'No,' she muttered finally. 'No, you're right. I'll, um . . . I'll go and talk to her.' And she left him to it.

She walked upstairs and gently tapped on Sadie's door. When there was no response, she walked in anyway. Her daughter looked tired – desperately tired. There was a haunted look about her, just as there had been when her father had passed on. Jackie had hoped never to see it again, but there had always been a nagging doubt at the back of her brain – a mother's instinct that Sadie was just bottling up her sorrow and that it could explode at any time. She sat on the bed, hugging her knees; Jackie noticed that the teddy bear she always hugged when she was upset was lying face down on the floor.

Mother and daughter looked at each other. Allen had called her a liar and a thug. She didn't look like that to Jackie.

And yet she had been suspended from school;

she had been fighting; she had been listening in on them the other night. Maybe Allen was right. Maybe Jackie should listen to him. And she didn't want to do anything to provoke that terrible temper of his.

'I'm going out now, love,' she said softly.

Sadie gazed up at her and shook her head slightly. 'But you said—'

'I know what I said,' Jackie snapped, before checking herself. 'I know what I said,' she repeated, more calmly now. 'But come on, love. Allen's right – I can't just bunk off work because you're in trouble at school, can I?' Christ, she was gasping for a ciggie.

Sadie didn't answer. She could see her mum's hands trembling.

'It's a punishment, anyway, isn't it?' Jackie started stumbling over her words, unnerved by the way Sadie was looking at her. She strode forward, kissed her daughter's hair and then left the house in a hurry. She was late as it was.

Sadie remained on her bed, sore from the abuse, yet strangely numb. Allen had been right. Why would anyone believe the word of a child against that of a grown-up? They wouldn't even believe that she had been in the right yesterday in the playground; why would they believe her if she told what had happened last night?

Anyway, she didn't want to tell anyone. Whenever the image of Allen pressing himself against her came into her mind, her face would wince and she would try to blot it out; but even if she managed to she would feel her skin tingle with shame at what she had allowed him to do.

The door slammed shut as her mother left the house, and she knew she was alone with him once again. The hum of the television set was vaguely audible in the background; otherwise the house was quiet.

Almost in a daze, Sadie slipped off the bed and pulled the soiled towel out from underneath it. She scrunched it up and quietly walked into the bathroom, where she dropped it in the bath and turned on the taps. The material filled with water, which drained away a pink colour, and Sadie knelt over the side of the bath trying to scrub the red stain out of the white towel. She scrubbed hard, and it hurt her hands, but she didn't care.

'You all right, pet?' Allen spoke from the bathroom door.

Sadie yanked her head back to look at him, shocked by his sudden presence. 'What do you think?' she asked, turning her attention back to the towel. She carried on scrubbing.

Suddenly she felt his hand on her shoulder. Her muscles tensed and she stopped scrubbing. 'You're a big girl now, pet,' he whispered. 'A very grown-up girl. You should be pleased.' His hand stroked her hair. Sadie barely moved.

And then he was gone. Sadie found herself breathless, shaking and suddenly filled with anger. She started rubbing the stained towel with more vehemence than before. The more she rubbed, the more frustrated she became: the towel just seemed to be in a worse state than ever. For the first time since the previous night, tears streamed down her cheeks and eventually she picked up the towel and flung it to the other end of the bath.

It was ruined. She had been stupid to think she could remove the stain.

It would be there for ever.

It would never go.

He didn't touch her for the rest of the day, nor the day that followed. Sadie stayed in her room, venturing out only when hunger overcame her: she would make a hasty sandwich and hurry back upstairs. She did not wash or bathe, as she was too scared that he would walk in on her. Her body began to smell, but she didn't care – perhaps it would keep him away, she thought. Even so, every minute of every hour she expected to hear his footsteps up the stairs. They never came.

The time passed agonizingly slowly, but eventually the weekend arrived and Mum wasn't working. Sadie felt safer now that there was somebody else in the house, but she still stayed in her room, unable to bear the way Allen's eyes followed her whenever he was near. When Jackie came in to check on her, Sadie would curtly tell her mum that she was fine, and then go back to staring into space. She desperately wanted to say what had happened, but fear and embarrassment held her tongue and she kept quiet. Once Jackie had left, however, she found that her sense of emptiness and desperation increased: with each lost opportunity to confide in her mum, confessing what had happened became harder to do and Sadie felt increasingly alone.

She was glad when Monday morning came and she could go to school. More than anything, she prayed that the bad blood that had existed between her and Carly and Anna would have cleared, and her heart gave a little leap when she saw them waiting for her in the playground. They grinned a bit sheepishly as she approached, and for a while none of them seemed to know quite what to say.

'We going to school, then, or what?' Anna asked finally.

'S'pose,' Sadie replied, and the three of them started walking.

'So,' Carly asked once they had left the playground behind. 'Martin gave you suspension?'

Sadie nodded.

'Wicked,' Anna observed. 'No school. What d'you do?'

Sadie licked her lips and looked straight ahead. 'Not much,' she told them. 'Mum made me stay in.'

Carly looked at her in genuine surprise. 'What for?'

Sadie shrugged, still refusing to look at them. 'What did I miss at school?' she asked, changing the subject.

Carly and Anna looked at each other with slight hesitation on their faces.

'What?' Sadie insisted.

Anna spoke. 'Your boyfriend, Jamie Brown—'

'He's not my boyfriend.'

'Yeah, whatever. Well, he wasn't in on Friday, was he?'

'So?' Sadie asked, trying to sound unconcerned but suddenly aware of an uncomfortable feeling in her gut.

'Everyone's gossiping, saying he's not coming back.' Anna looked piercingly at Sadie, clearly looking out for a hint of concern at this news. Sadie bit on the insides of her cheek to stop any emotion from showing.

'I asked Venables where he was, because I thought you'd want to know. She told me to mind my own business. Cow.' Anna managed to sound genuinely resentful.

For a brief moment, Sadie forgot about her own worries and remembered the bruising she had seen on Jamie's arm. She hoped he was OK, but she had a bad feeling about it.

The three of them walked on in silence. After a few minutes, Carly spoke. 'We going to show her, then?' she asked, addressing Anna.

'Up to you,' Anna told her. 'It's yours, isn't it?'

Carly looked around conspiratorially, checking that nobody in the street was watching them. She put her hand into the inside pocket of her old denim jacket and pulled out a slim, tightly rolled joint. Sadie paused only momentarily as her eyes flickered towards it; then she kept up the pace.

'Weed!' Carly said in a heavy whisper, causing Anna to raise her eyebrows at such a statement of the obvious.

'All right, Carly,' Anna said, wrapping her hands around her friend's fist. 'You can put it away now.'

'Let me guess,' Sadie said quietly once the joint was safely out of sight. 'Tom gave it to you, right?'

Carly blushed. 'Yeah,' she said weakly, before looking around again. 'I thought us three could do it tonight.'

'No thanks,' Sadie muttered. Then a thought came to her. He hated the smell of smoke – he was always going on at Mum about it. Perhaps if her skin smelled of it, he might . . . Sadie changed her mind almost immediately. 'Actually, yeah. After school, right?' Anna and Carly grinned at each other once more, and before long they were approaching the school gates with a crowd of other pupils.

Miss Venables' English lesson was first, and for the first time for as long as she could remember, Sadie found herself concentrating on what was going on. It was one way of getting the constant image of him out of her head. At the end of the lesson, she packed up slowly and was the last person left in the class. She looked up to see Miss Venables staring at her, one eyebrow raised.

'Suspension, Sadie Burrows?'

'Yes, miss,' Sadie said, somewhat shamefacedly.

Then she looked back into the kindly face of the teacher. She had urged Jamie to tell Miss Venables about what was going on at home; maybe she should listen to her own advice. She could talk to her, she thought. Confide in her. Trust her to do the right thing, to tell the right people, to make sure Allen Campbell was removed from her life once and for all. But before she could contemplate it any more, Miss Venables spoke.

'Sadie, love, I need to tell you something.' The teacher walked to the door, which was still slightly ajar, shut it, and then walked back and perched on the corner of Sadie's desk. Her eyes narrowed slightly. 'You look tired.'

Sadie didn't respond, and Miss Venables shrugged it off.

'It's about Jamie. You've probably heard that he's not been in school.'

Sadie nodded, her eyes wide with horrible expectation.

'Jamie won't be coming back to school, Sadie. John Martin . . . I mean, the headmaster doesn't want it to become common knowledge why not, but I think, after everything, that you deserve to know. Social services have removed him from his mother's care and placed him with a foster family out of the area. He was' – she hesitated –' quite badly hurt.'

'How badly?' Sadie demanded.

A shadow came across Miss Venables' face as she shook her head. 'You don't need to know that,

Sadie. I just thought you'd feel a bit better knowing that he's somewhere safer now, OK?' She looked towards the door. 'You'd better go, Sadie. I don't want you being late for your next lesson.'

Somewhere safer. Sadie supposed he was; so why was the blood running like ice in her veins? She remembered the look of horror on Jamie's face when she had suggested he tell someone what was going on. What was it he had said? 'I don't want her to get into any trouble. And they'd only get me kicked out, wouldn't they?' Everyone else might think this was the best thing for Jamie, but her heart ached at the thought of what Jamie must be feeling.

And then *his* voice rang in her head, as it so often did. 'I'll have you taken into care.' 'Put one step wrong and it'll happen. You know I can make it happen, don't you?'

Sadie felt her mouth going dry. It could happen. It did happen. If she put one step wrong, he would make it happen.

'Are you all right, Sadie?' Miss Venables asked, her face a sudden picture of concern.

Sadie blinked at her. 'Yes, miss,' she said quietly, before picking up her satchel and hurriedly leaving the classroom.

When school finished, the three girls met in the playground. Flushed with the excitement of what they were about to do, Carly and Anna had a nervous boisterousness about them and didn't seem to notice Sadie's quietness. They slipped out of the school gates and, instead of turning left towards the estate where people would recognize them, they turned right. Before long they arrived under the arches of a railway bridge, where the greasy car-repair garages had already shut up shop and there were few, if any, people hanging around, despite the fact that they were just off the main road. The three of them sat in a circle on the cobbled pavement, ignoring the old Coke cans and fag packets strewn all over the place. Sadie and Anna watched silently as Carly brought the treasured joint out of her pocket. From her trousers, she also pulled out a plastic lighter.

Doing her best to look as if this was something she did all the time, Carly put the joint in her mouth. She tried to flick the lighter into flame, but it just sputtered with an ineffectual spark. Anna tried to grab it, but Carly pushed her away, tried again and this time managed to make fire. She held it to the skin of the joint and breathed in. Sadie watched closely as the paper crackled, and the air was suddenly filled with a thick, spicy aroma. Carly sucked on the joint. After a few seconds the smoke billowed out of her mouth in a big cloud that would have indicated to Sadie and Anna that she wasn't inhaling had they but known it. Her eyes watered slightly and she passed the joint to Sadie.

It felt dry in her fingers, and the smoke made her eyes water too. As she put the joint to her lips she felt the wetness of the paper from where Carly had sucked on it. She drew in a deep breath, and the smoke instantly hit the back of her throat, making her cough and splutter. Carly and Anna laughed – Anna a bit half-heartedly, as she had not yet had her go.

'Pass it on, then,' Carly said.

Sadie shook her head. She took another puff, taking care to keep the smoke in her blown-out cheeks this time. When she exhaled, she made a special point of breathing over her clothes. Then, with a look of mysterious satisfaction, she handed it on to Anna.

It took ten minutes for them to finish it, and they did so in silence. Carly took the last puff, and then ground the butt into the cobbles and smiled at her friends. 'Well?' she asked.

'I don't really feel much different,' Sadie admitted.

'What?' Anna screeched. 'I do – it was wicked!' Sadie could tell she was lying, but chose not to say anything.

'Me too,' Carly added, avoiding Sadie's gaze. 'Tom said he can get it for us whenever we want.'

'Yeah, well,' Anna countered, not to be outdone, 'I know someone who can get it too . . .'

Carly shrugged. 'Whatever. I've got to go home – the little ones will be shouting for their tea.' She stood up and the other two girls followed suit; but at the thought of going home, the familiar feeling of sickness arose in Sadie's stomach. As they walked out on to the main road, she addressed Anna.

'Can I come back to your house for a bit?'

Anna shook her head. 'Nah, sorry. Mum says I'm not allowed to bring people home on week-days any more.'

'Oh,' Sadie said in a small voice. 'OK.' She started to drag her heels.

Anna shot her a slightly perplexed look. 'She'll probably have forgotten about it next week, though.'

'Right.'

By the time the three of them went their separate ways, Sadie was more wretched than ever. The joint hadn't made her feel that great, and she felt that every step she took back home was a step nearer the terrible punishment that she knew was waiting for her, although she didn't know what it was for. When she knocked on the door, she did so weakly.

As soon as Allen opened it she knew there would be trouble – he had that look about him. Wordlessly she walked in, straight up the stairs and into her bedroom.

He was there before she could sling her satchel to the floor.

Slowly and deliberately he shut the door behind him; then he turned to stare at her. His eyes had a slightly vacant look, as though he was under the command of urges he couldn't, or didn't want to, control. He licked his lips as he took a couple of paces towards her. Sadie shrank from him, but she knew she couldn't escape him; and she knew, without knowing how, what he had on his mind.

He was right in front of her now, his hand stroking her hair. He paused for a moment, wrinkling his nose and sniffing. His hand left her hair and he smelled it; then he narrowed his eyes at her.

'What've you been doing, pet?' he asked in a desperately quiet voice, fixing her gaze with his snakelike eyes.

The foolishness of her actions suddenly came crashing in on Sadie. She gulped and shook her head. 'Nothing . . .' she started to say.

'You think I don't know what that smell is? You stink like a fucking crack den.'

She bit her lower lip, trying to stop herself from crying.

'Who were you smoking it with, Sadie? A boy?'

Now Allen's hand was round her throat, squeezing. He bent down and whispered in her ear. 'If I find out that you've been with another boy, I'll kill you. Got it?'

Sadie tried to say yes, but all that came out was a choking sound.

When he finally let go, he did so roughly, with a push that knocked her to the floor. 'Upstairs,' he told her. 'Now.'

She clambered to her feet and, too terrified to do anything but obey, did as she was told.

It didn't hurt so much the second time, but

somehow it was worse knowing what to expect. She didn't bother trying to scream; she just lay there, hoping that if she didn't struggle it would be over more quickly. When he had finished, and rolled over on to his back as before, she crept to the bathroom, where she scrubbed herself, wincing with pain from the nail brush but desperate to remove all traces of him.

Back in her bedroom she put on her tracksuit and waited for him to come in again, as she knew he would. Sure enough, the door opened and he stood there, the same redness in his face that she had noticed after the first time.

'I can get it for you, pet, if you want,' he said.

'Get what?'

'The blow. The weed. I can get it for you. You've only got to ask.'

'Go away,' she told him.

Allen smiled. 'You shouldn't be so rude, pet.'

He stepped towards her and stroked her hair, as was his habit.

'After all,' he said, 'you wouldn't want your mam to know about your little secret habit, now, would you?'

CHAPTER 8

It didn't happen every day.

It didn't even happen every other day.

But once or twice a week, when Jackie was at work, Allen would present himself in Sadie's bedroom. Sometimes he made her wash while he watched her; other times he seemed unable to wait and ordered her immediately on to the bed he shared with her mother. Sadie could never walk into that room voluntarily now, even when Jackie was in there. It smelled of him.

As time passed, and Allen's attentions became increasingly regular, Sadie found herself concocting little ways of defying him. She knew how he hated it when she read books or did other schoolwork, so suddenly she found herself immersed in the homework her teachers gave her. And when, after it happened, he came into her room and tried to ingratiate himself with her – as he always did, no matter how aggressive and unpleasant he had been before the act – she never allowed herself to treat him with anything other than contempt, and he always left quietly. It was hardly a victory, but it was something.

Alone in her room, she found herself dividing her mind into little boxes. Every time she was called upon to satisfy his twisted needs, she would deposit the memory of the event in the box reserved for that part of her life. Hidden in the furthest corner of her consciousness, it was kept firmly shut. Sadie might have been young, but she knew full well that if she allowed herself to dwell on the contents of that box, she might very well go mad. And as long as she could keep the shame to herself, it didn't seem so bad.

It was three weeks after the first time that Sadie realized she had one more weapon in her arsenal. She arrived back from school to find him waiting at the door for her. By now he only had to nod his head to indicate that he wanted her to go upstairs; this afternoon, however, with a slight shudder of excitement and apprehension, she shook her head.

Allen looked flatly at her and slammed the front door shut. 'Get upstairs,' he told her.

Again Sadie shook her head. 'You can't.'

'What do you mean, I can't?' he asked, his voice dripping with contempt.

'It's my time,' Sadie said defiantly.

'What time?' His eyes had narrowed.

'My time of the month.'

Allen's lip curled into an expression of distaste. He seemed to be wrestling with something, and for an awful moment Sadie thought that he was going to go through with it anyway.

'How long does it last?'

Sadie shrugged, and even managed to look smug. As Allen turned round and walked back into the kitchen, he muttered, almost to himself, 'It won't be long.' He didn't look back as she disappeared upstairs.

Five minutes later she heard the front door slam. He had gone, she realized. She was alone in the house for the first time in weeks. Her face broke into a rare smile, and suddenly she felt positively carefree. Four or five days stretched ahead of her, glorious days during which she knew he wouldn't want to go near her. Wouldn't want to touch her. Wouldn't want to have his vile way.

Like a temporary stay of execution, however, the time passed quickly. Too quickly. Almost before she knew it, her brief moment of freedom was gone, and Allen was there to take advantage. He was especially rough with her the first time after her period, as though to remind her who was in control of the situation.

And when it happened, Sadie just shut the memory up in the little box, hidden away, where nobody could know about it.

Jackie stood nervously in front of Allen. She wasn't a good liar, but she had to put on a good performance now; otherwise she knew what she could expect: the hand round her throat, the blow to her stomach. He was always very careful never to hit her anywhere where it would show, and in any case she had learned how to stop him from losing his temper too much. But there were still bruises on her tummy, and she had no wish to add to them.

'I'm off out to work then,' she said.

He looked at his watch. 'You're early.' It was only midday.

'Yeah, well – they wanted me to fill in for someone, didn't they?' She turned and picked up her handbag from the back of the chair.

'Wait a minute, Jackie.'

She looked back at him over her shoulder. He was eyeing her suspiciously, and then he stepped forward and held her face in one hand. His fingers pinched into the skin.

'What's wrong, love?' she breathed.

'Don't be back late,' he told her, before letting go and walking back into the sitting room. By the time Jackie left, the television was already on.

Her cheap heels clattered down the pavement as she hurried through the estate. Her appointment with Miss Venables – the only teacher she had ever heard Sadie mention – was at twenty past twelve, and she didn't want to be late. She had been assured when she called her from the pub yesterday that if she arrived at that time Sadie would be in another part of the building and there would be no risk of bumping into her – she didn't want her daughter to think she was interfering. It was just that she had seemed so different in the past few weeks. Jackie was not the sort of mother who would normally go to the school for advice, but she couldn't think of anything else to do.

The school receptionist ushered her into Miss Venables' classroom, and the teacher stood up with a friendly smile. She wasn't at all how Jackie imagined her to be – casually dressed and with a softness about her face that made her immediately trustworthy.

'Have a seat, Mrs Burrows,' she offered, pulling up a plastic school chair to her desk.

Jackie sat down and almost instinctively pulled her packet of Rothmans out of her bag. 'Do you mind if I . . .'

'Actually, Mrs Burrows, it's not really the . . .'

'Oh, no, course. Sorry.' Flustered, she returned the cigarettes to the bag.

'So what can I do for you, Mrs Burrows?'

Now she was here, Jackie didn't quite know what to say. 'Um, well, the thing is, it's Sadie . . .'

'I see,' she replied patiently. 'Is something wrong?'

Suddenly Jackie felt embarrassed. Embarrassed about not knowing what was wrong with her daughter. She looked down to her shoes as she spoke. 'I'm just worried about her, is all. She's not talking to me, she's always up in her room with her nose stuck in some bloody book . . .'

With a smile, Miss Venables glanced at the pile of books on her desk.

'Oh, I'm sorry.' Jackie stumbled over her words. 'I didn't mean . . .'

'Please go on, Mrs Burrows.'

Jackie breathed in deeply, as though taking a drag on an imaginary ciggie. It made her bruising hurt. 'Well, that's it, really. She's just different. I thought maybe she was in trouble at school. Bullying, or something . . .'

Miss Venables let Jackie's voice peter out before she replied, 'Actually, Mrs Burrows, I agree with you.'

Jackie looked up at her in sudden panic, but Miss Venables held up a mollifying palm.

'I've noticed a change in Sadie too. She's more serious, and less inclined to cause trouble. She's a thirteen-year-old girl, Mrs Burrows, and she's had a lot to deal with over the last couple of years. Frankly, it would be a surprise to me if she didn't start displaying signs of changing. From where I'm sitting, it all seems perfectly natural.' She smiled. 'To be honest, I wish more parents would come in and complain that their children are spending too much time reading and doing homework. The standard of Sadie's work has sky-rocketed. You should be very pleased with her.'

Jackie blinked. This was not what she had expected to hear, and she could not help feeling a little surge of pride in her daughter.

'Tell me, Mrs Burrows,' the teacher continued, 'how is everything at home? If you don't mind me asking, that is.'

Jackie felt as if she was being caught slightly off guard, and she sat up straight in her chair. 'Fine,' she said quietly.

Miss Venables gave her a querying glance, and in the brief silence that followed, she found herself getting flustered again. 'Fine,' she repeated. 'I've got a new . . . I mean, there's a . . . there's a man in the house now.' She felt herself blushing.

'I didn't know that,' Miss Venables said mildly. 'Sadie hasn't mentioned . . .'

'No. But if she carries on the way she's going, I'd say she's thriving on having another man in the house.' She smiled that appealing smile again. 'I'm very fond of Sadie, Mrs Burrows,' she said warmly. 'I'll keep an eye out for her.' She looked up at the clock on the wall. 'The period's nearly coming to a close. If you want to keep our meeting a secret, I think you ought to . . .'

'Yeah,' Jackie agreed. 'Yeah, OK. I've got to get to work anyway.' She stood up and took Miss Venables' outstretched hand. 'Um, thank you.'

Her gratitude was well meant. As she hurried out of the school, she felt a sense of genuine relief. She had been so worried, but the teacher made perfect sense. Sadie was a teenager, for God's sake. They were supposed to be like that, weren't they? And if Allen's presence had made her more serious, that wasn't such a bad thing.

Was it?

Sadie was a day late, but that day seemed like a week. Of all her friends, she was the most regular. But not this month.

She spent every waking moment waiting for the

familiar cramps that hurt but were so welcome; and as she tried to concentrate on her schoolwork, her mind was preoccupied with waiting for her time of the month to come so that she could claim her days of release.

When she was two days late, she thought about lying to Allen, telling him that she was on. But she didn't, because when her period finally arrived she would have to admit to him the fact that she had misled him. If that happened, she knew, he would hurt her badly to make sure that it didn't occur again.

He had her that day, and Sadie didn't protest. She almost never did nowadays, as she found it was over much more quickly that way and she was allowed to scrub herself down in the bathroom in peace before hiding away in her bedroom once again.

On the third day she woke up feeling sick. Her instinct was to rush into the bathroom and put her head over the toilet, but she didn't, for fear of waking Mum and him. Instead, she left the house as quickly as she could and, rather than sitting on the swings as she waited for Carly and Anna, she walked around the playground, taking deep breaths and trying not to vomit. By mid-morning the sickness had subsided, but come lunchtime she still felt like keeping herself to herself, preoccupied and worried as she was by the dilemma that her late period presented her with. Now that her few precious days of safety had not come, she felt bereft, as though she had been expecting to go on a wonderful holiday but had been told at the last minute that she couldn't. It was too much to bear, and she decided to pretend that her period had come.

But not yet. Today was Thursday. He almost never touched her at the weekend because Mum was around, so if she could wait until Monday she could have a longer stint without him. And maybe by Monday it would have started anyway.

It didn't. But the sickness continued.

When she arrived home from school on Monday afternoon and gave him a meaningful shake of her head, she did so with trepidation, fearing that he would see through her lie. But he had been expecting it, and without speaking to her he left the house as he always did, pausing only to flash her the look of revulsion that her time of the month always seemed to elicit from him. Sadie went to her room and worried. Now that she had told him the lie, the delay in her period was causing her even more anxiety. If it didn't come soon, he would know she had deceived him, and she tried to put from her mind the kind of horrors he would inflict on her.

On Tuesday he wasn't there when she got back; nor was he on Wednesday. On Thursday he gave her an enquiring glance, but she shook her head and he looked angry and frustrated. On Friday when she did the same, he looked suspicious. Over the weekend, she knew, he wouldn't touch her.

But on Monday she would not be able to continue the pretence.

She tried to sleep on Sunday night, but she couldn't for fear and panic. And still her period refused to come.

School on Monday passed in a blur. When she arrived home, he was waiting for her, as she knew he would be. He had not had his way for nearly two weeks now – the longest she had ever gone since the abuse started. As if on autopilot, she walked up the stairs and into the bedroom, aware of his heavy breathing behind her. She knew what to expect.

At least she thought she did.

It was different today. His hands trembled more, and he seemed increasingly excited. He made her do things that he had not insisted on before, and that made her want to retch even more than the sickness that was becoming a common morning occurrence.

And then things returned to their horrible new normality.

When it became clear to Sadie that her period was not going to arrive, she put it to the back of her mind. It was a blip, she told herself. It happened sometimes. Anna had confided to her once that she sometimes went for months without one, and she reassured herself by slipping into the public library and finding a book on the subject. It was perfectly common for young girls to be irregular, she read with relief, before someone else walked down the deserted aisle and she hastily put the book back on the shelf and left with embarrassment.

There was still the sickness, of course, but she put it down to nerves.

When her second period failed to materialize, she almost felt relieved. There was no cause for concern, she told herself, remembering what she had read in the library book, and she had cottoned on to the fact that an imaginary period could last a day or two longer than a real one. An extra day to herself, without him. It was something to be relished.

The summer holidays arrived. Sadie had been dreading them. When she was at school, she was safe; at home, she never knew when he was going to walk into her room with that look in his eyes.

'I hope you don't think,' he had told her on the first day of the holidays, 'that you're going to be out gallivanting for the next few weeks.'

'What do you mean?'

'You know what I mean, pet. Those friends of yours – the ones you go out thieving with and smoking drugs. I want you here in the house, where I can keep an eye on you.'

On the few occasions when she did manage to get out to see Carly and Anna, she never stayed long. All her friends seemed to want to do now was to hide behind disused buildings and smoke the pungent joints that Carly's faceless boyfriend Tom was continuing to supply her with. Sadie had no desire to let Allen smell that on her again; but nor did she want to seem square in front of the others. In the end it was easier just to stay away.

Allen noticed her increased presence in the house with a smug satisfaction. He started giving her little presents. Chocolates mostly – not sweets from the newsagent's, but boxes of them with two trays and a little menu leaflet. 'Grown-up present for a grown-up girl,' he would whisper in her ear. Sadie never ate them; she just flushed them down the toilet, a couple a day, to make sure that he never got angry with her.

By the time she had missed her third period the sickness had subsided, but her anxiety had increased. Occasionally she sneaked into the library and read the section of the book from which she had drawn so much comfort all those weeks ago; but deep down she was not so foolish as to be unaware of what was happening. Telling anybody would be unthinkable, of course. The shame would crush her, and she would never be able to show her face at school – the one place where she felt safe. Anyway, maybe she wasn't pregnant. But if she was, she had an idea what to do about it.

It was during the last weekend of the holidays that she started to put her plan into action. She had spent all her time in her bedroom, as she always did now – Mum had given up even asking her to come out, aware that her refusal would only cause an argument in the house to which there could be only one winner. Mealtimes were the one exception, and she would gobble down her food and then return immediately to her self-imposed prison.

At about two o'clock on Sunday afternoon Jackie called up to her, 'Sadie, food's ready.'

She didn't reply.

'Sadie! Food!'

'Not hungry,' she shouted down.

Her mum trotted up the stairs. 'Come on, love. Come and eat.'

'I told you, I'm not hungry.'

Jackie looked as though she was preparing to argue, but at the last minute she stepped down. 'All right, love. Maybe tonight, eh?'

'Maybe.'

Sadie stared into the distance, trying to ignore the hunger pangs that she was feeling. She didn't hear the conversation downstairs; she didn't see Allen grabbing a clump of Jackie's hair and telling her that her daughter was a sulky little bitch who was walking all over her. All she knew was that Allen came and stood in her room, fire in his eyes, ordering her downstairs. She knew there was no way she could defy him, so she obeyed.

No one spoke as they sat around the table eating a microwave lasagne that was so hot that it burned their mouths. Sadie picked at her food, eating only half of it before asking if she could leave the table. 'Yeah,' said Allen. 'We're sick of looking at your sulky face.' Jackie remained silent as Sadie left the room.

Upstairs, Sadie walked straight into the bathroom. She knelt at the toilet and put her fingers down her throat. She didn't stop until she could vomit no more.

If she was pregnant, she decided, she would do everything she could to stop the child from being born. Starve it. Harm it.

Anything to relieve herself of the shame.

Anything to stop her from bringing *his* child into the world.

CHAPTER 9

In Sadie's dream, the baby was very much alive. Its arms and legs were thin, and it wailed for food. But there were no tears in its eyes. Just hunger. Sadie could not bear to look at them, but the baby never stopped looking at her. She did not know if it was a boy or a girl; nor did she want to. It was enough to know that it was his.

In her dreamworld, she would find herself wandering around the empty house, desperately trying to check that she was alone. She would look behind the doors and under the table; she would even look in the kitchen cupboards. Just when she had satisfied herself that the house was deserted, though, she would hear the scream. Sometimes the baby would emerge from Mum and Allen's room; sometimes it would crawl towards her from the end of her own bed. It would crawl and crawl, and scream and scream; but somehow it would never get any closer.

The screaming would become louder and louder. Sadie would put her hands to her ears to block out the noise, but it never worked. She would start screaming herself, louder than the child, trying to get the noise of its panicked, hungry voice out of her head. But she never could.

And just when she thought the noise could get no louder, just when she thought her head was going to explode, she would wake up, drenched with sweat and bolt upright, not knowing which was worse – the dream or real life.

For the next eight weeks, Sadie learned just how little food you could get by on. She barely ate, allowing herself only a few mouthfuls when the hunger threatened to overcome her. When she was forced to eat – by her mum mostly, but occasionally by him – she made sure it came back up again immediately in the relative privacy of the unlocked bathroom. Her face became gaunt as the weeks passed, and although her tummy had started to swell she managed to hide it; when she lay on her back it was impossible to tell she had a bump, so not even Allen noticed. At night she would lie on her front, hoping in her childlike way that by doing so she might be squashing the baby; and in her moments of greatest anguish she would punch herself in the stomach – not only to harm the child, but also to punish herself. How could she find herself in this situation? It was her fault, just as he kept telling her.

She told no one what was happening, of course. She just gave herself over to the impossible hope that she would be able to prevent the inevitable.

It was a cold day when it happened. At first, when the twinges started as Sadie was walking alone along the corridor from one class to the next, she thought – with a surge of elation – that her period was starting. But there was something different about this; something more intense. In the middle of the lesson she gasped with pain, causing snide giggles from the kids all around her. She asked to be excused, but when she left the classroom she did not head for the girls' toilets: she headed for the exit.

She might have been only six months' pregnant, but she knew what was happening.

Sadie stumbled home. The contractions were stronger now, and it was difficult to walk. As she reached the estate, tears pouring down her eyes and her breath coming in short, sharp gasps, the people she passed looked at her in horror.

One woman offered her help. 'You all right, love?' she asked.

'Get off!' Sadie whimpered, shrugging the woman's well-meant hand from her shoulder and continuing on her way.

When she got home, she banged on the door heavily and irregularly. Jackie answered. 'What the f –' she started to say; but her annoyance dissolved into shock as soon as she saw the state of her daughter. 'Oh my God, Sadie. What's wrong?'

Sadie just pushed past her and struggled up the stairs. Halfway up, she bent double and cried out; then she crawled the rest of the way. Jackie followed in desperate concern, but when Sadie reached the bathroom she slammed the door behind her and manoeuvred the dirty-washing basket in front of it, as she always did.

'Sadie, love, let us in.'

'No!' she shouted. 'Leave me alone.' And she dissolved into tears.

She held tightly on to the side of the bath. Each time the contractions came, she felt her legs buckle beneath her and saw her knuckles whiten as she squeezed the bath as tightly as her young muscles would allow.

And then Allen was there. He had pushed the door open, sliding the dirty-washing basket across the floor, and was now standing by the sink.

'What the fuck do you think you're playing at, Sadie? How dare you talk to your mam like that?'

The thirteen-year-old girl was in too much pain now to fear him. She looked back over her shoulders, and as soon as Allen saw the look on her contorted face something changed in his own expression. The anger and the arrogance fell away, and the lips tightened.

'Get . . . out . . .' Sadie almost growled the words, which were filled with the months of hatred and resentment that she felt towards this man.

For the first time ever, Allen looked wrong-footed. He started to say something, but before he could speak, Sadie was hissing at him, her voice horribly transformed.

'Get out! Get out of here! It's your fault! Get out!'

He stepped backwards out of the bathroom. Through the agony of another contraction, Sadie heard him rush down the stairs. 'I don't know what the fuck's the matter with her,' she heard him shout, and then the front door slammed shut as he left the house.

When Jackie appeared, Sadie was crouched in an agonized little bundle on the floor. 'For God's sake, Sadie,' she wailed. 'What's happening? Tell me what's wrong.' Her voice trembled as she spoke.

Slowly, painfully, Sadie knelt and shuffled round to face her. Her big eyes looked up at her mum – the pain had put her past tears now, but they were still raw – and she struggled to get her breath to speak. 'I'm sorry, Mum,' she managed finally.

'What do you mean, Sadie? What are you sorry for? What's happening?'

She breathed her way heavily and painfully through another contraction.

'I think I need an ambulance, Mum,' she moaned.

'But tell me what the—'

'*Now*, Mum.' And she collapsed again.

Jackie stood still for a shocked moment, and then nodded her head curtly and hurried off to make the call.

The baby was born before the ambulance could get there. Jackie was in the kitchen, worriedly smoking a cigarette, when it happened, having been hollered at from the bathroom by Sadie three times in the previous ten minutes. But when she heard the inhuman scream from upstairs, she could not stop herself from sprinting up to see what had happened.

The bathroom floor was covered in blood. Sadie sat in the middle, half naked, a look of stunned disbelief on her face. In her hands she held the impossibly tiny form of her desperately premature child, marble white beneath the smears of blood and other fluids on its skin. It was stone still. Jackie felt her veins turn to ice as she watched, her eyes tracing the line of the umbilical cord weaving its way to the purplish mass of placenta. She could not speak. Suddenly the silence in the room was shattered by the minuscule, birdlike cry of the baby.

Sadie, shivering, stretched out her fully laden hands. 'Take it,' she whispered.

Jackie didn't move.

'*Just . . . take it*,' Sadie breathed. Her eyes locked with her mother's as she refused to look at the crying baby.

The doorbell rang. For a second Jackie didn't appear to hear it, but then it rang again, followed by a sturdy rap at the door. 'I'll be back, love,' she whispered, and she ran down the stairs. Sadie heard her directing the ambulance men upstairs, and then they were with her – two of them. They gave each other a worried glance before one of them gently took the child and wrapped it in a towel. The other medic crouched down and put his arm around her.

'Can you stand up, sweetheart?' he asked, his voice calm.

Sadie didn't respond, but her shivering seemed to get worse as she stared ahead at nothing in particular.

The medic turned to Jackie, who had appeared at the door. 'What's her name?' he asked abruptly, speaking loudly over the cry of the child.

'Sadie.'

'Sadie!' He shook her slightly. 'Can you hear me?'

Infinitely slowly, Sadie turned her head to look at him. 'Get it out of here,' she told him.

'Sadie, sweetheart,' he persisted. 'You have to tell me how long you've been pregnant.'

'I don't know.'

'You must have some idea, Sadie.'

But Sadie's attention seemed lost again. The medic looked back at his colleague. The look they exchanged was grim. 'Special care,' he said shortly, and the man holding the baby nodded and left the bathroom. 'Sadie.' The medic continued to speak loudly, even though the child's screams were disappearing. 'You're very premature. We have to get your baby to the hospital quickly, and we have to get you there too . . .'

Suddenly she snapped out of her trance. 'I'm not going anywhere with it,' she stated flatly.

'Sadie, you're losing blood heavily. You have to—'

And then she was screaming and flailing, struggling away from the kind-faced medic and sliding further away from him along the bathroom floor. 'I'm not going anywhere with it!' she screamed. 'I never want to see it again . . . It's not mine . . . *I hope it dies . . .*'

'OK, Sadie, OK. Calm down. Take deep breaths.'

The girl did her best to obey, but her choking gasps remained irregular. 'My colleague's going to take the baby to hospital. I'll call for another ambulance and wait here with you while they arrive, but I need to go down now and get some things. I'll be back in two minutes, OK?'

She nodded as the medic stood up. 'Stay here with her,' he instructed Jackie. 'Don't let her move.' And he was gone.

Sadie buried her face in her hands, hoping to smother her shame by blocking everything from her sight. She felt her mum place a trembling hand on her shoulder, but she shrank from her.

'Sadie, love,' Jackie said through her tears. 'Why didn't you tell me?'

No reply.

'Who did this to you?' she insisted.

No reply.

'Oh, Sadie,' she was wailing again now. 'Why didn't you tell me?'

And in that instant, Sadie snapped. All the tension and secrecy and insecurity that had been wound up inside her for the last few months suddenly uncoiled, and she found herself saying the words that she had decided never to say. 'How could I tell you, Mum? How could I?'

'What do you mean?'

'It's his, isn't it? His child.'

Jackie stared at her, her mouth agape.

'It's your boyfriend, Mum. Your fucking boyfriend.

It's that bastard's, and I never want to see it again.'

Mother and daughter looked at each other, their faces barely inches apart. And then Jackie collapsed, her face flat against the bathroom floor and her fists banging to bruising point against the tiles.

The sound that came from her mouth didn't sound like her voice; it sounded like the sound of an animal in pain.

'I wanted to tell you, Mum,' Sadie said accusingly. 'But you always listened to him, not me.'

But Jackie barely heard her as her animal scream mutated into words.

'No!' she half yelled, half sobbed. 'Oh Sadie. Oh God, no . . .'

The house was quiet now. Horribly quiet.

Jackie had wanted to go to the hospital with Sadie, but her daughter wouldn't allow it. The dead look she gave her as she told her mum quite calmly that she didn't need her had felt like a thousand nails ripping through her soul; but Jackie didn't dare argue with her daughter. Not now. Not after everything that had happened.

'I don't want anyone to know,' she had whispered just before the medic had come back in with his swabs and his morphine.

'We've got to go to the police . . .'

'*No!*' Sadie had snapped. 'No police. Nothing. I don't want anyone to know.'

'Why not, love?'

'What do you mean, why not? Look at me. Don't you understand?'

Sadie's voice was getting louder again, and Jackie felt pierced by the suggestion that she did not understand her daughter – not least because the depth of her lack of understanding was only just becoming clear to her. 'All right, love,' she said, trying to mollify her. 'No police, I promise.'

'I never want to see him again,' Sadie added through gritted teeth.

Jackie shook her head mutely.

'Or the baby. I never want to see it again. It's his, not mine.'

That had been two hours ago. The nice ambulance man had told Jackie that Sadie would most likely be sedated for the rest of the day. Jackie should go to St George's in the morning, and they would look after her well in the meantime. Since her daughter had been taken away, Jackie had smoked most of her cigarettes – the last one was now burning in the full bowl she used as an ashtray – and swallowed the remainder of some vodka that she had found at the back of one of the cupboards. The empty bottle now sat in front of her on the table and she stared at it impassively.

From somewhere inside her reverie, she heard the doorbell ring. She ignored it. After a minute it rang again, and then there was a loud banging and a voice shouting; she couldn't make out the words. As if in a trance, she stood up. Her knees buckled slightly as she staggered to the door, and she had to steady herself against the wall while her alcohol-muddled body regained its balance. 'I'm coming,' she called, but the words came out as a barely audible rasp.

Finally she opened the door. Allen stood in front of her and for a moment they said nothing. Then he pushed past her and walked into the kitchen.

He launched in without catching her eye. 'I don't know what she's been saying to you, Jackie.' His voice was slightly slurred – much to Jackie's surprise. She had never known him drunk; never known him out of control. 'She's a fucking liar, you know that. Whatever games she's playing now, I've got a good mind to go up and give her what for . . .'

Jackie turned her back on him, her hands gripping the table to steady herself.

'Don't fucking ignore me, woman,' Allen spat, and she heard his footsteps approaching her from behind.

She didn't think twice about what she was about to do; it just seemed to happen. Her right hand grabbed the neck of the bottle and she swung round, her arm outstretched. When the bottle crashed against the side of Allen's head, he stopped in his tracks; and as the shards of glass tinkled to the floor, he put one hand against his cheek and dabbed his fingers against the hot wetness of the suddenly flowing blood.

'You stupid fucking bitch,' he whispered,

sneering unpleasantly. His bloodied hand started to clench.

But Jackie wasn't going to be scared by him. Not this time. Not now. She still held the bottle in her hand, and its edge was sharp and broken. She lunged at him, and he put his hands up against his face to protect himself. The longest glass spike stuck into his palm, and he hollered in pain as she broke the bottle away, leaving his skin splintered and bleeding. Allen staggered back, and Jackie bore down on him again.

'Get out,' she hissed.

'Don't be—'

'Get out,' Jackie repeated. 'I know everything. I know what you've done. The only reason I'm not at the fucking cop shop right now is because Sadie begged me not to.'

The accusation hung in the air, but not even Allen could withstand the fire in Jackie's drunken eyes for long. Without letting the sneer drop from his face, he stepped backwards towards the front door, Jackie matching his pace step for step. 'If I ever see you again—' she started to say.

'You think you know the truth about your daughter?' Allen interrupted her with a dismissive laugh. His face was white, his brow sweating.

'Get out.'

He was at the door now, fumbling as he tried to open it. Only when his escape route was there did he speak again.

'Well, I'll tell you the truth about her. She enjoyed it.'

Jackie's hand started to shake even more.

'I could see it in her eyes when I had her.' He licked his lips. 'She enjoyed *every . . . fucking . . . second*.'

'*Get out!*' Jackie roared, and she hurled the bottle at the monster in her doorway.

But it was too late: the remnants of the glass simply shattered against the inside of the door that he had closed swiftly behind him.

CHAPTER 10

'Just leave me alone!'

Jackie had lost count of the number of times she had heard Sadie say that over the past couple of weeks since she had got back from the hospital. Now she heard her screaming it up in her bedroom.

'Get out. It's nothing to do with you. Just go away!'

The social worker came down the stairs, grim-faced, and gave a nod of acknowledgement to Jackie, who had been standing alone in the kitchen, nails digging into her palm, all the while she had been up with her daughter. Christ, Jackie was sick of social workers, and doctors, and police – all of them looking at her as if she was the worst mother in the world. It wasn't as if she needed their supercilious glances to tell her that.

'I think we need to talk, Mrs Burrows,' she said.

Jackie led her into the front room, where they sat on the settee. The woman looked so damn prim with her knee-length skirt and her brief-case, Jackie found herself thinking. Made her feel like a slob. The social worker pulled a sheaf of papers out of her briefcase. Jackie felt her hand shaking as the woman spoke, and did her best to hide it.

'She says she just wants to read her book.'

'It's all she's done since . . .'

Instantly the social worker started making notes, and Jackie faltered under the scrutiny.

'I suppose Sadie still hasn't made any disclosure to you about who was responsible,' the woman asked.

Jackie shook her head and remained tight-lipped.

'Nothing at all?'

'Nothing.'

'Mrs Burrows,' she said without looking up. 'Somebody raped your daughter. If she makes a disclosure, it's a simple matter of a DNA test to confirm her accusation.' She forcefully tapped a full stop at the end of her sentence before looking up at Jackie again. 'Are you sure you've no idea?'

Jackie shook her head again. 'Probably one of the boys at school,' she replied neutrally. 'You know what it's like nowadays . . .'

'Yes, Mrs Burrows. I do.'

Jackie fell silent.

'I've tried to explain to Sadie the situation regarding the child,' the social worker continued, 'but she refuses to have the conversation. The doctors think it was born about three and a half months prematurely. I'm sorry, but its chances for survival aren't good. It will remain in the Special Care Baby Unit until . . .' Her voice trailed off. 'Anyway,' she resumed, 'if at any point Sadie changes her mind and wants to see her child, you only have to call me and I'll make arrangements.'

'I don't think it's very likely.'

'No, nor do I. But your daughter's gone through a trauma and you never quite know how people will react.' She stood up and put her notes away. 'The school has been informed. They say Sadie is welcome back there whenever she feels ready. But I wouldn't rush it. Now, is there anything else you want to ask me?'

For a second, Jackie realized with a pang that she hadn't even looked to see what sex the child was. She thought about asking, but something stopped her – the thought of what Sadie's reaction would be, probably.

'All right then,' the social worker said when there was no reply. 'I'll come back in a week's time, if that's all right with you. See how you're both getting on. Don't get up, Mrs Burrows. I'll show myself out.'

Jackie waited until the door had closed after the social worker before she went upstairs to check on Sadie. As the woman had said, she was sitting on her bed, reading a book, and she did not lift her eyes from it when her mother entered. Jackie walked to the bed and sat down next to her, but still Sadie acted as though she wasn't even there.

'You going to talk to me, love?' Jackie whispered.

Slowly Sadie put her book down. 'What do you want to talk about?' she asked numbly.

Jackie gave her an uncomfortable smile. 'Good book?' she asked.

Sadie didn't reply. She just picked the book up and started reading again.

'You didn't used to read so many books.'

'No.'

'So why . . .'

'Because *he* hated me reading them, OK?' Sadie hissed.

Jackie felt blood rising to her cheeks, and she couldn't think of anything to say. For a moment they were silent.

'Did you tell her?' Sadie asked eventually without lifting her eyes from the page.

'No, love,' Jackie replied in earnest.

'Good.'

'Look, love – if you'd just go to the police . . .'

'No.'

More silence.

'She said they'd told my teachers what happened.' Sadie still didn't look up from her book.

'You don't have to go back to school until you want to, love.'

'I'm going back tomorrow.'

'No, love, that's too—'

'I'm going back tomorrow,' Sadie repeated forcefully, as though she was the parent and Jackie the child. She gave her mother a faintly contemptuous glance. 'Why would I want to spend all my time here?' she whispered.

Jackie felt as if she had taken a blow to the stomach. With a curt nod, she stood up and left.

Down in the kitchen she found herself on edge, wanting to do something but not knowing what to do. There was a fresh, unopened bottle of vodka in the cupboard and as she paced the kitchen she found her eyes darting involuntarily towards it. She looked at her watch. Ten thirty. Too early for a drink. But the conversation with Sadie had left her all churned up. A quick one now would calm her nerves and leave her better prepared to cope with everything.

As quickly as a stone released from a catapult, she fetched the bottle, opened it with her trembling hands, took a dirty mug from the side and poured herself a glug of vodka. She gulped it down in one and closed her eyes as the warmth of the alcohol settled through her veins. She lit a cigarette and breathed deeply.

By midday, half the bottle was gone, the cup was on its side on the floor of the sitting room and Jackie was asleep on the sofa.

An hour later, she was oblivious to the fact that Sadie had been standing watching her for a good ten minutes, her face inscrutable.

She was not aware when her daughter placed an old blanket over her for warmth.

And she felt nothing as Sadie gently kissed her head and smoothed her hair, before quietly creeping back upstairs to her room and her book.

The night passed in its usual way, with Allen and his child visiting her in dreams that made her sit up in bed, afraid and sweating, almost hourly. When dawn came, it was a relief.

Sadie did not go to school via the playground that morning. She didn't know if Carly and Anna would be there, for a start; and anyway, she wanted to be by herself. Inside the school gates, she soon got used to the looks that the teachers gave her – surprise, followed by sympathy. They'd get used to her being there soon enough, she told herself. Miss Venables asked her to stay behind after lessons, but Sadie ignored her and simply left. She didn't want to talk to her about it any more than she wanted to talk to anyone else.

The other kids were more of a problem, but nobody seemed to know the real reason for her absence over the past couple of weeks and she knew their gossip would soon die down. Carly and Anna would be the most difficult of all, however. They ran up to her in the corridor after their first lesson, their eyes bright with anticipation.

'Where've you been?' Anna whispered.

'Home.' Sadie continued walking and did not even look at her two friends. 'Ill.'

'Ill?' Carly asked. 'For two weeks? What with?'

Sadie's face twitched momentarily. 'Tummy ache,' she said.

'Tummy ache?'

'Yeah, tummy ache.'

'For two weeks?'

Suddenly Sadie stopped in her tracks. 'Look, what's it got to do with you two anyway?'

The question hung in the air. 'Fine,' Carly said huffily.

'Yeah,' Anna backed her up. 'Fuck you.' And they walked away.

Sadie watched them go with a numbness that stopped her from feeling the desperation she might otherwise have experienced from knowing that she had just lost her two best friends. She didn't care. She had vowed not to tell anyone what had happened, and that included them. She felt different from Carly and Anna now. Their pre-occupations were not her pre-occupations; they acted like children, but she felt like an adult.

What was it he had said? 'You're a big girl now, pet. A very grown-up girl.' She felt as if she was, even though she didn't want to be.

She walked home by herself, just as she had walked to school. Back home, she opened the door with the key she had taken from her mum's bag without asking. Immediately her senses were assaulted by the thick fug of cigarette fumes. All the curtains in the house were closed, the television was on and Jackie was asleep in the bed that Sadie could hardly bear to look at. The stench of alcohol in the room made it perfectly clear what had knocked her mum out. Sadie looked at her dispassionately before going to her room and doing her homework.

By six o'clock she was hungry, and Jackie was showing no signs of waking up. Walking down to the kitchen and opening the fridge, Sadie found it empty, apart from two bottles of vodka that she was sure hadn't been there that morning. She hunted around for her mum's bag, opened her purse and found it empty.

Her stomach was groaning now, and now she had no reason to starve herself; but there was no food, and no money. She stood in the kitchen for a moment, chewing her lips in thought as she wondered what to do; then she opened the fridge again, removed the bottle and slung it into her satchel. Moments later she was walking purposefully towards the off-licence.

There was a queue when she arrived, and Sadie stood in line, ignoring questioning looks from the adults in the shop. When her turn came, the man behind the counter – who knew Sadie well from her frequent visits there on behalf of her mum – looked at her indulgently.

'Sadie,' he said, acknowledging her.

Sadie delved into her satchel and pulled out the still-cold bottle of vodka. 'Did my mum buy this earlier?' she asked.

The shopkeeper nodded.

'I want the money back,' she stated.

His eyes flicked to the queue of people behind her. 'What?'

'I want the money back.'

He smiled awkwardly. 'I can't just give you . . .'

'I want the money back now. Otherwise I'm going to the police to tell them you've been selling me under-age booze.'

The shopkeeper's eyes narrowed and everyone in the shop went quiet. 'Why don't you just fuck off home, Sadie?'

Sadie looked fiercely up at him, her jaw clenched. 'It's up to you,' she said implacably. 'I want the money back.'

Her demand seemed to hang in the air between them.

Then, reluctantly, the shopkeeper took the bottle. He opened the till and removed a handful of change, which he counted silently into Sadie's outstretched hand. Bending down so that he was face to face with her, he whispered, 'I don't want to see you or your alky mum in here again.'

Sadie didn't reply. The moment the money had been refunded, she stuck it in her pocket and without a further word turned and left, ignoring the stares of the other customers she passed. Then she went to the chippie on the outskirts of the estate and bought her dinner. She didn't bother getting anything for Jackie. There was no point – she knew she wouldn't be awake for hours.

Next morning, Jackie was already up when Sadie came downstairs. She was nervously looking in all the cupboards, and even checked the fridge three times. There was a sense of panic emanating from her, and Sadie left before her mum could question her about the missing bottle.

The money from the refund was soon spent. When Jackie realized what her daughter had done, she started to rant; but it took only one look from Sadie for the rant to dissolve into a mumble and for Jackie to leave the house so as to avoid the hot glare of Sadie's disapproval.

It didn't stop all the money they had going on Mum's booze, however. Sadie would eat as much as she could at school, and then prepare herself to go hungry in the evenings. The weekends were worst: only once in a blue moon Mum would buy something small for the fridge, and soon Sadie had lost count of the number of newsagent's she got chased out of for stealing a chocolate bar to stave off her hunger.

The weeks turned into months; Jackie's dependence became more extreme. Sadie had seen it happen before, so she knew what she was witnessing. There was on one to tell, though; nothing to do. She just had to get on with it.

Her fourteenth birthday passed, and Jackie didn't even mention it.

To take her attention away from everything, Sadie threw herself into schoolwork. It took her mind off being hungry, and she felt in her own small way that she was defying her tormentor. If Allen were still around, it would drive him wild that she was doing schoolwork in her bedroom, and somehow that made her feel better. Her results soared and her teachers seemed astonished and delighted at this turn of events.

Jackie seemed more distant than ever. Sadie only ever saw her when she was drunk, comatose or hung over. It was as it was before Allen arrived – worse even. She would disappear for increasingly long periods of time, even up to two days; when she returned and Sadie quizzed her on her whereabouts, she would just get angry. 'Don't fucking start, Sadie,' she would mutter, before finding further solace in booze if there was some, or sitting, trembling and unapproachable, while she waited for money to come in so that she could buy some more.

During one of Jackie's prolonged absences, on a freezing cold Saturday afternoon, Sadie found herself wandering aimlessly around the estate. As usual, the pangs of hunger were with her, and she had gone for a walk to try to forget about them. There weren't many people about, and she suddenly realized that she had left the boundaries of the estate and was walking up a road she didn't recognize. She stopped and looked around her, not quite knowing where she was or which way she had walked in order to get here. It was a dingy side street, with litter blowing around as a result of the wind being trapped into a channel by the high buildings on either side. There was nobody else there, and most of the shops, such as they were, were closed and had their sturdy metal grilles pulled down over their front windows. There was just one exception: the shop outside which Sadie found herself standing had blacked-out windows and the words 'Books and Videos' etched into them.

With a shiver, she realized how cold she was and took a step forward to take advantage of the warmth that was coming from the shop doorway. As she did so, two men walked out. Recognizing the stench of alcohol on them, Sadie wrapped her arms around her body and lowered her head as they jostled past her.

'Going shopping, darling?' one of them asked, and his friend sniggered.

Slowly Sadie turned round to look at them. They were unprepossessing types, with pallid, slightly podgy faces; and they each carried a brown paper bag that concealed whatever it had inside. They were leering at Sadie as they walked slightly unsteadily; as they caught sight of her pretty face and almond eyes, however, their expressions changed. Looking at each other, they smiled as though they thought their luck was in. One of them stumbled over to Sadie and started to put his arm around her.

'Tell you what, love, don't worry about going in there. Just come with—'

'Get your hands off me,' Sadie ordered, stepping away from his attempted grope.

The two men sniggered at each other again. This time both of them stepped towards Sadie, and the smell of drink on their breaths hit her once again.

What it was that made her go for them she didn't know. It was as if she had a reflex action. Involuntary. Of the two men, the one who had tried to put his arm around her was slightly in front.

With a sudden force that almost took her by surprise, Sadie jerked her knee up and struck him hard between the legs. With a gasp he doubled over. Sadie jumped back, strangely satisfied with her work but fearful of what was going to happen next.

And well she might have been. As the man struggled to an upright position, his features transformed from thoughtless drunkenness to blind anger. 'You stupid bitch,' he said through gritted teeth. 'That fucking hurt.'

His friend looked aggressive too, and the pair of them started to bear down on Sadie, who wanted to run but found her feet glued to the pavement. She cowered as the man she had kicked raised his hand to hit her. When he did, the blow to the side of her cheek was like a sharp sting. Sadie fell with a whimper to the ground and touched her face to feel for blood. There was none. Not yet. But the anger hadn't been dispelled from the man's face. He was giving his brown paper package to his mate so that both hands would be free to deal with the girl on the ground in front of him.

'All right, fellas. Enough.'

Sadie's assailants stopped, then turned round to see who had spoken.

The man standing in the doorway of the shop was not young – in his seventies, perhaps – and he was slightly overweight. The white hair on his head was like a cloud of cotton wool, and his clothes – jeans and a brown checked shirt – fitted him poorly. His face was deeply lined.

'Fuck off, Granddad,' one of the men said to him, before turning his attention back to the terrified Sadie. 'What are you, her fucking pimp?' One of the men barked a short, ugly laugh and spat at Sadie.

The older man had no qualms about attacking them from behind. They had clearly been so dismissive of him that they did not see the cosh in his hand; he whacked it forcefully into the side of each man and they both stumbled away, winded. 'Police already called, lads,' he told them in a clipped, abrupt voice. 'Best you go. Don't come back.'

With a final look of disdain back at Sadie, who was still sprawled on the ground, the two men continued to stumble down the road. Shivering from the cold, she watched them go, turning to look at the old man only when she heard them shout their parting shot: 'Fucking whore!'

The old man approached her, bent down and helped her up. 'Sorry,' he said, looking apologetically back at his shop. 'Sometimes get them. Nasty characters. Hurt you, did they?'

'It's all right,' Sadie muttered.

'Take you to the hospital if you like.'

'No,' Sadie said sharply. 'No. Thank you.' She started to dust herself down.

The old man squinted at her. 'You look freezing,' he said. 'Are you all right?'

Sadie just shivered at him in return.

Again the old man looked back at his shop. 'I'd

invite you in for a cuppa,' he said, 'but it's not really the sort of place . . .' His voice trailed off. 'Do your parents know you're out?' he asked suddenly.

Sadie nodded, avoiding the man's eyes as she did so.

For a while, neither of them spoke. 'Come on then,' the old man said finally. 'Can't stand outside here shivering in the cold.' He indicated with a sweep of his hands that Sadie should come inside with him.

She hesitated. Part of her wanted to run away, to get back to the relative safety of her home. But there was something about this man, a kindness in his eyes. And she was very, very cold. Slightly timidly, she followed him into the shop.

Once through the door, the man turned and locked it.

'What are you doing?' Sadie asked, panic rising in her chest.

'Locking up. We'll go out back. Not a place for young 'uns, in the shop.'

She looked around her. He was right. The walls were plastered with rack upon rack of adult magazines and videos. The pictures on the front seemed to Sadie to merge into one great mass of flesh – she could hardly differentiate one picture from another – but she found she didn't feel repelled by it. Just numb.

The old man saw her looking around. 'Like I say,' he said with insistence in his voice, 'not a place for young 'uns. Come on.' He led her through the shop, behind the counter and out to the back.

It could not have been more different there: whereas the main shop had been seedy, the lighting stark and the carpet thin and frayed, out the back it was comfortable, if a little shabby. There was a squishy sofa covered with a brown corduroy material, a scrupulously clean little kitchen area and a stand-alone gas heater, all three bars pumping out welcome heat. Mismatched lamps dotted around the room gave it a homely yellow glow, and a sports match of some description was being played quietly on the radio.

'I'll make us a cuppa,' the old man said.

Sadie never normally drank tea, but she sat down on the sofa, which threatened to envelop her, and sipped it, grateful for its warmth and sweetness.

'What's your name, dear?' the old man asked, breaking the silence.

'Sadie.'

'I'm Lionel. And do your parents really know where you are, Sadie?'

She shrugged. 'Did you really call the police?' she asked.

'Certainly not. I'm afraid the police couldn't care less about what goes on in places like this.' He smiled sadly. 'I don't really blame them.'

'Have you got anything to eat?' Sadie asked.

Lionel looked a bit flustered. 'I, er . . . I might have some biscuits somewhere. Tend to eat in the café. Not really one for cooking.' He stood up and rummaged around in one of his kitchen cupboards before coming back with half a packet of Rich Tea biscuits. He handed them to Sadie and watched thoughtfully as she started to wolf them down. 'You're not off the streets, are you dear? You do have a home?'

'I do,' Sadie said through a mouthful of biscuits, 'but my mum's not around much.' Suddenly she realized that she had eaten almost all the biscuits. 'She likes to drink,' she admitted in a small voice. 'It doesn't leave much money over for food.'

'I see.' Lionel appeared glassy eyed. He stepped out of the room, back into the shop, and came back a minute later clutching a ten-pound note. 'Take it,' he said.

A look of indecision crossed Sadie's young face. She wanted to accept the money, but she felt embarrassed to do so.

'Please,' Lionel insisted. 'Take it.' Sadie stretched out her hand and gratefully pocketed the cash.

Again they sat in silence, sipping their tea and feeling the awkwardness of their newfound friendship.

'If you come here next Saturday,' Lionel said after a while, 'I could give you a bit of work.'

Sadie blinked at him.

'Not out front,' he stuttered slightly. 'I wouldn't want you out front. Not a place for you. Course it's not. But back here. Stocktaking and the like. If you want to.'

His face reddened slightly as he spoke, and Sadie found herself becoming embarrassed too by such an unexpected act of kindness.

'I don't know,' she said, fiddling with her fingers. 'I think I'd better go home.'

'Yes,' Lionel stood up. 'Of course. Sorry. Anyway, hurry home. Cold out there.'

He led her back through the shop and unlocked the door, and Sadie walked out into the street. 'Thanks for the tea,' she smiled.

Lionel waved his hand dismissively. 'Go carefully, Sadie,' he said, before turning back inside. Sadie hunted for her way home, the ten-pound note clutched firmly in her hand.

It was Monday night before Jackie returned. Her face was bruised and she smelled of sweat and cheap booze. Sadie had spent some of her money on a big bag of pasta and some tomato sauce from a local shop, and so was able to prepare her worn-out mother a bowl of hot food when she arrived home. They sat together at the table, the silence between them speaking more eloquently than any words. Sadie didn't bother asking where her mum had been because she knew she wouldn't get a straight answer; she just watched quietly as Jackie picked unenthusiastically at her food with a trembling hand before slinking up to bed.

It was difficult to make the ten pounds last, but Sadie was careful and didn't spend the last of it until Thursday night. On Friday they went hungry.

As she sometimes did, Jackie stared into the empty fridge with annoyance, as though the lack of food was someone else's fault.

'Fucking money doesn't come till next week,' she muttered.

Sadie was standing in the doorway.' Maybe you should get a job again, Mum,' she suggested in a small voice.

Jackie turned on her, sudden fury in her eyes. 'Don't start, Sadie. You're as bad as him. He was always on at me to get a job.'

Sadie's face hardened, and in an instant Jackie realized what she had said. 'I'm sorry, love,' she said in apology. 'I didn't mean . . .'

'Forget it,' Sadie told her, before turning upstairs.

The next morning she left the house at nine o'clock and paced around the estate nervously before summoning up the courage to do what she wanted. Finally she retraced her steps back out of the estate towards the side street where Lionel's shop was situated. It was closed, so she knocked on the door. There was no answer. A couple of passers-by gave an odd look to this young girl banging on the door of such a place, but she didn't even notice them.

Instead, she decided to wait. She sat on the pavement by the door to the shop, her arms clutching her knees. After a few minutes, it started to rain, but she didn't move, ignoring the fact that her clothes and hair were becoming sodden.

It was nearly an hour before Lionel arrived. He didn't appear to notice her until he was right by the shop door; when he did, his eyes widened.

'Sadie,' he exclaimed. 'What are you doing? Sitting there. Out in the rain.'

'You said Saturday,' Sadie replied, her eyes wide and her damp hair sticking to her cheek.

'But I thought . . .' Lionel stumbled over his words.

'Please, Lionel,' Sadie implored him.

He smiled. 'Yes, of course, dear. Of course. Come in. Come in. Through to the back. Don't want you out here. There we are.' He ushered her through to the comfortable back room. 'Now then, first things first. Dry yourself by the fire and I'll make us a nice cup of tea . . .'

Sadie never told her mum where she went every Saturday, and Jackie never asked. But suddenly, with the thirty pounds that Lionel paid her every weekend for totting up lines of numbers, checking the occasional stock deliveries and making endless cups of tea, there was food in the fridge and washing-up liquid by the sink. She kept her week's money firmly in the pocket of whatever clothes she was wearing, because she knew what would happen to it if she left it lying around the house.

Each Saturday morning, she made her way to the shop and was ushered into the back by Lionel. He never let her out front – 'Not for young 'uns,' he'd repeat in his clipped way, seeming genuinely embarrassed by his line of work – so when Sadie had completed the few jobs he had given her to do, she would set her schoolbooks out in front of her and spend the time studying. Whenever a customer walked in, a little bell would ring; sometimes Sadie didn't hear the bell for hours on end and she knew that Lionel would not have earned enough money that day to pay her. But pay her he always did, brushing aside her offers to take less money with a wave of his hand.

It was strange work. Sadie kept quiet about it, not because she was embarrassed but because she knew that if people found out where she was, she would be forced to stop. She was too young even to work in a supermarket and if anyone discovered she was spending her Saturdays in a sex shop, there'd be hell to pay. She'd lose the money, people would find out about Mum . . . No, it was much better not to mention this to anyone.

Not that that was difficult. Carly and Anna never spoke to her now – they were too busy with their boyfriends and their spliffs to be bothered with Sadie and her moods and her new-found bookishness. The other kids at school avoided her too, aware that she had changed in some way, but knowing that she could fly off the handle and wasn't afraid to defend herself with her fists if they pushed her too hard.

It wasn't just the money that kept her going back to the shop. Lionel had a kindliness that seemed at odds with his seedy profession, and when trade was slow they sat out the back and chatted. Occasionally he looked at her with something approaching pity in his eyes, as though he sensed the sadness she had experienced; but he never probed too deeply, never tried to persuade Sadie to reveal things about herself that she didn't want to reveal; he just took her as she was, and treated her with respect.

And as time passed, they became friends. More than friends. Not father and daughter, exactly, but close . . .

One Saturday, not long before Sadie's fifteenth birthday, they were sitting out the back, drinking tea and chatting about nothing in particular. The familiar jingle of the bell indicated that someone had entered, so Lionel stood up with a sigh and walked into the shop. Sadie started reading her book again, but was suddenly distracted by the sound of raised voices. Concerned, she put her book down and crept to the dividing door. It was slightly ajar, and she could just see through it.

The man standing at the till was a lot younger than Lionel – mid-twenties, perhaps. He had a couple of days' stubble growth, his thick black hair was tightly greased back on to his scalp and there was a flatness in his eyes as he looked at Lionel with disdain.

'I haven't seen you in quite a while,' Lionel was saying. He was mumbling slightly.

'What a surprise,' the young man replied, his voice drenched with a thick cockney accent.

Lionel scratched his woolly head, a look of confusion coming across his face. 'Quite . . .' he muttered. 'I suppose you're not here to enquire about my health.'

The young man snorted.

Lionel nodded uncomfortably and opened the till. He took out a thin wad of notes, removed a twenty and a ten, and handed them over to the young man. 'This will have to do, I'm afraid, Michael. You'll spend it properly, I hope.'

But Michael didn't seem to be listening. Instead, he was greedily leafing through the notes with his finger, adding up how much Lionel had given him.

'Would you like a cup of tea?' Lionel asked falteringly.

'Course not,' Michael replied without looking up.

'No. No, of course. Tell me, how, er, how is she?'

'Mind your own business, old man,' Michael said with an unpleasant smile. He walked towards the door, but at the last moment he turned round. 'Oh,' he added, sarcasm dripping from his voice, 'thanks for the pocket money. Glad to see business is going so well.' And with another snort he left.

Sadie watched as Lionel remained stone still, his hands flat on the counter as he stared at the door. 'It's all right, Sadie dear,' he said suddenly, causing her to jump. 'I know you're there.' He turned round and gave her a sad little smile.

'Who was he?' Sadie asked quietly.

Lionel didn't answer. Instead, he walked into

the back room, took a seat and pinched between his eyes.

'Was that protection money?' Sadie persisted.

'No, dear. Not protection money.'

His voice sounded final, and Sadie chose not to press him any further. But before she sat down again, he spoke. 'That fine young gentleman, I'm sorry to say, was my son.'

'Your son?'

Lionel nodded.

'I didn't know you had a . . .'

'Don't really talk about him.' He lapsed back into his clipped way of speaking. 'Don't see him much. He prefers not to.'

Sadie blinked and waited for Lionel to elaborate if he wanted to.

'Grown-ups can be very complicated, Sadie,' he said, the sad smile coming back to his face.

'I know.' Sadie went and sat next to him, taking his arms in her hands. 'Try me.'

'Married his mum thirty years ago. Very happy for a while. Then Michael came along. Changed her. She took against me. Left with Michael and I never saw them.' The words had started to tumble out now. 'Oh, I could have tracked them down. Insisted on seeing my son. But that's not really my . . . not really my style. Thought she might have another man. Didn't want to interfere. Of course, you probably don't really understand, Sadie dear. About having a child, I mean.'

Sadie looked away briefly.

'Of course, all this happened before I owned this place.' He stood up suddenly and started to pace the room. 'Not proud of it, you know. Not how I wanted to earn a living. But it came along, and . . .' He shrugged. 'Michael first turned up about four years ago. Just walked into the shop and told me who he was. At first I thought he just wanted to know his father. But he soon put me right. That wasn't what he wanted at all.'

'Money?' Sadie asked.

'Yes. Money. And I gave it to him.'

'Why?'

For an instant Lionel's face softened. 'Because he's my son, Sadie.'

At that moment the image of Jackie, drunk and bruised and comatose, popped into Sadie's head. Would Sadie's mum do the same for her? she wondered. Probably not. All of a sudden she felt herself suffused with love and respect for the wild-haired man in front of her.

'I see him about twice a year. Give him whatever I can. And that's it.'

Lionel walked into the kitchenette area and put the kettle on; Sadie watched in silence as he made himself a fresh cup of tea and then came and sat down next to her.

'Who can blame him, really?' he said.

'What?'

'Who can blame him?'

'I don't understand.'

'Well, Sadie, look at it.' His arm made a sweeping

gesture towards the front of the shop. 'Who would want anything to do with a father who ran a place like this? Even I'm ashamed of it.' He put his tea down on the floor in front of him and buried his head in his hands.

They sat there in silence, Sadie not quite knowing what to say but feeling the need to say something. Finally she stood up and kissed the old man on the top of his head. 'I'd feel proud to have a father like you,' she whispered.

Slowly, Lionel raised his face to look at her; Sadie returned his gaze, jaws clenched. 'You are a very sweet girl, Sadie,' he said, smiling.

As he spoke, an uncomfortable prickle of shame shuddered down Sadie's spine, and images flashed in front of her eyes: little Jamie Brown's bruising which she could do nothing to stop; Allen's heavy body bearing down on her; the screaming baby in her arms that she had consigned to a near-certain death without a mother's love.

'You're a very sweet girl indeed.'

If only he knew, Sadie thought to herself.

If only he knew.

CHAPTER 11

The months passed.

Jackie and Sadie never spoke of Allen. It was as if he had never existed, as if he had never stepped foot in their house. Sometimes Sadie wondered if Jackie had a box in her head too where she filed away all the unpleasant memories.

When Sadie's fifteenth birthday arrived, she knew better this time than to expect Jackie to remember, and it passed without comment. Despite that, the two of them fell into a routine which was, if not comfortable, at least predictable. Sadie would go to school, come home and cook simple meals for the two of them if Jackie happened to be there, or just for herself if she wasn't. On Saturdays and during the school holidays she would spend the day in the shop with Lionel. Jackie would regularly disappear for a couple of days – usually just after the giro money came – and return home looking much the worse for wear. The daughter would never ask where she had been, and the mother would never tell. When she was at home, Jackie would barely speak, choosing instead just to sit and stare into space. Now and then she would break down in tears, telling Sadie how sorry she was, how sorry for everything. Sadie didn't know if she meant sorry about Allen or sorry about her present state, but it didn't matter. She knew she wouldn't change. She knew she couldn't change. Not now.

Sadie continued to work hard at school. The teachers seemed pleased by her efforts and the pupils disparaging of them in equal measure; she managed to avoid aggro by keeping herself to herself and ignoring the praise of well-meaning people like Miss Venables. Jackie was oblivious to how well her daughter was doing – mainly because she never attended the school parents' evenings, but also because Sadie never told her. As the summer of her GCSEs approached, Jackie seemed unaware of the important exams round the corner, and Sadie saw no reason to bang on about them. It would have meant nothing to her poor, drunken mother, who was more concerned about her vodka and trembling hands than her daughter's schooling.

And then the exams were upon her. Sadie was taking more subjects than anyone else in the school, and although she felt quietly confident, deep down she missed her mother's encouragement. On the morning of her final examination, she went into Jackie's bedroom. Her mum was sprawled on that hated bed, a full ashtray spilling over the sheets. She was fast asleep.

Gently, Sadie shook her on the shoulder and she

awoke groggily, as if not knowing where she was. 'I'm going, Mum,' she whispered.

Jackie collapsed back on the bed and shut her eyes.

'It's my last exam today.'

Again her eyes opened, but the look she gave Sadie was one of such blank incomprehension that she knew her mum had no idea what she was talking about. 'It doesn't matter,' she breathed; then she turned and left for school.

Jackie lay immobile on the bed. Although her eyes had closed again, she was listening for the sound of the door shutting. When she heard it, she didn't move. Not yet. Her limbs felt heavy and the familiar feeling of sickness in her stomach was overpowering. She needed something to make it go away. Groggily she pulled herself off the bed and stumbled to her knees, blindly feeling under the mattress until her fingertips came into contact with a small brown plastic pill bottle. There was a pharmaceutical label on the front, but the guy who had sold her these cheap amphetamines had been very far from being a pharmacist. She struggled to open the cap, and when she had managed it she hungrily swallowed a couple of the small pills – half black, half clear and filled with tiny spheres of dextro-amphetamine – and then lay on the floor as she waited for them to kick in.

She felt it first in her stomach: a tingling feeling that started to suppress any other feelings of sickness or hunger that might be there. After fifteen minutes her teeth were grinding and her eyes were open. She blinked furiously at the ceiling for a while – how long, she couldn't tell – before she found that the speed had given her enough energy to get up.

For half an hour she paced round the kitchen, wringing her hands and chewing on her lower lip. She needed a drink, but there was nothing in the house and the only money she had on her was the eighty-three pence in her pocket. But it was unseasonably cold outside, she noticed with satisfaction. It was always easier to get hold of booze when it was cold because you could wear heavier clothes. She grabbed her largest coat – a stained and torn anorak that used to belong to her husband – put it on and rushed out of the house, not noticing as she slammed the door behind her that as a result of her shaky fumbling with the latch it didn't close properly. Fuelled by her high, she practically ran off the estate. There was no way she could do what she was about to do close to home – everybody knew her, and they knew not to trust her.

The supermarket was not busy. Just the usual daytime lot – mostly pensioners on their daily trip to buy milk and bread. Jackie felt a sudden surge of paranoia and thought that people were watching her as she swept down the aisles, but maybe that was just the speed talking. She headed first for the bread section, and grabbed a small loaf at random; then she hurried round to the booze shelves. It was the clear alcohol she was after – vodka, gin, it didn't really matter to her. The bottles were arranged in alluringly neat rows, like glass soldiers standing to attention. Shiftily looking left and right, she reached out and took one of the larger ones before clumsily secreting it inside her coat. With another look around her, she started walking down the aisle to the checkouts.

As she walked, a voice came over the tannoy. 'Staff announcement, code 586 in aisle 11, please. Code 586 in aisle eleven.'

Jackie's frequently blinking eyes shot up to the sign suspended from the ceiling above the aisle. Number eleven. And behind her she heard the unmistakable patter of footsteps running towards her. She turned round to see two security guards tearing down the aisle. As she did so the loaf of bread fell from her hands and, clutching the bottle tightly to her body, she started running away from them.

The amphetamines had heightened her awareness, and she moved more quickly than she might otherwise have done. Tearing through an empty checkout lane, she activated a screaming alarm and knocked sideways an old lady who was packing up her groceries; but she was out of the shop before the security guards could collar her. Without checking what the traffic was doing, she ran across the road, causing horns to beep and brakes to screech, and then pounded along the pavement as fast as she could. It was a good couple of minutes before she dared stop and look back; when she did, she saw that she had lost the security guards.

Her chest and stomach were burning, her knees felt as if they would collapse underneath her and the knuckles on her hand hurt from clutching the bottle under her anorak so tightly. She fell against the brick wall of the street in which she found herself, waited for her rasping breath to calm down and then, with shaky hands, undid the top of the vodka bottle and took a mouthful.

She coughed as it went down, but that did not stop her from taking another.

Ten minutes later, half the bottle was gone and Jackie was staggering. The amphetamines were still coursing through her system, stopping the effects of the alcohol from being too much of a downer but making her aggressive. Angry. Occasionally a passer-by stared at her for a few seconds too long, and when that happened she let rip, shouting and swearing at them until they bowed their heads in embarrassment and went on their way.

The morning passed in a haze as Jackie wandered aimlessly and drunkenly. By midday the bottle of vodka was finished, but she still held on to the neck fiercely; now and then she forgot she had drunk it all and put it to her lips, cursing wildly when she realized that there was not even a drop left. She was off the beaten track now, away from the roads and walking alongside a small tributary of water that led north up to the Thames – not that she realized that.

It was a shabby area, grey and derelict. Jackie staggered through a disused car park that was full of the burned-out, scrap-metal shells of vehicles long since abandoned. At one end was a railway bridge. A seemingly endless freight train trundled across it as Jackie walked underneath and found herself on a litter-strewn towpath. To her left was the river, flowing brown and sludgy at the bottom of a high wall. To her right was the concrete husk of a disused warehouse. Jackie stopped. She needed to sleep, and inside this building would be as good a place as any.

Near by was a metal door. It had once been painted green, but the paint had almost all peeled off. Jackie stumbled towards it and pulled it open. The hinges were rusty, and it took a couple of good tugs before she could step inside; the door dragged along the ground as it opened.

The interior of the building was a large open space. Although it was the middle of the day, there was very little light in there; the windows, mostly smashed in, were small and high up and seemed to cast only a different hue on the pervading gloom. Along the walls were a series of dens fashioned from cardboard boxes, and around them sat their occupants – ragged down-and-outs – huddled in small groups. A few looked up, uninterested, at the new arrival, but mostly they seemed devoid of the energy to pay Jackie any attention.

For a few moments she stood there, blinking as her eyes got used to the semi-darkness. Then she staggered towards the nearest group of vagrants and collapsed heavily beside them. There were five of them – three girls and two boys. They were young, although their dirty faces and forlorn eyes made it impossible to say just how young – late teens, maybe. An almost empty tube of glue languished on the dirty ground in front of them, as did several old aerosols – their cheap fix having been administered, they had been crunched up and discarded. As one, the youngsters eyed the bottle in Jackie's fist.

'Share it round,' the boy said.

As if in a trance, Jackie raised the bottle to look at it, and then shook her head. 'Empty.' She dropped it on the floor.

As it became clear that she had nothing to offer them, the group's attention subsided. Somewhere, from the depths of her inebriation, Jackie felt the stirrings of sympathy. They looked so young, so hopeless.

But then, with the selfishness of the true alcoholic, her thoughts came straight back to herself, and her need for another fix.

She looked around, trying to determine if one of the residences in this cardboard city might house someone prepared to give her a mouthful of drink. With difficulty, she pushed herself to her feet and staggered to another randomly chosen down-and-out. She was younger than the others, and seemed less aware. Her skin was covered in angry red spots, especially around the nose, and she twitched occasionally and involuntarily. She looked up at Jackie with wide, bloodshot eyes, and the flickering flame of sympathy in the older woman reignited itself. She sat down beside the girl and gave her a brief smile of solidarity.

'I've nae got anything,' the girl said in a marked Scottish accent. Briefly Jackie wondered what she had been through to bring her so far from home, but that thought could not win against the look of disappointment that passed across her face.

'You know how to get something if you want it? A fix, I mean.'

Jackie shook her head numbly.

The girl pointed to the other side of the building and, as if summoned by that gesture, the silhouette of a figure emerged from one of the cardboard-box houses. 'Him,' the girl whispered.

Jackie squinted across the room. 'He'll give you whatever you want,' the girl was saying quietly. 'Well, whatever he's got. You just have to give him something back.'

'What sort of thing?' Jackie asked, her voice slurred.

'You know. Things.' The girl's coy answer seemed at odds with the state she was in. 'It doesn't take long, and if you need a fix . . .'

Her voice trailed away and Jackie watched as the figure made its way round the side of the building. There was something about his gait that chilled her; something about the shape of his silhouetted body that made the adrenaline pump through her veins and, for the moment at least, lifted the cloud of drunkenness from her.

She felt sick as he approached.

She didn't want him near her.

But he was drawing closer; and as he did so, Jackie realized that the shouted warnings of her instinct were on the mark, despite the chemicals in her system. It was only when he was a few metres away, however, that she saw for sure that it was him.

It had been eighteen months since she had last seen Allen's loathsome face, and it had changed in that time. His skin was more deeply lined, more weather-beaten; there were scars along one side; his hair was longer and flecked with grey; and he had a wispy, untrimmed beard. His eyes were the same, though. Dead. Flat.

She found herself frozen to the spot.

Allen didn't notice Jackie until he was almost upon her; and even when he did, it seemed to take a while for the fact of her arrival to register with him. When it did, his features creased into that familiar sneer she knew, despised and feared in equal measure.

'Hello, Jackie,' he said in a rasping voice. 'Down on our luck, are we?'

Jackie's drunkenness had suddenly been replaced by a sharp clarity, the like of which she had not known for months. Ever so slowly she pushed herself to her feet and positioned herself between Allen and the young junkie on the floor. One eyebrow raised, Allen looked archly over Jackie's shoulder at the girl. 'Don't worry about her, pet. She won't be talking to me for a while. Not till her little packet of snout runs out.'

Breathless with shock, Jackie said nothing.

'I have to say,' Allen continued, 'that you're just about the last person I expected to see here. Your tramp of a daughter, maybe. But not you.'

At the mention of Sadie, Jackie snapped. She raised her arm, ready to rain down blows upon him, but he was too fast for her, grabbing her by the wrists and squeezing mercilessly until the pain was too much to bear.

'Get off,' she whimpered. 'You're hurting me.'

'Believe me,' Allen grimaced. 'I'm not. Not yet.'

From behind her Jackie was aware of the girl scampering away from the scene.

'Have you got any idea how much trouble your little outburst with the broken bottle caused me?' He squeezed tighter. 'No, probably not.' Suddenly he let go, but Jackie was not allowed much respite from his violence: instantly he grabbed a clump of her hair. She wailed, and started trying to punch him, but he wrenched the hair round tightly and all she could do was raise her hands to her head as she screamed.

Allen started to walk towards the door, roughly pulling Jackie along as he did so. She stumbled behind him, tears of pain streaming down her face.

As they approached the half-opened door, however, she grabbed her opportunity. She barged forward, forcing Allen's bulk against the peeling green metal of the door's corner. The collision echoed round the building, and for a brief moment he let go of her hair as, slightly dazed, he staggered sideways.

Jackie slipped out of the door, but her head was not filled with thoughts of escape. Far from it.

She was going to do what she wished she had done last time she saw him; she was going to make good the regret and despair that had sent her spiralling into this pitiful condition; she was going to make him pay for everything he had done to her little girl.

She was going to kill him.

Swiftly, soberly, she scanned the ground for something – anything – that she could use as a weapon. Her eyes settled on half an old red brick and she grabbed it as Allen stepped outside, looking like the Devil himself. He hurled himself at her and she swiped the brick at his face; he roared in anger, but to Jackie's horror the old brick simply crumbled to dust in her hand. He launched himself on top of her and the two of them fell heavily to the ground.

Now his hands were round her throat. She felt them pressing into her jugular and squeezing her windpipe. As she gasped for air, she could smell his breath, pungent and rancid; but then her senses started to fade and her neck felt thicker and bloated. Desperately her hands scrabbled in the dust, trying to find something to defend herself with. Eventually her fingertips happened on a small pebble, and with all the brutality she could muster she cracked it against Allen's skull.

Allen maintained his grip, though the beast behind his eyes grew angrier.

She hit him again.

And again.

On the fourth blow he let go. Jackie scrambled to her feet and staggered back towards the river that ran along side them. Allen was bearing down on her again, blood streaming into his eyes from where the stone had cut his head. He was staggering now, and Jackie felt a burst of confidence. If he went for her, she could step aside and he would trip and fall from what was an alarming height into the water.

She just had to keep her cool.

Suddenly, though, her head started to spin. What it was – the booze, or the near asphyxiation – she couldn't tell. Her skin went hot and cold and her sense of perspective crumbled. She couldn't tell where Allen was – near or far. She started to stagger herself.

Then she felt it: his hand on her neck. And then his voice.

'So you never want to see me again,' he breathed. 'Well, guess what, pet. You're in luck. You never will.'

And he pushed.

As Jackie fell backwards over the side of the towpath, everything seemed to happen in slow motion. She saw Allen standing over her; then she saw the sky.

But as her head cracked against the wall of the river bank, the lights went out.

She didn't feel the cold as her body limply hit the sludgy water.

She could do nothing as the current started gently to pull her downstream.

And there was no way she could see Allen, watching her for a brief moment as her body turned face down of its own accord, and then running, without looking back, in the other direction.

Some days you wished you just hadn't got out of bed. For WPC Annie Macarthur, this was one of them. She'd spent the morning trying to move a vagrant on from outside Wandsworth station, but she had soon realized that he needed medical care. An ambulance had been called, but when the medics tried to take him in he'd gone for them. Turned out he'd been secreting a blade under his filthy clothes. The medic had been rushed off for a tetanus booster and would need an HIV, test in a couple of days. The tramp had been remanded in custody.

And now this.

Annie hated shouts like this. She walked briskly down the corridor with her colleague, PC Andrews.

Nice enough bloke, but not really cut out for the job. Too quiet. There was certainly no way he was going to do the talking today. That would be up to Annie.

The headmaster who was walking in front of them – a Mr Martin – had been badly shaken when she informed him of the news. His pale, thin lips had grown thinner and he had placed his arm over his eyes for at least a minute. He had then buzzed through to his secretary to find out where the pupil in question was. 'She's completing an examination,' he had said finally. 'Nearly finished. We'll go there now.'

The room in which the exam was being taken was a small hall – probably the gym, Annie deduced, as she looked through the small window in the door. The head pulled her back gently by the arm as she did so.

'Please, officer. Not a good idea. The sight of a uniformed officer is going to unsettle the children, and they haven't finished their exam yet.'

Annie apologized, and the three of them stood in silence outside the hall while they waited for the exam to end.

They didn't have to wait long. At half past three exactly, Annie heard a woman's voice call 'Pens down, please.' Instantly the headmaster opened the door, allowing the sound of the pupils' hubbub to escape into the corridor.

'I don't believe Miss Venables asked anybody to start talking,' the head shouted as he entered, and the noise softened for a moment. He whispered in Miss Venables' ear and the two of them came out again.

She had a nice face, Annie observed dispassionately to herself as she informed the teacher of the news. Then she stood back and watched the colour drain from that face.

'Oh my lord,' she whispered. 'The poor girl.'

'We need to speak to her now, Miss Venables,' Annie told her.

'Of course. I'll just . . .' She walked back into the room and raised her voice. 'You're all free to go home now. Er, Sadie Burrows, could you please stay behind for a couple of minutes?'

The pupils had realized by now that there were a couple of police outside, and Annie could see that Miss Venables was having difficulty making herself heard. Chairs started to scrape, and soon a crowd of boisterous kids started to file out. Annie ignored their stares and poorly disguised V-signs. Occasionally one of them shouted the word 'pig', pretending to disguise it with a loud cough. Water off a duck's back to Annie – she heard it every day of the week. Besides, she had something else to focus on now. The worst part of the job.

Once all the pupils had left, the two police officers stepped into the hall. It was empty now, apart from Miss Venables, the head and a solitary girl sitting at her desk, her eyes wary. Stacy looked at her colleague, nodded, and then walked towards her.

'Sadie Burrows?' she asked.

The girl nodded, and before Annie could speak again, she asked a question. 'Is this about Lionel?' she demanded sharply.

Annie shook her head. She didn't know what Sadie was on about, but she wished it was about some minor misdemeanour that had been worrying the fifteen-year-old.

'No, Sadie, love. I'm afraid it's about your mum.'

Sadie's eyes tightened.

'Your mother is Jackie Burrows?'

The girl nodded.

Here goes, thought Annie. She knelt down to Sadie's level and took the girl's hands in hers, but Sadie snatched them back as though burned by her touch.

'There's no kind way to put this, love. Your mother was found in the river about two hours ago.'

Sadie shook her head, but Annie continued implacably. It was the only way.

'I'm so sorry, Sadie. So very, very sorry.'

The girl's breath was heavy now.

'I'm afraid she's dead.'

CHAPTER 12

The next thing Sadie knew, Miss Venables had her arms around her and was walking her to the headmaster's office. The grown-ups stood around looking awkward – only Miss Venables seemed to Sadie to have any warmth about her – and somebody told her that they were waiting for social services to arrive. There was other conversation too, but Sadie didn't really take it in.

The social worker who arrived was a man. Tall, thin, with a shiny bald head and a protruding Adam's apple, he gave Sadie an inappropriate smile, pulled up a chair and sat opposite her. He took her hands in his, but she quickly pulled them away. The social worker raised his palms as if to reassure her that he wouldn't do that again, and then he spoke.

'I'm Graham,' he told her. 'I need to arrange somewhere for you to stay tonight.'

'I want to go home,' Sadie told him.

The grown-ups in the room looked uncomfortably at each other.

'You can't go home, Sadie,' Graham said. 'You understand why, don't you?'

No, Sadie thought to herself. I'm always at home by myself. But she didn't say that; she just found herself nodding mutely.

'Is there any family you can stay with? Grandparents? Aunts? Uncles?'

She shook her head.

'There must be someone, Sadie. Think hard – it's important.'

'There's no one, OK?' she snapped. From the corner of her eye she saw the headmaster open his mouth to speak, but he seemed to think better of it.

'All right, Sadie, all right,' the social worker said in a consoling tone of voice. 'Then we're going to have to find somewhere else.'

'Am I being put into care?'

'That's really not a phrase we like to use, Sadie. There are a number of foster families who are on standby for situations like this . . .'

'But I'm being put into care, right?'

Graham closed his eyes and nodded. 'For the time being, yes.'

The girl looked up at Miss Venables. For the first time since the news had been broken, she felt her lower lip start to wobble and tears ooze out of her eyes. 'Is she really dead?' she asked her teacher in a small voice.

'Oh, Sadie,' she whispered, and Sadie became aware that she was crying too. 'Yes, she really is dead. I'm so sorry.'

Sadie sniffed heavily, took a deep breath and

tried to steady her emotions. She half heard the social worker talking to her headmaster. 'There is lots of paperwork, obviously,' he was saying, 'but for now it's best if she just comes with me.'

Mr Martin nodded, walked to the door and opened it. 'If there's anything the school can do,' he said.

'Of course,' Graham replied. 'Come on, Sadie. Let's go.'

Sadie stood up. She gave a sad little smile at Miss Venables, and then walked to the open door without acknowledging anyone else.

The moment she was through it, she ran.

'Sadie!' She heard the voice of the social worker echo behind her, and maybe footsteps, though she couldn't tell above the noise of her own running and the occasional shouts of encouragement by the few pupils who were still left in the school. She clattered round the corner, running as fast as her shaky legs would carry her. Only when she had turned another corner and put some distance behind her did she allow herself to look back. The corridor in which she found herself was empty, but she knew that it led to a hall from which there was no way out. To her right, however, was an alcove full of coats on pegs and satchels on the floor. Without thinking twice, she rushed into the alcove, curled up in a corner and covered herself with a couple of coats.

As soon as she was hidden, she heard the unmistakable sound of footsteps. They rushed past her and burst through the door at the end of the corridor. Sadie allowed herself a few seconds to check that nobody else was coming; then she jumped out from the alcove and retraced her hasty steps. Two minutes later she was out of the school.

She kept running – not because she thought anyone was after her, but because she knew that if she stopped she would break down. The streets seemed to fly past her eyes, and she ran without any thought in her head other than the image of where she was going. Nobody would be able to find her there. Nobody would take her away.

As she burst into Lionel's shop, there was a solitary customer browsing the shelves. At the sight of Sadie, he hurriedly left. At first Lionel, sitting on a stool behind the counter, flashed Sadie a rare look of annoyance. It took only a moment, however, for him to realize that something was wrong. He looked enquiringly at her, standing in front of the counter and feeling for all the world that she had nowhere else to go.

'My mum,' she said simply, her voice wavering. 'She's dead.'

Lionel blinked at her in shock. 'What do you mean?'

'The police came to school to tell me. They found her . . .' – she could barely bring herself to say it – 'they found her in the river.'

Without saying a word, Lionel walked out from behind the counter, locked the front door and led

Sadie by the hand to the back. Still in silence, he sat her down and made a cup of hot, sweet tea. Only then did he speak.

'I'm so sorry, Sadie, dear.' He looked as if he wanted to say more, but Sadie understood that there was little else to say. She buried her face in her hands and wept for what seemed like an age.

'What happened?' Lionel asked finally, when she had regained her composure somewhat.

'I don't know. I only saw her this morning. She was, well, she didn't look like she was going anywhere. I suppose she must have found something to drink and . . . had an accident. Lionel, they want to put me with a foster home, but I don't want to go. That's why I came here. You'll let me stay with you, won't you?'

Lionel looked blankly at the weeping girl in front of him, and then stood up and turned his back on her. He didn't speak for quite a while, and when he did he still did not face Sadie, so he couldn't see her wide, red, raw eyes.

'Sadie, dear, you're fifteen. I can't just take you in – I'd be breaking the law. I could be banged up.'

'You could foster me,' she said hopefully.

Only now did Lionel turn round. The sympathy etched in his face seemed to be merged with something else now. Self-loathing. 'If I could, Sadie, I would. But look at my line of work. They would never allow it.' He sat down again next to Sadie. 'When you're sixteen, my doors will be open to you and I promise I will look after you like my own daughter. But until then . . .'

Sadie closed her eyes. It was two months until her sixteenth birthday, but at that moment it might as well have been two years.

'I ran away,' she admitted meekly. 'From the social worker, and from the school.'

Lionel nodded and took her hand in his. 'I think we should call them, don't you?'

'I suppose so.'

'Would you like me to do it for you?' he asked.

Sadie nodded.

Forty-five minutes later, he was leading the social worker through the shop and into the back room, where Sadie sat waiting for him. Graham's face told of his profound distaste at his surroundings, but he seemed relieved to find Sadie safe and well.

'I know it's a difficult time, Sadie,' he admonished her, 'but you shouldn't have run off. We're only trying to help you, you know.'

Sadie gazed at the carpet. 'Where are we going?' she asked.

'Well, like I told you before, we have a foster family waiting to look after you. They're very nice people.'

'I don't care how nice they are. I want to stay here with Lionel.'

Graham glanced back to the shop owner without hiding his disapproval. 'That's not going to happen, Sadie. You shouldn't be somewhere like this in the first place. Come on. Say your goodbyes, and let's go. And no running away this time.'

Sadie stood up slowly and walked to where Lionel was standing, one hand nervously clutching the other. She stood on her tiptoes and embraced him. Very quietly, so that Graham would not be able to hear, she whispered in his ear. 'I'll be back,' she said. 'I promise.'

The social worker had parked in front of the shop; he indicated to Sadie that she should get into the front passenger seat, but she preferred to sit by herself in the back as he drove her back to the estate. Word of Jackie's death had clearly already got out, because a few bunches of flowers were propped up by the garden fence. Sadie barely looked at them. She let them into the house and, rather ineffectually helped by Graham, packed a few random clothes into an old bag. Before they left, she took a picture of herself as a little girl with her mum and dad and stashed that away in her school satchel. Then she took the opportunity to look around the little house for a final time. Something told her she would not be coming back here again, and she did her best to imprint an image of everything on her mind: the frayed carpet, the kitchen table, even the bed that still gave her shivers to think about and the stark white bathroom where she had sat in a pool of her own blood holding *his* child. Did the social worker know all that? she found herself wondering. Would he tell whoever was going to take care of her?

The foster family to whom she was taken lived in west London, in a smart townhouse which seemed to Sadie more like a mansion – she felt dwarfed as she carried her small, scruffy overnight bag up the path. Feeling like a prisoner on death row, she waited while Graham rang the bell.

A woman answered. She was plump and immaculately dressed, and as she looked down at Sadie, her eyes filled with compassion. Graham introduced her as Mrs Caldwell, but as she took Sadie's hand in hers, she said, 'Please, Sadie, call me Laura.' Laura's hand was soft to the touch, and she had a faint, floral fragrance about her. As they shook hands, an old grandfather clock in the large, elegant hallway struck six. 'Come and meet the family,' Laura said with a smile.

Reluctantly, Sadie was led into an enormous kitchen. A man stood at the stove, wearing an apron and holding a frying pan over the heat. At the table sat a boy, about Sadie's age. He had curly, scruffy hair and a pleasing, open face. 'Sadie, this is my son Dan,' Laura introduced, 'and my husband Harry.'

Sadie nodded briefly at them, avoiding their eyes, before looking down at the spotless kitchen floor.

'Why don't I take you up to your bedroom?' Laura asked breezily once the ensuing silence had gone on for just a little too long.

'If I could just interrupt,' Graham said. 'Sadie, I have to go now. I'll come back tomorrow and see how you are.' He smiled an encouraging smile. 'And don't worry, everything's going to be all right.'

The look Sadie gave him mirrored the contempt she felt at his stupid comment.

Wordlessly, she was led up two flights of stairs to an enormous room with a double bed and its own TV. 'Just come down when you're ready, dear,' Laura told her, a little less chirpy now, and she left her on her own.

Sadie sat on the side of her bed. She felt uncomfortable in such a rich, well-furnished place. It was a million miles away from the little house on the estate she had woken up in that morning. She didn't move. As evening fell, she started to grow cold, but she simply sat there and shivered, thinking of her mum and the sleepy, unknowing look she had given her that morning. As time wore on, her skin started to tingle with the discomfort she felt at being in this strange house.

Suddenly there was a knock on the door. Another knock, and then the door opened slightly. In the light of the landing, she saw Dan standing there, holding a tray.

'I brought you something to eat,' he said quietly.

When Sadie didn't reply, he stepped inside. 'Shall I turn the light on?' he asked.

Looking around, she realized she had been sitting in the near darkness, so she nodded her head. Dan felt for the light switch, and when he had turned it on he stepped further into the room with the tray, which he placed gently on the floor by Sadie's feet. There was a sandwich there, and an apple, and a glass of orange juice, and instantly Sadie realized how hungry she was.

'Thank you,' she said grudgingly to Dan. She bent down, picked up the tray and placed it on her lap.

'I heard about your mum,' Dan said. 'I'm really sorry. If you want to talk about it . . .' He had a posh accent and all of a sudden she felt ashamed to speak, so she kept quiet as she chewed her sandwich.

'Can I sit down?' Dan asked, and before she could answer he took a seat by Sadie's side.

They sat there in silence while Sadie finished her food.

'If you want anything else . . .' Dan said, but she shook her head. Out of the blue she could feel the tears coming again. Before long the crying simply overcame her. She put her face in her hands and just let it come.

Just then, she felt an arm round her shoulder. It was Dan. He had shuffled up the bed towards her and now his right leg was touching her left and he was squeezing her nervously.

Sadie didn't even give him a warning. Like a shot she stood up, ignoring the plates as they shattered underneath the tray which had fallen off her lap. She pointed threateningly at him. 'Get your hands off me,' she whispered.

Dan had jumped to his feet, embarrassment creeping across his cheeks. 'No,' he stuttered, 'I wasn't . . . I was just . . .'

But now Sadie was shouting. 'I know what you want!' she yelled. 'You think I'm going to let it happen? Well, I'm not. Get out of here! Leave me alone! Get your fucking hands off me.'

Dan took a couple of faltering steps back, watching in undisguised horror as Sadie bent over, picked up the tray and held it up as though she was going to use it as a weapon. '*Get . . . out . . .*' she hissed again.

And then Dan's parents were there.

'Sadie,' Laura gasped. 'What on earth –'

But before she could finish her sentence, the father had stepped between Dan and Sadie. Harry looked furious, as though he was going to start shouting. Blinded by rage, Sadie went for him, hammering the tray down on the side of his arm and causing him to shout in pain before wrestling it from Sadie's hands.

'What the hell do you think you're doing, young lady?' he demanded in his patrician voice.

'If any of you put your hands on me . . .' she screamed.

Dan interrupted. 'I didn't do anything,' he said. 'I was just seeing if she was all right.'

The three members of the family were stepping backwards towards the door now. 'I know it's been a very difficult day for you,' Laura said, 'but you really need to calm down. We want to help you, but we simply can't have that kind of behaviour in our house. It's really not what we . . .'

'Just leave me alone,' Sadie interrupted.

The family fell silent, and with confused nods they left.

They left her alone for the rest of the night. At around ten thirty, Sadie heard the sounds of Laura and Harry making their way to bed, and then everything fell quiet.

That was what she had been waiting for.

She switched her bedroom light off and stood quietly for a few minutes while her eyes grew used to the dark. Then she silently opened the door and slipped outside. As she crept down the stairs, holding her breath, each creaky floorboard sounded a hundred times louder than it really was; it seemed to take an age for her to get downstairs. If anyone discovered her, she decided, she would smile sweetly, apologize for her earlier behaviour and tell them she wanted a glass of water.

But in fact she had very different plans.

A street lamp from outside illuminated the kitchen and she found she could see without too much difficulty. On the back of the kitchen chair was a large handbag. Sadie made straight for it, removed the fat purse that was inside and opened it. There was money in the note compartment: without counting it, Sadie removed it and slipped it into her back pocket.

Then she turned her attention to the kitchen drawers. There were lots of cooking knives there, good and sharp; she selected the smallest – a paring knife – and secreted it in the pocket of the tracksuit top she was wearing.

Now all she needed to do was get out of the house. This wasn't the place for her.

She was pretty sure the front door would be locked, and indeed it was. There were two options – try to find the key, or break a window. If she broke a window, she would run the risk of waking everybody up; but she would be away soon enough, and locating the key could take all night. She stood in the hallway, trying to decide which room would be the best to break out of.

Suddenly, something caught her eye: a flashing red light in the top corner of the hall. With a sickening feeling she realized what it was. A burglar alarm. There must be motion sensors dotted around the house, and she knew that she must have triggered them. As though in confirmation of her realization, she became aware of the flashing blue light of a police car drawing up at the front of the house.

Sadie ran back into the kitchen. On the other side there was an archway, leading to a utility area and the back door. The top half of the door was glass – double glazed and strong. She would need something sturdy to smash it. Sprinting back into the kitchen, she looked desperately around, even as she heard the banging on the door of the police. Her eyes settled on a heavy, state-of-the-art food mixer sitting on the counter. Straining, she picked it up; then she ran to the utility room and hurled it against the door.

The glass cracked, but did not break, and the mixer fell to the floor with a deafening clatter.

Sadie picked it up again and hurled it once more at the glass. This time it smashed, shards splintering everywhere. Urgently, she covered her hand with the end of her tracksuit and pushed the remains of the glass out; then she took a deep breath, clambered up through the glassless window and escaped. She winced as she felt a shard scrape against the side of her cheek, but the adrenaline was pumping too much for her to stop and give it any attention. She had to get out of there.

The garden was long – in the darkness she couldn't see to the end of it – and thin. Sadie's instinct was to run towards the darkness, because she knew it was only a matter of time before the family and the police came bursting through the back door. But something stopped her. It would be better, she decided, to climb over the low fence to her right and get into the neighbours' garden. She threw herself at it, and was two gardens along by the time she heard voices back at the house. They were talking loudly – loudly enough, certainly, for her to risk making a little bit of noise as she continued her escape.

Minutes later, she was at the end of the terrace. She soon scaled the low brick wall that separated her from a quiet side road; the moment her feet hit the pavement, and without stopping for breath, she tore down the road.

Refusing to stop until she had put a good deal of distance between herself and the house, she ran and ran. The streets were unfamiliar, and she sprinted down them blindly. When she did finally stop, she found herself in a small, open park with a railway bridge along one side. A tube train trundled over it as Sadie took a seat on an empty park bench.

Only then did her thoughts revert to her mother, dead and cold, and as she cried, her face and hands became smeared with a mixture of blood and tears.

Sadie seemed unable to stop the flow of either.

Lionel had barely slept.

He had closed the shop as soon as Sadie and the social worker left, and headed straight for home. He had no appetite, and he spent the evening pacing his small flat, wondering if he had done the right thing in sending her away. The look on her face had broken his heart, but there was no way he could have done as she asked. Giving her a bit of pocket money was one thing; hiding her from the authorities was quite another. Knowing he was right didn't make him feel any better, though, and the night passed slowly.

It was ten o'clock the next morning when he arrived at the shop. As he walked down the road, he could see that there was a small crowd of people outside. Unusual, so early in the morning, he thought to himself. Unusual at any time of day, come to think of it. It was only as he approached that he saw the distinctive blue uniforms of the coppers, and he walked up to them with his heart in his mouth. Police arriving at your doorstep first thing in the morning could never be good news.

There were two of them – a man and a woman – and with them was the social worker who had arrived yesterday to take Sadie away.

'Lionel Briggs?' the WPC asked as he approached.

'That's right.'

'WPC Annie Macarthur. This is my colleague PC Andrews, and I believe you know Graham Lewis.'

'We've met,' Lionel replied coolly.

'Can we come in?'

Lionel nodded and unlocked the door. As he led them through the bookshop, he was aware of their disapproving glances at the material on display, but he ignored that and took them immediately into the back room.

'What can I do for you?' he asked.

'Mr Briggs,' Annie replied, 'when was the last time you saw Sadie Burrows?'

He blinked at them. 'Yesterday. When' – he waved his arm at the social worker – 'Graham came to collect her.'

'You haven't seen her since?'

'That's what I just said, isn't it?' Lionel snapped.

Annie ignored the barbed comment. 'Can I ask, Mr Briggs, how you came to know Sadie?'

'Why?'

The WPC looked meaningfully back into the shop. 'Bit of an unusual hang-out for a girl of her age, wouldn't you say? Not on the pay roll, is she?'

'No,' Lionel lied smoothly.

'You're sure about that, are you?'

Lionel fixed her with a steely glare. 'What exactly is it that you're trying to say?' he demanded.

'Look, Mr Briggs, we know of enough places like this that act as a front for . . . other activities.'

'Ah.' Lionel nodded knowingly. 'Prostitution. You're suggesting I was pimping Sadie out, is that it?'

'I'm not suggesting anything, Mr Briggs. I'm just asking if you've seen her.'

'Then perhaps I could ask you a question in return, officer.' He looked at each of the three of them in turn. 'If I was Sadie's pimp, why do you think I called her school yesterday the moment she arrived here?'

They seemed to have no answer for that, so Lionel continued talking. 'So unless you want to tell me what is going on, perhaps you would be so good as to leave my premises.'

The policewoman nodded. 'All right, Mr Briggs. Sadie ran away from her foster home last night. She stole about two hundred pounds in cash and caused a good deal of damage to the property. She hasn't been home and nobody's seen her.'

Lionel felt his heart sink.

'Aside from the fact that she is now wanted for

theft and criminal damage,' Annie continued, 'I'm sure I don't need to remind you that the streets of London can be a very dangerous place for a young girl.'

'No, officer,' Lionel replied, a little more meekly now. 'You don't have to remind me of that.'

'And I would also point out to you that Sadie is not yet sixteen, which means she's still under the jurisdiction of social services. Any attempt to get in the way of that will carry a very heavy penalty indeed. So if you see any sign of her, just make sure we're your first call.'

'Yes, officer.'

'Good.' She nodded at her colleague and at the social worker. 'Thank you for your time, Mr Briggs. We'll show ourselves out.'

Lionel watched them go, and then collapsed on to the sofa. He felt nauseated by the accusation of the policewoman; but more than that, he felt desperately worried for Sadie. He didn't care about the police officer's threats; he just wanted to see her, to make sure that she was OK. If it were possible, he would have gone out at that moment and tried to find her.

But London was a big place, and she was just one person.

Oh, Sadie, he thought to himself. You stupid girl. You stupid, stupid girl. What the hell do you think you're doing?

CHAPTER 13

The park bench was hard, and the night air cold. Having used the stolen knife to cut a patch from her tracksuit top and use it to stem the bleeding on her face, Sadie had laid down on the bench – not out of tiredness, but more because she didn't know what else to do. She had occasionally drowsed, but the first tube train had woken her up and now she had decisions to make.

She couldn't go home, she knew that – they'd find her soon enough. And she wasn't going back to the foster home, even if she was welcome – which she very much doubted after her exploits of the previous evening. Lionel was out of the question too. He'd made it quite clear that he couldn't risk giving her a place to stay until she was sixteen and that was two months away. Surreptitiously she had counted out the money in her pocket: a hundred and ninety-five pounds. Not enough to pay for a place to stay, and in any case she wanted to stay anonymous. People would be looking for her – not only social services but also the police – and the last thing in the world she wanted was to be thrown back into some foster home where creepy guys could put their arms around her. She knew only too well what that could lead to.

Her cheek was stinging, but the blood had stopped flowing. It was only when she walked into a sandwich shop in the upmarket parade round the corner that she realized what a mess she must look: the woman behind the counter looked at her aghast.

'My God, dear. What's happened to you?'

'Nothing,' Sadie mumbled. 'I'm fine.' She paid for her breakfast with one of the stolen notes and left as quickly as possible.

She had to get out of here. If people were looking for her, she was too recognizable like this. But first she had to clean herself up.

It took ten minutes to find a fast-food restaurant. It was surprisingly crowded for the early hour, but the toilets were empty. Sadie looked at herself in the mirror, and she saw why the woman had been horrified. The gash on her cheek was long and jagged. It was puffed up and swollen round the edges, and although it was not bleeding, the wound was wet and suppurating. More shocking, though, was the smear of blood that was caked around the left-hand side of her face. She touched it gingerly, and realized it was dried. Strands of her long brown hair were stuck to it.

Sadie filled a sink with warm water. She winced as she splashed it over her stinging face; then she gritted her teeth while she meticulously scrubbed it clean and dabbed it with paper towels. It looked better by the time she had cleaned it up, but the cut was still prominent and sore. Sadie shrugged. It would heal, but at the moment she was more worried that it identified her too easily.

Her next stop was a department store, where she bought herself a top with a large hood that covered her face, and then she took a tube train into the centre of London.

It felt comforting to be surrounded by crowds. She was faceless here. Anonymous. She walked the streets all morning, not really knowing where she was going and caring even less. It was something she would have to get used to, she told herself. These streets were going to be her home for a while.

In the afternoon it started to rain. Sadie took shelter in a large record store off Piccadilly Circus, but after pretending to browse there for an hour, she noticed that a uniformed security guard had started to follow her around. It was still raining outside, so Sadie went into another fast-food restaurant, bought herself a large polystyrene cup full of tea and nursed it for as long as she could. But she couldn't stay there for ever, and as night fell, she wandered back out into the street.

It was still crowded – even more so now that the clubbers and tourists had congregated in the West End. There were drunken shouts all around her, and the smell of food being prepared on street corners. Suddenly Sadie didn't feel quite so comfortable, and she turned away from Piccadilly Circus. Without knowing where she was going, she found herself in the streets of Soho, with its bohemian mixture of late-night cafés and sex shops; but it didn't take long for her to find a less crowded street, where the ground was strewn with litter and the pungent odour of over-ripe fruit from the daytime market was thick in the air. The rain continued to pour, so Sadie nestled herself into the sheltered doorway of a closed shop and prepared to spend the night there.

It was desperately uncomfortable, and as she sat, huddled, she felt the cold arms of self-pity wrap themselves around her. How had she ended up like this? What had she done? As she closed her eyes, the image of Allen rose unbidden before her. This was his fault. Everything had been all right until he came along . . .

She was woken from her reverie by a voice. A woman was standing above her with a cigarette in one hand and a glassy look about her eyes.

'What you doing?' she asked aggressively.

'Nothing.' The rain had stopped now, and Sadie eyed the woman up and down. Her skimpy clothes were tight – too tight for her figure – and her lined face was heavily made up. She bent down so that she was face to face with Sadie.

'Don't "nothing" me, my lovely,' she said, her breath warm with the smell of booze and fags. 'You don't work this patch without the say-so.'

Sadie looked blankly at her. 'What are you talking about?' As she spoke, she flinched: the woman had reached out and pulled down her hooded top. She looked almost triumphantly at the scar on Sadie's face.

'Well, my pretty,' she sneered. 'Someone been a bit rough with you? That'll be knocking a few quid off your price, now, won't it?'

Suddenly it dawned on Sadie what the woman was talking about; and as it did so, she became aware of another figure, on the other side of the almost deserted road, lurking in the shadows.

'What's going on?' he called quietly.

The woman stood up quickly and turned around. 'Looks like she's working the patch, Jaz,' she said.

Sadie held her breath as the figure crossed the street. He had brown skin and several days' stubble, and a look that suggested he was not a man to mess with.

'This true?' he asked.

She shook her head.

Jaz appeared to think about that for a moment; clearly he decided he wasn't satisfied. 'Stand up,' he said. 'And come with me.'

'I'm not going anywhere.'

The woman smiled unpleasantly, but Jaz's face remained emotionless. He simply bent down and grabbed a clump of Sadie's hair. In seconds they were walking down the dark street. Sadie screamed, but the man soon put a stop to it by using his free hand to deliver a pounding blow to her stomach, winding her. It was all she could do now to keep on walking.

At the corner of the road was an open door leading on to a dingy staircase. A sign above the door read 'Model' and had an arrow pointing upwards next to it; the staircase itself was flooded with dusky light from a single red light bulb. With a sharp push, Jaz urged her upstairs.

The next thing she knew, she was alone in a room with him; the woman had disappeared at some stage – Sadie didn't know when. There was a single bed with a couple of grubby, unmade sheets slung over it; and a table with a box of tissues and several packets of condoms. Jaz shut the door and stood in front of it. Sadie's mouth went dry and with a shudder she realized that the same coldness was flowing through her veins that she used to experience before Allen had his way.

It wasn't going to happen again, she promised herself. She had the knife in the pocket of her hooded top. If he tried, she would kill him.

'Let me out of here,' she said clearly, her voice disguising her fear.

'Not yet, sweetheart. Is what she said true? You been working this patch?'

'No.'

Jaz nodded slowly. 'Empty your pockets,' he ordered.

Sadie froze.

'Do it.'

There was no option but to do as he said. For now. She reached into the back of her trousers and pulled out the wad of notes she had stolen the night before.

There was a silence between them.

'And where did you get that, you lying little bitch? On your paper round? Give it to me now.'

He stepped forward and Sadie gave him the money, but he didn't seem that interested as he slung it on to the bed. 'Now then,' he whispered. 'Let's get a few things straight. I own this patch. You want to work it, then I own you. Got it?'

As he spoke he continued to walk towards her, and Sadie stepped back until she hit the table. There was nowhere for her to go now, so she gently placed her hand inside the pocket of her top and gripped the handle of the paring knife. Her breath trembled. Jaz reached out and took her chin in the palm of her right hand; his left he placed flat on the table as he leaned against it. He smiled, and Sadie saw a gold tooth in his mouth.

Do it now, she told herself. Do it now, or it's going to happen again.

The speed with which she drew out the knife surprised even Sadie. As quick as lightning, she slammed the tip of the knife into the pimp's free hand. It sank into the flesh surprisingly easily, and even stuck a couple of millimetres into the table.

For a couple of seconds, he was too astonished even to shout out. When he did, his shout expressed such a mixture of pain and fury that he seemed even more terrifying to Sadie than he had before. She had to move quickly, while he was pinned to the table. Pushing the screaming man away, she ran to the door, opened it and hurtled down the stairs into the street.

The rain had started again. By the time she had no more energy in her to run, she was soaked to the skin.

It took her three days to stumble across a soup kitchen. By now she was starving and filthy. The scar on her face had white streaks of pus along its length, and the rest of her skin was sore and wind-chapped. Every time a passer-by looked at her, her heart lurched: in her mind, it was a policeman or an associate of the pimp she had stabbed; and as her paranoia grew worse, so she became increasingly aggressive to anyone who dared to speak to her.

The soup was thin and bland, but hot, and Sadie drank it hungrily, ignoring the way it scalded her lips. It was the first food to pass her lips in days, and she needed it. Only when the cup was empty did she look around. The vagrants queuing up to the back of the open van where volunteers were dispensing the soup were a hopeless-looking crowd. Nobody seemed to speak to each other; they just shuffled up the line to collect their food, and then shuffled away again. Sadie noticed, however, that they all seemed to walk in the same direction, so she decided to follow them. She had spent the past three nights in shop doorways, and her body was bruised, cold and aching. Now she was on the south side of Waterloo Bridge, and nobody paid her any attention as she followed the other homeless people down the steps of the subway and into the bowels of the cardboard city that existed beneath the bridge.

It was warm there, and smoky. Smouldering metal bins were filled with burning rubbish and debris, and small groups of the homeless gathered around them. The people returning from the soup kitchen seemed to melt away, disappearing into their cardboard-box homes and leaving Sadie to stand alone and ignored.

After a while she summoned up the courage to approach one of the fires. There were four people around it, three men and one woman. The scraggly beards on the men made it impossible to tell how old any of them were; the woman looked as though she was in her thirties, though her ravaged face suggested she might have aged prematurely. She was filthy and wrinkled, and had red, raw eyes and dreadlocked hair. She looked suspiciously at Sadie.

'What do you want?' she asked in a low voice that sounded more like a man's.

'Just to get warm,' Sadie replied.

The woman nodded gruffly, and Sadie approached a bit closer, keeping her hood firmly over her head to disguise her youth.

'Got any gear?' the woman asked.

Sadie shook her head, and the woman seemed to lose interest in her.

'Can I stay here?' Sadie asked after a few moments.

The woman snorted. 'Got a reservation, love?' she asked.

Sadie gave her a perplexed look.

'If I was you,' the woman continued, 'I'd fuck off home, all right?'

'I can't do that.'

'Well, don't expect any bleeding fucking hearts round here. Not many can.' She looked around. 'You don't ask to stay here. You do it because you haven't got anywhere else.' And as though Sadie's question had offended her, she walked abruptly away.

Sadie watched her go, but suddenly became aware that one of the men around the fire was leering at her. She gave him an aggressive stare, and then walked away, deeper into the heart of the cardboard city.

The dwellings that the homeless people who lived here had constructed were surprisingly elaborate: she noticed that one place even had a small washing line with clothes hanging out to dry, but where the washing had been done in the first place she couldn't imagine. Nobody gave her a second glance, and she found that reassuring; but neither did anyone give her a look of welcome, or encouragement, or sympathy. Why would they? They were all in the same boat.

The faces of all the inhabitants of the cardboard

city had the same look of numb hopelessness; but as Sadie walked and looked, she caught sight of one that, with a horrifying shock, she recognized.

It had been a long time since she had seen him – a couple of years, probably – and he had changed. His cardboard dwelling was small and seemed less well cared for than the others; and whereas most of the occupants of this subterranean city sat in groups, he was alone. He did not seem to notice Sadie as she approached, which gave her the opportunity to take in his pitiful appearance. He sat cross-legged, a disgustingly dirty blanket draped over him; his hair was long, and he would have seemed older than his years had it not been for the fact that the growth on his face was wispy and immature. But it was the eyes that shocked Sadie the most. They stared ahead and did not blink; the pupils were dilated and the rims were blood red.

And even in this stinking place, the smell that emanated from him was overpowering.

Sadie knelt down in front of him and did her best to smile.

'Hello, Jamie,' she said.

Jamie Brown didn't reply. He didn't even seem to see her. He just sniffed, and then became suddenly overcome by a hoarse, racking cough.

Sadie waited for the fit to subside, a lump forming in her throat.

Then she tried again. 'Jamie, it's me. Sadie. Don't you remember?'

Again there was no response from the boy. Sadie stretched out her arm and gently brushed her fingertips against the side of his face.

The moment she touched him, Jamie's demeanour changed. He scampered back, like a frightened animal, and scowled at his former friend.

'It's OK, Jamie. I'm not going to—'

But before Sadie could finish, she had to jump back herself. Jamie had scrabbled around by his side and grabbed something in his trembling fist: a small hypodermic needle, rusty and dirty, but still sharp enough to do damage. He held it above his head, his expression a terrible mixture of aggression and fear. There was no recognition in his eyes.

'All right, Jamie,' Sadie breathed. 'All right. It's OK. I'm going.' And she stepped slowly backwards. The further away she went, the calmer Jamie seemed to become, until he was once more sitting down, looking as though he had all but forgotten about his recent visitor.

Sadie watched him from a distance. He had started talking to himself now, and was flinching, as though something invisible was pinching his body. The needle was still firmly in his grasp.

As Sadie stared at him, a wave of pity crashed over her. But there was something else too. Anger. Determination. Jamie shouldn't be there. He shouldn't be in that state. And nor should she.

She would not go down that path.

She would not succumb to the oblivion that little Jamie Brown had clearly sought in that needle.

She would not let the street get to her.

She would not be building herself a cardboard-box house, because she wasn't going to be here for long enough.

She knew in her heart that Jamie was a lost soul. There was nothing that could be done for him now. Despite his young age, he had entered the winter of his life. Sadie could not – would not – join him.

Her eyes narrowed in thin determination as she looked back at him one last time; then she turned and walked away from the cardboard-box city for ever.

The weeks that followed Sadie's disappearance were like years to Lionel.

The day after the police visit, his son walked into the shop, demanding money. For the first time ever he considered sending him away, but at the last moment he relented. In losing Sadie he felt he had lost a daughter; he had no desire now to lose a son, no matter how errant he was.

For the first couple of weeks the police dropped in on him at irregular hours. Lionel knew they were trying to catch Sadie with him, and each time he told them the same thing: that he wished to God he knew where she was. They never looked as if they believed him, but he was past caring. Frankly, he cursed himself for turning her away.

Maybe he could have hidden her. Done the right thing. It wouldn't have been that hard, would it? What kind of man was he?

As the weeks passed, it became increasingly clear to Lionel that Sadie had gone from his life for ever. The very thought made him feel sick to the stomach.

And today would have been her sixteenth birthday. As he opened the shop, he remembered the day she had come into his life; he remembered her plucky but frightened face, and the sadness behind her eyes that betrayed more experience of the world than most adults would ever know. He imagined her begging on the pavement, learning the tone of voice that would encourage the most generosity in passers-by and using it to cajole as much change from them as she could.

If anyone could survive, it was Sadie. But it was tough on the streets, and despite everything she was just a girl – ripe pickings for the vultures and the predators. He put such thoughts from his mind and, as he made himself a cup of tea, he silently raised his mug and wished her a happy birthday, wherever she was.

As he did so, the shop bell rang. With a heavy sigh he put his tea down and walked through. He couldn't do this much longer, he told himself. Age was getting the better of him, and this was no place for an old man.

At first he didn't see the customer, and he

blinked around the gloomy shop, trying to see him. Suddenly he became aware of a figure moving up one of the aisles. His face was hooded and looked at the ground as he walked, and for a heart-stopping moment Lionel felt threatened by this quiet stranger, who approached the counter, raised his head and slowly pulled back the hood.

It was only then that Lionel saw it was not a man.

She looked more like a spectre. Her skin was sallow, her face filthy. A wicked scar, puffy and red, jutted along the side of her face. Her hair was matted and dirty, and she was desperately, desperately thin.

Lionel could not speak. It was as though his own daughter had returned from the dead.

'I'm sixteen today,' she said, her voice cracking as she spoke. 'They can't take me away. I can do what I want.'

Unbidden, a tear appeared in Lionel's eye. His old legs felt heavy as he stepped around the counter and bent down so that his face was at the same level as that of this wild, destitute girl. He stretched his arms out and pulled her towards him, enveloping her in a tight, fatherly embrace.

'Oh, dear Lord,' he breathed. 'What have they done to you? I thought you were . . .' He couldn't bring himself to finish.

Slowly, as though the very movement made her creak, he felt the girl reciprocate his embrace with her thin arms. 'I can do what I want now,' she repeated, as though begging for confirmation that this was true.

And Lionel nodded his head.

'Welcome home, Sadie,' he whispered. 'Welcome home.'

PART II

CHAPTER 14

Fourteen years later

A tall, slim woman, dressed in silk pyjamas, looked out over the city.

Her almond eyes were unblinking as she watched the sun rising, flooding everything with its peaceful glow; and her lustrous, long brown hair shone. Along her left cheek was a thin, almost imperceptible white scar, normally skilfully hidden under a light layer of foundation. Now it was visible only under close scrutiny, but that didn't worry her: nobody would ever get that close.

From her penthouse apartment she could see all the landmarks of London. The wheel, white and elegant; St Paul's cathedral, imposing and shapely; and in the distance the blinking light on the top of Canary Wharf. She liked this time of day, the stillness and the quiet, and made a point of rising with the sun. This morning was no different in that respect, although rather than get straight down to work, she allowed herself some time. Time to watch the dawn become morning. Time to think.

Sadie Burrows was no more. The frightened, plucky little girl was simply a memory, locked firmly away in the mind of this beautiful woman. She had changed her name on her twenty-first birthday. It had seemed symbolic at the time, and in a way, she supposed, it still did. The day she became Sadie Scott had not been the day she came of age; it had been the day she was reborn.

That had been nine years ago exactly. Today she was thirty. As dawn turned into morning, she dragged herself away from the cityscape and poured herself a glass of sparkling water from a large, gleaming stainless-steel fridge. This would be the only bubbly that would pass her lips today – or any day. Alcohol was permanently off the menu. She walked out of her state-of-the-art kitchen back into a comfortable sitting room with a large window overlooking London, and raised her glass in a silent toast to the photograph in an understated silver frame that sat on the ultra-modern coffee table.

Sadie could still remember the day that picture of her parents had been taken, and now it was the only record she had of their faces, the only means of stopping their features retreating into nothingness in her mind. Somewhere, hidden away, was a scrap of newspaper cutting. It told how Jackie Burrows had been found dead in the canal. A post-mortem toxicology report had revealed dangerously high levels of alcohol and amphetamines in her system, and a coroner had recorded a verdict of death by misadventure. How Sadie had wept when she first read that article; now, though, she kept it well hidden. She preferred to remember the Jackie who smiled out at her from the photograph, not the one described in those cold words.

She sipped her drink slowly, and then returned the glass to the kitchen and went through to her bedroom. It was time to get dressed – today might be her birthday, but she wasn't in the habit of giving herself the day off, and today was no exception.

Ten minutes later she emerged, dressed in an expensive but understated brown Prada trouser suit. She glanced at her watch. Nine o'clock. Her appointment wasn't until ten, so she had an hour to kill before then – easily done with the file of figures that needed to be gone through before she made her way to the office, and the time flew. Before she knew it, the concierge was buzzing up, announcing the arrival of her visitor. Sadie put her work to one side, adjusted her appearance in a mirror and went to open the door.

The woman waiting there was dressed remarkably similarly to Sadie, although her business suit was navy, not brown. There the similarities ended, however. She was shorter, stouter and older; her hair was flecked with grey, and her skin was beginning to show signs of ageing.

'Victoria Oliver,' she said, smiling and putting her hand out.

Sadie took it, but the smile did not fool her.

The hardness around this woman's eyes spoke of a certain ruthlessness, and Sadie had learned long ago to be extremely wary of journalists – especially those with the broadest smiles.

'Sadie Scott,' she replied. 'Please, come in.'

Sadie selected her interviews carefully these days. Ten years ago, when she was starting out, she had been grateful for any publicity she could get; now the tables were turned, and journalists were desperate to get any snippets they possibly could about the mysterious Sadie Scott. They seldom managed it – if there was one thing Sadie was even better at than running her business empire, it was keeping her private life private. But she'd been talked into this one. A homeless charity she represented had begged her to get them some much-needed publicity, and in the end she had agreed to their request. The prospect made her nervous, though: she knew this woman would want to talk about her, not the charity – and no good could come of that. Sadie was notoriously tight-lipped in these circumstances, but that didn't stop people trying; and this woman with her wide smile and wary eyes would be no different.

As Sadie led her through the large apartment, she was aware of the journalist's eyes looking around in a certain awe. It was something she had grown used to – she seldom had guests, but on the few occasions that she allowed anyone entry into her personal space, they were always impressed by the rich surroundings.

'Nice place,' Victoria Oliver said almost begrudgingly.

'Thanks,' Sadie replied. 'You're the first journalist to see it. Kind of a world exclusive.'

Her companion smiled thinly. 'If only you'd allowed me to bring a photographer.'

Sadie avoided her eye. 'You should have asked my office,' she said smoothly.

'I did.'

'Oh well. Perhaps next time.' Sadie knew the journalist realized there wouldn't be a next time, and that neither of them was convinced by her pretence, but it didn't matter. 'Have a seat.' She pointed to the comfortable leather sofa and took her own place in her favourite armchair.

'Wonderful view,' Victoria murmured as she fiddled with her Dictaphone, sitting back only when the green recording light was illuminated.

'I like it,' Sadie agreed perfunctorily. 'Shall we start the interview now? I don't have that much time.'

The journalist raised one eyebrow at Sadie's abruptness, but quickly recovered herself. 'Quite,' she said rather primly. 'Well, let's start with this.' She waved one arm around the immaculate room.

'I don't understand.'

'Where did it all come from? How does a girl from a south London council estate end up with all this?'

Sadie looked sharply at the woman. How did she know where Sadie used to live? Her past wasn't secret, exactly, but it was hardly common knowledge. The journalist seemed satisfied that for the first time she had the upper hand, and she played her advantage.

'You've been involved in the sex industry from a relatively early age. I wonder how that came about.'

'I . . .'

'Did you encounter a lot of pornography while you were growing up?'

'I beg your pardon?'

'I just wondered whether your business practices derived from . . .'

'I'm not a pornographer, Victoria.'

'Not now, perhaps,' the journalist insisted. 'But you can't deny that . . .'

'I'm *not* a pornographer,' Sadie repeated more firmly.

'Then how would you describe yourself, exactly?' the journalist asked in a calm, mollifying voice.

Sadie closed her eyes briefly. She hated interviews. Hated talking about herself. But the journalist was here now, and there was no reason why she shouldn't tell her the same story that had been in the press any number of times. She took a deep breath. 'I would describe myself,' she said, doing her best to keep her voice level, 'as a businesswoman.'

'But why this business?'

'I started working in an adult bookshop when I was in my late teens.'

'How old exactly?' the journalist asked. 'Can you remember?'

'My late teens,' Sadie replied emphatically. 'It was your standard sex shop, really; but the man who ran it was a long way from being your standard sex-shop owner.' At the thought of Lionel, Sadie felt a sense of crushing sadness, but she did her best not to let it show in her face. 'He died when I was twenty and left me the business.'

'Unusual,' the journalist observed.

'In what way?'

'Leaving the business to an employee.' She raised an eyebrow again, and her expression seemed to say 'unless you were more than that'. Or maybe Sadie was being paranoid.

'It was just a small shop,' Sadie said, diverting the conversation the way she wanted it to go. 'I knew I could do something with it, turn it around. So I got rid of the dirty magazines and the blacked-out windows and started selling lingerie instead. Business was pretty slow to start off with, so I diversified. Videos for couples, sex toys, that sort of thing – upmarket, though. Nothing seedy. And I changed the name of the place to "Sadie's Secrets". Within a year I'd opened a second shop, and I haven't really looked back.'

The journalist had heard it all before, Sadie could see that. She'd have read the profiles and articles, gone through the press cuttings. But like every journalist who preceded her, she would want a bit more. She would let Sadie tell her the story, and then she would start probing, trying to find something new. It was what they always did, but Sadie had become expert at fending it off.

'And what do your family think about the way you make your living?'

Immediately Sadie's face hardened. 'That's not something I want to talk about.'

'But there must be implications – they must have opinions . . .'

'I'm not going to repeat myself,' Sadie stated. 'We're here to talk about the charity. If you carry on asking me questions that are off-limits, I'll bring the interview to a close.'

Seemingly chastened, Victoria Oliver thought for a moment before asking her next question. 'I'd like to talk to you about your escort agency. How did that come about?' she asked.

'Just a natural progression,' Sadie said, shrugging.

'But it's exploitative, isn't it?'

'Not at all.'

The journalist seemed to ignore her. 'After all, it's little more than legalized prostitution.'

'Of course not,' Sadie responded shortly. She had been called upon to argue this corner more than once. 'The girls my agency represents are escorts, nothing more. They escort people. We are not in the business of selling sex.'

The journalist appeared fired up now, even indignant. 'That's the standard response,' she said. 'But everyone knows the truth.'

Sadie's eyes narrowed. She found herself filled with a sudden urge to kick this woman out of the flat, but she knew that would only give her ammunition when it came to writing her piece. 'Are you suggesting,' she asked, 'that I'm some sort of brothel owner? A latter-day Cynthia Payne?'

'No,' the journalist replied. 'Are you?'

'Absolutely not. And any suggestion like that and your paper can expect a call from my lawyers.'

Victoria nodded, and then spoke carefully, as though she was choosing her words with great precision. 'My question,' she said, 'is this. Many people believe that escorts are simply prostitutes under a different name. You're a well-known and influential figure in the industry. As a woman, some would find it surprising that you've made a move into this area, especially as – and correct me if I'm wrong – you only employ women in the management side of your organization.'

What do you know about it? Sadie wanted to say. What makes you such a fucking expert? How many pimps have you met? How long have you spent on the street? But of course she could say none of this. Instead, she leaned over to where the Dictaphone was lying and switched it off.

The journalist looked at her in confusion.

'Listen to me,' Sadie breathed. 'Some of my girls have been on the game; others haven't. The ones who have, they've been beaten up more times than you've had hot dinners. So don't you dare waltz in here and start accusing me of exploiting them.

None of my girls has to do anything they don't want to. But if they do choose to take things further, and anything happens to them, whoever did it most certainly comes to regret their actions.'

'You mean you get the police involved?' the journalist asked.

Sadie smiled thinly. 'Something like that,' she said. She looked down at the Dictaphone. 'Oh, and if you put any of that in your newspaper, I'll deny every word of it. OK?'

The journalist nodded, and Sadie looked meaningfully back at the Dictaphone to indicate that the journalist could turn it back on again. When Victoria asked her next question, however, she sounded a little less sure of herself.

'Um . . . what is the turnover of your business?' she asked.

Sadie was distracted. She'd crossed the line just then, she knew that. But she couldn't help it. It had been all she could do to resist a hollow laugh when this woman suggested that the police would be interested in a few hookers being knocked around. The version of life that she wrote about in her newspaper was very different to the version that Sadie knew. The real version. Real life.

'The accounts are available at Companies House,' she replied evasively.

The journalist inclined her head to one side. 'So let's talk about your charitable donations.' She checked some scribbled notes on a pad by her side. 'My understanding is that you make sizeable donations not only to this homeless charity, but to several others, as well as a children's charity and a drug rehabilitation centre for young people. And you've gone on the record as being an advocate of harsher laws against drug pushers. Why these causes? What makes them so close to your heart?'

Sadie looked coolly at the journalist. 'They're good causes,' she replied in a soft voice.

'Undoubtedly. But why them?' She looked sharply at her interviewee. 'What is there in the life of Sadie Scott that makes these charities so special to you?'

The question hung in the air, and with annoyance Sadie felt one side of her face twitch. Her interviewer was getting too close to the bone – too close to the kind of questions that Sadie really didn't want to have to answer. She looked – none too subtly – at her watch. 'I'm afraid that's a question for another day.' She stood up to indicate the end of the interview.

The journalist looked at her with a furrowed brow. 'I was told I'd get an hour,' she complained.

'I'm sorry,' Sadie smiled blandly. 'I've a hectic schedule. But I've enjoyed our little chat – we'll try and do it again soon.'

The woman looked as if she was going to respond, but ultimately thought better of it. With a nod of acknowledgement, she started gathering her things, put them in her leather bag and stood up. 'Thank you for your time, Miss Scott.'

They shook hands and started to walk towards the exit. 'I hope I didn't overstep the mark,' the journalist said, friendlier now than she had been during the interview. 'It's just that I'm expected to ask certain questions.'

Sadie didn't reply. It was the oldest trick in the book, she knew that. Get your subject to think the interview is over, lull them into a false sense of security and then persuade them to reveal something they didn't mean to. She sensed her companion bristle with annoyance when she refused to bite. 'Thank you for your time,' she said politely as she held the door open for her.

'Just one more thing.' Victoria Oliver had steel in her eyes now.

'Yes?' Sadie asked mildly.

'I wanted to come here well prepared in the event that we were able to have a bit longer.'

'As I say, a busy schedule . . .'

'Quite. Anyway, I took the liberty of finding out what I could about the young Sadie Scott. Would you believe I couldn't discover anything?'

Sadie jutted her chin out pugnaciously.

'I even went to Somerset House to look for a birth certificate. There were plenty of Sadie Scotts – one in Walthamstow, a couple in Chelsea and quite a few outside London. But none of them seemed to be you. Isn't that strange?'

'Not really. I daresay it wouldn't be the first time a journalist has overlooked something.'

Victoria Oliver smiled, almost in a motherly way.

'I daresay you're right. But perhaps you'd allow me to give you a small piece of advice.'

'You can give all the advice you want,' Sadie retorted.

'I've been a journalist for thirty years. You get to learn when someone's holding things back. It's amazing how skeletons can jump out of your cupboard when you're least expecting it. You're a well-known woman, Miss Scott, and people are interested in you. People like me.' She fished around in her jacket pocket and handed her a business card. 'Excuse my French, but if the shit ever hits the fan and you want to tell your side of the story, you know where to find me.'

Sadie remained stony-faced. 'Goodbye, Miss Oliver,' she said in a level voice, and she closed the door.

Alone again, Sadie started pacing around her flat. The journalist's piercing comments had shaken her, exorcizing ghosts for which she had no room in her life. And she was angry, too. She had blown the interview, that much was clear, and the profile, which was to appear in a major magazine, was unlikely to be sympathetic. But she hadn't been able to help herself. She was a success, someone who had made something of herself. Why was it that in the same breath with which people said that she had made the sex trade respectable, they were always out to portray her as some kind of seedy madam? Normally she didn't let it get to her, but today . . .

Something about what the journalist had said had touched a nerve. Maybe she'd been right. Maybe Sadie was stupid to be running from her past; stupid to think that with a past such as hers she had even a hope of running fast enough. She gazed at the business card for a full minute before snapping herself out of an encroaching maudlin reverie.

Damn it, she thought. I've done it for this long. Why revisit the past? It's water under the bridge, and murky, dirty water at that.

Why should she open the secret box in her head? She had a new life now, a million miles from the one she had escaped. She was Sadie Scott now. Sadie Burrows was dead and buried: there was nothing to be gained from bringing her back to life.

Some things are best kept secret.

With a hasty swipe of her hand, she threw the business card into a waste-paper bin and left for the office.

CHAPTER 15

Esther Davies was on edge.

She hadn't been working here for long, and she was shy at the best of times, but today she had more reason to be nervous than usual.

Suzy, Miss Scott's formidable PA and her own immediate boss, had caught Esther staring at her more than once in the hour or so they had been in the office that morning. Each time it had happened, her face had reddened and she had quickly pretended to divert her attention back to some imagined task at her desk; but in reality she had achieved very little other than pushing bits of paper around in an attempt to make it look as if she had been doing some work.

Esther couldn't work Suzy out. Listen to her talk and you'd think she was just another working-class girl from south London, but you'd be making a mistake. She was crisp, efficient and no-nonsense, the sort of person who could take you down several pegs with a few well-chosen words. A bit like Miss Scott. In fact, a lot like Miss Scott. No doubt that was why she was so good at her job, and why Esther was so wary of her. It wasn't that either of them was unpleasant to her – quite the opposite. But with some people, you could just tell: cross them, and you'd regret it.

And that was what made her predicament all the more dangerous.

'Everything all right, Esther?' She jumped and looked up to see Suzy standing by her.

Flustered, Esther shuffled through a pile of typing she had to do. 'Fine . . . Fine, thanks,' she stammered; then she flushed even more as she felt Suzy's inquisitive gaze on her.

'You sure?'

'Yeah, totally. Just a bit tired is all. She not coming in this morning?'

Suzy glanced over at the door that led to Miss Scott's office. 'She'll be in later. She's being interviewed for a profile this morning –'

But as Suzy spoke, the main door opened and Miss Scott strode in. There was something about her presence that made Esther doubly edgy. It was so commanding and determined, and everything Esther with her slightly dowdy clothes and mousy hair was not, that it paralysed her somewhat. It was like being back at school, when there was always some older girl whom you wanted to be friends with but were too scared to approach because you were sure they wouldn't want anything to do with you. And today, her face seemed unusually severe.

'You're early,' Suzy said by way of greeting.

'Interview finished sooner than expected,' Miss Scott said shortly.

Suzy raised one eyebrow. 'That your decision, or hers?' she asked.

'Don't start, Suzy.' Esther glanced at the PA to gauge her reaction, but it seemed to be water off a duck's back to her. She wondered how she did it: had Miss Scott spoken to her like that, she'd have crumbled.

But she needn't have worried. 'Morning, Esther,' she greeted the office assistant.

'Good morning, Miss Scott,' Esther replied timidly, blushing once more and getting back to her work.

'What time are we expecting him?' Esther's ears pricked up and the nagging sickness in her stomach welled up again.

Suzy looked at her watch. 'About an hour,' she said. 'I can always cancel him, you know.'

'No,' Miss Scott replied. 'I'll deal with him. What have you got for me in the meantime?'

The PA handed her a memo. 'The Confederation of British Industry want you to speak at their Women in Management dinner.'

'I'll think about it. Anything else?'

'Yeah,' Suzy said cautiously. She glanced over at Esther, and then nodded in the direction of Miss Scott's office.

'OK,' Miss Scott said crisply. 'Come on through.' And in an instant the two of them were gone.

It was a relief for Esther to be alone in the office, even if only for a few minutes. The paranoia caused by her guilt weighed heavily upon her, and she felt, whenever anyone else was in the room, as though she was being eyeballed.

As though they had their suspicions.

As though they knew.

With a shudder, she put that thought from her head and went back to work.

'What is it, Suzy?'

Sadie's office was like her apartment – a sleek, modern pent-house on the south side of the river overlooking the city. She dumped her leather bag on the desk and took a seat while her PA remained standing.

'The Brick Lane branch,' Suzy told her. 'Trouble last night.'

'What sort of trouble?'

'The usual. Bunch of pissed-up guys rolled in after closing time and started trying it on with the two girls behind the counter.'

'Who were they? The girls, I mean.'

'Sally and Elaine.'

Sadie nodded. She knew them – she knew everyone who worked in the organization. They were pretty girls, feisty, paying their way through university. 'How far did it go?'

'Far enough for them to call Old Bill. Course, by the time they arrived, the damage was done. Bunch of lingerie was nicked, along with a few other things, and Sally got a black eye for trying to stop it happening.'

Sadie nodded grimly. 'CCTV?'

'Got it all. Do you want me to forward it to the police?'

Sadie thought about that for a moment. 'No,' she shook her head finally. 'Don't. I want two of the lads in there, morning, noon and night. Plain clothes, looking like punters. Anything like this happens again, they know what to do.'

'They've got a free hand?'

She nodded. 'Carte blanche. Whatever it takes. I want word to get out about what happens to people who try this sort of shit on my employees. As for Sally . . .'

'She might want to press charges, you know.'

'Fine. That's up to her. In the meantime, she's to take a month off on full pay. And tell her she only has to come back if she wants to – it won't affect her money.'

Suzy nodded. 'Anything else?'

'No, that's it.' She looked at her watch. 'Let me know when he arrives.'

'Of course.' The PA turned to leave, but looked back at her boss at the last minute. 'Oh, and Sadie?'

'Yes?'

'Happy birthday.'

Sadie smiled briefly – it was a rare gesture and it lit up her face. 'Thank you, Suzy.' She picked up a file from her desk as the secretary left.

The meeting ahead was one she had been dreading for days, and there was something about what the journalist had said that made it seem all the more ominous. 'It's amazing how skeletons can jump out of your cupboard.' Well, she thought to herself, this one can rattle his bones at me as much as he likes. It's not going to get him anywhere.

Before she knew it, Suzy was buzzing through. 'He's here,' she said.

Sadie took a deep breath, and could feel the tense muscles in her already severe face harden into a stony expression that she knew instilled apprehension in people. This guy had a thick skin, though; she knew that from experience and from the relentless and offensive way in which he had badgered Sadie's staff into giving him an appointment. Exactly what he wanted she didn't know, but she could hazard a guess.

The door clicked open and Suzy ushered a man inside. Sadie recognized him instantly, and with a crushing sense of déjà vu she saw him, in her mind's eye, through the back door of Lionel's bookshop, standing in front of the counter with that disdainful look in his eye. He was older now, of course, and Sadie saw with a pang that those extra years had increased his likeness to his father. He didn't have Lionel's kindly, open features, of course; to Sadie's eye he was more like a grotesque caricature. He was paunchy under his leather jacket and polo shirt, and his greying, curly hair was cut short. His very presence in the room revolted Sadie.

'Michael,' she said curtly without standing up, trying to keep her voice level.

Michael nodded and stood awkwardly in the middle of the room. Sadie nodded at Suzy to leave them; once they were alone, they eyeballed each other for a full thirty seconds before she spoke. 'It's been ten years since your father died. You surprise me – I thought you'd have crawled though my door long ago. Now you're here, you'd better sit down.'

But Michael didn't sit. Instead, he started walking round the office with a patronizing sneer on his face. His fingers trailed lightly over the back of the leather sofa, and for a moment he gazed out of the window. 'Nice view, Miss *Scott*,' he said in his cockney accent, his voice dripping sarcasm.

Sadie's eyes narrowed. 'Listen to me,' she said, ominously quietly. 'You've been badgering my staff with abusive calls for two weeks. I've agreed to see you, but only out of respect for your father. You've got two minutes to say what you have to say, and then you can leave. Any more calls after that, and I'll get the police to issue a restraining order.'

Michael turned. 'Respect for my father? How sweet.' He walked towards Sadie's desk. 'Shame, though, isn't it, that the old man didn't have a bit more respect for his own family when he croaked?'

'From what I can tell,' Sadie replied flatly, 'he gave you far more respect than you deserved when he was alive. Those handouts were a hell of a sight more than I'd have given you in his position.' Michael's eyes flickered away from Sadie's gaze for a second, and she smiled. 'I thought so,' she whispered. 'You want money, don't you?'

Michael stared arrogantly at her once more. 'You've done very nicely for yourself, Miss Scott. Anyone can see that. But you've done it on the back of what should have been mine, and I want my share.'

Sadie pressed the tips of her fingers together and glanced over them at him. 'I suppose,' she said after a pause, 'that if I give you something, you'll promise me that I'll never have to set eyes on you again.'

Suddenly there was a gleam in Michael's eyes. It was obvious that he thought he was getting somewhere. He was close. Subconsciously he licked his lips, as though he could taste a pay-day. 'All depends really,' he said with forced nonchalance, 'on how much we're talking.' He took another step forward and sat casually on the edge of Sadie's desk.

She observed him for a moment, looking him up and down. 'Get off my desk,' she told him, without raising her voice.

'Thanks,' he said, 'but I'm comfortable where I am.'

Sadie nodded slowly. 'About thirty seconds away from this room,' she said, 'is a four-man security team. They'll be very bored at the moment – doing the shift in this office is the short straw for them, because nothing much ever happens here. Nothing that they'd be interested in, anyway.' She nodded at the intercom on her table. 'All I have to do is press a button there, and they'll be straight up. It really only takes a word from me, and they'll make you a lot more uncomfortable than you've been in a long time. They're very good at it.'

The two of them continued to stare at each other.

'I'm not going to ask you a second time to get off my desk,' Sadie said implacably.

With a sniff and a look on his face that suggested he was doing it of his own volition, Michael stood up and lazily wandered over to the window once more. When he turned to look at Sadie again, his eyes were flashing.

'I'm not impressed by all this,' he spat, waving one arm at the luxurious surroundings. 'Far as I'm concerned, you're just a chancer who used to work in a seedy sex shop and got lucky. But I want my piece of the action, and I'm going to get it. I'm his only fucking son, after all.'

Sadie's face remained calm and expressionless. 'It takes more than flesh and blood to be someone's son,' she said. 'Frankly, you sicken me, crawling out from under a stone with a demand like that, after the way you treated him.' Casually, she pressed a button on the intercom. 'How dare you claim to be family? I'll go to my grave before I ever give you a penny. Like I say, it's only out of remembrance for your father that I've given you the time of day. Get the hell out of my sight – I never want to see you again.'

Michael's lip curled up. 'Fuck you,' he breathed, but as he spoke, the door opened and two men walked in. Both wore identical suits – they might have passed for businessmen had it not been for their burly frames and the tattoo one of them had plastered on the back of his hand. They stared impassively at Michael.

'He's leaving,' Sadie stated. 'Now. Make sure he finds the exit.'

One of the men stepped aside and indicated with one hand that Michael should walk through the open door. For a moment he didn't; there was a tense silence and Sadie felt the threat of violence crackle in the air. Clearly Michael could tell the situation was hopeless, but as he walked away he held his head high. 'I'm not finished,' he hissed at Sadie.

She refused to allow any flicker of emotion show in her face.

As he walked through the open door, one of the security guys took him gently but firmly by the elbow. Impatiently, Michael shook him off; but, with some satisfaction, Sadie noted that he kept walking as one of her boys shut the door respectfully behind him.

Esther needed to take three different trains to travel east after work to the tiny flat she called home, and it was almost seven o'clock when she arrived. She pulled the front-door key out of her bag and placed it to the lock; but her hand was trembling, and she only managed to insert it with difficulty. The heavy door creaked open. There was a steep, narrow staircase with no banister which she had to climb in order to get up to her first-floor maisonette, and she cursed under her breath when she realized that the bare bulb had gone and she would have to go up in darkness. She closed the door behind her and walked up.

The door to the flat was ajar, and the sight of the light on inside gave her goosebumps.

It meant he was home.

Esther fixed her lips into what she thought was a friendly grin before stepping inside. Michael was sitting at the kitchen table. In front of him was a can of strong lager, and with a shudder she saw that there were four other empty cans, crushed by his strong fist, littering the table and floor.

But worst of all, he had that look in his eyes. She recognized it immediately, from the way he gazed at her without quite catching her eye. 'You're late,' he said, slurring his words.

Esther tried to be as breezy as possible as she put her bag down and removed her coat. 'I'm not late, Michael,' she said reasonably. 'I always get home at this time.'

Suddenly she started as Michael brought his fist violently down on the table, causing one of the crushed cans to fall on the floor. 'Don't fucking argue with me, Esther,' he hissed. 'If I say you're late, you're late.'

Esther flinched. 'All right, Michael,' she said as

calmly as she could, but she was unable to stop her voice wavering slightly. 'I didn't mean anything by it. Please don't get upset . . .'

But it was too late. She froze as Michael stood up, knocking the rest of the beer cans on to the floor with one furious sweep of his arm – including the full one, the contents of which fizzed over the lino. As he strode towards her, she shrank. She knew what was coming.

Experience had taught her not to cover her face with her arms, no matter how much it felt like the right thing to do. Michael was smart enough never to hit her there, because the telltale signs of his abuse would be too obvious. Once, when he was particularly drunk, he had left bruises round her neck and she had been forced to wear a polo-neck sweater for the next ten days while they healed; but he hadn't made that mistake again. Now, as she cowered, she wrapped her arms firmly around her, one across her abdomen, the other across her breasts: they were the areas he normally went for, and she had learned to protect them.

'Please, Michael,' she whimpered as he raised his hand.

Michael stopped. Although he was sneering at her, he seemed to be savouring the moment, relishing the anticipation of what he was about to do even more than he ever appeared to enjoy doing it. His voice slurring, he mimicked her. '*Please, Michael.*' She could smell the beer on his breath.

'You're so fucking pathetic,' he said. 'You can't even do the one thing I ask you.'

'I'm trying –' Esther started to say, but before she could finish, she felt him kick her hard on the side of her left leg, and she fell heavily to the floor.

She sobbed. 'Please,' she repeated as she turned on to her side and groaned. But her request fell on deaf ears.

The next kick struck her hard on the hand that was covering her tummy, so when Michael tried again, he moved his foot a couple of inches down her body. As it connected, she gasped, and then started desperately trying to catch her breath, but without success.

And then he was on the floor with her, kneeling down so that his face was only inches from hers and she could feel the warmth of her skin. 'I fucking mean it, Esther,' he said. 'If you don't find me some dirt on that stuck-up, thieving bitch you work for, you're going to think that a kick in the tummy is like a birthday present. Do you understand what I'm saying?'

Esther was in too much pain to answer.

'*Do you understand what I'm saying?*' Michael roared, his face turning red with fury. Still gasping, Esther forced herself to speak. She knew there would be no let-up if she didn't.

'Yes, Michael,' she whimpered. 'I understand. Please don't hit me again. I understand . . .'

CHAPTER 16

The next morning dawned unseasonably cold, and there was even a flurry of snow as Sadie arrived at the office at eight o'clock. As usual, Suzy was already there, immaculate and efficient. Esther was there too, which surprised her. She didn't normally start until nine thirty, but her eyes looked bruised with tiredness. Sadie walked up to her, aware that she was avoiding her gaze.

'You're in early, Esther,' Sadie noted.

The girl turned to look at her. Sadie noticed that she was biting her lower lip and had difficulty holding her gaze. 'I've got quite a lot to do . . .' she mumbled before her voice petered out.

Sadie nodded silently. 'Is everything all right?' she asked.

'Of course,' Esther said, just a bit too quickly. She looked flustered as she turned her attention back to the computer on her desk.

Sadie allowed herself a few moments to stand there looking at her, but it soon became apparent that her presence was making the office assistant uncomfortable, so she inclined her head and walked back towards the door to her office, indicating to Suzy with a nod that her PA should follow her in.

'What's wrong with her?' she asked as soon as the door was shut behind them.

Suzy shrugged. 'She's always been a bit quiet.'

'There's quiet and quiet,' Sadie noted. 'I'm worried about her.' She looked sharply up at Suzy, who was eyeing her with a look of half-amusement in her face. 'What?'

'You can't make everyone else's problems your own, Sadie,' Suzy said. 'I'm sure Esther's fine – she's probably just had an argument with her boyfriend or something.'

'Yeah, OK,' Sadie replied. 'You're probably right. Just keep an eye on her, will you?'

'All right. Look, Sadie. I know you prefer me to open your post for you, but I've got something here you might want to look at privately.' Suzy handed her boss a letter. It was weighty for such a small thing, thanks to the thick vellum of the envelope, and it was addressed by hand. Sadie looked at it with a sudden sense of foreboding. Written in fountain-pen ink in a scrupulously neat hand were the following words: 'For the personal attention of Sadie Scott, née Burrows'.

Sadie blinked, and then looked guiltily up at Suzy, who had stepped back a discreet distance and was standing with a tactfully blank look on her face. 'OK, thank you, Suzy.' She nodded at the PA to indicate that she could leave now, but as Suzy turned, Sadie spoke again. 'Suzy,' she said sharply, 'who's seen this?'

'Just the porter downstairs. I collected it from him. I don't, er . . . I don't think it would mean much to him.'

'OK. You won't mention this to anyone, I hope.'

'Of course not,' Suzy said quietly, and left the room.

Sadie took a seat at her desk and placed the letter in front of her. Nobody knew the name Burrows – nobody in her present life, at least. And that was the way she wanted to keep it. In a flash, the image of Michael leaving her office yesterday illuminated itself in her mind. 'I'm not finished,' he had said to her. With certain clarity, she realized that this was the next shot in his war of attrition.

She didn't want to open it, and she sat there looking at the envelope for a good five minutes, feeling sick at what the contents might contain. Opening that letter would be like opening Pandora's box; but as the minutes ticked past she found it irresistible. Eventually she picked it up and carefully, apprehensively, opened it.

There was a single piece of paper inside. Its edges were a bit wonky, which suggested to Sadie that it had been cut to size to fit precisely inside. As she pulled it out, she saw that there was a short note written in the same handwriting as that on the envelope; she shut her eyes for a moment before summoning up the courage to read it.

But read it she did. The message was simple, and stark.

> I know about the events of seventeen years ago. I will be waiting for you on Waterloo Bridge at midnight tonight.

And that was all. No name. No clue as to the author. Sadie read it again, and again, her mind numbed by a horrible mixture of shock and fore boding.

It couldn't be coincidence. First Michael, then this. He had tried to get his filthy hands on Sadie's fortune, and now he was upping the stakes. Well, if he thought she was going to play along, he had another think coming. He could fuck around on Waterloo Bridge for as long as he wanted tonight. Sadie wasn't going to be there.

But for all her determination, she couldn't help letting her mind wander. What had he found out? What did he know? Sadie had gone to great lengths to keep the past a secret; she had always known, though, that secrets were difficult to keep. One day, she would have to face up to her past. But today wasn't that day. She wasn't prepared for it. And she wasn't prepared to let it happen.

With a sudden surge of anger, she crumpled the note up and threw it into the waste-paper bin by the side of her desk.

Almost the second she did so, the door burst open. Sadie looked up in surprise to see Suzy striding in, her face grim. 'We've got a problem,' she said without preamble, and leaving the door slightly ajar.

'What is it?'

'One of our girls is in hospital. Roughed up by a client last night.'

'Who?'

'Mandy.'

Sadie nodded. 'Where is she now?'

'University College Hospital. She's just been discharged and she called me first thing. Sick fucker broke her arm and split her face at about three this morning because she refused him a blow job.'

'Do we know who he is?'

'Of course.'

'Good.' Sadie thought for a while, her face severe. 'First things first. Find Mandy somewhere safe to stay. I don't want this bastard going back for a second bite of the cherry. Soon as you've done that, get the boys to pay him a visit.'

Suzy's lips thinned.

'Don't look at me like that, Suzy.'

'You could just call the police,' the PA suggested.

'You're right,' Sadie stated. 'I could. And I'm sure they'll put all their resources into what they think is some hooker being roughed up. Even if they do, Mandy'll have to make statements and stand up in court. Why the hell should she have to go through that? It's only her word against his anyway.'

Suzy inclined her head in defeat. 'All right. What do you want me to tell them?'

Again Sadie was silent with thought for a moment. 'I want him in hospital,' she said finally. 'I want them to do to him exactly what he did to her. And they don't have to feel they need to cover it up – I want everyone to know what they can expect if they pull this shit. OK?'

'OK, Sadie.'

'Good.' She nodded in satisfaction. 'Do it. Now.'

'Good.' Esther stood close to Sadie's slightly open door, her ear pressed against the wood. 'Do it. Now.' The sense of determination in her boss's voice filled her with a strange mixture of fear and excitement. As quickly as she could, she scurried away from the door; she sat down just as Suzy walked back in, but with relief she saw that the PA hadn't even noticed her. She could feel her heart beating quickly, and adrenaline had made her breathless.

Suzy picked up the phone and started to dial a number; but as she did so she suddenly looked over at Esther and casually returned the phone to its cradle. 'I forgot to pick up the papers on my way in,' she said across the office. 'Nip out and get them for me, would you? The money's in petty cash.'

Flustered, Esther nodded, gathered up her bag and her heavy winter coat and took a tenner out of the petty cash tin. She was out of the office in less than a minute, her face burning and her hands trembling. The bruises below her stomach hurt, but she barely paid them any attention; all she could focus on was the fact that she had something to tell Michael. Tonight, maybe, he would be pleased with her for a change.

Five o'clock was a long time coming, and the journey home was cramped and slow. When she arrived back at the flat, she noticed with relief that Michael hadn't been drinking; he even appeared to have shaved.

'Going out tonight?' she asked him timidly.

Michael gave her a dangerous look. Mind your own business, it seemed to say, and Esther nodded, crushed. Hanging her head, she took her coat off and went to hang it up.

How had she got herself into this situation? she wondered – not for the first time. She was twenty years old; Michael was in his forties. Everyone had warned her about him – her parents, her friends – but she had ignored them all. Now she was too embarrassed to go running to them, admitting she was wrong. Too embarrassed and too scared. If she crossed him, she honestly thought he might kill her. And not doing what he told her to would be unthinkable.

Like a mouse, she crept back into the kitchen. He was standing with his back to her, putting a ready meal into the microwave.

'I overheard something today,' she said.

Michael appeared not to hear her, and Esther was unsure whether or not she should continue talking.

'At work,' she ventured.

He turned round to look at her, his face severe. 'So you going to tell me?' he asked. 'Or are you just going to stand there looking stupid?'

Esther's eyes flickered to the floor in embarrassment. 'Miss Scott was talking to Suzie,' she explained. 'I didn't hear the start of the conversation, but she . . .'

All of a sudden, Esther was struck by the disloyalty of what she was about to do. Miss Scott had been kind to her. Scary, but kind. This was no way to repay her. She faltered.

'Go on,' Michael said, his voice emotionless.

'It's probably nothing . . .' Esther's voice trailed away.

And then he was there, in front of her, grabbing her shoulder-length hair in his fist. It didn't hurt – not yet; but she knew what she could expect.

So she told him. Word for word what she had heard. As she explained the conversation, she even saw a flicker of a smile on his pale lips, and when she had finished, he released her without inflicting any pain. He looked curiously satisfied as he removed his meal from the beeping microwave and sat down to eat it at the table.

Esther looked on, not daring to speak, so it was Michael who finally broke the silence.

'I won't be here tonight,' he admitted.

She just nodded. There was no point asking him where he was going to be. He would only volunteer that information if he wanted to.

'I've got a meeting,' he continued, as though he

had read her mind. 'Late. Might not even be back till morning.'

And without a further word he stood up, pulled on a jumper and a heavy woollen duffel coat, and walked out of the flat, leaving Esther to clear up the dinner things, which were still strewn on the table.

Sadie sat alone in her office.

Night had fallen; everyone else had gone home. She gazed out of the huge window, watching as a thick blizzard covered the city with its silent frosting. None of the lights in the room was on, but the nearly full moon and the snow illuminated her nonetheless.

She glanced at her watch. Almost eleven. The note from this morning was still where she had left it, crumpled in the wastepaper bin, and she had forced herself not to pick it out again. But it was the elephant in the room – she knew it was there, and she knew, deep down, that she would not leave without reading it again. Cursing her weakness, she stood up and retrieved it. She flattened it out on her desk and reread it by the light of the moon, though in truth she had memorized the words that morning.

It made no sense. Sadie had been turning it over in her mind all day, and she couldn't fathom what he was up to. What would he want to say to her on Waterloo Bridge that he couldn't say in this office? Maybe he was going to blackmail her and he was scared that this place would be bugged

– but he didn't strike her as being that bright. Maybe he was going to attack her – but why such a public place? Whatever it was that he wanted, it spelled trouble for Sadie. The best thing she could do was ignore it. Grab a cab. Go home. Forget about it.

That's what she would do. But as she left the office she was very aware of the fact that she had slipped the note into her pocket.

The cab driver wanted to chat, but Sadie soon put paid to that by being unresponsive. Instead, she stared out of the window. It always surprised her how busy London was, even this late and even in the snow. The cab drove along the river and she drank in the sight of the bridges illuminating the flurries. They were beautiful, but they were also a lie. Sadie knew that well enough. They told of a London that was rich, colourful, grand, but they hid what lay beneath. Whenever the weather was bad and she looked out on to the streets, she remembered Jamie Brown. Where was he now? Was he alive? Probably not. Of all the faces from the past, his was the one that never seemed to fade in her mind, staring at her aggressively from his little cardboard dwelling under Waterloo Bridge.

Waterloo Bridge.

As if snapped out of a nightmare by that thought, she suddenly rapped on the dividing window of the cab. 'I've changed my mind,' she called. 'Waterloo.'

The cabbie shrugged and gave her an odd look, but Sadie ignored him. She looked at her watch.

A quarter to twelve. As she sat back in her seat, she realized she had been intending to do this all day.

It was a relief to Sadie that even at this hour the bridge was crowded – full of warmly dressed, hunched pedestrians going about their chilly business and long lines of traffic slowly creeping through the snow. Nevertheless, Sadie felt inside her bag for the small canister of self-defence spray that she always carried with her. Then she walked apprehensively to the middle of the bridge, and waited.

It didn't take much time for her to grow cold. Her fingers and toes became numb, and she stamped on the snowy ground to warm herself up. But it wasn't only the cold that was making her shiver. She felt uncharacteristically nervous: her mouth was dry, and she found herself chewing her lower lip anxiously. She tried to distract herself by looking across at the spectacular night-time view – St Paul's, the wheel, floodlit boats on the Thames – but it was no good. Nothing was going to put her mind at rest other than this clandestine meeting.

Twelve o'clock. Nothing. She looked up and down the bridge but nobody seemed to be paying her any attention. Why would they? Sadie felt suddenly foolish: what was she doing out here in the cold? She was already covered by a dusting of snow. Her breath billowed mistily in front of her, and she decided to allow herself five minutes. Then, if nobody was here, she would leave and put this evening's outing down to experience. She turned and looked resolutely out over the water.

The minutes passed. Five past twelve arrived and went. That was it. She was going home.

Sadie turned round to head towards the south side of the bridge – she'd be able to get a cab at Waterloo station. As she did so, she became aware of a figure out of the corner of her eye. The figure was wearing a heavy, grey woollen coat with a large hood that covered the eyes, and it was standing – ominously, somehow – about ten metres away. The minute Sadie saw it, she felt a sickening shock of recognition, and even though she was sure she had never seen that face before, she had to steady herself momentarily by reaching out to the low wall on the side of the bridge. She gripped the canister in her hand more firmly as the two of them faced each other, and she squinted to try to make out the features beneath the hood, without success.

And then the figure started walking towards her.

Sadie took a deep breath and pulled herself up to her full height. Her face was locked into that habitually severe expression of hers, and she held her head high. Even as the figure approached, however, she could not see its features: the hood was large, and whoever it was kept their face firmly to the ground. It stopped about a metre away from her.

'I take it you're my pen pal.'

No answer.

'Look, I'm not a big fan of party games,' Sadie said abruptly. 'Why don't you tell me what all this is about?'

For a moment, the figure did not answer. Then it spoke. 'Sadie Burrows?'

The voice was that of a woman.

'I don't go by that name any more,' Sadie said curtly.

It did not seem to worry the woman. Slowly she raised her right hand and pulled the hood from over her face.

As she did so, Sadie felt herself go weak, though she did not know why. There was something haunting about the woman in front of her. She was pretty, of that there could be no doubt: her skin was clear, and her eyes shapely. Her dark hair was long and glossy and was swept round her neck to drape appealingly over her right-hand shoulder. It was difficult to tell how old she was at a glance, but she couldn't have been more than a teenager.

'My name is Alicia,' she said in a throaty voice that wobbled slightly as she spoke. 'My friends call me Ali.'

'Good for you,' Sadie replied. 'And what the hell's that got to do with me?'

Momentarily, Alicia looked away, her gaze flickering over the river. But soon their eyes became locked again.

'A lot,' she said.

Sadie waited for her to elaborate.

'It's got a lot to do with you,' Alicia said a bit more firmly, as though she had mustered her courage. 'Because I'm your daughter.'

CHAPTER 17

'What are you talking about? What kind of sick joke is this?'

It was suddenly as if there were no other people on the bridge, just the girl and her: Sadie could not hear the roar of the traffic; nor was she aware of the passers-by who jostled them as they stood in the middle of the pavement. As if from nowhere, all the old feelings of shame and resentment seemed to saturate her very being, as though the secret box in her mind had been ripped open, destroyed. She couldn't decide if she wanted to run or stay.

'I'm your daughter,' Alicia repeated. Her voice was clear and middle class – patrician almost. A long way from Sadie's accent, at any rate.

'Don't be stupid,' Sadie stated flatly. 'I don't have a daughter.'

But even as she spoke the words, she found herself becoming unnerved by the presence of this young woman. She was calm, and held Sadie's belligerent gaze with a coolness that the older woman had rarely encountered. It was more than that, though. For an unreal moment, Sadie felt as if she was looking into a mirror that showed her a reflection of herself as a teenager. The brown hair, the almond-shaped eyes: there were differences too, for sure, but there were similarities. Enough similarities for Sadie to know, deep in her gut, that this stranger was telling the truth.

And the truth, she realized with a twist of her stomach, repulsed her. If what this girl was saying was true, it was not *her* daughter that was standing in front of Sadie; it was *his*.

The distaste must have shown on Sadie's face, because as they stood wordlessly together, Alicia's calm expression became suddenly crestfallen. 'I'm sorry about all this,' she said in a small voice, waving her arm to indicate the bridge and the snow. 'I tried to make contact before, but it's impossible to get hold of you.'

'You could have written me a letter,' Sadie whispered accusingly. 'A proper letter, I mean.'

Alicia nodded. 'I could have, it's true. And what if you'd just ignored it? I wanted to meet you, to see what you look like. And I wanted you to see me too.'

The two woman scrutinized each other. Finally Sadie spoke. 'This is mad,' she said. 'Who the hell are you? What do you want from me? If you're trying to blackmail me, then you'd better think again.'

'I'm not trying to blackmail you,' Alicia replied. Sadie wasn't sure, but she thought that she could detect tears in her eyes, a slight catch in her voice. 'I only wanted to meet my mother. I'm sorry if I upset you, but I've known you were out there for some time now, and it just got too much.'

Sadie found it difficult to maintain eye contact, but she forced herself to do so.

'Look,' Alicia continued. 'I don't want anything. I don't want money and I don't expect you to welcome me with open arms. In fact, I don't expect you'll ever want to see me again. You made that clear seventeen years ago.' And then, almost as an afterthought, she handed Sadie a piece of paper. 'My phone number,' she explained. 'Call it if you want to; but I'll understand if you don't.'

And with that she pulled the hood back over her head, nodded once at Sadie and walked away towards the north end of the bridge.

'Wait!' Sadie shouted. She found that she was trembling all over, a kind of fury surging through her veins. As though in the control of some other force, she ran towards this stranger who thought she could swing into her life and mess with her emotions like that. Roughly, she grabbed the girl's arm and held her tightly, but not with affection. 'Listen to me,' she hissed. '*I don't have a daughter*. I don't know who told you this stuff, but the baby I gave birth was too young to survive, and good riddance. So you can take your scams and your cynicism and fuck off. Do you understand me?'

Alicia didn't reply. She just looked calmly out from under her hood and waited for Sadie's anger to run its course. Self-consciously, the older woman let go of her arm.

'You'll never hear from me again,' Alicia whispered. She stared hard at Sadie, as though she was trying to imprint her features on her brain for all time. Then she turned away once more, and walked.

This time Sadie did not call her back. She just stood there, frozen but not by the cold, and watched in stunned, sickened silence as the figure merged with the other passers-by walking on the bridge, became indistinct through the haze of the snow and finally disappeared from sight.

Sleep, of course, would not be possible. Every time Sadie closed her eyes, the images came flooding back. Allen. The bed. The bathroom. And most of all the tiny child in her bloodied hands. It had been seventeen years ago, yet still the scene was as clear in her mind as if it had been just last week. She could remember the grim look on the face of the medic, the look of hopelessness. This child is too tiny, it seemed to say. It can't survive.

And that was what Sadie had believed; or was it just what she had wanted to believe?

For an hour, maybe longer, she sat on the sofa with the framed picture of her parents in her hand. Could it really be that Jackie, in her addled, depressed state, could have kept the truth from Sadie? Could she have filled in adoption forms on her behalf, deceiving her? Or may be the bleeding-heart social workers had taken it upon themselves to ensure that the child had not been allowed to be part of that broken, unhappy family. For a while Sadie felt resentment that this might have been the case, that decisions had been taken all that time ago that had prevented her from being prepared for this bombshell. But soon a more reasonable thought entered her head. Would she have wanted to know? Would she have wanted contact with the child? She had to admit that the answer was probably no.

As the snow fell thickly outside, Sadie paced around her flat. She did not want to believe a word this girl who called herself Alicia had said; yet somehow she knew she could not deny it.

The night drew on. Sadie found herself haunted by the memory of Alicia's eyes, wide and unblinking, as they looked at her on the bridge. And she found herself haunted in other ways too: the more she stared at the picture of her mother, the more she felt as if Jackie was in the room with her. It had taken her years to recover from her death, from the trauma of not being able to say goodbye. No child should have to go through that. But Alicia didn't want to say goodbye; she just wanted to say hello. Why, then, could Sadie not feel even the stirrings of maternal affection towards the young woman who claimed to be her daughter?

In a flash, she realized that she had answered her question herself not forty-eight hours previously. What was it she had said to Michael as he stood before her in the office? It takes more than flesh and blood to be someone's son.

Alicia was forced on her. Sadie was no more a mother today than she was yesterday. She owed this girl nothing. If she wanted a parent, let her find her father.

And that thought made her stop.

She shivered slightly as she remembered him. The eyes, the sharp sideburns, the pleated trousers. She remembered his face only inches away from hers as he laid himself upon her on the bed. She remembered the firm grip of his hand.

Was he alive? Was he dead? Sadie didn't know and she didn't care. The last time she had set eyes on him was when he had stormed out of their little house on the estate, never to be seen again. But if he was alive, there was no way she could let Allen Campbell into the life of any young woman, whether a daughter of hers or not. And there was no way she could leave Alicia to listen to the self-serving lies of that man.

Just before dawn, Sadie knew what she had to do.

The piece of paper Alicia had given her was still in her pocket. She took it out and toyed with it for some time before plucking up the courage to go down the path from which she knew she could not return. But eventually she dialled the number.

The phone was answered immediately, and despite the early hour Alicia did not sound remotely sleepy.

'Hello?' she said warily. Had she been up all night too? Sadie wasn't going to ask.

'It's me.'

A silence.

'I didn't think you'd call,' Alicia said finally.

'Nor did I.'

'I'm glad you did.'

Sadie wasn't going to be drawn into a sentimental conversation. 'You've handled this badly, you know,' she said.

At the other end of the phone Alicia breathed heavily. 'I'm sorry,' she conceded. 'I did the best I could.'

Sadie found herself shrugging, even though there was nobody there to see it.

'We could meet,' Alicia suggested in a small, nervous voice.

Sadie closed her eyes. 'Where?' she said after a moment.

'Well, I could come to you. To your house.'

'No.' Sadie spoke a bit more sharply than she intended. She didn't want Alicia coming here. 'No. There's something I want to show you.' She gave the girl some directions. 'I'll meet you there in an hour.' And with that, she hung up.

Sadie seldom drove, but it was early, the streets were empty and she wanted to be in control, so she dressed warmly against the snow and took the lift downstairs to the underground car park where she kept her silver Mercedes convertible. Soon she was heading south.

The estate on which she had grown up was deserted now. The tower blocks were empty, their windows smashed in and the cement crumbling. As Sadie drove her expensive car round the familiar roads, she passed the rusting shells of other vehicles, covered in a thick blanket of snow. Hers were the only tyres that had made tracks in the snow; nobody else came here now.

Alicia was waiting for her in the playground. How she had got there Sadie did not know, nor how she had arrived so quickly, but she looked lonely in the grey light of dawn. As the strong headlamps of the Mercedes illuminated her, Sadie saw that she was stamping her feet against the cold and she felt a sudden urge to hurry her into the warmth of the car. But that wasn't what they were here for. She pulled up alongside the playground, turned off the ignition and stepped outside.

The girl looked tired, perhaps a little frightened at being in such an unwelcoming place, but relieved to see Sadie, who realized with a sudden insight that Alicia had not been sure she would appear – and equally clearly that there was no way she would have left her here alone.

Alicia smiled winsomely. 'Not necessarily the place I would have chosen for an emotional reunion,' she half-joked.

'That's not what this is,' Sadie replied, aware that she was deliberately misreading Alicia's intention but unable to pierce her own defensive shell.

'I know,' the girl replied awkwardly.

Sadie looked at the run-down remains of the

playground. 'I used to come here,' she said. It was years since she had last been here. The swings on which she and her friends used to sit were no longer there, though the frame from which they were suspended was – rusty and rickety. It gave her an odd feeling to see it again; a feeling she didn't like. 'Come with me,' she said. 'There's something I want you to see.'

As Sadie led the way, she locked the car with her key fob; the clicking noise it emitted echoed in the empty, snowy road. They walked in silence for a few minutes, Sadie almost on autopilot as she led the way past the derelict buildings to the house in which she used to live, her skin tingling as they approached.

It was boarded up now. The windows were encased in beige metal shutters, the front door reinforced to stop squatters from taking the place over. The roof was disintegrating, with large holes that had allowed the snow to pile in, and the front garden was overgrown and litter-strewn. Sadie looked at it impassively; then she turned to the shivering girl next to her.

'You sound to me like a nice girl,' she said. 'Posh accent, good home. Am I right?'

Alicia nodded mutely, and Sadie looked back at the house. 'This is where you were born,' she said bleakly.

Alicia looked up, unable to hide the look of shock in her face. 'It's not quite what I pictured,' she stuttered.

'I didn't think it would be. Of course it wasn't always like this.' She looked Alicia up and down. 'But I don't think it was ever somewhere you'd have felt comfortable.' And then, more quietly, 'I know I didn't.'

'So why have you brought me here?' Alicia asked.

'Because I want you to understand something. I want you to understand that the past isn't always what you expect it to be. Sometimes it's best just left alone.'

They stood in silence for a minute.

'You must have a thousand questions to ask me,' Sadie continued. 'But questions like that sometimes don't need to be answered. I promised myself years ago that I would keep my past a secret for as long as it is in my power. I don't intend to go back on that promise. Not for you, not for anyone. I don't care if you are my daughter.'

Alicia nodded her head slowly, as though she was struggling to understand. 'Is this the last time I'm going to see you?' she asked starkly.

Sadie took a deep breath before she answered. 'No,' she said. 'We can see each other. Now and then. But don't expect us to be best friends. Don't expect cosy little evenings in wine bars and intimate chats, because that's not how it's going to be.'

'What should I call you?' the girl asked apprehensively.

The older woman's jaw clenched. 'My name is Sadie.'

'You're younger than I thought you would be, Sadie,' Alicia ventured.

Instantly, Sadie turned on her heel and started walking back to the car. Alicia ran behind, slipping slightly on the frozen pavement. 'I'm sorry, I didn't mean to . . .'

'Forget about it,' Sadie instructed.

As she spoke, her mobile phone rang. She almost felt relieved, ignoring the fact that it was too early for most normal people to be calling as she pulled it from her coat pocket and flicked it open. 'Yeah?'

The person at the other end waited a few seconds before speaking. 'Hello, Miss *Scott*,' the voice said, in a slow, lazy drawl.

Sadie stopped dead. She recognized the voice, of course. It was Michael's. 'How did you get my number?' she demanded.

'Oh, I know all sorts of things about you that you don't want me to know,' he said flatly.

'I've told you already – I've got nothing to say to you.' She glanced at Alicia, who was observing her worriedly.

'Oh, I think you might be interested to hear what I have to say to *you*.'

'I doubt it.'

'What if I was to tell you that I've got evidence that you've been – how can I put it – taking the law into your own hands?'

Sadie found herself momentarily lost for words.

'Of course, it's all very sad, one of your hookers being knocked about a bit. But wouldn't people be interested to know that you've instructed your own staff to have the poor bloke put in hospital?'

Sadie's eyes narrowed. She stepped away from Alicia, out of earshot. This wasn't something she wanted her to hear. 'What do you want, Michael?'

'You know what I want, Miss Scott.'

'Then we need to meet.'

'I'll come to your office now.' His voice was sneakily triumphant.

'No,' Sadie said sharply. 'Not my office.'

'Where, then?'

'There's a place I use for business meetings I don't want my staff to know about.' Quietly, so as not to be overheard, she gave him directions. 'I'll be there in an hour,' she said.

'You'd better be,' Michael replied. The phone went dead.

Sadie took a deep breath to steady her shaking hand, and then turned back to Alicia.

'Is everything all right?' the girl asked uneasily. 'You look worried.'

Sadie avoided the question. 'I have to go,' she said shortly. 'Get in the car. I'll drop you at a tube station.'

Alicia's adoptive father hadn't been at all sure that trying to find her birth mother was a good idea. Maybe he knew something he wasn't telling her; maybe he was scared of losing his only daughter. Whatever it was, however, he was well enough acquainted with her wilfulness to know not to stop her from doing what she wanted.

As Alicia arrived back at their comfortable family home in Islington, she felt overcome with exhaustion and the emotion of the previous twelve hours. She sneaked into her bedroom without her dad hearing and then flopped down on the bed and stared into space, for how long she didn't know. Gradually she became aware of the fact that her hand was resting on a piece of paper. She picked it up, unfolded it three times and started reading the words in immaculate copperplate writing on her birth certificate. *Mother: Sadie Burrows. Father: Unknown.*

It was rare for adopted children to be able to trace their natural parents; that much she knew. Maybe someone had messed up in making this document available, but her father had told Alicia the truth about her past when he felt she was old enough to deal with it, and the birth certificate had been in her possession since she was fifteen. It had been only in the last few months that she had started trying to trace her mother, but she had fantasized about their reunion for a long time now. In her mind it had been tearful, emotional. Her mother had taken her into her arms and accepted her without question.

The reality had been quite different.

Sadie Burrows, or Scott, or whatever she called herself now, was a hard woman. A difficult woman. Alicia was honest enough with herself to admit that she was a bit scared of her.

But there was something else. Something that

she couldn't quite put her finger on. The surreal nature of the morning's events had made Alicia uneasy, and she found herself repeating in her head every word this strange woman had said to her. What was it about the past that she was so desperate not to revisit? What was it that she was running from?

There was a knock at the door. Alicia answered almost absent-mindedly: 'Come in.'

'It's only me, Ali, love.'

Her father looked old now – Alicia had only started to notice it in recent months. His wife, Alicia's adoptive mother, had died not long after they had adopted her – from a rare and vigorous cancer that still cast a shadow over her dad's face whenever it was mentioned – and he had been left to bring her up alone. For all that time he had done his duty with a love and care that could not have been more absolute had Alicia been his own flesh and blood. He had never raised his voice or his hand to her, and he had never given her any reason to believe that he found being left alone with her to be a difficult twist in the story of his life. But now that she was almost of age, Alicia felt that the strain was beginning to show. As if he was a piece of elastic that had been stretched once too often, his sprightliness had deserted him and he was starting to look like what he was becoming: an old man.

'Hi, Dad.'

'So? How did it go? Did you see her?'

Alicia paused. 'Yeah, I saw her?'

'And how did she take it?'

She thought about that. How *had* she taken it? It was difficult to know. 'About as well as could be expected,' she said noncommittally.

'It can't have been an easy thing for her,' her Dad said kindly. 'Did you get on?'

'Mmm . . .'

'Would you rather not talk about it?'

Alicia felt suddenly guilty. This wasn't easy for her dad, either. For all her life he had referred to her adoptive mother as 'your mum'; there were pictures of her and Alicia all around the house. But since he had told her about her adoption, Alicia had wondered anew what it would be like to have a mother. Try though she might, she had never really felt a bond with the woman in the photographs.

'It's all right, Dad,' she said, sitting up and patting the bed to indicate that he should come and sit with her. 'I don't mind talking about it. To be honest, I don't think she's the sort of person you get on with.'

'Did you like her?' Her dad's honest face spoke of its nervousness.

Alicia hesitated. It was a good question; for a moment she didn't know how to answer. 'Yes, Dad,' she said finally. 'Yes, I think I did. But . . .' Her voice trailed off.

'But what?'

She took a deep breath. 'There's something

about her, Dad. She wants to make you think that she can take care of herself, but . . .'

'Go on, love.' He took her hand and squeezed it gently.

'But I think she's in trouble,' Alicia blurted out, somehow surprised by her sudden insight. 'I really think she's in a lot of trouble. And I don't know what I can do about it.'

Michael called a minicab. It wasn't something he did often – too expensive, and they were always driven by foreigners. He hated putting his money into the pockets of the blacks and the Asians. But this morning was different. He wanted to be there in good time, and anyway his fortunes were about to change for the better. The smug bitch was running scared, and all he had to do was name his price.

The cabbie had given him a distrustful look as he climbed into the back of the Laguna, and Michael knew why. He'd been drinking all night, celebrating his good fortune. Actually, that was bollocks. Good fortune didn't come into it. He'd been grafting for this for ages now, and all his hard work was about to come to something. It felt good to know that he would be able to ditch that thick muppet Esther pretty soon. She'd served her purpose, and it infuriated him the way she crumbled into a hysterical mass every time he so much as glanced at her. But she wouldn't learn, would she? She drove him to it, every fucking day.

Happily the cab driver didn't seem to want to speak. As they made their way towards the address on the outskirts of Dulwich that Sadie Scott had given him, Michael started to feel queasy – a mixture of the booze and the pungent smell of the air freshener hanging round the rear-view mirror. He opened his window slightly, ignoring a tut from the driver.

They were there quickly. Reluctantly paying the cabbie, he stepped outside and looked at his watch. A quarter to seven – he was twenty minutes early. No harm in that, he thought. Check the place out. He looked up and down the road: it wasn't at all what he had expected. The other office had been in a tall glass building with porters and water coolers; this was a shabby side street with nondescript doors and crumbling brick walls. There were no pedestrians, although Michael noticed in his semi-drunk haze that the snow had been recently disturbed outside the door he had been directed to. He raised his hand to knock, but then he saw that the door was slightly ajar, so he pushed it open and stepped inside.

The room in which he found himself was small, stark and at least as cold as it was outside. There was an empty table and an old metal filing cabinet, but they gave the impression that they were seldom used: that this was a place masquerading as an office, not a place where anyone actually did any work. On the other side of the room was another door, and this too was open. Michael felt a sudden twinge of apprehension. Where was she? Why wasn't she here to greet him? Should he go through? Looking back over his shoulder, he reassured himself that the front door was still open – he could get out if he needed to – so with a loud sniff he stumbled across the room and stepped through the second door.

Michael found himself in what looked like a warehouse, and it surprised him – from the front you would have had no idea that this place existed. The ceiling was high and vaulted, and it was a good fifty metres to the other end of the room. There was strip lighting hanging from the ceiling, but it was not switched on, which made the concrete and brick interior particularly gloomy and threatening. The only source of light was from smeared windows high up. Through one of them, the morning sun was starting to gleam, shooting a diffused beam down on to the ground.

And standing in the light, half her face illuminated by the sunbeam, the other half obscured and shadowy, was the woman he had come to see.

Michael breathed out contemptuously, and his breath steamed in the cold air. Then he walked slowly towards her.

She was dressed in black – a long woollen coat, long black boots that still had traces of snow on them – and she held her head high as he approached. She was sneering at him, but he didn't give a shit about that. She could sneer all she liked, as long as she paid up.

He was right in front of her now, inches from her face. She was taller than him, just, and looked at him with flat, dead eyes. There was a small white scar along her left cheek – something he hadn't noticed before – and he felt momentarily nervous of the look he was receiving. He couldn't let it show in his face, though.

'Why don't we talk business?' he said.

Sadie Scott's lip curled into a sneer. 'I don't know how many times I have to tell you before you get it into your stupid head,' she said, 'that I don't have anything to discuss with you.'

Michael's eyes narrowed. 'What do you mean?'

'I think I've been pretty clear.'

Michael felt a sudden surge of fury in his veins. If it had been Esther standing in front of him, he'd have had her on the floor already. How fucking dare she speak to him like that? His clenched his fists, but struggled to control his anger. Even in his bleary, alcoholic state, he knew that that was not the way to deal with this. Much as he'd like to beat the crap out of her, he had to think about the bigger picture.

'Fine,' he said. 'Then I'm going to the police, to tell them what I know.' He had nothing but Esther's word, of course, but she didn't know that. She wouldn't be calling his bluff anytime soon. He smiled an unfriendly smile at her and then, suddenly, spat in her face.

Sadie's head didn't move. It was as though he had spat at a statue.

Quickly, he turned round to walk back towards the door; but as he did so, he stopped.

Two men were standing there. They were broad-shouldered and grim-faced, and they looked towards Sadie, as though waiting for something. Michael looked back at her just in time to see her giving a firm nod. The men started to walk towards him.

The wooziness that Michael had been feeling immediately left him. 'You're not going to fucking scare me,' he said to Sadie, but as the men approached, he took a step backwards. He kept his eyes on them as he heard Sadie talking.

'I don't know where you get your gossip and half-truths from,' she said coldly. 'But you've got nothing on me – I'm too careful for that. And even if you did, who's anyone going to believe – me or a scumbag like you?'

The men were upon him now, each grabbing one of his arms. 'Get the fuck off me,' he railed at them, as one of them jerked his right arm behind his back. It hurt like hell.

'You'll probably find,' Sadie continued, 'that these gentlemen do what I ask them, not what you ask them.' She stepped closer to him, almost nose to nose. 'If you ever try a stunt like this again, then believe me – what these men will do to you will be ten times worse than what they're about to do.'

Michael started to struggle, but there was little he could do – if he moved too much the pain became intolerable. '*Get the fuck off me*,' he whispered again. This time he was aware that he sounded frightened.

And then Sadie Scott gave her men another nod.

The bone in Michael's arm cracked as it broke, and the scream of pain that came from his lips echoed around the warehouse long after he was thrown roughly on to the cold concrete floor.

CHAPTER 18

Sadie walked out of her office, a magazine in her hand. Esther and Suzy glanced up.

'What do you think?' she asked, addressing the room in general.

Esther, of course, was too timid to give an opinion, but Suzy shrugged. 'You lie down with dogs, you get up with fleas,' she told her boss.

'I didn't lie down with her, Suzy. I gave her an interview and it didn't last more than twenty minutes. How the hell did she fill up ten pages with this shit?' She flung the magazine down on Suzy's desk, open at the headline 'AN AUDIENCE WITH THE QUEEN OF SLEAZE'. A three-year-old black-and-white publicity shot of Sadie in a business suit adorned the article that she had only skim-read. It was the usual collection of gossip, supposition and inaccuracies that she was used to but which nevertheless filled her with fury whenever she read it.

'Why don't I just file it away?' Suzy said tactfully.

'Good idea,' Sadie replied. 'I'm going out.'

Her PA looked down at the diary. 'There's nothing in,' she observed.

'Guess what, Suzy,' Sadie said lightly, 'sometimes I go out without asking you.' And with that she was gone.

For two weeks after she had taken Alicia to the estate, Sadie hadn't heard a word from her. Maybe the little trip down memory lane had done its trick, though she wasn't quite sure what that trick was supposed to be. Had she wanted her to stop all contact? If anyone had asked her, Sadie would probably have said yes; but as the days passed, and the call didn't come, she found herself wishing that it would. Every time her mobile rang, she jumped.

And then Alicia had rung. She was relieved to hear her at the other end of the phone, though for some reason she couldn't quite explain to herself, she went out of her way not to let that pleasure sound in her own voice.

'I thought I could repay the favour,' her daughter said brightly.

'What do you mean?'

'Show you where *I* was brought up.' She sounded a bit less sure of herself after Sadie's less than encouraging response.

And so it was that Sadie now found herself in a black cab, doing her best to calm down after reading the article and heading towards north London while admitting to herself that she was curious – excited, even – to see something of Alicia's life.

The snow had melted, though the weather was still cold, and Alicia was wrapped warmly in a dark overcoat and colourful scarf as she waited outside the closed restaurant on Upper Street. Sadie noticed how the girl smiled when she saw her, and she allowed a smile to flicker back as she paid the cab driver. She greeted Alicia with a curt nod, and the two women started walking down the street, neither of them appearing quite confident enough to break the ice.

It was not until they had crossed the road at a zebra crossing that Sadie spoke. 'So where are we going?'

'It's not far,' Alicia said.

They turned off the main road and into a side street. On the corner, and old man sat on the pavement. His skin and clothes were grubby, his face grizzled, and he stank. He had an old polystyrene coffee cup in his hand and, lying on its belly by his side, was a lean black Labrador that looked at least as dejected as the beggar. Sadie stopped and looked at him, and Alicia halted by her side. For a moment he didn't seem to notice the two women towering above him, but when he did he immediately and automatically intoned the words 'Spare some change.' It was almost like a reflex action, and his voice was monotone and robotic.

Sadie crouched down to his level and looked directly into his eyes. 'Where are you staying tonight?' she asked him, her voice uncharacteristically gentle.

The man eyed her suspiciously. 'You a copper?' he asked warily.

'Do I look like one?'

The man's face twitched, and he mumbled something in a growly voice that Sadie couldn't make out.

'Where are you staying tonight?' she repeated.

'I'm staying here, lady,' the beggar said tetchily. 'Till I get moved on.'

'There are hostels,' Sadie said insistently.

The man instinctively reached out and stroked his dog, who whimpered slightly at his touch. 'Not for both of us, there aren't,' he said, and then he looked away, as though his attention had been lost by the fact that this woman clearly wasn't going to give him any money.

But Sadie was reaching into her purse. She slid two new twenty-pound notes out of their leather compartment; vaguely aware that Alicia's eyes were firmly on the money, she pressed them into the hand of the vagrant. 'Get something warm,' she instructed. 'No booze, OK?'

She stood up and walked away before the tramp could answer – she didn't want him to be forced to give her his thanks. That wasn't what it was about. Alicia trotted behind to keep up with Sadie's brisk step.

'He's always been there,' she told Sadie.

'No he hasn't,' Sadie said. 'Not always.'

'Well, for as long as I can remember, anyway,' Alicia conceded, chastened. 'Do you often give money to people in the street?'

'How far are we?' Sadie replied, diverting the conversation.

Alicia stopped. 'This is it.'

They were outside a red-brick mansion building, with a small car-parking area at the front. 'I've lived here all my life,' Alicia said. 'Well,' she corrected herself with a grim smile. 'Nearly all. Would you like to come up? My dad's there.'

For a heart-stopping moment, the image of Allen flashed through Sadie's mind and she thought the girl next to her was playing some kind of sick joke; then, equally quickly, she realized that Alicia was talking about her adoptive father. 'No,' she said, for some reason unable to look at her daughter. 'No, I don't think I'm ready to meet him.' She looked around and saw a greasy-spoon café across the road. 'Let's go there. We can talk.'

It was warm and welcoming inside the café, and not too crowded, so the two women could sit out of earshot of the other customers. When they had two steaming cups of tea in front of them, Sadie spoke.

'It's not as grand as I thought it might be,' she said.

'What?'

'Your house. I thought . . . Well, I don't know what I thought.'

'My mother – my adoptive mother – died when I was small,' Alicia explained. 'Dad was always struggling a bit to work and look after me. He did all right, but . . .' Her voice trailed away and she took a sip of her tea. 'I wanted to ask you something.'

'What?'

'Did you ever give me a name? In your head, I mean?'

Sadie looked down and started to pick at her well-manicured nails. For an uncomfortable moment she thought she felt tears threatening to come, and she fought off the sensation with all her might. What could she tell this wide-eyed girl sitting opposite her? The truth? That whenever she thought of her, it was as if she was in the middle of a nightmare?

'No,' Sadie replied. 'You never had a name.'

Alicia gave a stoical little nod. 'I just wondered,' she said quietly.

They sat in silence for a minute, sipping the scalding tea.

Finally, Alicia blurted out the question that had clearly been on her mind since they had first met. 'Why did you leave me? I mean, it's OK . . . I don't blame you or anything . . . I just wanted to know . . . I mean, I was just a little baby . . .'

'It's more complicated than that, Alicia,' Sadie snapped, and as she did so she felt a dreadful wave of déjà vu crash over her. Suddenly she was standing in the kitchen of the house on the estate, looking up to Jackie and asking her why it had to be her who went to work. Why couldn't it be him? '*It's more complicated than that, Sadie,*' her mother had said. Sadie flushed. 'I . . . I'm sorry,' she stuttered, embarrassed.

'It's OK,' Alicia replied, an apology in her voice if not in her words.

'I don't understand why you want to know all this,' Sadie said to her. 'Isn't it obvious that whatever I'm going to say isn't going to make you feel any better about things?'

'You don't know how I'm going to feel, Sadie,' Alicia complained, her voice irritated now.

Sadie stood up. She didn't have to listen to this. 'I have to go,' she whispered.

But Alicia stood up too, her face determined. 'Where's your mother?' she asked in a clear voice.

Sadie stopped. 'She's dead,' she said tersely.

'And what would you do if she walked into this café right now?'

'What do you mean?' Sadie hissed. The girl had gone too far.

'Sit down and I'll tell you.'

There was steel in her eyes; to Sadie it was like looking in the mirror. Slowly, reluctantly, Sadie returned to her seat.

'I spent my whole childhood without a mother.' Sadie opened her mouth to defend herself, but Alicia raised a hand to stop her. 'I don't mean you,' she said. 'My adoptive father's an amazing man and he did a good job, but all my life, I wanted my mum. Then, when I was fifteen, I was told that you existed. You came back into my life just as surely as if your own mother walked into this café now. I'll ask you again: what would you do?'

Sadie could not find the words to speak. She closed her eyes and her mind was filled with a vision of Jackie, standing with them in the middle of the café. What would she say? What would she do? Cry, certainly. Scold her, perhaps. But most of all, she would want nothing more than to wrap her arms around her in a fierce, loving, daughterly embrace. She would want to feel her warmth. She would want to feel her comfort.

Slowly she opened her eyes. Alicia was looking expectantly at her. 'I'm sorry,' she said quietly.

Alicia nodded. The blaze in her eyes had subdued a little, and she took another sip from her mug of tea.

On a whim, Sadie reached into her handbag and pulled out a chequebook holder with the words 'Coutts & Co' engraved on it, along with a fat fountain pen. 'I want to give you something,' she said as she opened it. 'It's –'

But her daughter's hand had shot across the table and firmly closed the chequebook before Sadie could put pen to paper. 'That's not what I want,' she whispered. 'You don't understand, do you?'

But Sadie thought she did understand, and she felt guilty as she sheepishly put the chequebook to one side. When she looked back at Alicia, she saw tears in the young girl's eyes.

‘I don’t want your money,’ she said in a quiet voice. ‘I don’t want anything from you except your respect. One day, maybe, your love.’

Sadie looked away.

‘When you took me to the estate,’ Alicia said, ‘and you took that phone call, who was it?’

‘No one you know,’ Sadie said curtly.

‘You looked worried.’

‘I wasn’t worried.’

‘You looked it.’

‘It’s nothing. OK? It’s dealt with.’

Silence.

‘You know, Sadie,’ Alicia said after a while, ‘I can’t force you to be my mum. But there’s nothing you can do to stop me from being your daughter.’

Sadie took a deep, shaky breath. ‘I was thirteen,’ she whispered. ‘I thought you were dead. What did anyone expect me to do?’

‘I don’t know,’ Alicia said. She stretched out her arm and took Sadie’s hand; to the older woman’s surprise she did not find herself moving it away. ‘But you’re not thirteen any more. Perhaps the time has come for you to deal with it.’

Alicia held her breath. There was an honesty to her face, Sadie noticed with a certain impassivity – you could tell what she was thinking. Alicia didn’t know what her mother’s reaction would be. She thought she might have overstepped the mark; she knew that Sadie was not the sort of woman you spoke to like that.

And Sadie herself did not know how she would

react. She was as surprised as Alicia when, unable to bottle it in any longer, she broke down into an uncontrollable flood of devastated, body-shaking tears.

Tonight was the night. Esther had promised herself over and over. Tonight was the night it stopped.

She'd been building up her courage all day. It had been a relief when Miss Scott had left the office unexpectedly. She hadn't come back – much to Suzy's annoyance – but at least it meant that Esther hadn't had the additional worry of having her boss around. When five o'clock came, though, suddenly she didn't want to leave; the office seemed safer. Michael might have a broken arm – how it came about, he wouldn't tell – but he would still go mad when Esther ordered him out of her flat. She had to do it, though. She couldn't put up with it any more.

The time soon came when she could no longer stay in the office without Suzy asking questions, so she slowly packed up her things and with a meek 'goodbye' made her way to the tube station. Once underground, she allowed a couple of full trains to depart that she would normally have squeezed herself on to: there was no hurry to get home today.

As she approached her front door, she felt her heart thumping. Half of her wanted to run away, but she knew that was not an option. She had to go through with it. She had to make it stop.

Esther unlocked the door and climbed the stairs. Tentatively, she walked into her flat.

The kitchen was empty. Rather than take her overcoat off, however, she walked to the drawer where the knives were kept and chose a small one, which she secreted up her sleeve. There was no way she could ever use it, of course, but it still made her feel a bit safer.

'Michael,' she called, doing her best to keep her voice steady. 'Michael, it's me. Esther.'

There was no reply.

She looked round the flat: each room was empty. God knows where he was, or when he would be back. Esther felt curiously deflated as she went into her bedroom. She needed to do something, anything, to calm her nerves, so she decided to get changed out of her work things. She put the knife down on the dressing table, removed her coat and got undressed. Moments later she was standing, naked apart from her underwear, in front of the full-length mirror on her wall.

It was not a pretty sight. Her slight abdomen was covered in huge, purple bruises. Now that he only had the use of one arm, Michael had taken to beating her with whatever implement came to hand: it had been a stick a few days ago; then last night a wire coat-hanger, which had caused angry welts all over her belly and the tops of her legs. She had wanted to wear tights this morning, because of the cold, but she hadn't been able to: her legs hurt too much. Esther gazed at herself, at the wreck her body had become, for some time, with a look of distaste on her face; eventually she could stand the sight no longer and got dressed.

Taking the knife with her, she went to the kitchen table and sat down. The sight of her ravaged body had given her encouragement, and she knew that there was nothing for it but to sit and wait.

Eight o'clock came and went. Nine o'clock. Ten o'clock.

It was almost midnight when Esther was shaken from her drowsiness by the sound of footsteps coming up the stairs. They were heavy but unsteady, and she knew what that meant: he had been drinking again. One look at him as he lurched into the kitchen confirmed that: his eyes were unfocused and the moment he appeared the stench of alcohol filled the room. His bandaged arm hung limply in a sling that was greying and stained. He looked at her contemptuously.

'What are you doing still up?' he asked.

'Waiting for you,' Esther mumbled.

'What?'

'Waiting for you,' she repeated, louder this time.

'Yeah, well, sorry, love – I'm not in the mood.' Michael barked an ugly laugh at his own joke.

Esther took a deep, tremulous breath. 'I want you to leave,' she whispered.

Michael appeared not to hear her. He stumbled to the other side of the kitchen, where there was a half-empty bottle of Scotch on the side. Clumsily he poured himself a glass.

'I want you to leave,' Esther repeated more forcefully.

'Yeah, I heard you the first time.'

'So?' she asked breathlessly.

He turned round, put his glass to his lips and downed the lot, his eyes staring at her over the rim of the glass. 'So, don't be so fucking stupid.'

Esther felt her cheeks redden. 'I mean it, Michael. I've had enough.' Her fingers crept towards the kitchen knife and she wrapped them round the handle. Michael caught sight of her movements, but they seemed to do nothing but increase his contempt for her.

'What are you going to do?' he asked with a sneer. 'Stab me?' He walked right past her towards the other side of the room.

Esther stood up, still holding the knife. But, quicker than she would have expected of him in his drunkenness, Michael grabbed the broom that was leaning against the wall. Swinging it round, he pressed the rough, bristly end against her neck and pushed. She dropped the knife in surprise; then she staggered back as he used the broom to force her against the sink, knocking her chair over behind her. There was a wildness in his eyes now, a madness that he had hinted at before but which Esther had never seen quite so explicit. He suddenly dropped the broom and bent down to pick the knife up off the floor with his free hand.

In an instant he was upon her. The knife tip

pressed gently into the warm flesh of her neck, like a finger pressing lightly on jelly.

'You stupid, stupid cow,' he growled. 'You think just because I'm laid up you can try a trick like that on me? Do you think I'm an idiot?'

Esther just stared at him with terrified eyes.

'*Do you think I'm an idiot*?' he repeated.

'No, Michael,' she choked. 'I didn't mean it. Please don't cut me. I'm sorry.'

'Sorry?' he snorted. 'You fucking will be sorry.'

Esther whimpered, but it had no effect on Michael.

'I'm telling you,' he said, 'try any shit like that again and I swear to God, I'll cut your filthy fucking throat.'

And Esther had no doubt whatsoever in her terrified mind that he meant it.

They had spent the day together, mother and daughter, walking the chilly streets. Long silences passed between them, but they didn't matter; in a way, those silences were as necessary as the conversation. A glue. Something to bind them together. When they did speak, it was of unimportant things. Neither of them mentioned the way Sadie had broken down in the café, and for that she was very grateful. Such emotions were not something she felt comfortable displaying in front of anyone. Even Alicia. Especially Alicia. She had been vulnerable once before; she didn't want to be so again.

The two women ate lunch in a restaurant; Alicia tried to pay, but Sadie wouldn't have it. And then they walked some more. Occasionally, she felt her arm brush against her daughter's as they strolled side by side; when that happened, she instinctively shrank from her, afraid of what would happen if they got too close. As the afternoon wore on, however, and evening fell, she found she did not want the day to end.

'Would you like to come back to my flat?' she asked Alicia hoarsely.

Her daughter gave her a weak smile. 'I'd like that,' she said.

The taxi struggled through the central London traffic. By chance, their route took them through Soho, past one of Sadie's shops. It had not been her first, but in a way it was the one of which she was most proud, situated as it was a stone's throw from where the teenage Sadie had had her violent encounter with the pimp all those years ago. She had done well, she congratulated herself; she had brought some sort of respectability to an industry that fed on more vulnerable and weak women than it should. What did Sadie care if people chose to judge her harshly for that? What did they know?

And as these thoughts passed through her head, she looked at Alicia. She had never asked Sadie about her business, but she surely knew what it was. Not once had she expressed disapproval. Not once had she wanted to ask difficult questions. She just seemed to take her as she was.

When they arrived at the flat, the concierge gave Sadie a curious look and she knew what it meant – visitors were rare, and likely to raise eyebrows. She ignored him and ushered Alicia upstairs. The younger woman's expression said it all as she walked into the expensive apartment, drinking in the lavish modern décor and the comfortable surroundings. Sadie led her straight through into the sitting room.

'Sit down,' she said. It was more of a command than an offer.

Alicia did as she was told, and Sadie felt a little lurch in her stomach. She knew, suddenly, what she wanted to do; but now the moment was upon her, it seemed impossibly difficult. She turned and looked out of the window; her mouth felt dry, and her voice cracked as she spoke.

'You deserve an explanation,' she said quietly.

Alicia didn't reply.

Sadie took a deep breath. 'Only one person knows what I'm about to tell you,' she whispered, 'and I don't even know if he's still alive. Frankly, I hope he isn't.' She turned to look at Alicia, who stared back at her with wide, rapt eyes; she almost looked scared by what she was about to hear. 'Your father raped me.' Sadie said the words quickly, hoping that it would make it easier, but it didn't. 'I was thirteen; he was thirty, or thereabouts.' She fell silent.

The look on Alicia's face was heartbreaking to see: such shock. She shook her head imperceptibly, as though refusing to believe what she was hearing, as though she couldn't bear to hear any more. But now that Sadie had started, she found she could not stop. For years this had been inside her; now the cork had been released, and the truth about her past exploded from her like a bottle of poisonous champagne. She told Alicia about everything: the rape, the birth. 'The medics, the social workers – everyone said you could never survive. You were too premature. And . . .' Her voice petered out.

'And what?' Alicia asked.

'Nothing. It doesn't matter.'

'You hoped I was dead, didn't you?'

Sadie looked her daughter full in the eyes. 'Yes. I hoped you were dead.'

The admission hung in the air for a while before Sadie continued to speak. In short, staccato bursts she told of Jackie's descent into alcohol abuse. Holding back tears, she recounted the day that Alicia's grandmother was found floating in the water, her blood stuffed full of booze and amphetamines.

'Did she commit suicide?' Alicia asked in a shaky voice.

Sadie shrugged. 'Who knows? Perhaps. More likely, I think, she was drunk and fell.' She looked to the floor. 'She was always drunk, after . . .' She couldn't bring herself to say the words. 'After your father left.'

'What did you do?'

'I ran away. I lived on the streets.' Sadie did not

mention the foster family, or the encounter with the pimp; but she told her daughter all about Lionel. 'That's where all this came from,' she looked around her. 'If it wasn't for him, chances are I'd be that guy sitting on the corner of your street begging for money – if I was still alive, that is.'

When Sadie had finished talking, she walked out of the room. Alicia would need time to take in everything she had heard, and Sadie herself wanted to be alone, so she went into the bathroom and stared for several minutes in the mirror. Half of her knew what Alicia's question would be when she returned to the sitting room, and she wasn't sure she had the heart or the inclination to answer it. She couldn't stay in the bathroom for ever, though, so when she had composed herself she walked back.

Alicia had her back to her, and was looking out of the window. For a moment it took Sadie's breath away – it was like looking at herself, as though she had stepped out of her own body for a moment and could see how she appeared to other people.

'I want to know his name.'

Sadie's stomach lurched – that was the question she didn't want to answer. 'It doesn't matter, Alicia.'

'I want to know his name.'

'Forget it. I'm not going to tell you. It's not going to happen.'

As she spoke, however, Alicia turned round, and the uncanny feeling that Sadie had of watching herself multiplied tenfold. Her eyes were like granite, and her features were set in a look of such stony determination that Sadie was momentarily taken aback. 'If you don't tell me,' she said slowly, deliberately, 'I'll find out somehow. You know that, don't you?'

The two women stared at each other.

'If I tell you,' Sadie said, 'I want you to promise me that you'll never go looking for him.'

Alicia hesitated.

'I meant it, Alicia.'

'OK. I promise.'

Sadie nodded her head slowly. 'All right then. His name—' She felt her face contort into an expression of the deepest loathing, and she realized that she did not even want to speak his name. Instead, she took a pen and a piece of paper from the side, and in shaky, indistinct handwriting wrote the name: 'Allen Campbell.' She handed the paper to Alicia, who drew a heavy breath, nodded and turned back to look out of the window.

'You need to know one more thing,' Sadie said firmly.

'What?'

'I don't care if he's your father. And I don't care about all this. I didn't always have money, and I wouldn't miss it if it went. But if I ever see that man again, I promise you, I will kill him. And nothing you, or anyone else, can do will stop me.'

CHAPTER 19

It was the small hours of the morning, but often those were the busiest and the A&E department of the Manchester Royal Infirmary was crowded. There were a few worried-looking mothers holding listless, tired children, but they were in the minority. The pubs had long since chucked out, and the hard seats were largely filled with drunken men suffering a colourful array of injuries. Some of them had cuts on their faces; some had wounds to their arms or legs. A few shouted intermittently at the harassed-looking hospital staff; others were just asleep. All of them looked as if they had been involved in vicious, drunken fights.

One man, however, was neither shouting loudly nor snoozing. He was in his early fifties, paunchy with closely cropped, balding hair. He had walked in a couple of hours ago, his face bruised and a deep gash on his forehead, doing his best to stem the blood flowing from it with a handkerchief. It was fast becoming saturated, however, and soon he would need something else.

The man had given his name and address to the

woman on duty at the reception desk; she barely glanced up at him as she asked what the matter was.

'I've got a bit of a tummy ache,' the man growled, causing the receptionist to look up at him and his bleeding face. The sight of so much blood didn't seem to worry her – clearly she was well used to people arriving in that state – and she tapped something into her computer with a bored look on her face.

'How did you receive your injury?'

The man paused. 'I tripped up over my shoelaces.' The words were flippant, but the way he said them was not; either way, they had no effect on the receptionist.

'A doctor will call you when they're ready.' And with a curt nod the man took one of the few seats remaining.

The bleeding had stopped now, which meant that the man had both hands free, so he stood up and went to a pile of magazines sitting on a table by the wall. He grabbed the first one that came to hand, and then went back to his seat; but he didn't look at the magazine for a while. A young girl – maybe twelve, maybe older, it was so difficult to tell these days – had approached the vending machine at one end of the A&E waiting room. The man watched impassively as she put a pound coin into the slot and then spent a good minute making her selection. Eventually she chose a packet of crisps, which she released from the machine before taking her change and walking back towards where everyone else was sitting, and allowing the man to get a proper look at her. She had long hair – he liked that – and slim hips. His head followed her as she walked past, and he smiled to himself as she went out of sight. Half of him wanted to get up and follow her, but of course he didn't. It was a hospital. There were too many people around. He touched his fingers to his forehead to check that the bleeding had not started again; then he turned his attention to the magazine in his hand.

The picture on the front made him stop and blink, and he felt a sudden surge of excitement as he looked at it. Immediately he fumbled with the magazine, opening it to find the cover story. He found himself almost holding his breath as he read the headline: 'AN AUDIENCE WITH THE QUEEN OF SLEAZE'. Unable to resist, he read on.

> Her clothes are from Prada; her fingernails are perfectly manicured; as we shake hands there is a gentle waft of expensive perfume. The woman in front of me could be a Hollywood actress or a tough, millionaire banker. But she isn't. In fact, nothing could be further from the truth. As I am ushered in, my first thought is that the archetypal image of the sex-shop owner has come a long way.
>
> Sadie Scott is the darling of the sex

industry, and if there's one thing she has made perfectly clear in the moments since I have arrived in her sumptuous London apartment, it's that she doesn't want me to be here. Famously shy of publicity, she seems unwilling to talk about the seamier side of her business empire. Miss Scott has an estimated personal fortune of £10 million, a fortune she has built up from scratch by lifting the grubby sex shop – once the domain of seedy men in large overcoats – out of the gutter and into the high street. Business has boomed, and now she has extended her operations to include a high-class escort agency. A posh phrase for the oldest profession.

I suggest to her that most escort agencies are just a front for prostitution, and immediately her hackles are up. Certainly it would do her standing in the business community no good at all if it were believed that this is what her new venture amounts to. But one thing is sure. If the comfort in which Sadie Scott lives reveals anything, it is this: sex, most undoubtedly, sells. And this is why Miss Scott is in a position to make such substantial charitable donations. But at what cost?

As he read, a thick drop of blood splashed on to the page. It fell on to the bare neck of the woman in the picture that accompanied the article, and soaked slowly into the glossy paper. The man touched his forehead with his fingers once more and they became smeared with red wetness. But the wound on his face was suddenly the last thing he was thinking about. Over at the vending machine, the young girl, clearly bored, had returned to see what else she could afford with the change in her hand; but even that failed to hold his attention. Instead, his eyes darted over the next few pages of the article, and he skim-read the text, which was becoming stained with the marks of his bloodied fingertips. It was the pictures, however, not the words that filled him with a grisly fascination. They were taken in moody, grainy black and white, and in each one the same face stared out of the page at him.

It was her. There was no doubt about it. It was her.

She was older, of course, but there was no mistaking the almond eyes and the lustrous hair. She looked just like her old self; and she looked very like her mother, too, he noted impassively. And just as there was no mistaking the eyes and the hair, so there was no mistaking the insolent look that did not seem to have been softened by adulthood. If anything, it had developed into something more threatening. But whereas most people, he knew, would see the hard business-woman, this man just saw the little girl. And he had seen that look enough times, after all, for it not to have an effect on him.

The man became aware that his lips had curled into a sneer. 'Sadie Burrows,' he whispered to himself. 'Sadie Burrows. Who'd have fucking thought it?'

Suddenly his eyes stung as the newly flowing blood dripped into them. He used one hand to wipe the blood away, but with the other he firmly gripped the magazine. There was no way he was going to let it go – it filled him with too much of a desperate thrill. But the blood was flowing heavily now, and he knew he needed to see a doctor.

It was then, just in time, that his name was called. He didn't hear it at first above the hubbub of the other people talking and his own racing thoughts, and the Indian doctor standing a few metres away had to repeat himself.

'Allen Campbell,' he called. 'Is there an Allen Campbell waiting here?'

Allen rolled the magazine up and stuck it under his arm; then he stood up and walked towards the doctor, his face expressionless and devoid of all the feelings that had just been fired up inside him.

Sadie had said she would kill him, and at the time Alicia had felt goosebumps on her skin. But people often say that, she persuaded herself. They said it all the time. It was a turn of phrase – they didn't necessarily mean it.

Did they?

It was a week since they had spent the day

together, and the young woman had still not quite recovered from the shattering news about her parentage. She had promised herself over and over, when she first embarked upon this, that whatever happened her dad – her adoptive father – would still be her dad. But now she knew the truth, she felt split in two. Half of her was filled with hot revulsion, not only for the man who had done such things to her mother but also for herself as the product of all that; and yet the other half was curious. Curious to know if he was still alive; curious to know what he looked like. Even if she found out more about the man, she didn't have to make herself known to him; she didn't have to meet him; she wouldn't really be going back on her word to Sadie.

Would she?

As the days passed, she began to persuade herself that she would not be doing anything wrong if she just satisfied her curiosity. Who could it possibly hurt? He wouldn't know anything about it; Sadie wouldn't know anything about it. It would be Alicia's secret. After all, surely she deserved to know a bit more about her birth father? It was her right.

Wasn't it?

She knew his name. She knew he was in his fifties. She knew where he had lived for a short time many years ago. And she knew he was a paedophile. Alicia was a bright girl, but even she knew that this wasn't much to go on. She soon established that the sex offenders register was no good: ordinary people like her had no access to it, it only listed those who had offended in the last ten years and who was to say that he had a conviction anyway? The electoral roll listed fourteen Allen Campbells. She made a list of their addresses, and then found herself at a dead end. It could be any, or none, of them – she had no way of knowing. Short of stalking each of them, there was little more she could do. She was going to have to think hard.

It took her two days to come up with a plan.

The first thing she needed was a P.O. box. That was easily done. Next she needed headed notepaper. She would not use her own name, of course, so instead she came up with a pseudonym: Alice Kaye Associates – Private and Corporate Investigators. That was how such people seemed to refer to themselves, her research told her, and as she designed her letterhead with the P.O. box address and her own mobile number, she felt quietly satisfied with the result. She had fifty copies professionally printed at the shop round the corner. There would be no need for more than that.

The difficult bit would be writing the letter. It had to sound confident, authoritative enough for nobody to suspect it was a scam, but also intriguing and irresistible. It needed to appeal to someone's greed. Alicia spent a long time drafting it, and when it was ready, she printed out fourteen copies.

Dear Mr Campbell

We have been engaged by a firm of solicitors to locate a Mr A. Campbell in relation to the matter of an outstanding bequest for a will they are administering. We have been informed of the last known address of the correct Mr Campbell, and would be grateful if you could fill in the attached form with your address(es) during the years 1990–91. Please also fill in your date of birth. We will be in touch if you appear to be the person we have been instructed to locate.

Yours sincerely
Alice Kaye

Would it fool everyone? Would it fool anyone? Maybe, maybe not – Alicia just didn't know. But there was only one way to find out. Nervously, she posted the letters.

There was no point in checking her P.O. box the following day, but the day after that she was queuing up when the sorting office opened. She was disappointed to find nothing there. The next day was the same, and she began to fret that her letter had been too transparent. No one was going to fall for it, surely.

But on the fourth day, there were three envelopes waiting for her.

Alicia hurried home with them. She locked herself in her bedroom and then carefully opened each letter. The forms had been carefully filled in, and none of them matched the address of the house Sadie had taken her daughter to weeks before. Indeed, none of them was even a London address, and in any case the date of birth of the respondents indicated that they were unlikely to be the man she was trying to find. She crossed them off her list. During the course of the day she received a couple of phone calls from Allen Campbells, all scrupulously polite and wanting to check that this wasn't some trick. Alicia spoke boldly and brightly to them, and they seemed satisfied that she was for real. Impatiently she waited for the next day's post.

There were another five letters when she returned to the post office, and three the following day. A couple of them gave the right age, but none gave the correct address, so Alicia crossed them off her list. And as each letter arrived, she wrote back, informing the respondent that they were not the person in question and thanking them for their time.

Only three replies were now outstanding. A day passed without any more mail; two days; a week. Alicia began to despair of narrowing down her hunt any further, but then, ten days after the arrival of the last letter, two more arrived. Alicia opened them with trepidation; a thin smile spread across her face when she realized that neither of the respondents was the man she was looking for. She crossed them off her list and looked triumphantly at the one remaining address: Allen Campbell, Flat 33A, Stockton Road, George Bernard Shaw Estate, Manchester.

That was him. It had to be. That was Alicia's father. All she needed was a letter to confirm it.

But that letter never came. Alicia's satisfaction at eliminating all the others on her list soon turned to anxiety. What if she'd made a mistake? What if this wasn't the right man? And even if he was, what was she going to do with the information now she had it?

These questions began to preoccupy her as she did her best to keep the rest of her life normal. Her adoptive father clearly noticed a change in her – she could tell by his concerned glances and the way he kept asking her if she was all right. Alicia would smile back at him, doing her best to put his mind at rest. But how could she tell him what was wrong? How could she tell him what she was up to? It would truly devastate him. Alicia found, though, that she could think of nothing else. It was like a worm, eating away inside her: she hated her father, but somehow she just had to set eyes on him. She consulted a map to see where the address she had was; she even went so far as to check out the train times to Manchester. But at the last minute, something always held her back.

That something was a promise she had made.

Since the night Sadie had told her daughter everything, Alicia had seen her infrequently. Whenever they met, the older woman never seemed to be able to regain the same level of intimacy they had achieved that day; and although she was never actively dismissive of Alicia, she could tell that there were times when her mother found her presence trying. It would come, she told herself. She just had to be patient.

It was while she was waiting for the one letter that Alicia received an invitation from Sadie to come for coffee in her office. This, she thought, was a breakthrough – her mother had never yet suggested meeting in the company of anybody else she knew, and presumably there would be other people there. Sure enough, when she arrived at eleven o'clock on the appointed day, there were two other women in the office: a formidable but friendly enough PA who introduced herself as Suzy, and a timid woman not much older than Alicia who said her name was Esther but didn't say much else. Both of them looked at her somewhat quizzically – clearly they had no idea who she was – and Alicia noticed the way Suzy's eyebrow shot up when Sadie ushered her into her room without introducing her properly to the girls. She sat down on the comfortable sofa while Sadie silently poured her a cup of fresh coffee from the machine by her desk.

'They don't know who I am, do they?' Alicia asked.

'Of course not,' her mother replied, rather harshly to Alicia's ears. 'Don't take this the wrong way, Alicia, but it's not something I want to be shouting from the rooftops, is it?' She looked over at her daughter. 'And it's not something you want to be common knowledge, trust me. You'll have the papers camped outside your house for days. Try explaining that one to your mates.'

Alicia kept quiet. Suddenly Sadie seemed to become a little nervous. 'I've got something to ask you, actually.' She walked over to the window and looked out over the skyline. 'You've, er . . . You told me you've finished school, right?'

Alicia nodded. She had left at sixteen, feeling no compulsion to return to the place where she always felt like an outsider.

'So what are your plans?'

The younger woman smiled. 'What is this, Sadie?' she teased. 'A mother–daughter chat?'

A flicker of annoyance crossed Sadie's face. 'No,' she said sharply. 'Actually it's a job interview.'

Alicia blinked.

'If you want it, that is. You can come and work here. For me.'

'I don't know, Sadie. Don't take this the wrong way, but it's not really the sort of career I've ever thought about. I'll have to think about it.'

'Of course you'll have to think about it, and more carefully than you might imagine.'

Alicia didn't understand what she was saying, and her expression made that clear.

'Look, Alicia, I'm not going to pull the wool over your eyes. It's a dangerous trade, and where some industries can count on the support of the police, I can't. I have my own security, and sometimes I have to' – she hunted for the words – 'look after things by myself. You're going to have to be comfortable with that, because you won't be able to pretend it's not happening.'

'Pretend what's not happening? I don't understand what you're saying.'

Sadie seemed to size her daughter up, as though judging whether or not she could trust her to hear what she had to say. Clearly she decided that she could because, leaning back on her chair, she started to speak. 'I run an escort agency. You know that, right?'

Alicia nodded.

'Got a problem with it?'

'Not really.'

'Good. A couple of weeks ago one of my girls got beaten up by a client. What do you think I should have done?'

'Gone to the police,' Alicia said firmly, without even needing to think about it.

'Well, welcome to the real world. The police couldn't care less about a hooker being roughed up.'

'I didn't think she was a hooker.'

'She's not – unless that's the way she wants the evening to go. But the police don't believe that.'

'So what did you do?' Alicia didn't like the way

this conversation was going, and she wasn't sure she wanted to hear the answer to her question.

Sadie shrugged. 'As I say, I have security. Not for me, but for my girls and my staff. I won't tolerate stuff like that going on, Alicia. Why are you looking at me like that?'

Alicia was shaking her head dubiously. 'I don't know, Sadie. You can't just take things into your own hands like that. What would happen if everyone went about everything in the same way?'

'Don't be so naïve, Alicia,' Sadie retorted angrily. 'If you knew half the things that went on—'

'I'm not being naïve,' Alicia said, riled. But as she spoke, Sadie was already buzzing through to her PA.

'Suzy,' she ordered. 'Bring me the pictures of Mandy, would you?'

There was a long silence between the two women while they waited for Suzy to come in. Finally she did, wordlessly placing a file on the table before leaving. Sadie picked it up, and then walked over to where Alicia was sitting and dropped it on her lap. 'Look at those,' she said shortly.

Her brow furrowed, Alicia opened the file. Inside were three A4 pictures. The first was a close-up of a woman's face. It was a pretty face, you could tell; but it was damaged. Her lower lip was split, and there was still a trace of congealed blood about her mouth. One of her eyes was bruised; the other had a scar along the side where an angry slash had been patched up with adhesive medical tape. The second picture showed her neck, horribly bruised, and the third was a full-frontal. She was wearing an evening dress, but it had been ripped along one side, and her arm was in a sling. Alicia felt herself shudder.

'What happened to her?' she asked.

'A man called Andrew Lyons happened to her.'

'And what happened to him.'

Sadie gave her a flat look. 'Let's just say he won't be doing it again.'

Alicia thought about that for a moment. 'I'm sorry,' she said finally, 'but that doesn't—'

As she spoke, her mobile phone rang. She looked apologetically at Sadie before answering. 'Hello?'

At first there was no answer; thinking it must be a crank call or a wrong number, she prepared to hang up. But before she did so, there was a voice.

'Alice Kaye?'

Alicia's heart stopped, and she felt a chill in her veins. 'One minute,' she stuttered. She excused herself from the room with a glance at Sadie, and ran out of the building on to the street. 'Who is this?' she asked.

Again that pause, before the low northern accent spoke again. 'I think you know perfectly well who this is.'

Alicia felt sick. What could she say? Words tumbled from her mouth. 'I don't know . . . I mean, I don't know what you mean . . . Who is this?'

'Alice Kaye Associates – Private and Corporate Investigators,' the voice said as though reading from a sheet of paper. 'Doesn't exist, does it? I checked. Not too difficult. You must think I'm stupid.'

'I don't think you're stupid,' Alicia said a bit too quickly. 'I'm Alice Kaye, and I'm sorry if—'

But the voice interrupted her. 'Serious business, this, pet. I'm sure the police would love to hear of it.'

Alicia responded with a guilty silence.

'I think you're something to do with Sadie Burrows,' the voice continued. 'Why else would you ask me where I was living back in the day? What's that fucking tramp up to now?'

Alicia felt her cheeks flush as her little game was suddenly exposed. What could she do? What could she say? Panic overwhelmed her, and before she knew what was happening, she had flicked her phone closed. Her skin went hot and cold, and she felt nauseous. There was no way she could go back into Sadie's office – not in this state, not with the knowledge of what had just happened. And so, ignoring the fact that her coat was still inside, she ran as fast as she could. Within an hour she was in her bedroom, head in her hands, her body shaking and her mind doing somersaults.

What could she do? What the hell could she do?

Alicia barely slept that night: she kept expecting the phone to ring and for that implacable, monotonic voice to start asking her questions she didn't want to answer. More than that, however, she was scared that he would get in touch with Sadie to tell her everything that Alicia had been doing. What her reaction would be Alicia could only guess – but it wouldn't be good. Jesus, it wouldn't be good. Would Sadie want to see her again? Probably not, and who could blame her?

In the small hours of the night, that one thought haunted her more than any other.

As the sun rose, Alicia felt as if her head was stuffed with straw. She got dressed, and went into the kitchen to find her adoptive father already there.

'You're up early, love,' he noted.

'Couldn't sleep,' Alicia murmured as she put the kettle on for some tea.

'Me neither.' He sat down, and Alicia could feel his eyes on her. 'Something's wrong, isn't it, love?'

She didn't answer, unable to trust her voice to sound convincing.

'It's all right, Ali,' he said gently. 'You don't have to tell me. Just remember I'm always here to listen if you want to talk, that's all.'

Alicia turned round and smiled gratefully at her dad, suddenly suffused with a feeling of unbounded love for this man. Ignoring the fact that the kettle had just boiled, she went and sat next to him, taking his hand in hers. 'Thank you, Dad,' she said, smiling at him.

A silence fell between them, and Alicia started

to bite her lower lip. She felt out of her depth – a child in an adult's world. 'If you've done something wrong, Dad,' she said finally, 'you should do whatever you can to make it right, shouldn't you?'

His face became shadowed with worry. 'What have you done, Ali?'

For a moment, Alicia considered telling him everything; but she knew how much it would upset him. In that instant, however, she realized what she had to do. She stood up suddenly. 'I've done something I need to put right. I have to go out, Dad. I'll be back later.' She pulled on a jumper, and was out of the house in seconds.

It was still early, but the tube station was busy nevertheless as she bought a ticket to Euston station. Once she was there, her eyes widened slightly as she was told the price of a fare to Manchester; it would be cheaper, she was told, if she waited a couple of hours, but she didn't want to do that. What needed to be done had to be done quickly, so she paid the money and found herself a seat on the train. It seemed to take an age to leave, and Alicia found herself silently urging the driver on; when the train juddered into motion, however, her stomach lurched. There was no going back now.

She stared out of the window as the suburban scenes melted away and were replaced by fields and satellite towns. As she gazed, sleep overcame her and with a start she awoke to find the train sitting at Manchester Piccadilly. Ignoring the crick in her neck, she shot up and ran off the train just in time – as she hit the platform she heard all the doors slamming and the blowing of a whistle. Crowds swarmed around her, and she became a little light-headed as she looked around for a taxi rank. She found it soon enough, though, and as she climbed into one of the waiting vehicles she recited the address that was embedded in her mind: 'Stockton Road, George Bernard Shaw Estate.'

The cab driver gave her a look. 'You sure, petal?' he said in a dubious tone of voice. 'That's a pretty rough part of town – you shouldn't go wandering round there by yourself.'

Alicia was taken aback, but she tried not to let it show. 'I'm sure,' she replied.

The cab driver shrugged and started the engine.

The mid-morning traffic was heavy, and it took a while to struggle through to the outskirts of the city; the nearer they got, however, the more anxious Alicia felt and the more she started to doubt the wisdom of what she was doing. Something drove her on, though – something that not even the grim, grey wasteland of the council estate she now found herself in could dispel.

Stockton Road was not so much a street as a collection of towering council blocks. As the cabbie approached it, he flicked a switch that automatically locked all the doors of the car. He pulled up behind another vehicle which was rusting, with smashed windows and missing wheels. The man seemed anxious to get away, so Alicia paid him a twenty and then let herself out; the cab moved on even before she had shut her door.

Alicia looked around to get her bearings. There weren't many people, but those that there were looked at her unfamiliar face with suspicion – including a gang of boys, all hooded, who wolf whistled as she passed. 'Any chance of a blow job, pet?' one of them called. Alicia hurried on, her jaw set, and she approached a board showing a plan of the estate. It was worn and graffitied, but she could just about work out where she needed to go.

Flat 33A was four storeys up one of the tower blocks. The lift was out of order, so Alicia walked up the concrete stairwell, her footsteps echoing as she went. When she found the door she was looking for, she took a deep breath.

Did she really want to do this?

Was it the right thing?

She paused, and knocked.

At first there was no reply, so she knocked again. From inside there was the sound of movement; then the door opened.

The man who answered had clearly just woken up. His face was pasty and bore the remnants of a nasty cut on the forehead. His hair was cropped, and he was paunchy – a fact that was highlighted by his clothes, a pair of pleated trousers and a vest. A musty odour wafted out of the flat as the door opened, and Alicia found herself breathing through her mouth so that she didn't have to smell it. The man eyed her slowly up and down, his eyes lingering on her breasts and thighs. Her flesh tingled with revulsion.

'Allen Campbell?' she asked in an attempt to get his attention.

The man nodded slowly. 'And who the fuck are you?'

Alicia felt her tongue stick in her throat. She had come here to tell him the truth, but now that she saw him in front of her, she found she wanted to keep the truth to herself. 'Alice Kaye,' she said, unconvincingly.

A smile flickered across Allen's face, and Alicia shuddered at the sight. He stepped to one side. 'You'd better come in, then, Alice Kaye,' he said.

Alicia stepped inside. She couldn't be sure, but she thought, as the door closed firmly behind her, that she heard it being locked too. She spun round. 'Unlock the door,' she ordered, silently cursing her voice for wavering as she spoke.

One of Allen's eyebrows shot up.

'I said, unlock it.'

Allen inclined his head; with an arrogant smile, he turned the key in the door. 'Go on through, pet,' he told Alicia, indicating the room at the end of the corridor. 'Make yourself at home.'

Alicia walked into what was clearly Allen's sitting room. The thin curtains were drawn, and none of the lights was on. Suddenly he was behind her, too close. She stepped forward as he flicked a switch and a solitary light bulb hanging from the ceiling illuminated the room.

She looked around it in distaste.

The furniture was old and tatty; an antique computer was set up in one corner, but it did not seem to be on. Opposite the sofa was a large, bulky television with a VHS player and a DVD player attached to it. Open video cases surrounded the machines, but Alicia could not make out what they were.

'Like I say,' Allen said from behind her, 'make yourself at home. Miss *Kaye*.'

Alicia took a seat, and something caught her eye. On the wall, by the television, were some photographs. Black and white. Grainy. Cut out from a magazine. Alicia recognized the woman in the photograph instantly, of course. It was Sadie. She couldn't stop her mouth from opening in surprise as she saw the pictures, and Allen clearly noticed.

'I thought so,' he said quietly. 'That stupid cow is a friend of yours, is she?'

His words caused a sudden surge of anger to rush through her. 'That stupid cow,' she said, doing her best to keep her voice level, 'is my mother.' Alicia stood up. 'And she's told me all about you.'

Allen barked a short, ugly laugh. 'Sadie Burrows was a lying bitch from the moment I first set eyes on her. Do yourself a favour and don't believe a word she said.'

'I'll be the one who chooses what I want to

believe,' Alicia replied, but Allen didn't seem to listen to her. Instead, he looked at her closely, as though seeing her for the first time.

'Who the fuck are you,' he repeated, 'and what do you want? What was all that shit with the letters?'

'That shit with all the letters was just a way of finding you.' She looked back at the pictures of Sadie on the wall. 'I'm Sadie Burrows' daughter, and I wanted to know what my father looks like.'

A silence fell on the room as Allen's eyes narrowed. 'I don't believe you,' he spat. 'If you're really her daughter, seems to me that you're just as much of a lying bitch as your tramp of a mother.' There was a tension in his voice.

'You threatened me yesterday,' Alicia replied. 'You said you'd go to the police. Well, let me tell you this. You make any attempt to mention this to anyone – including my mother – and it'll be me going to the police. And I think they'll be rather more interested in what I've got to say than what you've got to say. Don't you?'

Allen just smiled. He closed the door to the sitting room and leaned back against it. Alicia's eyes flickered around nervously: there was no other way out.

'You know what,' he said with a nasty sneer. 'A few weeks ago, I might have been slightly worried' He glanced at the pictures on the wall. 'Tell me, sweetheart, why has it taken so long for you to come crawling through my door?'

‘I was adopted,’ Alicia hissed. ‘Not that it’s anything to do with you.’

‘Ah,’ Allen nodded. ‘You must have been made up when you realized your real mum had a bob or two.’

‘That wasn’t why I got in touch with her.’

‘Course it wasn’t, pet. Perish the thought, eh?’

‘*That wasn’t why I got in touch.*’ He was getting to her now, and she hated the feeling it gave her.

Allen took a couple of steps forward. ‘You must have thought about it though, eh, pet? She must be worth a mint. Wouldn’t be too much to ask, would it? Slip a few quid her daughter’s way.’

Alicia stepped forward. ‘Shut up,’ she said. ‘I don’t think you realize how much trouble you’re actually in. It only takes a DNA test, you know. Then everyone will realize what you did.’

‘What I am?’ Allen laughed again. ‘It’s all my fault, is it? Well, maybe you should learn a few home truths about Sadie Burrows. Maybe you should think about whether it wasn’t all her fault to start with.’ Suddenly he walked right up to her and grabbed her face in one hand. Alicia breathed out sharply, but something stopped her from screaming. ‘She was a minx – a fucking prick tease. And she got everything that was coming to her. If I was you, I’d sting her for as much money as you can, because she hasn’t got anything else to offer you.’

He was hurting her now. ‘If you don’t get your disgusting hands off me,’ she breathed, ‘I swear I’m going to the police to tell them all about you.’

Allen looked hard into her eyes; then he gradually let go, but there was nothing in his face to suggest repentance. 'No,' he said with a faint grin, 'I don't think you'll be doing that.' He walked back towards the door and leaned against it again. 'She's quite the star, isn't she, your mummy? I didn't realize till I read about her in a magazine. And do you know what I think? I don't think she'd like it at all, her bastard child coming out of the woodwork and announcing to the world that she's nothing more than a gymslip mum who left her baby for someone else to bring up. What do you think?'

Alicia struggled to keep her emotions from her face. It was difficult, because Allen's words were like a knife in the guts. She knew every one of them was true. She knew Sadie would never condone her going to the police – it wasn't the way she worked. The only reason she was here was to stop this man getting in touch with Sadie; to stop her mother from finding out what she had done. And now all that seemed to be collapsing around her.

'I thought not.' Allen took her silence for the acknowledgement that it was. The smile returning to his face, he slowly opened the door. 'I suppose you'll want to be leaving now.'

He was right. Alicia wanted nothing more than to be out of there. Away from this man and his seedy surroundings. Away from his lies and his insinuations. She stormed towards the door, but before she left the room she turned to look at him.

'I loathe you,' she said. 'I just want you to know that.'

Allen just looked back at her, his face unreadable.

But as she walked along the dark corridor towards the front door, he spoke once more. 'What's your real name, pet?' he asked.

She stopped and turned. 'Alicia,' she said.

'Alicia what?' He was trying to sound nonchalant, but it didn't work.

'You don't need to know,' the young woman replied quietly. 'You don't need to know, because you're never going to see me again.'

It may have been a trick of the light, but as she turned to leave she thought she saw an expression on his face that she would not have expected. A sad expression. A look, almost, of regret. She didn't pay it any attention as she slammed the door behind her and ran out into the concrete stairwell and on to the street.

Alicia didn't look back. Something told her he would be on the balcony, watching her go, and it wasn't a sight she wanted to see.

CHAPTER 20

There was no such thing as a mother's instinct.

Sadie had lost count of the number of times she had told herself that over the course of the day. If there was, her own mother would have twigged that something was wrong when Sadie most needed her help all those years ago. No, mother's instinct was a con. Make believe. If anyone knew that, Sadie did.

So why, then, had she had this sick feeling in her gut ever since Alicia had left yesterday? How was it that she knew, beyond a measure of doubt, that all was not well? The phone call Alicia had taken had surprised the girl, wrong-footed her, even scared her. At some level, Sadie had wanted to grab the phone from Alicia's hand the moment she saw the look on her face, to protect her from whoever the hell it was she was talking to. But of course she would never have done that. Of course she wouldn't.

And why, she had asked herself any number of times throughout the day, had she felt so crushed by Alicia's disapproval of her business methods?

Plenty of people had a problem with them, she knew, and she knew equally well that she was comfortable with the things she did. Comfortable with the people she dealt with. Comfortable with the justice that she dispensed. But why was it that, when she could ignore the opinion of almost everyone else in the world, she could not ignore the opinion of this slight seventeen-year-old girl. There had been something touching about her innocence, something disarming. It had made Sadie hanker after a time long past.

Rain was falling heavily as she arrived home that evening. The black cab stopped right outside her block of flats, and she had a large umbrella to protect herself from the downpour. 'Nasty weather, Miss Scott,' the concierge observed as she clattered into the foyer area; Sadie just nodded her agreement without really looking at him. Inside the flat, she turned on the hot water tap of the bath and then went into her bedroom to peel off her work clothes. There were no mirrors in her room – she couldn't bear to look at her naked body any more than she had to – and she quickly pulled on a thick towelling dressing gown and hung her business suit up in the ample cupboard. Just then, she heard the familiar buzz of the intercom. Cursing under her breath, she walked out into the corridor to answer it.

'I'm sorry, Miss Scott.' It was the concierge, and he was gabbling. 'She just walked straight past me. She's on her way up now.'

'Who?' Sadie asked. But as she spoke, there was a knock at her door. 'Never mind,' she said, replacing the receiver. She walked to the door and looked through the spyhole; somehow she was not surprised to see Alicia standing there.

Sadie opened the door. Her daughter was soaking wet: her sodden hair was splayed over her face and her drenched clothes were dripping – they had created a substantial puddle on the marble floor tiles even in the short amount of time she had been standing there. Sadie looked her up and down, noting the redness around her eyes that indicated she had been crying, and the look of desperate panic in her face. She stood to one side and ushered the girl into the flat.

'The bath's running,' she said. 'You'd better get in.'

Alicia shook her head, but her teeth chattered as she did so – whether because she was cold or for some other reason, Sadie couldn't tell.

'For God's sake, Alicia,' Sadie said impatiently. 'Just get in the bath. I'll find you some clothes.'

Fifteen minutes later, her daughter was transformed. Wearing a pair of jeans and a pale pink cashmere jumper that fitted her surprisingly well, she walked into the sitting room, where Sadie was waiting for her; but no amount of hot water or expensive clothing could hide the aura of trepidation that she emitted as she stood awkwardly in the doorway.

'What's happened?' Sadie asked plainly.

Alicia took a deep shuddering breath. 'I'm sorry,' she stuttered through a sudden burst of tears. She clearly could not look directly at her mother.

'What?' Sadie asked. A cold dread had suddenly crept over her skin, like an awful suit of paranoia.

'I was never going to try to find him.' She took an earnest step forward. 'I promise, Sadie, it was never going to get that far. I just wanted to know where he was. But he turned it all round. He turned it all on its head.'

With crystal clarity, Sadie knew without doubt who she was talking about. 'Jesus, Alicia,' she whispered. 'What the hell have you done?'

Huge, heaving sobs overcame Alicia's body at the sound of her mother's unforgiving voice. At first she seemed unable to speak, but eventually the words came, tripping over themselves as she explained in desperation everything that she had done – the letters, Allen's threat to go to the police, her trip to Manchester to try to head that off. As the whole sorry tale unfolded, Sadie felt every muscle in her body become increasingly tense; and as her words dissolved into nothingness, Alicia stood before her, a frightened and exhausted child.

Whether it was anger or fear that led to what happened next, Sadie couldn't have said. She started pacing the room, her hands shaking and a hotness in her blood that she could not restrain. As she passed the coffee table, she grabbed the first thing that came to hand, the silver-framed picture of her parents, and in the grip of some kind of fury, she hurled it against the window. The pane cracked, and the glass of the photo frame shattered on to the carpet. Shocked by her action, Sadie simply stared at the debris of her outburst; the only sound in the room was that of her staggered, irregular breathing.

'How dare you tell him you'd go to the police?' she demanded.

'I'm sorry,' Alicia begged. 'Truly sorry. I just wanted to stop him from touching me.'

'How dare you? Don't you think that if I'd wanted this thing public, I'd have gone to the police years ago? Don't you have any idea what he did to me? Don't you understand?'

'Sadie,' Alicia started to say. 'Trust me . . .' But at one look from the older woman, her speech melted into silence.

'Trust you? How can I possibly trust you? The one thing I asked you not to do. The *one* thing!'

'I –'

'Shut up, Alicia! Shut up, and get out.'

'But –'

'Go!' Sadie suddenly screamed. 'Take your wet clothes and just go. Don't come back. I don't want to see you again!'

Alicia stared at her mother in horror. 'Please, Sadie,' she whispered. But the look Sadie fired back in return was intended to leave her in no doubt whatsoever that she meant what she said.

'You're not going to do anything stupid, are you?' Alicia managed one final question.

'*Get out!*' Sadie shouted.

Unable to stop a series of juddering sobs escaping from her lips, Alicia turned and left the room. Sadie stood there without moving as she heard her going into the bathroom to collect her clothes; and as the front door slammed she remained still.

How long she stood there she couldn't have said. She felt paralysed, sick. Slowly she turned her head to look down at the shattered photo frame on the floor; then she bent down to pick it up. But her hands were still shaking, and as she reached for the photograph she cut the end of her finger on a treacherous shard of glass. 'Shit,' she muttered beneath her breath, but it didn't stop her from picking up the picture. The blood from her cut smeared over Jackie's body: Sadie tried to wipe it away, but that only made things worse and now her dad was bloodied too. With her good hand, she made another attempt to wipe it clean; and another. The photo was crumpled now, and her eyes were so full of tears that she could not see it properly.

With an anguished shout, she threw the thing back on the floor, and then collapsed on to the carpet. Her hands covered her face as the blood, which was still flowing, ran into the warm tears that she could not stop from coming.

Esther looked up from her desk. The door had opened and Miss Scott walked in. The very sight of her made the office assistant catch her breath.

Normally she was so immaculate – perfect make-up, stylish clothing, not a hair out of place. Today, though, as she stormed into the office under a cloud, she looked quite different. Her face was stark and unmade-up, for a start; her eyes were raw round the rims and with bruised rings around them. Her long brown hair was frizzy and knotted, and although she was wearing one of her usual business suits, it was clear that it had been slung on without her usual care. There was no acknowledgement of either Esther or Suzy, no 'good morning'. Suzy appeared to open her mouth to say something, but she clearly thought better of it, as Miss Scott simply crashed through the room and walked into her office, slamming the door behind her.

The two women exchanged a glance. Esther still felt nervous of Suzy, and wary of her; but in the past couple of weeks she had grown to like the severe PA. She was straightforward, if nothing else; you knew where you stood with her. She could be fierce, certainly; but she could be fiercely loyal too. It was not a character trait Esther was used to seeing: she respected it, and it filled her with guilt. Guilt that she knew, deep down, that she did not live up to Suzy's own high standards; guilt that she was betraying these hard-faced women she worked with.

The phone rang. Esther's arm shot out to answer it and she winced as the bruising under her arm shrieked with the sudden movement. 'Sadie

Scott's office,' she announced, with forced brightness so as to drown the discomfort she was feeling.

There was a pause, and then a man's voice. 'I want to speak to her.'

'Miss Scott is in a meeting just at the moment,' Esther recited the mantra that she must have said fifty times a day. 'May I take a message?'

Another pause. 'I didn't ask if she was in a meeting,' the voice said quietly. 'I said I wanted to speak to her.'

Esther flushed, and her eyes flickered over to Suzy, who seemed to be watching her intensely. Occasionally you got one like this, a head case. Best thing to do was to be firm with them, Suzy always said, although the nervous office assistant found it difficult to do that. 'I'm sorry, sir,' she stuttered. 'I'm afraid Miss Scott isn't available.'

There was no reply.

'Hello?'

He had hung up.

Esther smiled awkwardly at Suzy, who was still looking at her. 'Crank,' she said shortly in explanation; but almost immediately the phone rang again.

'Sadie Scott's office.'

'Put her on the phone, now.' It was the same voice.

'I'm sorry, sir,' she flustered. 'I can't. She's –'

'Don't argue with me, you stupid bitch.' His voice was trembling – he sounded almost excited. 'She was always too fucking self-important for her own good, that girl. Now put her on the line before I come down there and stick that phone down your pretty little throat.'

Esther found herself biting her lip; gradually, though, she became aware of Suzy standing next to her. 'It's OK,' the PA mouthed to her. 'Let me handle it.' She took hold of the receiver.

'This is Suzy Thomas,' she said in her most abrasive south London accent. 'I'm Miss Scott's PA. How may I help you?'

Suzy's eyes hardened and her lips thinned as she listened to whatever it was the caller had to say. 'I'm going to put you on hold,' she said finally. She bent over and pressed a button on Esther's telephone, causing a red light to flash. Then, with a serious kind of glance at the office assistant, she turned and walked straight into Miss Scott's room without knocking.

Sadie blinked as Suzy burst into the room. 'What is it?' she asked abrasively.

'There's a man on the phone. Says he knows you from way back, but won't give his name. He's already nearly made Esther cry, and he told me to fuck off about three times in thirty seconds.'

Sadie stared ahead as a horrible premonition enveloped her. 'Allen Campbell?' she asked tersely.

'He didn't give his name. Look, we can't keep taking calls like this, Sadie,' Suzy complained vigorously.

'Shut up, Suzy!' Sadie closed her eyes and bowed

her head. 'I'm sorry,' she apologized. She looked at the handset on her table with the flashing light. 'That's him?'

Suzy nodded.

'OK. Thank you. I'll take it.'

The PA turned and left.

Sadie stared at the flashing light for a full minute, a riot of emotions stirring inside her. It could be anyone at the other end of the phone, but somehow she knew exactly who it was. Suddenly she was a little girl again, waiting in her bedroom, listening to the sound of his footsteps up the stairs. Waiting for the door to open. Waiting for him to have his way.

Waiting.

Waiting.

The light blinked.

The room seemed to spin.

Slowly she stretched out her hand, picked up the receiver and pressed the button next to the flashing light.

As she put the receiver to her ear, she didn't speak; but she could hear her own breath, heavy but steady, being amplified in the mouthpiece. And she could hear his breath too, tremulous, excited. And in her mind he was on top of her, that same breath hot on her face, his foul, pallied skin sweaty.

'Hello, pet,' he said.

The voice was the same – the intervening years had done nothing to remove the quiet smugness and the sense of restrained threat. Sadie would have known that voice anywhere, anytime, and on hearing it, she felt all the strength sap from her body.

'Aren't you pleased to hear from me?' he asked once it was clear Sadie was not going to reply.

'What the hell do you think?' she whispered.

'Manners, Sadie. Wasn't your mam always telling you to mind your manners?'

Sadie tried to retort, but the words stuck in her throat.

'She's a pretty girl, your daughter,' he continued. 'Prettier than her mam was. Oh, I'm sorry – was that supposed to be a secret?'

'What do you want?' Sadie asked in a dead voice.

'"With Sadie Scott, certain questions are strictly off-limits."' It took a moment for Sadie to realize that he was reading from the magazine article. '"I ask her an innocent question about her family, and she shrinks away, like an oyster sprinkled with vinegar." Very poetic, eh? Must have been a good little performance you gave there. Or maybe you really don't want people to know too much about the things you got up to in the past.'

'What do you want?' Sadie repeated through gritted teeth. She felt she barely had the strength now to hold on to the telephone.

'I'm a bit upset with you, to be honest. I'd have thought you'd have looked me up, all things considered.'

'What things?'

'The things I taught you, pet. You do remember, don't you?'

Sadie suddenly found it almost impossible to believe what she was hearing.

'Still, you've done well for yourself, pet. Very well. I'd have thought you'd want to share your good fortune with them as helped you on your way.'

Her head continued to spin, but gradually, like a man walking slowly out of the fog, it began to dawn on Sadie what he was trying to say.

The things I taught you.

Could it really be that he thought of what he did to her in those terms?

Did he really think he'd been doing her a favour?

Was he really that sick?

'Listen to me.' From deep inside her, Sadie felt a glimmer of strength and her lip curled imperceptibly. 'I've spent the last seventeen years hoping you were dead. That silly girl has robbed me of my delusion, but don't get it into your head that I want anything to do with you. I'm putting the phone down in twenty seconds unless you stop the shit and tell me what it is you want.'

'Temper, Sadie,' he replied in a sing-song voice. 'Temper, temper! You always did fly off the handle, didn't you?' He laughed briefly at his own joke before continuing in a more serious tone of voice. 'Money,' he said shortly.

'What?' Sadie was incredulous.

'If it wasn't for me, pet, you wouldn't be where you are now. I taught you everything you know.

Everything. I turned you from a girl into a woman, and now I want something back.'

'You're mad. You could be banged up for years for what you did to me.'

'Oh, I don't think that'll happen, pet. I don't think you'll want people to find out the truth about what you are, now any more than you did then.' Sadie suppressed a shudder as his voice seemed to echo in her head. 'I know you, Sadie. I know you like no one else does. I know you don't want people to think you're a dirty little slut, but that's what they will think, Sadie – the moment you open your mouth and tell them what you did.'

'Shut up!' Sadie said sharply; then she silently admonished herself. He was getting to her. He was right, damn him. He always knew which buttons to press.

'You know I'm right, Sadie.'

'I said, *shut up*!' Panic overwhelmed her. Panic, and shame. It was just as it used to be. She might be surrounded by the trappings of wealth, but in her heart she was still a terrified girl hiding under her duvet, praying for her mum to come home and make things right.

But no one ever made things right. Not for her.

It was that thought that snapped her out it, as surely as if somebody had slapped her round the face. Sadie was silent again but not, somehow, out of dread this time. Instead, she was shocked: shocked by the delusions of this man; shocked by his arrogance; shocked by his request. He was sick. The years had only compounded that sickness and now, as it had been once before, it was all directed at Sadie.

But she was not that scared little girl any more; she was not helpless; she was not hopeless.

This time, she was in a position to fight.

Suddenly refuelled with the strength that had previously deserted her, she sat up straight in her chair, her eyes flashing. 'Then we need to talk,' she said quietly.

'Good girl,' Allen replied. 'That's more like it. I'll come to you, shall I? It'll be just like old times.'

'There's a place I use,' Sadie said flatly, ignoring his comment. 'A place for meetings I don't want anyone to know about.'

'Anyone would think you were ashamed of me, pet,' Allen drawled.

'Shut the fuck up,' Sadie commanded, 'and write this down.' Slowly she recited the address of the south London warehouse where she had seen to Michael only a little while previously. 'I'll be there tomorrow. Midday.'

Allen started to say something, but Sadie could not listen to any more. She slammed the phone down and took several long, deep breaths as she tried to calm her nerves. Staring into space she repeated the conversation she had just had, once, twice, ten times. How often she had imagined that conversation, how often she had vowed to herself that she would say certain things; but the grisly fantasy had finally been thwarted by the actual moment.

Sadie sat in silence. Everything seemed to be crashing down around her. The life she had constructed for herself seemed to be collapsing. She had been living a lie, and that lie had started to haunt her, just as she had always known that it might.

And in the turmoil of Sadie's mind, she realized with a sudden clarity that there was only one thing she could do to put it right.

She knew what had to be done.

To do it, she would be risking everything. Her business, her money, even her liberty. But liberty was nothing, she realized, when it was blighted by the chains of the past.

She knew what had to be done.

For an instant, the image of Alicia flashed through her mind. Her disapproval of what Sadie had in mind would be complete, that much was sure. She had already lost her daughter; in doing this she would put her far beyond reach. But it didn't matter.

She knew what had to be done.

Sadie buzzed through to her PA. 'Suzy,' she said firmly, 'wipe everything from the diary for tomorrow and the next day.'

'But—'

'Just do it, Suzy. And ask the boys to come into my office, please.'

Suzy hesitated. 'Can I tell them what it's about?'

Sadie thought for a second. She could ask her security guys to go so far but no further. The rest would be up to her.

Sadie smiled gently to herself – a smile without pleasure or humour. A grim smile. 'Just say I've got a job for them,' she said.

CHAPTER 21

Only when you are in the presence of a monster, Alicia had realized on the interminably long train ride back, do you understand what monstrosity is.

The only monsters she had had to encounter so far were the ones in the fairy-tale stories that her adoptive father had read to her over the years. Even when she was quite old, she had hidden under the warm duvet, terrified that the wolf she had seen staring lasciviously out of the page, its teeth like daggers in the sun, would be made flesh. More than once she had cried herself into a terrified sleep, or woken up in the middle of the night full of fear.

Fear.

That was what she had seen in her mother's eyes last night. Naked fear. Sadie, she finally understood, had had her own real-life wolf to contend with. She had woken in the darkness to see that all her nightmares had come true.

And all because of that one man. Alicia could not allow herself to picture his face; she could not bring herself to think of him as her father – the very thought seemed to pollute her mind. Before Alicia had met him, his actions sounded horrific, certainly; but it was only on being in his presence, on seeing his eyes, on listening to the insidious way he twisted things that she even began to understand the true nature of what he had done. And if she could not bear to think of him, what must Sadie be experiencing now that the wolf's lair had been disturbed by her selfish, childish, idiotic actions?

How could Sadie ever forgive her?

How could Alicia ever win her back?

She was numb. What had she done? What the hell had she done?

She felt quite sure that the look of horror Sadie had given her the previous night would remain with her for the rest of her life. That one look had spoken more eloquently than any words of the terror that Allen Campbell had inflicted upon her, and of the dreadful thing her daughter had done in resurrecting it.

She shivered all night in her bedroom, and by morning her skin was blazing with fever. Her head was thick and her throat was barbed wire. She kept the cashmere jumper on, however, despite her temperature: it had a distinctive smell about it that she found somehow comforting. She was emotionally and physically exhausted, though, and every movement was a challenge. As dawn turned into day she lay on her bed, repeating last night's scene over and over again in her head; she found she could recite every word by heart. And each time, when it came to the bit where Sadie ordered her from the flat telling her she never wanted to see her again, she felt a lurch in her stomach, her eyes screwed up tight and the tears came.

She was a little girl, crying for her mum. Just as she had been all those years when she was growing up.

There was no way she could let it happen. She had only just found her mother; to lose her again would be more than she could bear. She had to speak to her; and yet she knew she would crumble if she heard those words of rejection on Sadie's lips again. They cut into her, as surely as the knife that had cut into the skin of the woman in the picture she had shown her yesterday morning. But there was no one there to patch Alicia up: that job would be her own.

The morning ticked on and Alicia's fever increased. She had spent too long in the rain last night; too long prevaricating; too long finding the courage to admit what she had done. Now her body was paying the price. But as her temperature increased, so too did her determination. She had messed up – of that there was no doubt – but she wasn't going to let Sadie waltz out of her life that easily. They had come too far for that. With difficulty, she hauled herself off the bed, and picked up her mobile. She doubted her mother would reply, but at least she could leave a message. Start the ball rolling. With trembling hands, she dialled the number.

To her surprise, Sadie answered. 'What is it, Alicia?' Her voice was hard, unforgiving.

'Sadie, I—' Now that she was talking to her, she couldn't think what to say. 'I'm so sorry.'

Silence.

'I really didn't mean to—'

'It's a bit late for that, isn't it?'

Alicia closed her eyes gently. 'Yes,' she admitted, her tired voice subdued. 'Yes, it is.'

'Is there anything else?'

She swallowed hard, and winced from the rawness of her throat. 'Yes,' she said. 'I want to come and see you. This morning. I want to sort this out between us, to get back to where we were.'

'It's too late,' Sadie replied, though this time her voice sounded slightly less forceful. Sad, even.

A horrible notion struck Alicia. 'Did he call you?' she whispered.

Sadie didn't answer. Her momentary silence was response enough, however. 'You can't come here, Alicia,' she said after a pause. 'Not today, not ever. But especially not today.'

'Why?'

'Because I say so. You've ignored my wishes once – please don't ignore them again. Things are going to happen today, Alicia. Things you must know nothing about. It's important. For your own safety. Do you understand me?'

'I—'

'I haven't told anybody about you.' Sadie interrupted. 'Nobody needs to know we are related.

Nobody should *ever* know we're related. Is that clear?'

'Why?' Alicia felt tears coming.

'Because if they do, they'll ask you questions you don't want to answer.'

'What are you going to do, Sadie?'

For a moment there was no answer. And then, abrupt and businesslike, Sadie said, 'Trust me, Alicia. This is the best way.'

There was a faint click as she hung up.

Desperately, Alicia redialled the number. There was no ringing tone – the call just switched straight to voicemail. Her mouth, already dry from the fever, became positively arid.

What was her mother up to?

What was happening?

She had to find out.

But how?

Sadie felt nothing.

She hadn't eaten; she hadn't spoken to anyone; she had barely even looked at anyone. The arrangements had taken ten minutes to make. The security guys Bryn and Tomas had accepted their instructions without even a flicker of disagreement: they were well paid, and good at what they did. But even they did not understand quite how far Sadie intended to go. Quite how far she had to go. Ever since she had decided on this course of action, she had been like a train travelling with increasing speed along a straight track; there was no way she could swerve now.

At home the previous evening, she had opened the safe hidden in the wall of her wardrobe. There was very little there – she wasn't one for expensive jewellery or trinkets – but there was a metal petty cash tin that she had owned ever since Lionel had died and she had taken over the first shop. Carefully she removed it, placed it on the bed and opened it. Her well-manicured fingers wrapped themselves around the handle of the Heckler and Koch semi-automatic pistol that she had bought on the black market all those years ago. It had never been fired – at least not to Sadie's knowledge – and had stayed in that tin, unlicensed and illegal, ever since she had acquired it. The gun-metal grey was as immaculate as it had ever been, and the bronze-coloured cartridges gleamed in the reflection of the bright down-lighters on the bedroom ceiling.

It was heavier than she remembered it being, and somehow that made it feel better in her hands. For the first few minutes she just sat there holding it, getting used to it; after that, she tried to cast her mind back to the day she had bought it, to the explanation given her by the shady guy who had insisted on coming to the shop, rather than her coming to him. He had spoken in jargon to start with: only when it got down to the serious business of how to fire the thing had Sadie started to take proper notice. Checking that it was not loaded, she extended her arm and squeezed the trigger. She jumped slightly as the weapon emitted a clicking noise.

Again she tried it.

And again.

When she was confident with the movement, she loaded the gun and engaged the manual safety lever. Then she returned to her wardrobe.

It took a couple of minutes of rummaging for her to find what she wanted, but soon her fingertips fell upon the smooth leather of her old school satchel. Once comforting, it now gave her an uneasy feeling. It always reminded her of him – of the way he would look through it without asking, as though making the point that there was nothing she could hold private, that she had no secrets from him. Somehow it seemed grimly appropriate that she should transport her weapon in that bag, and she felt a sense of satisfaction as she buckled it up and hid it under her bed, ready for tomorrow and whatever the day would bring.

And now the moment was nearly upon her.

It was rare for Sadie to take the underground, but today she did – she was too on edge to drive, and it seemed unwise to get a cab driver to take her directly to the place where it was all going to happen. The rush hour had subsided now; Sadie felt self-conscious as she sat in the juddering carriage, the loaded weapon concealed in the beaten-up leather satchel which was so out of place with the severe business clothes she was wearing;

she couldn't help but think people were staring at her suspiciously.

You didn't lightly carry a loaded gun halfway across London, no matter how much you knew you were in the right.

The streets were busy when she emerged, but it didn't take long for her to get away from the crowds as she walked down the side street in which the warehouse was located. It was an unprepossessing road, and people barely ever came down here. That was why she liked it. Her heels clattered down the cobbled street as she strode purposefully down.

The front door was locked, which meant that Bryn and Tomas were not there yet. Good, she thought as she slid her key into the lock. It gave her time to get things ready.

It was cold inside. Sadie took a wooden chair and dragged it into the main warehouse area. The scrape of the wood against the concrete floor echoed around the cavernous building; Sadie hardly heard it as she placed the chair firmly in the middle of the room before walking back towards the far wall and gently placing her stachel on the ground. She bent down, undid the buckles and then pulled out the gun. It felt reassuring to have it there. And only she would know.

Silently, she put it back into the bag and stood up. She took a deep breath, turned round and started to pace the vast warehouse.

Eleven o'clock. An hour to wait.

What was an hour, after seventeen long years?

How many times had she fantasized about the moment she would take her revenge? How many nights, when the darkness had engulfed her, had she prayed to the god she didn't believe in to bring justice to the man who had ruined her life? By the light of the moon, she had even sometimes decided to hunt him down, to take her retribution to his door; but by the light of the sun, such resolve had always crumbled.

But now her hand had been forced.

He was coming to her.

And by all that Sadie held dear, she vowed that he was going to pay for what he had done.

Alicia burst into the office. 'Where is she?' she demanded of the PA – Suzy, did she say her name was? – whose head had shot up to look at her. Suzy stood up, her eyes surprised but her face determined. 'You can't just come running in here,' she said. 'You need an appointment. You need to—'

But Alicia was ignoring her. She looked around; then her eyes fell on the door to Sadie's office and she strode intently towards it. Suzy rushed out from behind her desk to head her off, and the two women practically collided just by the door. Alicia looked directly into her eyes: they looked as determined as she felt.

'Where is she?' she repeated.

'You can't go in there,' Suzy told her.

Alicia pushed her out of the way.

'Stop it!' Suzy cried, but to no avail as Alicia opened the door and walked into her mother's office.

It was empty.

She looked around, desperately trying to see some sort of clue that would tell her where she had gone, but she didn't even know what she was looking for. Taking a deep breath to calm herself down, she spun round and walked back out.

Both women – Suzy and the quiet office assistant – were warily watching her. Alicia silently cursed herself for having been so abrupt: they weren't on her side now, and she was going to have to talk fast to get them to give her any information at all. She glanced sidelong at Esther. If she was alone with her, she would be able to get her to speak: that much was obvious. But she was too timid even to open her mouth while Suzy was there. No, the PA was her target. Alicia smiled apologetically at her. 'I'm sorry about that,' she said. 'Are you OK?'

Suzy brushed herself down. 'As I said,' she replied waspishly, 'she's not here.'

Alicia took a step towards her and quickly grabbed her by the hands, which she squeezed in a comradely way. 'Suzy. It is Suzy, isn't it?'

The PA nodded.

'Suzy, you have to tell me where she is. She called me half an hour ago, begging me to come and see her. She sounded as if she was in trouble, but we got cut off.'

Suzy looked dubiously at her, one eyebrow raised; Alicia willed an expression of authenticity on to her face with all her might. She had to look convincing. Suzy couldn't know she was lying. 'Have you tried her at home?'

'Yes,' Alicia lied. Her instinct had told her that Sadie wouldn't be there.

'Then I can't help you.' Suzy released her hands and turned back to her desk. 'Maybe you should call the police.'

Alicia strode up to her again. 'Come off it, Suzy. You must know her feelings about the police better than I do. You *have* to tell me where she is.'

At first Suzy avoided Alicia's eye; but then she saw the PA glance nervously over at Esther. She was cracking. 'Please, Suzy,' she pressed.

The two women eyeballed each other; but after a few moments Suzy looked away. 'I honestly don't know where she is,' she admitted quietly. 'I haven't seen her since yesterday morning. She looked awful. She had a meeting with—' She hesitated momentarily before carrying on, her voice a little stronger. 'She had a meeting with security, and then she left. All she told me to do was to clear her diary.'

'What about the security guys?' Alicia urged. 'Can you get in touch with them?'

'I've tried. No luck – their phones have been switched off since last night. In any case—'

'What?'

'They wouldn't tell me anything if Sadie had

instructed them not to. They do whatever she says – they're completely loyal.' And then, in a more subdued voice, she said, 'We're all completely loyal.'

As Suzy spoke those words, Alicia happened to see Esther from the corner of her eye. The office assistant bowed her head, went back to her desk and sat down. Somehow it seemed odd, but Alicia couldn't worry about it. 'You must have some idea where she could be, Suzy,' she pleaded.

'Honestly, no.' Then she stopped.

'What is it?'

'There is a place.' Suzy glanced at Esther. 'I need to talk to you privately.'

'No,' Alicia replied abruptly. 'There isn't time. What place? Where?'

'It's a kind of' – Suzy struggled for the word – 'warehouse. I've never been there, but I know she sometimes uses it for . . . security issues.'

The image of the cut-up escort girl flashed through Alicia's mind. 'Where is it?'

Quickly, Suzy rummaged through some spiral-bound address cards, and scribbled an address on a sticky yellow post-it note. Alicia was heading out of the door almost before it was in her hands.

'There's something else.' Suzy voice stopped her.

'What?'

'Yesterday, before she called in security . . . Look, I really don't think I should be telling you this.'

'Tell me, Suzy. It could be important.'

Suzy breathed out with frustration. 'Yesterday, before she called security, she took a call. It seemed to – I don't know, frighten her.'

'Who was it?'

'He didn't tell me his name. But she mentioned someone. I think it was' – she screwed her face up uncertainly – 'Allen Campbell?'

Alicia felt a wave of dread sweep over her. 'Jesus,' she whispered in horror, almost involuntarily. 'She'll kill him.'

Again she turned. Again Suzy called her back. 'Alicia?'

'I have to go.'

'Just one thing.' The PA stood up at her desk. 'Who *are* you?' she asked, and her eyes, for once, were wide and uncertain.

Alicia stared grimly back. 'I'm someone else who is loyal to her,' she whispered. 'A friend.'

And in an instant, she was gone.

The silence that filled the office after the strange encounter with the girl who called herself Alicia was prickly. Esther watched Suzy carefully; for once, the PA seemed to be finding it difficult to keep her emotions from her face. She refused to look at Esther; instead, she nibbled her nails and stared blankly into the middle distance, her eyes occasionally flicking towards the door. They sat there, Esther not knowing what to say, for perhaps two minutes before Suzy breathed out heavily, stood up, grabbed her coat from behind her chair and stormed out of the door, putting the coat on as she went.

Panic rose in Esther's breast. If Suzy had rushed out to catch Alicia – and it certainly looked that way – she would surely be too late. That meant she would be coming back, and soon. There wasn't much time. She hurried over to the PA's desk, where her address cards were still open at the one she had written down for Alicia. Esther wrote it down and then returned to her own desk where, her hands shaking, she started rummaging about in her handbag. It seemed to take ages to find her mobile phone, but once it was in her hand, she started dialling Michael's number. Then momentarily she stopped.

What was she doing? She wanted to be like Suzy. She wanted to be like Miss Scott. So why was she about to betray her?

It was a sudden thought, but an emotive one, and she felt a hot flush of shame envelop her.

But then she remembered the broom with which he had beaten her, and the coat hangers that had dug into her flesh. She remembered the kicks and the punches. And she could feel the bruises, of course. She always could.

Maybe this was her way out. You couldn't work for Miss Scott for any period of time and not realize that her working life was punctuated by violent moments – moments when she put herself on the line. Perhaps this was one of them. Perhaps if she told Michael what was happening, he would treat her kindly – if only for a little while . . .

She closed her eyes, took a deep breath and, with one eye on the door, pressed the connect button.

Esther half hoped that she would not hear the ringing tones. But it was not to be . . .

Michael didn't smile as the dozy bitch gabbled away at him. It was what he wanted to hear, of course, but it wasn't as if he could trust her not to get it all wrong.

'Are you sure that's what she said, Esther? If you're fucking making this up, you know what'll happen, don't you?'

'It's what she said,' Esther replied at the other end of the phone. 'I can only tell you what she said, can't I?'

'Don't get cocky with me, you stupid cow. And don't fucking well start crying again. If that moronic PA comes back and sees you in floods, she'll twig something's up. Where did she say it's going to happen?'

There was a pause.

'I'm not going to ask you a second time,' Michael told her in a dangerously quiet voice.

'A warehouse,' Esther sobbed. 'She said it was in a warehouse. I think I know where it is.' Through her tears she recited an address, but Michael only half listened. He knew the place well enough – he still had the sling around his arm to prove it. As Esther finished, he nodded quietly to himself.

'OK,' he said grudgingly. 'Good. Don't be late

home tonight. This place is a shit hole. You've let it go. Fucking let yourself go too. Anyway, tomorrow you'll be looking for a new job.'

'I'll be back as soon as I can,' she said quietly.

'Yeah, you will.' With that he hung up, and it was bliss not to have to listen to her whimpering voice any more.

For a short while he just sat there, fiddling with his phone in his good hand and staring, dead-eyed, at the yellowing kitchen wall. He hated this place. He deserved better, but he was never going to get it with that drip Esther and her dead-end job in tow. What he really needed, he thought to himself, was money. Sadie Scott's money. He was owed it. It was his. But she had humiliated him in his attempts to get his inheritance, and he was fucked if he was going to let that slide. If he couldn't get the money, he could get the next best thing: revenge.

It wouldn't be sweet, but at least it would be revenge. And now, thanks to his careful planning, he had a bit of ammunition. And he had a plan.

He'd have to make the call from somewhere else, somewhere he couldn't be traced. As he stood up and made for the door, he reflected on the fact that Esther had probably been exaggerating. It was just like her to make a mountain out of a fucking molehill. Murder? He didn't think so. Sadie Scott was a coward – she didn't have the guts even to do her own dirty work, let alone kill someone. But that didn't mean he shouldn't exaggerate a little himself; in fact, if he was to do this right, he was going to have to. Get someone on site. Catch her red-handed. Because whatever Sadie Scott had planned in her concrete warehouse, it was unlikely to be a tea party – he knew that from experience.

Hurriedly he walked down the road and stepped into the nearest phone box. It was plastered with calling cards for local prostitutes, and his lip curled as he breathed in the malodorous smell of urine, but that didn't stop him from lifting the receiver and dialling 999.

'Listen carefully.' He spoke clearly, subconsciously toning down his cockney accent to disguise his voice. 'This is an anonymous tip-off. There's going to be a killing, and it's going to happen in the next half-hour. Take down this address if you want to get the police there in time . . .'

CHAPTER 22

Bryan and Tomas had arrived. They hadn't spoken much. There wasn't a great deal to say. They knew why they were here – they had done this sort of thing before – and they were ready.

The form was always the same: the boys would stay in the corner of the warehouse, hidden by the gloom. Sadie would stand in the middle. When the visitor arrived, it would invariably be her who caught their attention, so Bryan and Tomas could walk quietly to the open door and stop them from fleeing.

It was amazing how often they tried.

It was gone twelve now. He was late. Of course he was late. Arriving on time would have meant he was doing what Sadie told him to do, and that wasn't his style. The boys were in position; Sadie was in position. She shivered as she stood waiting. All was silent; even the faint hum of the traffic in the background had receded into nothingness in her mind. It was all too unreal. Part of her had to fight the urge to run, to escape back home and hide under the covers as she had so many years before; part of her, with a sick fascination, wanted to see what had become of the monster.

Part of her, though, just wanted to get it over with. It wouldn't take long. Just a few moments. A few moments to eradicate the years of hurt.

Her lips were dry. She moistened them with her tongue, and waited some more.

It was the voice she heard first.

'Who's there?' It echoed from the anteroom into the main warehouse, and the moment she heard it any remaining warmth sapped from her body as the familiar sensation of icy dread spread through her veins. She didn't answer. He would soon find his way into the warehouse. They always found their way into the warehouse.

And then he was there, standing in the doorway, his eyes blinking as he looked straight ahead at Sadie.

He was smaller than she remembered, and chubbier. He had a few days' growth on his face – something that would never have happened seventeen years ago – and his clothes were tatty. But she would have recognized that face anywhere. There was the same look in his eyes, the same lazy arrogance, the same sneer on his lips.

'Hello, pet.'

All the responses that Sadie had prepared in her mind abandoned her, and for those first few terrible moments, it was all she could do just to stay standing. Her silence pleased him, she could see. He smiled, the same smile that always played on his lips whenever he knew he was in control, and he slowly walked towards her.

Behind him, seen only by Sadie, the two security men walked softly towards the door.

'I'd have thought a grand businesswoman like you would have somewhere a bit classier to catch up with old friends,' he taunted.

Still Sadie said nothing; she just kept her eyes on his approaching figure.

'Or perhaps you're not quite the big cheese you pretend to be. Once a liar, always a liar, eh, Sadie?'

'Shut up,' Sadie responded, her voice a strangled whisper. 'Shut up and sit down.'

Allen looked down at the chair as though noticing it for the first time. A flicker of puzzlement passed his face, but he soon mastered it. 'Thanks,' he said sarcastically, 'but I think I'll stand.'

He was close to her now, close enough for her to smell him. He carried with him the stale aroma of unwashed clothes, but there was something else too. The stench of him. When she was a child, it seemed to pervade everything. It clung to her clothes, to the furniture and of course to the sheets on his bed.

'It's not a request,' she said as she struggled to overcome a wave of nausea. 'It's an instruction.' Her eyes flickered over his shoulder and she became aware of Bryn and Tomas stepping gradually nearer.

'An instruction?' Allen laughed contemptuously.

'Who the fuck do you think you are? I don't take instructions from sluts like you, Sadie Burrows. Your expensive clothes don't fool me, you know.'

They were right behind him now, but he was so caught up in his insults that he didn't even notice.

'Sit down,' Sadie whispered. 'It'll be easier that way, believe me.'

But Allen wasn't listening. With a dismissive snort of laughter, he turned on one heel to walk away – and practically stepped into the two burly men standing a metre behind him.

He froze.

Tomas raised an enquiring eyebrow at Sadie; she simply nodded.

'What the fu—' Allen started to say, but with a deftness that belied their burly size, each man grabbed one of his arms. He started to struggle, but he was no match for the strength and resolve of the two of them. Fury in his face, he was dragged towards the chair. Tomas held him in front of it; Bryn let go of one arm, moved to face him and with sudden, brutal violence raised his knee and struck Allen sharply in the groin. With a shocked grunt, Allen bent double in pain; it took only a gentle push for him to collapse heavily on to the chair.

Swiftly, Bryn removed a length of sturdy rope from the pocket of his heavy coat, and in a matter of seconds the struggling Allen was tied up, his hands behind him and his legs bound to those of the chair. All the while, he was breathing in short, staccato bursts – clearly the agonizing pain from the kick had failed to subside completely, and though he evidently wanted to shout out, he was unable to do so.

Sadie stood by, trying to feel some kind of satisfaction in the grisly scene that was unfolding at her instruction before her; but she couldn't. Not yet, at least. It was going to have to go further than this.

It took a minute for Allen's gasps to subside; while that happened, Bryn walked back into the anteroom and returned a few seconds later with a heavy bag. He dropped it in front of Allen, and bent over to open it. As he did, Allen made a noisy gargle at the back of his throat and then spat at Bryn's bowed head. The man looked up to see Allen staring defiantly, loathingly at him. Without a word, Bryn put his hand into the bag and pulled out a heavy wooden cosh – similar in shape to a baseball bat, but shorter and thicker.

Then he stood up and silently waited for Sadie's instructions.

Alicia's taxi crawled through the streets of London with infuriating slowness. She had already asked the driver three times how far away they were, and now he had stopped answering her question. She sat on the edge of her seat, as though that would make the car travel faster, and willed herself to be at the address Suzy had scribbled down for her.

Finally, the taxi turned into a small, deserted side street. 'This is it, darling,' the driver told her, and she thrust some money his way before he could even tell her how much she owed. She got out of the cab and ran down the street without another word. Only when she reached the door she was looking for did she stop to catch her breath.

It was closed. Slowly she tried the handle and it twisted open.

Alicia crept inside. The small, bare office in which she found herself was empty, but as she closed the door behind her she heard a sound from the adjoining room. A roar. A man's voice.

She held her breath. It had started.

As silently as she could she approached the door on the other side of the room. Her skin tingled with goosebumps, and when she saw the scene that awaited her, it made her stop, statue still.

Allen Campbell was tied to a chair. One man stood in front of him, carrying what looked like a baseball bat; another was behind him, his arm fully around Allen's throat, perhaps to silence the scream that Alicia had just heard. And Sadie was there too, looking grimly on. Allen's face was bloodied and sore. The lower lip was split, and blood had leaked profusely down his chin and over his pale beige shirt. As Alicia watched, the man in front of him walloped the cosh hard into his stomach; he was unable to bend double to ease the pain, or even to shout out on account of the arm round his neck, and his face screwed up into a paroxysm of agony.

Alicia stepped forwards. This time she made no attempt to be silent, and both Sadie and her two security men spun round immediately. The man with the baseball bat strode immediately and purposefully in her direction, his face grim and determined.

'Stop!' It was Sadie's voice. 'Leave her alone, Bryn. It's OK.'

The man came to a halt, but he still looked at Alicia suspiciously, and she felt the threat of unspoken violence crackle in the air.

'I told you to leave me alone,' Sadie called imperiously. There was a tremor in her voice.

'I'm sorry, Sadie,' Alicia replied clearly. 'I couldn't do that.'

Silence. Just the wheezing of the man tied to the chair.

'Isn't this nice?' Allen said in a breathless, pained tone of voice. 'A family reunion.' But as he spoke, the man holding his neck squeezed a little harder, and his words dissolved into a strangled sound. Alicia found herself gazing at him. His eyes had turned towards her and his face was filled with a furious madness. Sickened, Alicia tried to drag her gaze away: she did not want to look at this man, but somehow she couldn't stop herself.

She became vaguely aware that the man called Bryn had positioned himself between her and Sadie, and he was brandishing the baseball bat almost nervously, ready to use it at any minute; strangely, though, she didn't feel threatened by him, despite Sadie's aggressive reprimand. As she dragged her gaze away from Allen, she looked defiantly at the thick-set heavy.

'It's OK, Bryn,' she heard Sadie say. 'She's all right.'

Suspicion still in his eyes, Bryn stepped aside and, as though in a dream, Alicia walked towards her mother and father. Allen's breath was heavy, rasping, still restrained by the force of the man's arm; but it was almost inaudible to Alicia as she stepped up to her mother. 'What's happening?' she breathed softly so that only Sadie would hear.

Sadie's eyes tightened and she jutted her chin out in defiance. 'Bryn, Tomas,' she instructed in a voice that echoed around the cavernous warehouse. 'Leave us.'

'Miss Scott—' Bryn started to say, but Sadie immediately interrupted him.

'Just leave us, Bryn. Get out.'

He inclined his head slightly, and then nodded to Tomas, who abruptly let go of Allen's neck. Allen struggled desperately for breath as the two men walked out of the warehouse; by the time they were gone, he was still breathing heavily, but could at least speak.

'For fuck's sake, Sadie,' he growled. 'Untie me.'

It horrified Alicia to hear this man speaking to Sadie in such a familiar way; it was like a sudden confirmation of everything that she knew. Sadie didn't even reply. She looked over to the door once more as though checking that they were definitely alone; then she hurried over to the other side of the room. There was a leather bag there, old and beaten up, which Alicia had not noticed before. Sadie picked it up and brought it back to where Allen was sitting. She placed it gently on the floor, opened it and pulled something out.

Alicia blinked. It was a gun.

She had never seen a handgun before; but that didn't stop her from realizing, as Sadie slowly raised her arm to point the weapon at Allen, that her mother was not used to holding it. Despite the look of dead determination in her face, her gun hand was trembling, faintly but noticeably. Allen saw it too. The look of shock that had passed his face at the first sight of the gun soon turned to a contemptuous sneer when he saw that Sadie was not as confident as she wanted to appear.

'You wouldn't fucking dare,' he taunted. As he spoke, Alicia felt the now familiar chill of hatred run through her, and noticed that the movement of his lips had forced more blood to seep from his mouth. She became aware that she was holding her breath. All it would take was one shot. She knew it. Sadie knew it. Alicia had come here wanting to stop her mother from doing the wrong thing; but just one look at her face told the young woman that may be this wasn't the wrong thing. It was what Sadie had been waiting for, what she had wanted to do all her adult life.

She had said she would kill him, and now she was going to.

And as Alicia looked at the brutalized form of Allen Campbell sitting on that chair, she wondered if the world would really miss him. Surely it was better to rid the planet of this disease before he had the chance to infect anyone else with his vileness.

Alicia opened her mouth to speak, but Sadie got there first. Her voice was shrill, tense.

'Don't judge me, Alicia,' she said, taking her eyes off Allen and turning to look at her. Slowly she lowered the gun. 'Don't you dare judge me for this. You've no idea what it was like. I want him to know. I want him to understand the pain he inflicted. I want him to know what it feels like to be abused.'

Suddenly Allen made a sound, and both mother and daughter spun their heads round to look at him. He blew out at them contemptuously – a kind of half-spit – and blood sprayed from his mouth. Despite his sorry state, there was a loucheness about him, as though he was past caring what anyone did to him. 'You want to know?' he asked of Sadie, half chuckling. 'You want me to know what it feels like to be abused? Perhaps we should ask your mother. Ask that pathetic tart Jackie.' Then his eyes opened in mock innocence. 'Oh, but of course, you can't, can you? Last time I saw her, she was trying to swim.'

His words seemed to echo round the room. '*She was trying to swim.*'

Had Alicia misheard?

Had he said what she thought?

A kind of rictus spread over Allen's face, and he closed his eyes, as though his brutal confession had filled him with satisfaction.

But Sadie seemed frozen. Her face was blank, and she appeared not even to be breathing.

The gun fell from her hands and clattered on to the concrete floor of the warehouse.

Alicia felt her own trembling breath echo in her ears, and she watched as Sadie walked with agonizing, determined slowness towards Allen. She stopped only when she was centimetres in front of him.

'What did you say?' she breathed.

'You heard me,' Allen replied. His eyes were still closed, and he looked almost serene.

As she listened to the conversation between her parents, a sensation overcame Alicia: it was almost as though she was not in control of herself, not in control of her own actions. With a sudden draining of emotion she watched Sadie spin round and thump Allen round the side of his face with the back of her hand; as though she was divorced from her body, she saw her mother look with distaste at the smear of his blood on her skin.

She stepped towards where it was happening. It was clear to her now. Her mother needed her. Her mother needed her to do what she herself could not. She bent down and picked up the gun from the concrete floor. It was cold and heavy, but she grasped its handle firmly and pointed it at Allen.

Her parents stared at her.

'I want you to trust me,' she told Sadie in a level voice. 'I want to be a daughter you can be proud of. You only have to say the word.'

And as she spoke, she looked into the eyes of Allen Campbell. Her birth father. For the first time ever, she saw fear in his eyes. Genuine dread. He knew she meant it.

Unlike Sadie's, Alicia's hand was steady. She wound her index finger tightly around the trigger and prepared herself to do what she had to do.

The call had come in twenty minutes ago, but these things always took more time than they should. The emergency operator had immediately forwarded the anonymous tip-off to Scotland Yard, but DI Callum Mackenzie was fucked if he was going to go in without an armed-response unit. It had only been a few months since a friend of his had been pensioned off by some junkie dealer with a revolver. That was the sort of thing that focused your mind on safety procedures, and as his car blazed its way through the streets of London, sirens screaming, he felt a lot better knowing that at least two unmarked transits with heavily armed officers were making their way to the same location.

He licked his lips nervously. 'Tell me what he said again,' he asked the sergeant sitting next to him.

DS Willits took a deep breath to calm his frustration. 'Hardly anything, guv,' he said in a level voice. 'He said there was going to be a killing, that it was going to be in the next half-hour, and he gave us the address.' He looked out of his window. 'Sounds like a crank to me. I could do without it – the DCI's given me paperwork up to my eyes.'

Typical, Mackenzie thought to himself. Typical of the kids coming through – they'd rather do paperwork than police work. Besides, it wasn't a crank call. It was too brief, too precise. Crank callers tended to be more elaborate in their fantasy scenarios.

'Don't be so sure, kiddo,' Mackenzie said tersely. 'When we get there, wait for the ARU boys to do their thing. If there's going to be gunfire, let the guys with flak jackets take the hits, all right?'

That got his attention. Willits looked at his boss in a serious kind of way, and sat up a bit straighter. Good. They were getting close now, and he needed to be on his guard. With a flick of a switch, Mackenzie killed the siren. No point in alerting the suspects now that they were near by.

He licked his lips again as he felt a cold rush of adrenaline surge through his veins. He'd had a bad run in the last couple of months: three arrests and no convictions.

But today all that was going to change. He could sense it. This was a live one. He could feel it in his bones.

* * *

'I want to be a daughter you can be proud of. You only have to say the word.'

Sadie stared at Alicia. It was like looking in a mirror and seeing her own determination staring back at her.

Then she turned to look at Allen. There was desperate terror on his face. It felt good to see it. It felt good to see him suffer.

One squeeze of the trigger. That was all it would take. One squeeze of the trigger and it would all be over. That thought suddenly salved the numbness that had paralysed her body. She bent down and faced Allen, the anger rising in her once more. 'Tell me what happened,' she whispered.

Allen shook his head; Alicia's actions seemed to have dissolved the arrogance in him. 'I was joking,' he stuttered.

But Sadie could tell he was lying. 'Tell me what happened,' she repeated. 'Or I promise we'll kill you now.'

The threat hung between them, but Allen crumbled almost immediately. 'She was drunk,' he practically whimpered. 'High. On fuck knows what. She attacked me, and I pushed her into the river. It was self-defence, pet, I swear to God.'

With surprising swiftness, Sadie's hand flashed out and grabbed him by his hair – it was not long, but long enough to get a decent grip. She twisted it, just as he had hers all those years ago. 'Don't give me that poison!' she hissed. 'I've heard enough of it and it doesn't work any more. You're a murderer, On top of everything else, you're a murderer. And not just of my mum. You murdered me long before that. Why the hell should you walk out of here alive?'

Allen tried to say something, but her grip on his hair was so strong that all he could do was grimace with pain.

Now was the time. One word and it would be done. Now she could finish it and move on.

And then – what?

Sadie took a deep breath and looked back over her shoulder. Alicia was still standing there, the gun in her outstretched arm still pointing at Allen. She seemed so calm, so intent on doing this thing. With a crushing realization, it dawned on Sadie just how far she was willing to go for her. Just how much she *could* trust her.

Just how wrong she had been.

It was horribly appropriate, somehow, that Alicia should want to pull the trigger – as though things had come full circle. Why, then, was there a rising feeling of nausea in Sadie's gut?

She let go of Allen's hair, looking down in distaste at the few greasy strands that had come away in her hand. Then she turned round. 'Give me the gun, Alicia,' she said quietly.

Alicia shook her head. There was a blankness about her demeanour, as though she had put herself in a place from which she could not return.

'Give it to me,' Sadie repeated.

Alicia sniffed, but kept the gun where it was. And so Sadie stepped sideways to place herself in front of Allen. Right in the line of fire. Everything was clear to her now.

'He's ruined enough lives, Alicia,' she said urgently. 'I'm not going to let yours be the next one.'

'You can't let him go,' Alicia whispered. 'Not after what he's done.'

'I'm not going to let him go.' Sadie took another step towards her, and then another. Soon she was close enough to stretch out her hand and lower the gun. 'Believe me, Alicia, I'm not going to let him go. But this isn't how we're going to do it.'

Alicia's eyes narrowed.

'I can trust you,' Sadie persisted. 'I see that now. But you have to trust me too.' She watched as moisture suddenly welled in Alicia's eyes and a lone tear dropped down her cheek. With infinite slowness, she brushed a finger against her face to wipe it away, and had to fight a sudden urge to swaddle her in her arms. 'I can't let him ruin your life as he ruined mine, Alicia. He's robbed me of my childhood; he's robbed me of my mother; don't let him rob me of my daughter.'

Alicia looked down at the gun in her hand and then over at Allen. Sadie followed her gaze. He was pale, drawn. She realized that he could not hear what they were saying, and for that she was grateful.

'You're not going to let him go, are you?' Alicia repeated her question quietly.

'No, Alicia,' Sadie said. 'I'm not going to let him go. Believe me, he will never be free of me. Now give me the gun.'

Sadie held out her hand, and with visible relief Alicia handed the weapon over. As she did so, Sadie felt the warmth of her touch against her skin. Even here, even now, it soothed her. Calmed her. She knew that what she was about to do was the right thing.

'There's another way,' she told her daughter.

Alicia smiled nervously. She gripped her mother's hand tentatively, and then squeezed a little tighter. Then, for the first time since they had met all those weeks ago on Waterloo Bridge, they hugged. It was not a long hug, and it was tense. But it was a start.

And for a few precious moments, Sadie even managed to forget that her abuser was there in the room with them.

The squad car edged nervously along the kerb.

At the other end of the road, Mackenzie could see that the two featureless white transits had parked either side of an unprepossessing door, no different from any other door in this dingy side street. He ground the car to a halt, and as soon as he did his radio crackled into life and a terse voice came over the airwaves. 'We're in position,' it said, 'awaiting your order.'

Mackenzie and Willits glanced sidelong at each other. 'Still sure it's a crank?' Mackenzie asked the younger officer under his breath. Willits's cheek twitched slightly, but he didn't say anything.

Mackenzie picked up his radio handset. 'When you're ready,' he said shortly.

Then he sat back and watched.

Within ten seconds the rear doors of one transit van swung open, and a four-man team jumped out of it. They wore black helmets and body armour, and carried weapons – Mackenzie couldn't see what they were, but he knew them to be MP5K semi-automatic machine guns. He found himself holding his breath as two of the ARU team took up positions on either side of the door while the remaining two entered stealthily.

Then everything around seemed to fall silent.

Ten seconds passed.

Twenty seconds.

Thirty.

'What's taking them so long?' Willits asked. But Mackenzie had no reply.

Suddenly there was movement. One of the team guarding the door touched a finger to his lapel, appeared to listen, and then made a gesture to the squad car. A thumbs-up.

'Let's go,' Mackenzie said shortly. He opened his door and ran towards the building; Willits followed, but not that closely.

The ARU team were all inside now, so Mackenize could be fairly sure that any suspects had been disarmed; he wasn't going to go barging in, though – he knew what could go wrong when guns were involved. He stood at the open door for a moment and listened.

Nothing.

Willits was with him now. Together they entered carefully.

They found themselves in a small office-type room. Empty, with an open door on the other side. Mackenzie took the lead, striding across the room to the door. The moment he entered the vast warehouse beyond, there was a click of machinery as all four members of the ARU team trained their guns on him; but when they realized who it was, there was a sudden release of tension.

Mackenzie looked at the scene before his eyes. Then he looked at Willits, standing quietly beside him. And then he walked forwards.

Apart from the ARU team and the two officers, the warehouse was empty. In the middle, lying on its side, was a wooden chair; next to it were two lengths of rope, knotted in places and frayed in others where they had been cut through with a knife. Mackenzie approached it, hotly aware of stares from everyone else in the room.

There was something else on the concrete floor. Spots. Stains. Sticky, and a deep brown-red. Blood.

He looked back, grim-faced, at his partner, and then around at the ARU team, still clutching their semi-automatics.

Something had happened here, of that they could all be sure. But whatever it was, they were too late to stop it now.

CHAPTER 23

The curtains were closed. They were always closed now. He seldom went out of the house since coming back to Manchester to lick his wounds.

It was a month since Sadie had had her crazed power trip – she and those meatheads with the baseball bats. It had taken till now for the bruises to clear and the cuts to heal, but the physical marks of the encounter he could deal with. It was the way those two bitches had fucked with his head that made him wake up from his fevered sleep in a cold sweat.

The very thought made him shudder. They had almost killed him. They had been that close.

The flat was beginning to smell – even Allen could tell that now. Soiled clothes, and the remains of the microwave meals that he sneaked out after dark to buy and ate at strange times of the day and night. Together they made a musty, putrid stench. Earlier, while pacing the flat, he had accidentally stepped on one of the well-watched videos that littered the floor. It was ruined now, but he didn't dare put it in the outside bin for fear that someone might discover what was on it. Maybe he should do something about the mess. But as he sat on his ragged old sofa, wearing nothing but ten-day old jeans and a stained vest, he knew that he wouldn't get round to it today. He didn't have the energy for it.

She had scared him. He could admit that to himself now. Scared the shit out of him. Not just with the gun, but afterwards too, when she let him go. There had been a look in her face that he didn't understand. Self-satisfaction perhaps. She had even smiled at him – not a friendly smile, of course, but a sinister one. The sort of smile that you'd never forget. 'You'll be hearing from me,' she had said. But he hadn't. What the hell had she meant?

He lay back and put his fingernail in his mouth, but there was nothing there to chew on. Whenever he thought about that moment, he had to suppress a shudder. She had something else planned: something worse than a bullet. But what could be worse than that? In the first few days he had panicked about what she had in store for him; but when time passed and nothing happened, gradually he managed to became a little more at ease. With any luck he wouldn't hear from either of the stupid bitches again.

He closed his eyes, but they flickered open immediately when there was a knock on the door. His stomach lurched. Nobody ever came here. Nobody ever knocked. It was probably just a door-to-door salesman. Or kids. Fucking kids were always larking about, winding him up – and never the ones he wanted to see. No, never those ones. He closed his eyes again. He would ignore them. They'd go away soon enough.

Another knock. Harder this time. Something about it made him sit up. Something instinctively told him that it wasn't a child's knock. It was too firm, too intense.

And then he heard it. A man's voice. Sharp. 'Police! Open up!'

He blinked, and a sudden surge of panic rose in his chest. Shaken from the lethargy of the past few days, he stood up and started looking around as though checking to see if some other exit had magically appeared in the flat he knew so well. Of course, his eyes saw no way out; they fell instead on the videos lying all over the floor. Hastily, clumsily, he gathered them up in his arms. If the police seized them, that would be it. Curtains. They'd throw away the key. But where could he put them? Frozen with panic, he looked around, desperately trying to think of a hiding place. But no hiding place presented itself.

Suddenly the door thumped. He found himself holding his breath. There was a pause; then another thump. Then another, and the door crashed open. Footsteps up the hallway. And then they were there: three male police officers, one female. He dropped the videos, and they clattered on the floor all around him.

One of the officers stepped forward. Even before addressing him, he indicated the old computer in the corner of the room. 'Seize the PC,' he instructed, and the woman strode over to start disconnecting it.

'What the fu—' Allen started to say, but he was interrupted.

'Allen Campbell?' the officer asked. His voice was neutral, but purposefully so, as though he was trying to hide the emotions he truly felt.

Slowly, Allen nodded his head.

The officer exchanged a glance with one of his colleagues before continuing.

'Allen Campbell,' he intoned. 'I am arresting you on suspicion of sexual assault and rape of a minor. You do not have to say anything, but it may harm your defence if you do not mention when questioned something which you may later rely on in court. Anything you do say may be given in evidence.'

When the officer had finished speaking, a silence fell on the room. Allen felt his eyes bulging; then the familiar sensation of heat rising in his neck.

'What's she been saying?' he whispered, loathing in his voice.

Nobody answered.

'She's a lying bitch!' Allen heard his voice rising in volume. 'She always has been. She's a lying fucking bitch!'

The officer looked down at the video cassettes strewn around the floor. 'I think you'd better come with us, sir,' he said mildly.

A dismissive grin flickered over Allen's face. 'I'm not going anywhere with you,' he spat.

'Yes you are, sir.' There was a hint of steel in the officer's voice.

Stand-off. But Allen was damned if these pigs were going to stand in his flat and give him this. With sudden violence, he launched himself at the officer, landing a crashing blow on the side of his face. The officer fell to the floor, with Allen on top of him, crushing his neck with his dirty hands. Allen felt his fury spilling out, all directed against this smug copper and his smarmy words.

Within seconds, though, he was being pulled off. His legs and armed flailed viciously, connecting sharply against the bodies of the other two male officers with whom he was now struggling. He felt his fingers being crushed as, while he was still on the floor, his hands were dragged behind his back. There was a strained fumbling, and he felt his wrists being forced into a pair of handcuffs. Two clicks and the handcuffs were closed.

That didn't stop him from struggling, though. Roaring with anger, he pushed himself up on to his knees; then he started shouting, cursing – he didn't even know what he was saying. As the obscenities spouted forth, the officers took a step back, looking at him with undisguised contempt. Out of the blue, one of them moved forward and kicked him sharply in the stomach.

Winded, Allen collapsed on to the floor, gasping for air. Get your hands off me, he wanted to say as the policemen tugged him up to his feet and started dragging him out of the flat. But he couldn't. He couldn't say anything. He was in too much pain.

He tripped his way down the hallway and over the threshold of the flat, blinking and squinting as he stepped out into the harsh daylight, which he had not seen for many days.

'Too bright for you?' he heard a voice saying. 'Well, don't worry. You won't be seeing much of the outside where you're going.'

And with that he felt another push, and staggered further along the concrete corridor of the estate, his head a flurry of violent thoughts: thoughts of escape; thoughts of revenge; thoughts of what he would like to do to that slag – that stupid, scheming *fucking slag* – Sadie Burrows, if he could only get his hands on her.

There was a knock on the door of Sadie's office. 'Come in!' she called, but she needn't have – the door opened before she had finished speaking, and Alicia walked in. She smiled affectionately, and Sadie smiled back as her daughter took a seat on the comfortable sofa.

'Well, Ali?' Sadie asked, a slight hesitation in her voice. 'Do you want to see it?'

Alicia shrugged. 'I suppose,' she said.

Sadie stood up and picked up a bound document from her desk. The cover page was plain, simply carrying the words 'DNA Report' in a bland typeface. She handed it to Alicia. Her daughter looked at it for a moment, before putting it to one side. 'I don't suppose I need to read it,' she said. 'No great surprises there.'

Sadie shook her head. It had been a simple matter to have someone perform a DNA comparison between the few strands of hair that she had torn from Allen's head and a sample taken from Alicia. Hearing the results had been the hard bit – even though she knew what they were going to say – and taking the report to the police.

She looked at her watch. 'It should have happened by now,' she said. 'He should be in custody.'

Alicia nodded. 'You sure you want to go through with this?' she asked.

'I am if you are. It's as much about you as it is about me.'

Her daughter smiled. 'It's important, I think. That people know. But you don't have to do it. You can stay anonymous.'

Sadie shook her head. 'If I stay anonymous, he stays anonymous. That's what he wants. Why should I give it to him? Why should I be the one who suffers the humiliation and not him? And besides—' She hesitated.

'Besides what?'

'I've kept too many secrets for too long. I've had enough of them. It's time for me to tell the truth.'

There was a silence. 'I'm proud of you, Mum,' Alicia said.

Sadie looked away. She hadn't got used to being called that, but she was honest enough with herself to admit that she quite liked it, despite it making her feel awkward.

To her relief, the moment was broken by the buzzing of the intercom on her desk. Sadie answered it. 'Yes, Suzy?'

'She's here,' Suzy's voice came over the loudspeaker. 'Downstairs, in reception.'

Sadie nodded mutely. 'OK. Send her up.' She looked over at Alicia. 'Shall we go out and meet her?'

Alicia inclined her head, and together they walked out. Sadie smiled at Suzy, and then looked over to acknowledge Esther. On catching her eye, however, the office assistant immediately lowered her head, as though she was pained by any kind of contact with her boss.

Sadie's eyes narrowed. Something wasn't right. Come to think of it, something hadn't been right for a while now. Why was Esther so nervous? A thought began to form in Sadie's head.

'Esther, can you come into my office for a minute?'

Esther's face flushed, and Alicia looked confused. 'But she's just on her way—' she started to say.

'Then she'll have to wait,' Sadie interrupted vigorously. 'Come with me, Esther.' She turned and walked back into her office, closely followed by the assistant. 'Shut the door,' she instructed shortly.

Esther did as she was told, and then stood up straight in front of her. She wore a grey woollen skirt and matching polo-necked top.

'You've been avoiding my eye for weeks,' Sadie said, and as she spoke, Esther looked away again. There was fear in her face.

'Is there anything you want to tell me? Now would be a good time.'

No answer.

Sadie approached her. 'It's a warm day for polo necks, Esther.' she commented, and the girl shook her head slightly. Gently Sadie stretched her hand out to the top of the polo neck. Esther recoiled. 'It's OK,' Sadie said quietly, her voice kinder than she would ever normally let it be, and Esther looked at her in surprise before turning her head away again. Slowly, tentatively, Sadie peeled back the rim of the polo neck, and could not stop a small gasp escaping her lips. The bruising was marbled and mottled – dark purple in places, elsewhere yellow. Esther winced slightly as Sadie let the fabric cover it again. 'Who did this to you, Esther?' Sadie asked softly.

Esther didn't reply, so Sadie turned and walked to the window. For a moment she stared out over the city, choosing her words carefully.

'There's a man called Michael,' Sadie said in a flat voice. 'He tried to blackmail me. He had information that only someone in this organization would have had access to.' She turned and gave her a penetrating stare. 'You don't know a man called Michael, do you, Esther?'

The question hung in the air.

'No.'

Sadie didn't let up. She knew it wouldn't take long.

Gradually Esther's eyes started to flick nervously around the room. She winced subconsciously and her face started to flush.

And then she crumbled. It was a terrible sight – such fear and panic in her eyes. Fear and panic that nobody should have to experience. A desperate sob escaped her lips.

'He said he'd kill me,' she whimpered.

Sadie nodded her head quietly.

'I'm sorry, Miss Scott. I'm so sorry. I didn't want to do it. I wanted to tell you. But you don't know what he's like.' She buried her face in her hands. 'You don't know what he's like,' she repeated.

Sadie watched as the girl dissolved into a flood of tears, her body shaking dramatically. It was a pitiful sight. She strode to her desk, pressed the intercom buzzer and spoke. 'Suzy, would you ask security to come up, please?'

Her words had an instant effect on Esther. Her body, previously hunched, straightened; and although she could not stem the flow of tears or stop the great wrenching sobs that surged through her body, she seemed to be doing her best to maintain her dignity. 'It's OK, Miss Scott,' she managed to say. 'I don't need escorting off the premises. I'll get my things and go.' She turned towards the door.

'Sit down, Esther.' Sadie spoke with such authority that the office assistant could only do as she was told, though she looked even more frightened now. Just as she took her seat, however, the door opened and the familiar sight of the two security guys appeared. As they walked in, they did not seem to notice Esther, and just looked enquiringly at their boss.

'Guys,' Sadie said briskly, 'you know Esther. I want you to take her home. She's going to get a few things together, and there might be someone there. If he causes any trouble, you know what to do.'

The men nodded, and Esther looked wide-eyed at Sadie. The tears had suddenly stopped. Sadie went and sat down next to her and gently took hold of her hands.

'Here's what we're going to do,' she said softly. 'Get some clothes together, whatever you need; then the guys will take you back to my flat. You can stay there for as long as you need, and in the meantime we'll find you somewhere to live. After today, you never have to see him again, OK?'

Esther was shaking now. 'He'll go mad,' she stammered.

'He can go as mad as he likes. It's not your problem any more.' Sadie looked up at the security guys. 'Don't take *any* shit from him,' she ordered, and the two men nodded grimly. Gently she helped Esther to her feet and walked with her towards the door. 'It finishes,' she whispered to her. 'Now.'

The girl nodded timidly, and left with the two men.

Sadie watched her go and then took a deep, shaky breath.

The sight of Esther's bruising had upset her more than she had imagined it might. But there was no time to dwell on it now. Esther would be all right; she'd see to that. If Michael was unwise enough to pick a fight with her security people – and half of her hoped he would – he would most surely regret it. In the meantime she had to concentrate on what she was about to do. It was important. Important for her and, in a way, important for Esther too. In the next few minutes she was going to free herself: from the hold that men like Allen and Michael had over her, from her own past. She was going to take control. She was going to ensure that the person who knew about her past did not have power over her any more.

Sadie opened the door and stepped out of the office into the room beyond.

The woman she had been waiting for was there. The sight of her amplified the familiar sense of sick nervousness in Sadie's gut.

It had been an eventful few months since she had last seen Victoria Oliver, the prickly journalist who had interviewed her for the magazine feature, and Sadie could tell immediately that she was suspicious of her motives for bringing her here. 'Victoria,' she said, smiling at her as warmly as she could manage and shaking her hand. 'Thank you for coming. Let's go into my office.'

The journalist nodded and followed her in. 'Coming, Alicia?' Sadie called, and Alicia joined them too.

Once the door was closed behind them and they had all taken seats, the journalist spoke. 'I'm a bit surprised to be asked here, to be honest.'

Sadie bowed her head contritely, and gritted her teeth. There was no going back now, she told herself.

No going back now.

She took a deep breath. 'When we last met,' she said, 'you said something to me. You told me that skeletons can jump out of your cupboard when you least expect it.'

Victoria Oliver shrugged and looked meaningfully at Alicia.

'I'd like you to meet my daughter,' Sadie said quietly.

The journalist looked surprised. 'Your daughter?'

'That's right.'

'Um, don't take this the wrong way, but you look too young to have a daughter of that age.'

'Yes,' Sadie replied. 'I am too young. Much too young.' She looked over at Alicia, who gave her an encouraging smile. 'What I'm about to tell you, Victoria, I've kept a secret for far too long. That can't continue. I don't want what happened to me to happen to other people. I want it to stop. So I want you to tell the world about it. Do you think you can do that for me?'

Victoria looked cautiously at her. 'It depends what you're going to tell me,' she replied.

Sadie closed her eyes. And as she did so, her life seemed to flash before her, in a series of scattered, disjointed images. She remembered her father, and the warm safety of his embrace; she remembered the tears streaking down her mother's cheeks when he died. She remembered the playground, and Carly and Anna; she remembered the day she first went home to find Allen waiting for her. She remembered with a shudder the first time he raped her; and she remembered all the times after that, each one distinct and horrifying in its own way.

She remembered the birth.

She remembered Lionel and his kindness; she remembered being told that her mother was dead. She remembered the streets, and the hooker, and the pimp.

And then she remembered that night barely months ago when Alicia had walked back into her life.

As she opened her eyes to see her daughter sitting there calmly, serenely almost, she felt a renewed sense of strength.

Of vigour. Of purpose.

She took a deep breath and smiled at the journalist.

'Everything,' she said. 'I'm going to tell you everything.'

EPILOGUE

One year later

Dinnertime.

The corridors of 'A' wing were full of lags coming to and from the dining room. As they passed Stuart Macleod, a new screw with only three weeks' service under his belt, they occasionally barged shoulder to shoulder into him. They knew he wouldn't do anything about it, not only because he was green and one of the least strict screws on the landing, but also because he was carrying a tray of food and had his hands full.

Macleod clattered up a metal staircase into the corridor above. The cell he was heading for was at the end of this row, and he walked quickly so that he could get this part of his job over and done with. He'd learned a lot in three weeks, but the thing that had surprised him most was how quickly he'd come to share the inmates' view of the world and come to form the same judgements as them. It had been only three days ago that he'd spent an hour chatting to a lifer with a twenty-year minimum recommendation for a double murder, and had come out quite liking the guy. Murderers were human too, he'd soon realized.

Sex offenders, though – they were a different matter.

Everyone despised Allen Campbell – or inmate VS1385746, as Macleod preferred to think of him. Screws, lags, everyone. On his first day, Macleod had been briefed about this particular inmate. Since his conviction, he'd suffered three beatings from other inmates, and on one occasion had been cut so badly with a blade carefully extracted from a safety razor that he'd had to be invalided out to the local hospital for ten days. He'd made several requests to be moved to a nick with a VP wing – vigorously supported by the governor, who wanted the guy off his patch – but prison numbers being what they were, he'd simply had to stay put. Now he barely ever ventured out of his cell. The governor had adopted special measures for him: in the morning he had to wait for everyone else to use the showers and toilets before being accompanied there by three screws; he was allowed his hour in the exercise room only when the others were locked up; and he took all his meals in his cell.

Nonces never had a good time inside, Macleod reflected as he approached the cell door with the meal tray – everyone knew that; but this guy had it especially rough. Not that it surprised him. He was a creepy fucker. Having anything to do with Allen Campbell as part of the duty rota always meant you'd drawn the short straw.

He placed the tray on the floor in front of the iron door, and then jangled the large bunch of keys that were firmly attached to his belt. 'Dinner, Campbell,' he shouted, knowing that there would be no reply. 'I'm opening up.' He rummaged through the keys, found the one he was looking for, and unlocked the door before bending down and picking up the tray.

As he stood up, his eyes met Campbell's.

The inmate's bed was set against the far wall. He sat on it, his back against the wall, and stared out unsmilingly as though he hadn't even noticed the screw at the door. His eyes were bloodshot, his skin pallid. He wore regulation trousers but no shirt, and his paunchy abdomen bore an angry scar where he had been cut from just above the belly to his neck. It wasn't unusual for cells to smell, but this one was worse than most. Macleod took a deep breath so that he wouldn't have to inhale too deeply once he was in there, and prepared to step inside.

Suddenly he was aware of someone approaching from one side. He looked and saw three people – or was it four? – striding towards him. Macleod couldn't put a name to the faces – he hadn't been there long enough – but he had enough time to recognize them as troublemakers before one of them careered into him and knocked him to the floor with one vicious punch to the side of his face. As he hit the hard ground, he felt the food tray being yanked from his fist before he was booted hard in the stomach – so hard that he was unable to shout out for help. He lay on the floor, gasping in agony; and it was from that acutely uncomfortable position that he witnessed what was happening next.

One of the lags had grabbed the blunt knife from Campbell's meal tray. It was made of a sturdy plastic and had a short serrated edge. As the other three bore down on Campbell, his face grew horribly pale. He tried to say something, but the words did not appear to come, and in any case one of his attackers soon had a burly fist around his throat.

It all happened so fast. Campbell's head was sharply whacked against the hard wall behind the bed. By this time Macleod had struggled to his knees, so he had a better view of what was going on. And by God he wished he hadn't, for he knew the scene before him would stay in his mind for as long as he lived.

Campbell was being held down by three of the inmates, his mouth covered by one of their hands. The fourth – the one with the plastic knife – looked in contempt as Campbell wriggled like a dumb animal who knew he was going to slaughter. And then he went to work.

The knife was not sharp enough to cut through Allen Campbell's jugular at the first slice, and the way he squirmed and fought made it even more difficult. It took several attempts to draw blood.

Once that happened, of course, it was all over.

One stab.

Two stabs.

With each brutal blow, Campbell's body shuddered. By the time a third blow had been struck, the inmates clearly thought their work was done. They spat at him, before dismissively brushing past Macleod and leaving the cell, their faces as flushed as their blood-stained hands. 'Fucking Broadmoor for you,' one of them told the lag who had done the stabbing, and the others laughed.

Macleod didn't laugh. And he didn't shout for help, or for a lock-down. He couldn't – his muscles seemed to freeze. Still on his knees, as though praying at an altar, he watched in cold horror as the knife that was still embedded in Campbell's neck throbbed to the beat of his failing pulse.

Blood, deep red, saturated the bedclothes.

A grotesque, animal rasp escaped Campbell's lungs. A death rattle.

Pulse.

Pulse.

And then nothing.

Campbell's arm fell limply by his side.

He should call a doctor, Macleod thought. And quickly. But something stopped him.

What was the point?

He didn't need a doctor to confirm that the man in front of him was dead.